Edwin De Leon

The Khedive's Egypt

The old house of bondage under new masters

Edwin De Leon

The Khedive's Egypt
The old house of bondage under new masters

ISBN/EAN: 9783337396480

Printed in Europe, USA, Canada, Australia, Japan

Cover: Foto ©Andreas Hilbeck / pixelio.de

More available books at **www.hansebooks.com**

THE KHEDIVE'S EGYPT;

OR,

THE OLD HOUSE OF BONDAGE UNDER NEW MASTERS.

By EDWIN DE LEON,

EX-AGENT AND CONSUL-GENERAL IN EGYPT.

WITH ILLUSTRATIONS.

LONDON:

SAMPSON LOW, MARSTON, SEARLE & RIVINGTON,

CROWN BUILDINGS, 188, FLEET STREET.

1877.

PREFACE.

THE AUTHOR'S APOLOGY.

——◦◦◦——

WHAT can anybody have to tell us about the Nile-land that has not already been said or sung *ad nauseam?*

Painfully conscious of the fact, that the collected bulk of all the writings on Egypt, if laid one above the other, would rival the height and magnitude of one of the smaller Pyramids, the present writer pleads as an apology, for contributing another stone to the tumulus, his exceptional advantages of many years' residence in Egypt in an official capacity, his intimate public and private relations with the last three Rulers—including the present Khedive—and his recent return from that country, which he left in April last. He therefore believes he has much to say about the Khedive's Egypt that is new, and, as he trusts, interesting—not only to the general reader, but to the thoughtful student of man and history as well. Written in no partisan or partial spirit, this book professes to give a photographic picture of the changes wrought in the old "House of Bondage" by Mehemet Ali and his successors; and its true condition, social, political, and economical, to-day,

when the second dawn of a new civilisation seems breaking over that portion of the East which hailed the first,
long ere Greece or Rome had emerged from the "double
darkness of Night, and of Night's daughter, Ignorance."

In this belief he entrusts his book to the tender mercies
of the public, and the tougher charities of the critics—
admitting in advance, most cheerfully, that it is not "one
of those books no gentleman's library should be without,"
against which Charles Lamb so solemnly cautioned his
young friend. All the facts and figures this book contains have been collected on the spot, and verified, as far
as possible ; and the writer is quite sure that, as he "has
nothing extenuated," neither has he "set down aught in
malice," concerning a country and a people, for both of
which he entertains a sincere affection.

LONDON, *July*, 1877.

CONTENTS.

CHAPTER VIII.

THE KHEDIVE'S EGYPT.

CHAPTER IX.

HELOUAN.

CHAPTER X.

THE KHEDIVE ISMAÏL AS A PUBLIC AND A PRIVATE MAN.

CHAPTER XI.

FOUR NATIVE MINISTERS AND HEKKEKYAN BEY.

CHAPTER XII.

THE LAND OF EGYPT AND ITS PRODUCTIONS.

CHAPTER XIII.

THE FELLAHEEN.

CHAPTER XIV.

SCIONS OF THE ROYAL HOUSE OF MEHEMET ALI.

CHAPTER XV.

IRRIGATION AND THE BARRAGE.

CHAPTER XX.

EGYPTIAN NIGHTS' ENTERTAINMENTS.

CHAPTER XXI.

THE SOUDAN.

CHAPTER XXII.

IMPROVEMENTS AND PUBLIC WORKS IN EGYPT.

CHAPTER XXIII.

THE ARMY OF EGYPT.

CHAPTER XXIV.

THE SHADOW OF THE STRANGER.

LIST OF ILLUSTRATIONS.

THE KHEDIVE'S EGYPT.

ERRATUM.

Page 46, foot-note, *for* " Appendix B " *read* " Appendix A."

ing it and the young cities which have sprung up, like Jonah's gourd, upon its banks within the last ten years.

Our steamer was one of the largest of those which pass through the canal, a magnificent specimen of naval construction in all respects,

B

LIST OF ILLUSTRATIONS.

THE KHEDIVE'S EGYPT.

CHAPTER I.

EASTWARD HO! FROM SOUTHAMPTON TO PORT SAÏD.

Leave Southampton on P. and O. steamer—The three chief routes to Egypt—"Biscay's sleepless bay"—Sudden step from winter to spring—The Rock and "Rock scorpions"—Remnants of Spanish and Moorish occupation—Fruit and flower markets in mid-winter—Malta and the Maltese—Marine theatricals—Port Saïd—First glimpses—The peculiarities of place and people—Off by canal by moonlight, for Ismaïlia.

LEAVING Southampton, under the cold and cloudy skies of a November morning in 1876, on the Peninsular and Oriental steamship *Khedive*, bound for Port Saïd, Suez, and India, we sailed for the Suez Canal—that eighth wonder of the world—with a view of examining it and the young cities which have sprung up, like Jonah's gourd, upon its banks within the last ten years.

Our steamer was one of the largest of those which pass through the canal, a magnificent specimen of naval construction in all respects,

B

combining power, speed, space, safety, and comfort in an eminent degree; and our long run was more like a pleasure trip than a sea voyage, owing to the admirable arrangements of the company. Even the *cuisine*, which is not generally the strong feature on English boats, left nothing to desire; and the bath arrangements were most ample and satisfactory. We carried one hundred and thirty first-class passengers, and could have comfortably accommodated a score or two more.

We chose the long route to Egypt for the benefit of the sea voyage of fourteen days' duration, in preference to the faster lines, *via* Brindisi or Marseilles, by which Egypt may be reached in half the time. Last year I dined one Thursday evening at London, and lunched at Alexandria on the ensuing Thursday, taking the P. and O. Brindisi steamer. The route *via* Marseilles and Naples, in the French *messageries* steamers, takes about two days more from London, and you are six days at sea instead of three. The fare by all these lines is very nearly the same; the cheapest route is by Liverpool screw steamers to Alexandria, and the Cunard, Moss, and Leyland lines, from the former place, are said to be well-appointed and comfortable: making the run in from twelve to fourteen days, at little more than half the price of the other lines already mentioned.

From Southampton to "Biscay's sleepless bay," where the "winds were rough," as in Childe Harold's day, our voyage was monotonous; but, on reaching that well-known point, we were "rocked in the cradle of the deep" in a most satisfactory or unsatisfactory manner; and the yawning gaps at the hitherto well-filled table testified that tribute was being as faithfully paid to Neptune, as though the worship of the heathen gods still prevailed. From lips brimming over with song and jest but the day before, now proceeded only sounds of woe, not "most musical," though "melancholy;" and the possessor of "sea-legs" was happier than he of more symmetrical but more unsteady supporters. This game of pitch and toss continued until we ran under lee of the land approaching the Spanish coast, where Cape St. Vincent boldly looms up from afar: with its watch-tower perched on its highest cliff like an eagle's eyry, and barracks in which some Spanish troops are stationed for the protection of the customs duties.

We had left Southampton on Thursday, and on the ensuing Tuesday the grim frowning Rock of Gibraltar (*Gebel el Tarik*, or *Rock of Tarik*) looked down upon us, as we rapidly steamed along the shores of Spain, and finally cast anchor beneath the shadow of the mountain at early morning, while sunshine and warmth, like those of early spring, bathed his bald old brow. For we felt we had gained another land and another climate than those we had parted from but four brief days before, and had made a sudden plunge into sunlight, and an earth covered with verdure and flowers. The little boats that rowed off to meet us were filled with ripe luscious fruit and fresh flowers; while the vendors of such souvenirs of Gibraltar as the place could boast of boarded the steamer immediately, with clamorous proffers of their wares in broken bits of several languages—English, French, Italian, and Spanish.

Of course I shall not attempt to describe the famous "Rock," whose history and prominent features are so familiar to everybody. Yet even here the intruding Saxon has made his mark, until the grim old Moorish pirate, Tarik—who has left it his name—would not recognize his eyry, were he permitted, like Hamlet's father, to "revisit the glimpses of the moon," and look upon it again.

The fortifications constitute the chief feature, yet a drive through the town, that nestles down by the seaside under their protection, will richly repay the traveller by the curious contrasts of character, costume, and race which will everywhere meet his eye. Like Malta, the place has a most hybrid aspect, and so have the population—half Oriental, half European, with a strong infusion of the Spanish, which is *sui generis* and most characteristic.

The English here, as at Malta, have only encamped, not colonized. They have not fused and mixed in with the native population, as has been usually the case with Anglo-Saxon settlement in other lands. " The Rock scorpion " of Gibraltar, like the Maltese, does not hold social intercourse with the English residents, who constitute a society within themselves apart from the foreign element ; and as it was in the beginning, so it is to-day, and will be to-morrow, on both the rocks referred to ; held by force and by fear, not by affection or by choice, as appanages of England.

Among the " Rock scorpions " (as the officers term the native population) the Spanish type is strongly marked in men and women, with an occasional infusion of Moorish blood, which, in fact, is perceptible throughout the whole of Spain.

The men are lithe, swarthy, and sinewy, with black hair and flashing eyes; the women, especially the younger ones, decidedly pretty and gipsy-looking. It was a *fête* day, sacred to some saint, when we landed, and many of the children were dressed in white for their first communion, and presented a most pleasing picture. The women, still wearing the Spanish mantilla, filled the narrow pathways going to or returning from chapel, and added to the picturesqueness of the scene to eyes, which for days past had rested only on the tumbling waves of the dreary sea.

The streets are steep and narrow, with tall stone houses of quaint architecture hemming them in—with glimpses of green gardens, in which gleam the golden oranges among the foliage, through open gateways. The public buildings are by no means remarkable, except for their mean appearance, contrasting thus most unfavourably with the other rock, Malta, where the grand palaces of the old knights have been appropriated for the purpose. At Gibraltar the British Government has pushed simplicity to meanness, in the Governor's palace and other public buildings, not having had any old knights' palaces ready at hand.

But the market-place struck us most, with its rich supplies of ripe fruit displayed in tempting profusion—orange, lemon, banana, blended with the fruits of less tropical regions; while the baskets of roses and other fresh flowers persuaded us that we must have been suddenly transported from November into June.

At mid-day we sailed away from this garden-spot in the waste of waters, whose grim fortifications contrast so strongly with its green gardens that cover the slopes below, as though War and Peace were disputing the ownership of the spot: and whose summer-like sun, even at this wintry season, gilded and warmed impartially the two. One cannot wonder that Spanish pride chafes at the English occupation of a spot so favoured, the key to two seas; and that even the "Rock scorpions," whose blood is Spanish, although profiting by the garrison and the expenditure it involves for their benefit, should equally resist denationalization, and look longingly forward (as I am told they do) to the day when the flag of Spain shall replace the banner of St. George on that lofty height. The British Government, however, shows no disposition to relinquish its grasp on this stronghold, which it still keeps strengthening, and it would be idle to dream of wresting it away by force; while seven years' provisions for the garrison, stowed safely away, forbid the possibility of starving out the place by investment.

We had six hours' detention at Gibraltar, which we passed most pleasantly, repairing to the beautiful and shady gardens, which do so much credit to the public spirit of the people; and, with a basket of fruit at our feet purchased for two or three shillings, sitting in open air, surveying the beauties of earth and sky. Gazing up to the frowning rock, at its summit we could discern the sentries pacing to and fro, reduced to the size of small children, on that airy height; from which, in very windy weather, one would imagine they might be blown off bodily into the sea; and turning our eyes still further upward, could rejoice in a vision of that blue unclouded canopy of sky, which we had lost sight of for many weary weeks before in dear old dingy, grimy, cloud-covered London.

For the rest of our trip we sailed over smooth seas, under sunny skies—the blue expanse of water unruffled by a blast, resembling more a placid lake than the ever-restless and unquiet sea; reaching Malta on the fourth day, and passing six hours there, which, of course, we spent on shore.

This half-way house between Europe and Africa has been so often and so well portrayed, that it would be an impertinence to reiterate a thrice-told tale in describing its frowning forts bristling with guns on the sea side, and the wide stretch of rocky plain, unrelieved by trees or verdure, which lies behind the town or towns, and the fortifications, which look strong enough to repel any foe, however numerous or however bold; nature and art having combined to render Malta, or rather Valetta, as impregnable almost as Gibraltar.

With these two keys to the Mediterranean, and the additional latch-key to Port Saïd, that sea may indeed now be regarded as an English lake, and John Bull's India house perfectly protected against either burglars or sneak-thieves. What the energy and foresight of Lieutenant Waghorn first provided in the "overland route" through Egypt, in shortening the road to India, the supplementary work of M. de Lesseps has made even easier and safer, under all contingencies. But without the possession of the keys already mentioned, with the additional pass-key of the Red Sea, the Great Bear might contend with the Lion for the future possession of Asia—a conflict now seemingly indefinitely postponed.

Of the steep rocky streets, which you have to scale by actual steps cut in the stone (by some approaches apparently as high as the dome of St. Peter's), with tall stone houses shutting in the narrow streets, showing a strip of blue sky above and a glimpse of the sea at each end ; of the ever-increasing escort of ragged native beggars, which precedes and follows the stranger's steps, whining piteously for alms in all the languages of the Levant, which are those of Babel ; of the preponderance of the military element in the streets when you reach the Strada Reale of Valetta, on which stand the

Governor's palace, the Guard House, the Library, the clubs, and the hotels and cafés;—are not all these familiar to the Indian traveller, the Egyptian voyager, and even the more enterprising of the tourists chaperoned by Messrs. Cook and Gaze?

But Malta presents more curious contrasts and more interesting studies, than those which first strike the stranger's eye, after landing and sauntering slowly through its unsavoury streets, where a congress of smells, as well as of languages, seems ever in permanent session.

The conflict of races, and their refusal, not only to amalgamate, but to meet and co-operate with each other—the evident stamp of subjugation on the one, and of imperious domination on the other part—is even more perceptible at Malta than at Gibraltar; and the mutual repugnance of the two races more strongly evinced in speech, in act, and in print. You cannot pick up a local newspaper without getting proof of this; and the language employed by these local editors is not even loyal, much less flattering to their local governors, or the government they represent. From the Governor down to the lowest official, the language of denunciation and dispraise is freely used; and assertions that would be regarded as libellous or actionable elsewhere freely indulged in, and greedily devoured by the Maltese portion of the population. A winter spent at Malta enables me to speak understandingly of place and people; and the result of my observation was, that if England depended solely or chiefly on the loyalty of her Maltese subjects to retain the island, her tenure would be insecure indeed!

The native Maltese are a curious race— Italian, with a strong infusion of Arab or Moorish blood in them: and with a most miscellaneous mixture of the blood of the different orders of foreign knights, who formerly lived and loved on the island, some of whose vows were notoriously regarded more "in the breach than the observance." Like their rocky home, the people are a kind of half-way house between the West and the East; but in them the Eastern element predominates. They have even invented a language on the same principle—half "Lingua Franca," half Arabic—unwritten, yet currently spoken and understood among themselves. They seem almost amphibious—the boys diving down into the sea and bringing up the pennies thrown into the water from the ship's side; and the boatmen looking half fisherman, half pirate, as they paddle across from Valetta to Sleima for a twopenny fare; the same boatmen, by the way, having this peculiarity, that they are so strongly saturated by the garlic they eat, that it penetrates not only their skin, but even their clothing, so that when the wind blows from them to the passenger in their boat, he scents not "the sweet south wind breathing o'er beds of violet," but the breath of Boreas blustering over the garlic fields, and redolent of that most potent perfume. Yet they are a good-tempered, hard-working, quick-witted race, even when uneducated; and the higher classes, who are chiefly descended from Sicilian nobles, and still bear their titles, possess the pride of race in a high degree; and among them may be found ladies and gentlemen of the highest refinement and culture, fitted to shine in any society. But they are jealously exclusive, and reciprocate the disrespect shown them by the English officers, by not mingling with them and their families more than they can possibly avoid.

At a ball given by one of these, descended from the old noblesse, out of several hundred guests, there were not more than a dozen English present or invited.

On this occasion the national dance of Malta, which is performed in the old peasant costume, to an old national air, was danced by some very handsome young girls and their partners; and the music, which was wild and strange, seemed to fit in to every movement. It resembled more an English country dance than a Scotch reel, and was danced with great spirit.

But to resume our voyage.

Over these smooth seas we glided, the throb of the great heart of the engine pulsing audibly our progress, during the silent watches of the day and night, until on the fourth morning after leaving Malta, at sunrise we sighted the light-house of Port Saïd, on the low flat shore which there meets the Mediterranean. The night before we had an amateur theatrical perform-ance, in which two well-known professional *artistes*, Minnie Walton (an exceedingly pretty and jolly woman and charming actress) and young Sothern, who inherits much of his father's talent, kindly participated — quite a brilliant success; collecting a considerable sum for the benefit of a charity fund, to which the proceeds were appropriated.

We parted with the ship and passengers, after our two weeks' experience of both, with reluc-tance; for it has seldom been my lot, in the course of wanderings more varied and wide, though not so much confined to one sea as those of the much bedevilled Ulysses, to have passed on board ship a more agreeable fort-night. But as we were not bound to China or India, and the captain declined the responsi-bility of dumping us down at Ismaïlia as his boat passed by, we saw no use in going through to Suez; so we gathered our luggage together, descended the ship's side, and embarked ourselves and what the Romans properly termed *impedimenta*, on the small boat which was to take us to the shore, where an expectant crowd, in baggy breeches, and no clothing worth mentioning, with very brown and exceedingly dirty faces and persons, seemed waiting to welcome—and, alas! to plunder us.

But a half-score of years ago, when the Suez Canal was as yet an uncertainty—*in posse* not *in esse*—where now stands a thriving and growing town were but a few scattered buildings for the use of the workmen and machinery of the Canal Company. But five years earlier, the site now occupied by piles of public and private buildings, surrounded by blooming gardens filled, even at this wintry season of the year, with green trees and tropical flowers in full bloom, was but a barren sandy waste, whose rugged coast offered no available harbour. But with the opening of the canal, "as though by stroke of an enchanter's wand," the desert was made to blossom as the rose, the groaning sea recoiled, a safe harbour was created, in which great ships might safely ride, and the twin towns of Port Saïd and Ismaïlia (the one at the Mediterranean mouth, the other at the central point of the new water-way) sprang into sudden and lusty life, and have been growing into manhood, with a rapidity truly marvellous to contemplate in so old and slow a country as that in which they were incubated out of the desert sands.

Although M. de Lesseps obtained the concession for the canal in the year 1854, shortly after the accession of Saïd Pacha, supported only by the Dutch and American consuls-generals in his application — even the French consul-general, like the English, then ridiculing and opposing the project in consequence of the opposition to it from England and Constantinople — it was fully five years before he got a fair start, and the birth of Port Saïd may really be dated from 1859. It was a very rickety child long after, and it was only in 1869, with the opening of the canal, that its real growth began. Since that time its march has been onward.

We landed at the wharf of Port Saïd among a motley crowd of native porters, all shriek-ing, yelling, and jostling each other in true Egyptian fashion, in desperate efforts to get possession of our luggage. Everybody got per-sistently in everybody else's way, and each separate piece of luggage created a harmless battle for its possession, similar to that so vividly described by Homer, as having raged over the body of Patroclus, it being fortunate, in both

cases, that the objects contended for were in-
animate. We were protected in our persons by
the inevitable Dragoman, who promptly took
possession of us, and resolutely refused to
abandon us, in spite of our protests, until we
left the place at midnight; standing sentry outside of our door when we "sported our oak"
against him, when inside the hotel, and squab-
bling for more "backsheesh" when we last saw
him gesticulating wildly on the canal shore by
moonlight. Civilization immediately stared us
in the face on landing, in the shape of a Custom-
house; and Orientalism in the backsheesh bribes
we had to pay the *employés*, for *not* examining
our various parcels and packages.

This ceremony over, escorted by a rabble rout
of porters and the friends of porters, each
striving to touch some part of the luggage
carried by the others, to establish a .claim for
payment, we proceeded to the Grand Hotel du
Louvre—a French hotel of rather a barracky
appearance, but whose table was really Parisian
and comforting to stomachs kept on the plain
British *cuisine* of the P. and O. steamer for
the two preceding weeks. Here we remained
from 8 a.m. until midnight, and found the hotel
—with two exceptions—comfortable enough.
These exceptions were the villainous smells
that permeated and pervaded it throughout from

imperfect drainage, and the hungry hosts of musquitoes which banqueted upon us without a moment's cessation. These winged leeches were small, black, and voiceless; giving no " dreadful note of preparation," as is usual with their bolder brethren elsewhere, but settling down in silence on face or hands, and giving the first indication of their visit by the presentation of their " little bills," until we were driven out into the open air to escape them. We also found human musquitóes, in the proprietors of the hotel, who proved almost as bad bloodsuckers as the winged ones, on presenting their " little bills " also at parting. But keeping an hotel at Port Saïd must really be no joke, and the few outsiders who can be caught in transit ought not to grumble at high charges under such exceptional circumstances; and therefore let us dismiss both men and musquitoes with a benediction, and the expression of a hope that we may never be subjected to the tender mercies of either again, during our Eastward pilgrimage.

As there are but two daily departures, *viâ* the canal, for Ismaïlia, forty miles distant, by small steamers—one early in the morning, the other at midnight—and we had missed the first, we spent the day in strolling over the town, which is decidedly French in aspect, and well and compactly built. The foreign population also seems

chiefly French—people in some way connected
with the Isthmus works; and the language also
in the shops was French, instead of Italian, as
is generally the case at Alexandria or Cairo.

Port Saïd is rather a pretty, though not over
clean place, with a large public garden in the
centre of the town, filled with rare Eastern
trees, shrubs, and flowers, all looking as fresh
and blooming as though the season were July,
not November. The heat of the sun also was
so oppressive that we had to resort to umbrellas
for protection. The town is remarkable as the
growth of so short a time, not only in its solid
blocks of buildings and blooming gardens, but
also for the magnitude and beauty of many of
the private residences, with their large verandahs
extending all around them, as in Havana—the
ceaseless clouds of tobacco smoke rising from
the mouths of the residents, completing the
resemblance to the "ever-faithful island."

Many of these planter-like residences are
occupied by the agents of the numerous steamship lines, of all nationalities, trading with India
and China through the canal; one of the effects
of that great artery's being opened having been
the destruction of the previous British monopoly
of the trade of the East. Now an eager and
active competition is carried on by other nationalities and by private companies, to the great

diminution of value of the P. and O. stock, which used to command very high premiums when that pioneer line enjoyed the monopoly of the overland transit through Egypt.

Viewing these snug residences, and reflecting that, for at least a portion of the year, the lives of the foreign residents must pass in almost as unbroken apathy and repose as those of Tennyson's "lotos-eaters," it occurred to us that the noiseless though persistent musquito of Port Saïd may have been provided by Providence, to prevent the blood from stagnating in so torpid a place; acting as a substitute for the immemorial "barber-leech" of Italy and Spain. We were surprised to find such numerous and excellent shops at Port Saïd, and the extreme youth of the place insured the freshness of the supplies. The streets are broad and well laid out; and although walking on the pavements, or the ledge representing them, is not unaccompanied by the drawbacks of sleeping dogs and much unremoved rubbish, common to all Eastern towns, yet, on the whole, a lady wearing short skirts can contrive to pass over them in comparative safety.

At midnight we left the hotel for the small Egyptian mail steamer, which was to take us through the canal to Ismaïlia. We were not kept waiting much over an hour beyond the appointed time at the office, and again were confronted with civilization, in the shape of weighing luggage, and heavy charges for alleged extra weight in addition to our regular fare, almost doubling the tariff price. Orientalism also took leave of us in a chorus of lamentations, sounding strangely like curses, from Dragoman and porters, already heavily overpaid for real or imaginary services forced upon us : as the small steamer splashed away towards the canal, under a moonlight almost as bright as daylight.

The steamer looked like a toy boat, reminding us, both from its size, and its wheel at the stern instead of the sides of the vessel, of the small boats that ply up and down the bayous in Louisiana. A very diminutive cabin forward, with no berths, but simply divans, sufficient to accommodate six persons stretched out at full length, constituted the first-class accommodation. Fortunately there were in all but four first-class passengers, so we were comfortable enough. As we were favoured by bright moonlight—so bright that one could easily read by it—I spent the larger portion of my time on the small outside deck, looking out upon the strange scene, and the narrow canal through which we were almost noiselessly paddling at the rate of about eight miles per hour. The great sea walls outside, built out into the sea several miles, to resist the encroachments of the Mediterranean, as well as the opening or mouth of the canal itself, are well worth seeing and examining more closely than our time allowed us; for they are proofs of the wonderful ingenuity and skill of engineering science in resisting the wars of winds and waves against its artificial bulwarks.

But the greater part of the transit to Ismaïlia from Port Saïd, when the first novelty is over, is monotonous in the extreme—almost a run through a large ditch, which, however, is far wider than one would have imagined from merely reading a description of it; since it looks wide enough to permit several steamers of large size to pass at the same time. Part of the canal is simply a trench cut through the desert, which is gritty, not sandy, and the deepening of the channel through salt lakes already existing; but too shallow for navigation. The rest consists of heavy cuttings through hills, whose rugged outlines on either side break the dead level and uniform monotony of the banks. Approaching and leaving Kantara—a station where a short stoppage is made—the latter is the case.

Yet the scene is unique and utterly unlike any other; the southern bayous, whose water-way resembles the canal, being fringed with great trees draped in moss, waving from them like banners in some old cathedral, and lined besides by dense underbrush. Here the dead silence and solitude, the grey wastes around unrelieved by tree, bush, or shrub, looking still more ghostly under moonlight, with only the plashing of the little steamer to recall the sounds of life, made it a solemn and weird spectacle, though a monotonous one, during the six hours of our transit.

VIEW NEAR LAKE TIMSAH.

To face page 21.

CHAPTER II..

ISMAÏLIA—THE DESERT—CAIRO.

Reach Ismaïlia at sunrise—First view.—The Custom-house nuisance again—The faith in things unseen—The Hotel Paris—A truly Parisian *cuisine* —Stroll over the town—Its public and private gardens—Peculiar charms of. this oasis in the desert—The railway route, *via* Zagazig, to Cairo—Along the Fresh-Water Canal—Should the Chinese coolie be imported?—The Suez Canal and Euphrates Railway route—Some facts and figures about. the Suez Canal—Mention of one of. its founders.

WE reached Ismaïlia about sunrise,. and passing ashore with our luggage, found ourselves under a leafy bower of shade trees, forming an avenue of acacias and wild figs which, although yet youthful, had attained already sufficient pro-portions to do honour to the Champs Elysées; although they, as well as the little city which we saw at the end of the leafy vista, half a mile distant, occupied the space which was sandy desert a few years before. For nature here is indeed a bounteous mother, wherever water is brought to the soil;. no other fertilizer seeming to be needed in this country of contradictions.

Here, again, we were most unexpectedly
arrested by the Custom-house nuisance, to
which we had already been subjected at Port
Saïd but twenty-four hours before. Why or
wherefore the superior powers alone can tell;
but the wayfaring man, though not a fool,
may not. Argument and expostulation were in
vain, and more francs had to be offered up on
the shrine of Backsheesh the Insatiable, whose
worship has succeeded that of Isis and Osiris in
the land of the Pharaohs, before we were permitted to pass the imaginary barrier, where
there is a gate barring the road, and an excessively dirty and stolid Egyptian acting as toll-
gatherer. On we marched, with unopened
trunks borne on the shoulders of several Arabs,
towards Ismaïlia and breakfast; and wearied
with our night journey, hailed the sight of the
Hotel Paris, which had been highly recommended to us, and richly merited the recommendation.

Ismaïlia (so named in compliment to the
Khedive) is a far prettier, though much smaller,
town than Port Saïd, which the completion and
successful working of the Fresh-Water Canal,
that connects it directly with Cairo, and
promises to act as a great feeder of produce to
the Suez Canal by diverting the transportation
thither, bids fair to expand into much larger

proportions, and make the centre of a brisk trade in native produce. Even now it is an attractive and pretty place—a wonderfully precocious child of eight years of age—with its public garden in the centre of the city, blooming even in mid-winter with rare exotics and evergreens, and with a large fountain of fresh water furnishing the inhabitants with a full supply of that luxury. Its Khedivial palace, and the pretty chalets of M. de Lesseps and others, embowered in gardens filled with flowers and fruits, and its snug little shops filled with Parisian knicknacks, give it the air of one of the small towns in the environs of Paris bodily transported into the desert—an impression which the prevalence of the French tongue, even on Arab lips, tends also to enhance. Here the "Father of the Isthmus," as he loves to be called—M. de Lesseps, that well known " *Vieillard qui ne se vieillit pas* " (as his French friends say)— holds his court for three months every year, and dispenses hospitality on the most lavish scale; and at the patriarchal age of seventy-three, exceeding the Scriptural term, with his young wife and houseful of young children, seems to bloom like a century plant.

Ismaïlia, as already stated, enjoys the exceptional privilege of an excellent hotel, the Hotel Paris, kept by an old French resident, who

boasts the same name as the gay capital of
France, and who proves himself entitled to that
highest eulogium of "knowing how to keep an
hotel." So well is this appreciated in Egypt,
that many of the visitors to, and residents at,
Cairo are in the habit of running up to Ismaïlia
to enjoy the *cuisine* and the climate, both of
which, except at midsummer, are exceptionally
good. Our experience of the place was limited
but to a few hours, but a better breakfast, on
short notice, could not have been served at
Paris—delicious fish fresh from the lake being
one of the most attractive features, served up
with a sauce justifying the French *gourmet's*
eulogy: "Monsieur, with this sauce one might
eat his father!"

Ismaïlia is famous for its fish, with which the
Cairene market is supplied; and its fruits and
flowers also are almost unrivalled.

The town itself is European in appearance,
reminding one of Auteuil or Passy, with a dash
of the East thrown in by the semi-tropical
vegetation. The shops are chiefly kept by
French men or women, who constitute the bulk
of the population, although of course the
evidences of Egyptian residence are not wanting.
The climate in winter is said to be very equable
and agreeable, though I should suppose that
the vicinity of large bodies of water would

render it somewhat damp. This, however, the residents will not admit, and my own experience was too limited to contradict their positive and patriotic vindication of their climate. Certain it is that Ismaïlia is a very pretty place, and for those who love peace and quiet, and can dispense with society, might prove an attractive residence during the winter months; although few Oriental features present themselves there beyond the gardens and the climate. Its proximity to Cairo also tends to render it accessible to civilization and society.

We spent only a few hours at Ismaïlia, and then took the railway, *viâ* Zagazig, to Cairo—a most dusty and fatiguing journey of about seven hours, rendered apparently longer by the frequent and almost interminable stoppages at the small railway stations, or rather sheds, every half-hour. Zagazig, at which we stopped *en route*, is really a pretty place, and apparently a prosperous one, with its well-built houses, and storehouses for produce, and its mosques and minarets of much pretension, to meet the spiritual wants of its population, which is chiefly Egyptian. Out of 40,000 inhabitants of which it boasts, not more than 300 can even put in a claim to foreign European origin. It is the chief city of the province of Charkyé, which numbers nearly half a million of inhabitants. Among

other large cities in the Delta are—Daman-
hour, with 25,000 inhabitants; Mansourah, with
16,000; Tanta (where the great fairs are held),
with 60,000; Rosetta at the Nile-mouth 15,000,
and Damietta 29,000; so that there are cities to
be seen outside of Cairo and Alexandria, though
seldom visited by tourists.

For more than half the way after leaving Ismaïlia, the transit is through the desert—the most
bare, bleak, and dreary scene the eye of man can
rest upon; the very "abomination of desolation"
spoken of in Scripture; unrelieved for miles by
the slightest trace of man's presence or occupation, deserted even by birds and beasts,—an arid,
shrubless waste of ever-shifting sand. Yet experience has proved that even this desert waste
can be made "to blossom as the rose," simply
by the use of water, without other fertilizers;
and one of the great uses of the Fresh-Water
Canal will arise from the irrigation it will supply,
and the belt of fertility it will create, along the
whole line of its course. The blooming gardens
of Port Saïd and Ismaïlia, so lately redeemed
from the desert by similar agency, would seem
to afford ample confirmation to this claim; especially since the canal has passed into the hands
of the Suez Canal Company, at least for a time,
that corporation having obtained the control of
it from the Khedive. The opening of this new

water-way has already been celebrated with much pomp at Ismaïlia in April, 1877; and the Khedive has promised formally to inaugurate it in the autumn.

Statements have been made, in English and foreign journals, that the Fresh-Water Canal from Ismaïlia had been purchased from the Egyptian Government by the Suez Canal Company; but this is a mistake. Like most of the great public works of Egypt at this moment, it has only been hypothecated to creditors, as are the railways and the harbours and docks.

A debt of 2,500,000 francs being due to M. Paponot, the contractor, and to the Suez Canal Company, for advances made to the Khedive, it has been agreed that a commissioner shall be appointed by the Canal Company to take over a portion of the tolls collected from the New Fresh-Water Canal, until the liquidation of this debt; though the Suez Company will have no power to control the management, but merely to collect a portion of the money accruing therefrom, as it is paid into the treasury.

The receipts of the new canal are estimated at about 1,000,000 francs per annum, which would clear off the company's loan in three years and a half. But, of course, this calculation is based on the popularity of the new canal as a means of transit for the produce of the interior, hitherto conveyed by other routes. As to its profits from irrigation, they probably will not be immediate nor great, for reasons already stated; and, in reality, with the diminishing force of labourers, which the war will necessarily cause, both by the drafts from Constantinople, and the necessity of keeping up an army in Egypt to guard the canal and meet other possible contingencies, some time must elapse before more land will be needed for cultivation in Egypt.

What is needed to effect the redemption of thousands of acres more of the waste lands of Egypt, in addition to canals for irrigation, is labour, and the judicious employment of it; instead of the slovenly and wasteful system that now prevails.

Egypt is sparsely populated, even for its area of already cultivable land; and of its five and a half millions of inhabitants, probably one-third of its adult male population reside in the larger cities and towns, and are not agricultural labourers or cultivators. Cairo swallows up half a million, Alexandria a quarter of a million, living by petty trades or industrial pursuits other than agricultural. The large towns of the Delta, which have increased , enormously in size and population under the present reign, swallow up many thousands more. A rigorous system of conscription also drafts largely from the rural population its young and able-bodied portion, the very bone and sinew of the country, to perish by disease or battle in Turkey or Abyssinia, or become unproductive consumers at home. The standing strength of the Egyptian army has been estimated at from 60,000 to 70,000 men, although recently the Khedive has reduced the *cadres* largely, and wisely sent back his warriors into that field where pruning-hooks take the place of swords. The new acquisitions in Soudan and Central Africa have called for, and must still demand, large expeditionary corps, many—perhaps most—of whom are destined never to return; falling victims either to the pestilential climate (almost as fatal to the Egyptian as to the European), or to the ferocity of the savage warriors of interior Africa, a race seemingly as untamable as the Comanche Indians. How to supply this pressing want, underlying the progress and prosperity of Egypt, is one of the many problems now vexing the active and restless brain of the Khedive, who has inherited much of the energy, as well as the throne of his grandfather, Mehemet Ali—the Napoleon of the East—founder of a line which bids fair to outlive that of the Sultan's.

By his equatorial annexations (now welded

together under the rule of the adventurous
and indefatigable Gordon Pacha (to whom absolute governorship for life has recently been
given), the Khedive has thus far gained a large
increase of territory and of population nominally, but no material advantage, nor addition
to his labouring population. For it is more
than doubtful, if the barbarians of Central Africa
even were colonized in Egypt, that they could
be made to work in the fields as regular labourers.
Their native indolence, as well as their savage
training, would render the result of such an
experiment (even if attempted on a large scale)
more than problematical. The tiger cannot be
made to plough in the same furrow as the ox ;
and the savage Central African nomad, compared with the peaceful, drudging Egyptian
fellah—a serf and born thrall for centuries—is as
the tiger to the ox. In this strait the attention
of the Khedive has been directed, by thoughtful
Europeans in Egypt, towards the teeming and
industrious millions of China ; and a scheme for
the introduction of coolies into Egypt has been
proposed to and considered by the Khedive
himself, who has inclined a serious ear to the
proposition, but has interposed doubts as to the
feasibility or propriety of the scheme proposed,
suggesting a plan of his own for the purpose.
He has responded that the idea was not a bad

one, but the experiment of introducing the coolies at his own risk and expense might prove a costly one to him, should it result in failure; and that it might prove highly difficult to enforce contracts with them, after they were in the country. "But," he added, "if they will come of their own accord, and at their own expense, entailing no charge, present or prospective, upon my government, they shall be warmly welcomed; be given employment, or, should they prefer it, be allowed to occupy and reclaim vacant or wild lands, which shall be free from taxation for a term of years."

The initiatory steps have thus been taken, the seeds have been sown, and it is more than probable that a short time only will elapse before the "heathen Chinee" will show his yellow face in Egypt, and add one more to the many types of race already there. For there are many reasons why the Chinaman should feel himself more at home in Egypt than in California, or in other Western lands into which his cupidity has led him. In the first place, soil, climate, and productions, as well as modes of cultivation in Egypt, assimilate more closely to those of the land of his birth, than those in the Western Hemisphere. In the second place, the prejudice of colour, caste, and race, as well as of religion, will not weigh so heavily upon him among

the Moslems, as among the "pale-faces" and
Christians, whose "charity" does not cover his
"multitude of sins" (real or supposed), in the
West. Put him down among the rice fields of
Rosetta or Damietta, or on the sugar plantations
at Minieh, among the copper-coloured labourers
there assembled, and but for the difference of
language and dress he might fancy himself at
home. There is really no such sharp dividing
line of character, custom and race between the
Coolie and the Fellah—no such insuperable barriers as those existing between the former and
the European ; and in the former case amalga-
mation, as well as association, would not seem
impossible, or even improbable. In short, viewing the matter in every aspect, the proposal to
introduce the Coolie into Egypt, to fill the labour
void, seems to offer the speediest as well as most
satisfactory solution of the problem.

This train of reflection was irresistibly induced
by what the new canal is expected to accomplish.
For what use will land be, however capable of
culture, without the hands to utilize it ? And
should the Mongol ants swarm into Egypt for this
purpose, how great a revolution in American as
well as Egyptian interests may they not effect ?

Since the Suez Canal ceased to be an engineering question, by its successful completion
and working, it has passed into the other phase

of a financial question. "Can it be made to pay?" is now the problem which thus far, owing to the enormous subsidies extorted from successive viceroys (now for ever ended), has never been fairly tested until recently.

We are very much in the dark as to many points of the administration, and as to the actual expenses of the concern; it having been very much of a close corporation, under French control, until intermeddling *"perfide Albion"* insisted on putting her finger into the pie, and assuming a share in the direction of the enterprise, to which she contributes about nine-tenths of the support. My own brief examination of the canal showed me how incessant must be the wash upon the sides, and the filling up of the narrow channel, through ordinary wear and tear. But there are other and extraordinary influences also at work on the canal, owing to its peculiar situation and surroundings, as the following statement clipped from the London papers of May 1st will conclusively show:—"The Peninsular and Oriental Company's steamship *Poonah*, with the India and China mails, which arrived at Southampton yesterday, experienced, while in the Suez Canal, *a severe sand-storm, which commenced at sunrise, and continued, more or less furious, until five in the afternoon.* During the storm she laid right across the canal powerless. *Tons of sand were thrown on the deck,* and the masts and gear were covered with a thick coating."

The effects of a series of such storms on the canal must be obvious to every one, the peculiar position and character of that work being taken into consideration.

From a general statement of the affairs of the canal, made to the shareholders at their general meeting at Paris, towards the close of the year 1876, by M. Charles de Lesseps, son of "the founder," and vice-president of the company, we derive some information as to its actual working. He assumes only to give " an interesting forecast of the probable financial results of the year's working " (to quote the language of the journal from which this statement is extracted), " as follows " :—

"In 1875, he said a net profit of 1,061,000 francs (£42,440) had been earned, which was sufficient for the payment of a dividend of 1f. 88c. per share. It is expected, however, that the free revenue of 1876 will amount to 1,500,000 or 1,600,000 francs (£60,000 to £64,000), and this increase of about 50 per cent. in the profits will admit of the payment of a dividend of about 2f. 80c. per share, which, added to the 25 francs of interest, gives a revenue of about 28 francs per share. But the company may be said to have made even greater progress than is shown by these figures. The increase in the traffic receipts for 1876, as compared with those for the previous year, amounted to 1,100,000 francs (£44,000), while the working expenses had actually diminished. On the working of the canal, therefore, there had been an increased profit not of 50, but of fully 100 per cent.; but, owing to the commercial depression in Egypt, the company had not been able to dispose of its lands so readily as in former years, nor to invest its money on such advantageous terms. M. C. de Lesseps, however, hopes that as the commercial situation improves these two last sources of income will become more prolific, and that, if peace be secured, an immediate and important increase of traffic may be expected. That increase, too, he believes, will not necessitate any augmentation in the working charges."

This statement, it must be borne in mind, does not come from M. Ferdinand de Lesseps, the head of the company, but from his son, lately promoted to the post of vice-president, and therefore cannot be regarded as a formal official *exposé* of the actual condition and prospects of the company, which has recently been strengthened, or weakened, by £4,000,000 of British gold, and the appointment of two English members of the Board. To practical people, this "interesting forecast" will not be as satisfactory as it seems to have proved to the able editor who reports it; the facts and figures not being so roseate of hue, as the hopes and beliefs of Lesseps the younger, based partly on political and partly on speculative assumptions, which may, or may not, prove fallacious. The jarrings and jealousies which have recently manifested themselves between the old French and new English stockholders have not tended to constitute "a happy family" out of the directory; nor has Mr. Disraeli's grand *coup* increased its harmony. The Lion, not the Eagle, now guards the entrance to, and protects the passage through the canal, which, but for Napoleon III. (who wrung the millions of indemnity out of the recalcitrating viceroy), would never have been completed. Never was the irony of fate more curiously exhibited than in the history of this enterprise which, planned and perfected by French pertinacity and French francs, eked out by Egyptian indemnities and contributions, has finally resulted in the almost exclusive use and benefit of England, so long its contemptuous critic and opponent.

That which one of the greatest English ministers, with the greatest English engineer at his back, contemptuously pooh-poohed in Parliament, with all England applauding him, an equally audacious successor in the premiership, encouraged by equally loud popular acclamation, has recently disbursed millions upon ; and a young prince of the blood royal has been sent in his ship, to keep watch and ward over its Mediterranean mouth, against all comers. For the canal now is more English than French ; and probably the most bitter reflection that passes through the mind of the representative Frenchman who, in conjunction with two other Frenchmen (the engineers Linant and Mougel Beys, who supplied the engineering skill in which the ancient diplomat was deficient), planned and perfected the canal, must be the knowledge of this fact; as well as the painful conviction that although, during the term of his natural life, he will still be the figure-head of the company, his destined successor must inevitably be an Englishman—from the preponderating interest of that nationality in the work, whether in peace or in war.

The cost of the canal from first to last seems to have amounted to £19,000,000, about £6,000,000 of which had to be paid to the company for concessions made by the Khedive, which he had to withdraw and pay for in this very liberal manner. These concessions consisted of large bodies of desert lands ; but the company still retains large tracts around its chief centres of traffic, Port Saïd and Ismaïlia. It has been proved that this landed property may be made cultivable by the use of water, and must therefore materially advance in value.*

In one respect all the visions of its projector have not been fulfilled. He was so sanguine of the substitution of steamers for sailing vessels in the trade with the East, that he laughingly said one day that he believed, after a short time, a sailing ship would become as great a rarity for general traffic by water as a stage-coach for land travel; nor has his other idea that sailing vessels would be towed through the canal been more correct. Steam has merely superseded sails in the Red Sea traffic, and there are still sailing vessels.

Hereafter, when the gratitude or the means of the company shall prompt them to raise some memorial to the founders of the canal, alongside of that which will commemorate the name and fame of Ferdinand de Lesseps—already so world-wide in this connection—should be placed another of equal magnitude, to commemorate the services of S. S. Ruyssennaers, consul-general of Holland, and first vice-president of the company, whose shrinking modesty has hitherto veiled from the public eye his claims to an almost

---

* See Appendix A for other particulars as to cost of canal.

equal paternity of the great enterprise, which without him might, and probably would, never have proved a success.

I speak of what I know, and of what many others in Egypt also know, when I assert that from the earliest inception of this enterprise, before and after the concession was obtained (in which he took a leading part), as well as in his constant mediation and management in all its stages, wherein his tact, temper, and influence with two successive viceroys had to be often and strongly exerted to save the scheme from utter ruin, the final success of the enterprise is as much due to him, as to the indomitable pluck and energy of his better known and more fortunate co-labourer, to whom the public has accorded all the glory.

I mention this fact with no wish to tear one leaf from the well-earned chaplet of M. de Lesseps, one of whose earliest friends and supporters (when his friends were few) I claim to have been, in act as well as profession. But surely there is glory enough in so great a success to bear division? and in what I have alleged the testimony of many old Egyptians will bear me out—as well as the records of the company itself. So sensible was the Khedive himself of this obligation, that in the photograph he caused to be prepared for presentation to the crowned heads of Europe, in commemoration of the inauguration of the canal, unsolicited by any one, he assigned one of the most conspicuous places, next himself in that picture, to the photographic likeness of M. Ruyssennaers, in recognition of his great services in regard to the work; and Christendom and the company surely cannot afford to be less grateful than the Khedive, when the hour comes for their public recognition also.

Suez has also profited by the canal, although not so much as her younger sisters on the Isthmus. Before the Suez Canal was a success, Suez had a certain impulse given to it by the transit, and its connection with the P. and O. line of steamers, then and for a long time the monopolists for the Indian voyage; after the enterprise and energy of Waghorn had demonstrated the superiority of the overland transit to the tedious passage round the Cape.

In those early days Suez was a crumbling old Arab town, with a sparse population of natives, and not a dozen European residents; possessing, it is true, a large rambling hotel, built by the P. and O. Company, which gave the returning Indian traveller a foretaste of European entertainment again. But there was a general air of desolation and decay about the place, which was rather disheartening.

With the new influx however, through the

HUYOT.

PORT OF SUEZ.

To face page 42.

canal, a revival has taken place, although it is sad to record the fact that two-thirds of the resident foreigners are men; the gentler sex apparently shunning Suez, or being dispensed with by the ungallant males who have congregated there, and made it a kind of Eastern bachelors' hall. The population now comprises about 2500 foreigners, and about 11,000 Arabs, in all 13,500; the floating population is impossible to esti-mate. The vicinity to the Red Sea, and the connection of several sites in the vicinity with Scriptural story—notably the supposed point where Pharaoh and his host attempted, and the Israelites successfully accomplished, the passage of the Red Sea, the well of Moses (*Ain el Moussa*), and other traditional places—give Suez the only interest it can boast of to the tourist.

The Euphrates Valley Railway road to India, which once shared public interest with the Suez Canal, for which it was proposed as a sub-stitute, seems to have lost the favour it once enjoyed. Five years since, the British House of Commons appointed an able committee to inves-tigate the subject, and obtain the opinions of the most eminent public men, whose experience had qualified them to form a correct judgment as to the necessity and practicability of that route. Among these were Lord Sandhurst and Lord Strathnairn, both formerly commanders-in-chief.

in India, and Sir Henry Rawlinson, than whom there could be no better authority. The committee also examined many other distinguished persons, whose experience or researches gave weight to their utterances.

The result of this inquiry was, that the committee came to the conclusion that the first cost of construction would be £10,000,000. Politically and strategically, there was an agreement of opinion that such an alternative line, in case of war, would be useful. The military witnesses differed widely in opinion as to the value of such a line as a means of sending troops to India. Lord Sandhurst expressed his preference for sea transportation. Several others doubted the expediency of sending troops over a line passing over 900 miles, from Scanderoon to the Persian Gulf, through a foreign country, liable to be disturbed by European complications and local disturbances. "The Indian Government, in a despatch to which are subscribed the names of Lord Mayo, Lord Napier of Magdala, Sir John Strachey, and Sir Richard Temple, 'earnestly desired that it might be found practicable to carry out the project, which would be of considerable, but not paramount importance to India,' and were '*decidedly averse* to any promise of pecuniary assistance being made.' It was added: 'We cannot consider the project of such vital and paramount importance to the interests of India as would justify us in placing a charge upon the resources of the Empire for its construction or maintenance.' "

Since the report of this committee, the monopoly of the Suez Canal route, as the best short route, seems to have been firmly established; and British diplomacy has therefore been seriously occupied with it, to the exclusion of all others.

The war has raised some important questions relative to the Suez Canal, and there has been much talk of " neutralization," in its broadest sense; but the expression of British opinion on this matter, through Lord Derby's utterances in Parliament, has shown, that the nation which has made the canal its highway to India, and supplies three-fourths of the tonnage passing through it, will never consent to this; because it would bar the passage of its own war vessels and troops, in certain contingencies.

The transit through the canal is governed by the concession of January, 1856, which regulates the relations of the Canal Company with Egypt and Turkey, the proprietors of the domain, of which the following is the text :—

" ART. XIV.—We (Khedive) declare solemnly, for ourselves and our successors, the Great Maritime Canal from Suez to Pelusium, and its dependent posts, open for ever as neutral ways, to every commercial vessel, proceeding from one sea to the other, without distinction, preference, or exclusion, either of persons or nationalities, subject to payment of dues," etc. etc.

But this privilege, it will be seen, covers only commercial vessels, not those of war; and the Porte and Khedive have so construed it, by giving notice that Russian war vessels shall not be allowed to pass. The war vessels of friendly Powers, on making requisition, have never been denied the privilege, although there is nothing in the concession to give them a right to do so. In the Abyssinian war England made effective use of the canal. The canal is still included in Egyptian territory—the right of "eminent domain" never having been conceded to the company—and has been leased to that company for ninety-nine years, at the expiration of which term the Egyptian Government may enter into full possession, on paying to the company the value of the plant and material.*

Unless the financial condition of Egypt should greatly improve in the interval, the property is not very apt to change hands and revert to Egypt, at the expiration of that term.

* See Appendix  B.

CHAPTER III.

OLD AND NEW CAIRO.

Approach to Cairo—Sights and scenes *en route*—Wayside views and voices—"Backsheesh, Howadji!" the same old tune—Nature and man unchanged—Startling changes in the environs of Çairo—Disappearance of walls and appearance of new boulevards, *à la Haussmann*—Surprises in store for the returning pilgrim after ten years' absence—What cannot now be seen from Shepheard's balcony —Cairo as it was and as it is—The old quarter and the new.

WE approached Cairo about sunset, hot, tired, and dusty after our ride through the desert, the fine sand of which, blown by a strong steady wind, drifted in through the crevices of the closed windows, and powdered our persons and dresses with a perfect coating of impalpable dust. After reaching the cultivated region we were freed from this annoyance, and the latter half of our journey was very agreeable. The general appearance of this cultivated country, and the sights and sounds that greet you at each successive railway station, are much the same as of yore, and familiar to all old

Egyptian tourists. These seem stereotyped, and you still see the same flat garden-like country, with its eternal carpet of verdure of different shades in patches, presenting the appearance of a vast farm from the absence of trees. You pass numerous Arab villages, with their clusters of mud-huts, swarming with chickens and children, crowned by the domes and minarets of the small mosques, which give a pictorial aspect to their squalor. You see long lines of laden camels swinging, and hideous water-oxen plodding by, and the inevitable old Arab in the single blue shirt jogging by on the donkey, so small that the man's legs with difficulty avoid touching the ground. At each station, looking out of the window of your carriage, you encounter the usual salutations from the small and exceedingly dirty orange and water vendors, all children; and dirty hands of professional or amateur beggars are thrust in the window, with hoarse, guttural prayers for "backsheesh!" the owners of all of which voices seem clad in the same old blue rags they wore years before. An adjunct to this scene is usually a group of soldiers, either just enlisted or just discharged, who are squatting on their hams, chewing sugar-cane or smoking—always waiting for something or somebody, and distinguishable from the surrounding crowd only by being cleaner and better dressed. They are the mildest mannered soldiers in the world.

It is unlucky for the traveller, and for the population, that during his transit by rail he comes in contact with the idlest and least attractive portion of the natives, who hang around the stations to pick up a few paras or piastres. Taking these as fair specimens, his estimate of the population would be low indeed.

But it is on approaching the Cairo station that the great improvement of that city and its suburbs, becomes perceptible to the visitor who has been absent for several years. He rubs his eyes, and almost distrusts his vision; for, looking up the Shoubra road which leads into Cairo, as well as outside the former limits of the city, where formerly stretched for miles fields under cultivation, he now sees, far as his eyes can reach, in every direction well-built and even palatial residences, surrounded by gardens, adding on new cities, for several miles. The old Cairo was formerly surrounded by high and massive walls, and entered by a wide gate, both of which have disappeared, while broad boulevards open an easy way into the city and out to the desert. Passing over where wall and gate used to stand, new surprises await the returning visitor. The old has given place to the new; and blocks of high buildings have replaced the picturesque old tumble-down erections of mud and wood, four stories high, with jealously latticed windows jutting out into the street.

But when you descend at Shepheard's Hotel, your astonishment reaches its climax, and you rub your eyes as hard as Rip Van Winkle; for the great characteristic feature of the Cairo of old, the Ezbekieh—the pride, the glory of the city and people—has utterly vanished! Where once waved the branches of the stately syca-mores planted by Mehemet Ali, are now to be seen only solid blocks of stone houses, with arcades in imitation of those of the Rue de Rivoli at Paris. Over three-fourths of the space formerly occupied by that primitive garden-wilderness, so dear to the memory of its old *habitués*, who used to sit every evening and night under its grand trees, sipping coffee and smoking nargilehs, on those Cairene nights brighter than western days, while an endless procession of natives and Levantines passed under its leafy arcades, are imitation European houses and shops. The garden has vanished like a dream. The same change has swept over the aspect of all four sides of the square which sur-rounded that great park, or garden, whose dis-appearance I have lamented. The quaint old Eastern buildings, with their latticed windows, and entrances beneath by a small door pierced

in a thick wall, through which you passed into
an inner open court in which was tethered a
donkey, passing up a flight of break-neck, narrow
winding stone steps to enter the house—all
these, too, have followed the Ezbekieh, and their
fronts at least are now on European models:
square, formal, uniform, hideous-looking imita-
tions of the ugliest architecture in the world,
replacing the most picturesque, if not the most
comfortable or convenient. A small portion of
the old Ezbekieh has been saved from the
building mania, but so "translated" that its
oldest friend scarce recognizes it as an acquaintance; for, originally the least wooded and most
unattractive portion of the old open space, it
has been converted into a French or German
tea-garden, under the auspices of a French ornamental gardener, partly on the trim Versailles
model, partly in imitation of the Bois de
Boulogne, with even its little artificial lake with
swans in it, and small mock-steamers for sailing
over three feet of water.

The garden, however, which boasts of about
forty acres, enclosed in a high railing, is a very
pretty one, and in hot weather affords a most
pleasant retreat from the dust and glare of the
outside world. It has rock grottoes, and restaurants, and also an open-air theatre; and every
afternoon one of the military bands " discourses

most excellent music " for public benefit. But
the foreign population is too lazy or too busy to
come every evening; and the band, punctiliously
performing daily, wastes its sweetness generally
on the heedless ears of a few nurses and children,
reinforced by an occasional traveller. On Sun-
days and religious festivals, however, there is a
crowd; and a very motley crowd it is, composed
of all the numerous races that go to make up
the nationality we designate the Levantine.

The natives—especially the lower class—have
abandoned the spot, squatting, smoking, and
story-telling elsewhere, in more shady and less
formal precincts. To find them at home, you
must now either go into the country, or burrow
down into those portions of the city, which the
march of improvement and the Khedive have
not yet reached.

Passing through this garden, and under the
long colonnades of the new buildings that hem
it in, you emerge on the old Mooskie—as the
quarter of European shops is called—and here
you recognize an old acquaintance, but little
smarter or more European than formerly. The
fine new shops (many of them worthy of Paris
or London) are in the Ezbekieh quarter, newly
built; while here the small Levantine traders
and shopkeepers still vend their miscellaneous
wares in unchanged dirt and squalor, in the

midst of crowds of natives, waddling along on foot, or mounted on donkeys, circling around the unclean street like flies, with apparently as little industrial effort—a good-tempered, dirty, un-improvable tribe, whom water and improvement never touch.

But the banished old Ezbekieh of twelve years ago is not the only lost vision for which the returning pilgrim vainly strains his wonder-ing eyes. Other equally familiar friends, once daily visible in his walks and rides about the city, have equally disappeared.

As he was wont to sit under the stately syca-mores of the Ezbekieh, there used, at eventide, to prance gaily by a cavalcade of gay and gal-lant-looking Eastern cavaliers, splendidly habited in Oriental costume, mounted on Arab steeds of great beauty and price, whose crimson velvet Turkish saddles were stiff with cloth of gold, and whose silken bridle-reins were studded with precious stones. Preceded by the running Berber syce, in his picturesque costume of white shirt, crimson sash or belt, and bare legs of ebony, and attended at the stirrup by pipe-bearer, nargileh in hand, whose long flexible tube was often in the hand of the rider, these proud-looking beys and pachas used to file slowly by, looking neither to the right nor the left, to the admiration of the motley crowd ever circulating about or squatting under the trees of the Ezbekieh.

Then also, ambling past on their sleek donkeys —huge bundles of black silk like unto balloons, and with impervious veils, through which only two bright eyes were perceptible, escorted by the zealous eunuchs—could be seen in part the ladies of the hareem : disdainful of side-saddles, and riding astride like men, as a yellow shoe perceptible on each side of the donkey conclusively proved.

To these sights on the Ezbekieh there were added many others of a purely Oriental character ; such as the long string of laden camels, with their serpent-like neck and crests, grunting hoarsely as though in complaint or wrath, as they swung along their ungainly bulk and burdens, moving the two legs on the same side simultaneously. Occasionally, but very rarely, the carriage of some European or Europeanized pacha passed ; but that was the most unusual kind of locomotion. The small coffee-houses on the Ezbekieh—mere booths or sheds as they were—constituted an attractive feature on summer evenings, when all the Levantine, and much of the Egyptian world—that strange amalgam of all races—came to sip coffee or fiery "raki," smoke and talk scandal, in front of these booths where chairs were placed ; while a band of Italian exiles made music at intervals, passing round the hat for contributions.

At the opposite side of the Ezbekieh, nearest the Mooskie, or street of Frank shops, the Arab population were accustomed nightly to assemble, squatting on their haunches in primitive Arab fashion, in a circle around some favourite story-teller giving them a re-hash of the "Thousand and One Nights' Stories," still current coin throughout the East; only with added coarseness, adapting them to coarser audiences. Here, too, came the dancing and singing girls, to win piastres or paras by the display of their respective crafts, in the open air, to delighted audiences. But, like the mirage of the desert, with the old Ezbekieh these sights and sounds, so truly Oriental, have passed away from the vision of the traveller, as he sits on the verandah of his hotel. All is now decorous, dull and European in the prim gardens, which usurp a portion of that vanished pleasure-ground, which, picturesque as it was, must be confessed to have been a public nuisance in many respects, however "sentimental travellers" may bewail the substitution of cleanliness and order for dirt and disorder, savoury for unsavoury smells. Much sentimental rubbish has been written about this improvement of Cairo; but, in a sanitary and progressive point of view, no sensible man or woman, however sentimental, can deny the improvement and growth of Cairo, under the demolishing tendencies of the Khedive. The change in the modes of conveyance, however, may merit regret; for now, instead of "mounting barbed steeds," the pachas and beys, and other native gentlemen, who used to be seen prancing by in all their bravery, loll lazily back in open victorias or barouches, drawn by sorry jades, and driven by very dirty Arab charioteers, smoking strong cigars of German origin, and habited in Frank dress, with only the red fez cap to mark their nationality.

The carriages of the Khedive, of his sons, and of some of the ministers, are well appointed, with fine horses, and still preceded by running syces, and accompanied by guards in uniform; but the great majority of these turn-outs would not pass muster on London cab-stands. It must be confessed, that to see Egyptian officials and private gentlemen lolling back in carriages, and smoking cigarettes or cigars in place of pipes, does bewilder old Eastern travellers; and that such will also mourn the disappearance of the pipe and nargileh, formerly the symbol and pledge of Eastern hospitality, since the chibouque was always tendered to every guest by public and private persons, until another *régime* abolished them. They have been "improved" away; and, save in the public coffee-houses and among the common people, the cigar and cigarette have superseded them.

In the outdoor life, the only touch of the Orient left is afforded by the constant apparition, or rather flitting by of the hareems, whose fair representatives very freely take the air, and pass and repass constantly in front of the great hotels, wherein the travellers do congregate, in their well-guarded carriages—one of the last relics of the old system visible to the eye. Yet their habits, too, have undergone a great change. No longer are they ambulating or equestrian balloons of black silk perched on donkeys, or concealed in closed carriages; although the inevitable and irremovable black guards still " guide their steps and guard their rest," as in the days when Byron sung of them. Standing in the front of your hotel, you see the veiled fair ones of the hareem slowly borne past, at morning and eventide, in the neatest Parisian or English *coupés*, drawn by the finest English horses, and dressed in the latest Parisian modes —all except the face, which, half-hidden, half revealed, is covered with a gossamer veil, which also drapes the bosom. This veil, of the most cobweb lace, does not prevent their seeing and even saluting occasionally the passing stranger, to the great disgust of their sable guards; and the intensity with which they regard the outer world from the windows of their carriages, augurs well for their thirst for information. All the follies of European fashion have been, I am told, transferred to the East; for European costume is now the rage in the hareems, and Lyons silks of brightest colours, and French boots with impracticable heels, have succeeded the flowing draperies and shuffling slippers and baggy breeches of the Eastern fair ones. Frank women who have visited freely in the hareems for the last two winters, deprecate this change, fully as much as any of our sterner sex can do: and declare that it not only robs the hareem of all its romance, but most decidedly diminishes the peculiar beauty of its inmates.

The Ismailieh quarter of Cairo is entirely a new creation within the last six or seven years, and is one of the prettiest portions of the city. In order to encourage the erection of good houses for the European and Europeanized residents, and to attract new ones from abroad, the Khedive offered to give building lots, of the value of £2000 and upwards, to every person who would build thereon a house of a fixed value; rising in proportion to the estimated worth of the gift. The bait took, and the lots mapped out in the rear of the great hotels, where there were no buildings, on the

outskirts of the city, in the direction of Boulak—
the old port of Cairo—were soon snatched up;
and a new town of several thousands of houses
soon occupied the site.   Most of these are good
substantial houses, in imitation of Swiss *chalets*
or English houses, and some are very fine,
costing as much as £20,000.   Almost all have
gardens surrounding them, some very spacious
ones; for reserved lots were purchased by enterprising natives in the vicinity.   These latter are
chiefly the native or Levantine bankers, who
are the richest class in the community; and
some of the pachas have also built large houses
on the Eastern plan, hareem accommodation
included.   One of the largest and finest of the
Frank houses is that of Mr. Remington, the well-
known arms-manufacturer, who has armed the
Khedive's troops.   The Duke of Sutherland is
another foreign real estate proprietor at Cairo;
the English Club occupying one-half of the large
house he caused to be built.

I do not know the exact population of the
Ismaïlieh quarter; but it includes a greater
portion of the foreign population of Cairo, with
a large sprinkling of richer Levantines.   Some
of the dwellings are quite palatial in their proportions, and there is very little of the Eastern
element perceptible about them generally in this
neighbourhood; even the inevitable black Boab

(or door-keeper) of former times, in loose shirt, naked legs, red morocco shoes, and ample turban, with shaven head and snowy beard, having disappeared. His sole duty used to be his real or supposed guardianship of the gate or door leading into his employer's house; where, night and day, he was to be seen squatting or stretched at length on his *cafass*, or palm-twig seat and bed, the Cerberus of the establishment. But he was a solemn old fraud as to his police functions, I am sorry to say, although a most pictorial one—a Cerberus not even requiring a sop to silence him: habitually asleep all day, and generally requiring to be awakened by visitors of good intentions; and either revelling, or prowling about like a dissipated old mouser, at night, when he was supposed to be the guardian of the gate, in reality as well as in name. Still he was a necessary adjunct to Eastern life, and especially to the picturesque presentation of it.

He was evidently the parent and progenitor of the French *concierge*, and like him or her a domestic spy, paid by the occupant of the house he does not protect; and in all disagreeable features the European imitation is a greater nuisance than the Eastern—the latter, at least, being civil to his master and to strangers; the former, like the ancient Roman, regarding every 'stranger as an enemy. Yet I confess I miss, at Cairo, the grisly old vagabond "dweller of the threshold."

The last Government census of Cairo dates from 1868; and in the interval of nine years, as the natural increase, especially among the native population, is rapid, the figures in that return mostly fall far short of the actual numbers to-day.

In that table the number of strangers resident at Cairo is given as 19,120, but the list includes some strangers of Eastern origin. The total population of the capital at that date is estimated at 350,399, males and females, although of course the female population must be taken on trust by the census takers; owing to the domestic arrangements of the native Cairenes.

It struck me—returning after an absence of several years, three seasons since—that the climate had perceptibly changed, being colder in winter and hotter in summer than formerly. It certainly is more damp; and rainy and cloudy days, which used to be very rare apparitions, are now not unfrequent in winter, and fires, morning and evening, quite necessary for comfort during such changes of the weather. This is accounted for by the larger space of water open to evaporation all over the Delta and through the desert, by the canals of various kinds, which have been so greatly increased in number and size during the last ten years.

Finally, with all due respect to the "spirit of the age," as exemplified at Cairo, and the Khedive's improvement of my favourite city, I must express the opinion, that for that climate the old system of narrow streets, and exclusion of too much sunshine, together with the old plan of Eastern building, were best suited to the climate, place, and people.

CHAPTER IV.

THE FOUNDERS OF THE DYNASTY.

Mehemet Ali—Soldier of fortune—Satrap and viceroy—Parallel between the Napoleons of the East and of the West—His strange career—Dreams of an Arab empire, like that of the caliphs—Why he failed in establishing it—England's interposition—Rage of the trapped lion—Cloudy close of a bright day—Personal traits and anecdotes of Mehemet Ali—His son Ibrahim, regent and successor—His short lease of power—Can his dream be now fulfilled?—Reasons for the establishment of an Arab empire at the present moment.

AUGUSTUS boasted that he found Rome of brick, and left it of marble.

Mehemet Ali, founder of Egypt and of the present Egyptian dynasty, within the memory of men yet alive, found Alexandria a mass of ruins and rubbish, a nest of needy fishermen and pirates, and left it a city. He found all Egypt a chaos, he left it a country.

The Egypt of the Pharaohs, familiar to all readers of the Old Testament, and the Egypt of the early Christians, so vividly depicted in Kingsley's " Hypatia," where Goth, Greek, and Roman struggled for the mastery, differed not more widely from each other in all respects, than from the country we know by that name to-day ; which, in its turn, varies as widely from the Egypt of the Mamelukes, known to the previous generation.

For the impress of the first Napoleon was not more strongly stamped on the empire he founded, than that of Mehemet Ali upon the country and the dynasty of his creation : wrung from his trembling suzerain, the Sultan, at the sword's point, and welded together by one man's genius and courage.

As the bronze equestrian statue of "the Napoleon of Egypt" looks proudly down to-day from the Grand Plaza of Alexandria, seeming to keep watch and ward over the city of his love : so the mighty shadow of its founder still seems to rule Egypt from its urn, and protect it from the shortcomings and sins of some, if not all, of his successors.

There are curious coincidences in the characters and careers of the two "men of destiny" in the East and in the West. Both were aliens in blood and birth to the countries and people over which they established their rule, and founded their dynasties. Both were soldiers by profession, and statesmen and lawgivers by intuition. Both were crafty, cruel and unscrupulous, never sacrificing the end for the means, nor

shrinking from acts of ruthless cruelty, when policy
or self-preservation prompted their commission.
The ambition of each was to found an empire,
and to obtain the succession for his son and his
son's sons for ever; and this too both seemingly
accomplished. What is stranger still, is that
the heritage left by the rude Eastern soldier of
fortune, has lasted longer than the far greater
one bequeathed by the mighty genius of modern
Christendom, whose puppets and playthings were
kings and crowns. As though to complete the
parallel, the two were almost as kindred in fate
as in renown; the end of each being equally
tragic. The Corsican ate out his own heart in
exile on the barren rock of St. Helena; the
soldier from Cavalla died a prisoner in his own
palace, the ghastly wreck of his former self, his
fine mind and iron will shattered by madness,
alternating between moody despondency and
frenzy, until his practical deposition became a
State necessity, and his warrior son, Ibrahim
Pacha, was compelled to seat himself in the
chair of his yet living father. As though to
make this sad story sadder still, it is said the
madness came from a potion administered
through superstition or mistaken kindness by
one of his daughters, who was told she could
thus restore the old man's waning powers, but
whose fatal draught consigned him to a living

F

death. True or false, the story is still repeated
and believed in Egypt.

His dream of empire he soon converted into
a reality. From insubordination to the Porte,
he soon broke out into open rebellion; and not
only seized on the Egyptian provinces, but
invaded both Arabia and Syria, through his
warlike son Ibrahim, and even menaced Constantinople. His troops actually occupied Syria,
and his purpose was to found an empire like that
of the caliphs, over all the Arabic-speaking
people; leaving the Porte those only who spoke
the Turkish tongue. But then a greater power
intervened between the rebellious vassal and the
powerless lord; the Great Powers of Europe
(with the exception of France) interposed, and
by menace and force of arms wrested the prey
from the old lion, and compelled him to renew
his allegiance, and renounce his projects of extended empire.

It required the presence of an English fleet at
Alexandria, to compel him to sign a treaty of
peace with his sovereign, and resign his conquests; tearing out handfuls of his white beard
in his wrath, under the compulsion, while he did
so. But he insisted on the retention of the
viceroyalty in his line for ever, and for quasi-
independence of the Porte in the same treaty
guaranteed by the Powers which compelled the
act of abdication.

What Mehemet Ali did, in and for Egypt, has passed into history. He created not only an empire, but a people, out of the dozen different nationalities which then, as now, constitute the strange amalgam we vaguely term Egyptians. Everywhere throughout Egypt and its dependencies, the hand of the mighty master is still to be seen in the traces it has left—from the Mahmoudieh Canal, connecting the waters of the Nile with the Mediterranean, to the fairy-like pleasure gardens of Shoubra, near Cairo; from the gigantic, but still uncompleted barrage, or breakwater of the Nile, to the grand old sycamore trees, which give their beautiful shade to the gardens and the roads around Cairo and Alexandria. The career of Mehemet Ali is as familiar to every one as that of Napoleon, whose footsteps he followed in the conquest of Egypt; and whose fiercest foes (the Mamelukes) he crushed at one fell blow, combining craft, cruelty, and treachery in the act which self-preservation dictated. The man's character should not be judged by this episode alone, nor weighed in our balance; for he was capable of being swayed by high and generous impulses— with more of the lion than the wolf in his nature—and the necessity was very pressing and very sore. So it is but fair to judge him by the canons of his own time, place, and people, which condoned his crime, and the terrible retribution dealt on the savage oppressors and spoilers of Egypt, who menaced his life, and meditated against him the treachery in which he anticipated them.

Rid of this impediment, by alternate force and fraud he worked his way doggedly on to place and power: subduing first one province, then another, in the name of his suzerain, the Sultan, and welding together into one mass, and under one rule, the scattered and warring tribes and factions composing Egypt. Nor did he confine himself to those limits, but carried fire and sword and the terror of his name into the desert, among the tameless Bedouins, then, far more than now, the scourge and terror of the peaceful peasant who had aught to pillage. Having done all this in another's name, he began to be weary of vassalage to his inferior in mind and manhood, and commenced to plot and plan for shaking off his fetters, and founding an independent empire.

He brought order out of chaos; he invited and encouraged. European immigration, and especially European merchants, to develop the rich resources of the country, neglected and despised by the warlike chieftains, who had been ruling it with a rod of iron, and making it the theatre of perpetual little local wars. Yet his

mistakes, like his successes, were on a great
scale; and inherited by his successors too.
Entertaining the notion, so common to uneducated minds, that a country to be independent
and prosperous should produce within its own
borders everything requisite for the use of its
population, he sought to put this idea into
practice in Egypt.   Nature had made Egypt
agricultural, Mehemet Ali determined she should
be manufacturing too! Regardless of expense,
he imported large quantities of costly machinery,
with skilled operatives at high wages, erecting
vast mills all over the Delta, that manufactures
on a large scale might be produced.   The
skeleton ruins of those mills, many of them still
filled with the rusty remains of the machinery
left there when the failure was manifest, attest
the cost of the lesson given this Eastern Canute,
whose will was to override all natural laws.   His
successors have not profited, as they should have
done, by this useful lesson; for similar wreck and
waste may be witnessed to-day all over the
country, both of mills and machinery, of later
date than the days of the great founder of the
line of viceroys in name, but kings in reality,
one of whom still sits upon the throne of the
Pharaohs.

He also strained the finances of the country
by his lavish expenditure, and it is curious to

read in the annals of his contemporaries of the straits to which he was often reduced, and his sudden and inexplicable command of money from no visible source. History in Egypt repeats itself more curiously than elsewhere, as well as the personal traits of its rulers, and the mystery which envelops the proceedings, not only of its officials, but of its finances, which have ever appeared and disappeared in a truly wonderful and inexplicable manner.

The early period was the golden age for the foreign merchants, invited by Mehemet Ali to develop the commerce of the country, to whom he gave very large commissions for the purchase of what he required, and great facilities for enriching themselves. Englishmen, Greeks, and Italians came at his call, and established great houses, and were merchant princes indeed, their scale of living being proportionate to their vast operations and immense gains. They lived in houses as large as palaces, kept large retinues of servants and retainers, entertained magnificently and with the greatest profusion, and were lavish in expenditure. One of these, a Tuscan, kept twenty carriages, that he might always be able to send them to convey his guests to and from their residences; his palace, surrounded by magnificent gardens, being four miles out of town. Another reserved every Friday evening, during the winter season, for a grand ball at his mansion, in addition to grand dinners three times a week. The latter relic of those good old days survived to the patriarchal age of 90 years, in full possession of his faculties ; and continued his hospitalities down to the third generation of his guests.

Grand as were the prizes offered, and great the fortunes accumulated in the days of the earlier viceroys, strange to say the number of Europeans attracted there was comparatively small always. As late as 1852 there were not more than 20,000 foreigners at Alexandria, and 2000 at Cairo. Yet the absolute rule of Mehemet Ali may be said to have commenced full forty years before.

If the viceroy was lavish of the earnings of his subjects, he was not sparing of their flesh and blood ; and the condition of the fellah, or agricultural labourer, then was very much worse than his lot to-day, for he was then treated as a slave and serf (*adscriptus glebæ*), whose labour was compulsory, paid by enough coarse food to keep body and soul together, and enough rough covering to conceal partially his or her nakedness. He could not leave his native village to settle elsewhere without special permission from the governor of his province. If he ventured he was caught, bastinadoed, and

taken back to his usual toil in the usual place,
if not sent to the army or the galleys. By forced
corvées he was compelled to labour on the public
works without pay, and often without food,
unless he brought it with him, through the
rascality of the subordinate officials, who robbed
him of that which the Government was supposed
to supply, but never stinted him of the basti-
nado. In fact, he was treated like a brute, and
compelled to live like a beast. His lot is certainly somewhat ameliorated now, yet there is
still great room for improvement in the condition and treatment of the Egyptian peasantry—
the most amiable, patient drudges in the world,
constituting as they do the bone and muscle
of the country, and the source of all its wealth
and productiveness.

When Mehemet Ali caused the Mahmoudieh
Canal to be dug by fellah labour, cutting a broad
ditch to connect the waters of the Nile with the
sea at Alexandria—a work of vast utility before
the railway communication existed—he is said
to have sacrificed to it the lives of many thousands of these poor wretches; set to dig with no
proper tools, under the burning sun of Egypt,
labouring day and night under cruel taskmasters, without food or shelter. The pyramid
of skulls erected by the savage Eastern warrior,
was not a sterner *memento mori*, nor a more

tragic record, than the Mahmoudieh Canal. The
terrible burden of the old song—

> "A pickaxe, and a spade, a spade!
> Ay! and a winding sheet,"

might have been chanted by these poor
wretches of the Nile, who thus dug their own
graves while digging this canal. But on this
subject I shall have more to say when treating
of the fellah as he was and as he is; not the
"fellah" of M. About's charming fiction, but
the grimy and oppressed reality, owing all the
blessings he enjoys chiefly to God's good grace,
and his hardships to "man's inhumanity to
man," which does literally "make countless
thousands mourn" in the old house of bondage,
where the nominal slave has not really the
heaviest fetters to wear.

To return to the maker of Egypt. Although
totally uneducated, and therefore destitute of
much general information, the natural genius of
the man and his quick mother-wit supplied to a
great extent his want of culture. His readiness
of retort was worthy of a French wit. One
illustration may suffice to show its quality. A
French engineer being asked what he thought of
the plan of the Mahmoudieh Canal, while it was
in course of completion, ventured this criticism:

"Your Highness must pardon my suggesting
that your canal will be very crooked."

"Do your rivers in France run in a straight line?" abruptly responded the Pacha.

"Certainly not," answered the astonished Frenchman.

"Who made them? Was it not Allah?" again questioned the Pacha.

"Assuredly, your Highness," replied the Frenchman, who thought his questioner's wits were wandering, and could not comprehend what he was aiming at.

"Well, then," answered Mehemet Ali, triumphantly, "do you think that either you or I know better than Allah how water ought to run? I imitated him in my canal; otherwise it would soon have been a dry ditch, not a canal."

The Frenchman was silenced, if not convinced; and the canal is certainly very crooked still.

Like all Eastern rulers, the grim old warrior, nursed from boyhood in the lap of war, was to a certain extent a voluptuary, although he never allowed his pleasures to interfere with his duties or his ambitious schemes. The gleaming white walls of the palace of Ras el Tin, which first strike the traveller's eye on entering the harbour of Alexandria, mark one of his favourite resorts. Another was the garden of Shoubra, near Cairo, in which he built a spacious kiosque of white marble, embowered in tropical foliage,

where the golden orange glows in the midst of
the dark green foliage, and the senses ache with
the perfume of roses and other fragrant flowers.
It was a lofty building in the form of a hollow
square; and in the central open space, over
which there was no roof, like the old impluvium,
was an artificial lake, about four feet deep,
paved with marble, with an elevated marble
resting-place in the centre.

Here, when his beard was like snow, and his
blood circulated more slowly, the old man was
wont to repair, to relax mind and body from
the fatigues and cares of State.   Perched on
this central seat, he would amuse himself for
hours, watching the gambols or the fright of his
hareem women, who he would cause to be rowed
or paddled about in small boats around this
mimic lake, at a secret signal from himself to
the boatmen causing them to be upset into
the water, and witnessing with delight their
struggles afterwards.   Strange contrariety of
human nature! that this grim old soldier,
whose savage nature and fierce eye (as we see
in his latest portraits) even years could not
tame or subdue; stained with the blood of the
slaughtered Mamelukes, and surrounded by
tragic memories, should have found pleasure in
such childish sport as this, even when trembling
on the verge of the grave!

But in every Eastern nature—which essentially differs from the Western—we find the extremes of ferocity and levity blended incongruously together; and the Pacha who inspires you with fear or with admiration one moment, by some childish act converts both into contempt or pity. But Mehemet Ali was an exceptional man, both in the evil and the good he wrought in and upon Egypt, of which the latter predominated. Let us bury the former and forget it; in memory of the latter, which lives after him, and embalms his memory in the annals of modern Egypt.

Of his successor for a short term, his warrior son Ibrahim, who swept like a flame through Syria and Arabia, and was the sword-hand of his father, his military genius was his chief characteristic, and the record of his battles the record of his life. The pious care of his son, the present Khedive, has erected a fitting monument to his memory, in the spirited equestrian bronze statue, which he has caused to be placed at Cairo, overlooking an open square near the Mooskie, or quarter of European shops. Mounted on his war-horse, which seems to snuff the battle afar off, with outstretched arm pointing out farther conquests to his fierce followers, he looks every inch a soldier, and born leader of men on the battle-field. What his abilities as a civilian or viceroy may have been he did not reign long enough to develop ; and he has therefore left no mark upon Egyptian administration or Egyptian affairs ; though, during his administration as his father's representative in Syria, he is said to have displayed considerable administrative ability. Personally he seems to have been a bold, frank man, a warm friend, and equally good hater, though not vindictive or cruel ; but, as before remarked, it is as a soldier chiefly that he will be remembered. He once visited London, and was known to the ragged boys of the metropolis, to whom a Turk was then a rarity, as *Abraham Parker !* into which they translated his patronymic, on the phonetic principle.*

In view of recent events, and of the impending disintegration of that huge colossus, by courtesy styled the Turkish Empire, over whose broken fragments there must be a European scramble ere long, the question now suggests itself, whether the Power which thwarted the project of Mehemet Ali, might not now wisely resuscitate and perfect it ?

An Arab empire, with Egypt at its head, embracing Syria and Palestine on the one side, and Arabia on the other, under a protectorate of two or more of the Great Powers, would oppose a

* His reign lasted but seventy days after his inauguration.

breakwater to Russian aggression on the one hand, and relieve that alien race from the exactions and misgovernment of the Porte, which has amply proved its unfitness to govern, and which in fact does not govern them; the limits of its authority being those of its garrisoned towns, outside of which protection from native sheiks is essential for the traveller's safety, and of whose nominal rule. the tax-gatherer is the only representative. Such a rule as has made Tunis a responsible government, and is redeeming Egypt from its " Slough of Despond," by the introduction of real, not sham, improvements in its internal administration, could as readily be established over the countries I have named, combined into a federation, whose centre would be Egypt, as the Arab-speaking country, already so far advanced on the march towards civilization.

It seems equally impossible now, to allow the rich countries named to languish much longer under the sickly beams of the waning Crescent, to be annexed to the Russian Empire even in part, or to be allowed to relapse into still greater anarchy than that which reigns therein to-day, in view of their importance strategically and commercially, lying as they do in part on the route to India. Among the various propositions made as to the partition of the Turkish Empire, it strikes me as surprising, that British statesmen have not, as in the case of the Suez Canal, reconsidered and reversed the policy of their predecessors, and made the dream of old Mehemet Ali, which they so rudely dissipated, a reality in the hands of his successors; under good and sufficient guarantees and proper securities that the powers thus conferred should not be abused, but exercised for the benefit and improvement of the most intelligent, docile, and laborious of all the races of the East, whose only ties to the Turk are now, as they ever have been, those of faith, subjugation, and taxation.

My own experience of these countries and people convinces me, that the accomplishment of this scheme would be comparatively easy now— far easier, in fact, than that which the gallant Gordon is now attempting, in the interests of civilization and humanity, among the savage negro races of Central Africa.

CHAPTER V.

ABBAS PACHA.

Accession of Abbas Pacha—Personal description of him—His peculiar character and habits—A Turk of the Turks—Contrasted with Saïd Pacha—His treatment of his people—The new "house of bondage" under him—His closing tragedy—A dead man's drive—His son El-Hami—A fated family line.

MEHEMET ALI and Ibrahim Pacha were before my time in Egypt, and of them I speak merely from history and from hearsay, having associated subsequently with those who had been intimately acquainted with both these rulers of men. All of their successors I have known well, and have been brought into intimate official and private connection with for many years. Of them therefore I can speak from personal knowledge, including the Khedive Ismaïl, who inherits many of the traits of his great progenitors as an administrator and manager of men, but whose ambition, though equal to his ancestor's, does not work through the sword or through force, but through diplomacy and persuasion.

Between the reigns of Ibrahim Pacha and the Khedive's two others intervened, those of Abbas Pacha and of Saïd Pacha, who though partaking of the same blood, and members of the same family, differed from each other in every particular and in every quality, physical and moral. Far as the poles asunder were these two men, and as opposite the impression made and left by each of them upon their common heritage. Abbas was a sullen, suspicious, timid tyrant, hating and fearing the European element his grandfather had introduced, and striving to put back the shadow on the dial-plate of progress moving in the direction of European civilization. Though born and bred in Egypt, he was a Turk of the Turks.

His complexion was much darker than that of the majority of his family, most of whom are fair, with reddish beards. Abbas was swarthy, with a scanty beard, short and stout of figure, with a bloated, sensual face, and dull, cruel eyes. Yet there was both energy and intelligence manifested in this repulsive countenance, when warmed into interest or animation on any matter that touched him nearly. His manners, like those of all high Turks, were bland and polished; for in all that constitutes perfect good breeding the Eastern surpasses the average Western man. Of his morals the less said, the

G

better, if Alexandrian and Cairene gossip can be relied on. But on this point I cannot testify from personal knowledge, not having ever been on the same intimate terms with him, socially, as with his two successors.

He understood and spoke no European language—an exception in his family, all the rest of whom have a thorough knowledge at least of French—and therefore always conversed with foreign agents, whom he saw as seldom as possible, through the medium of an interpreter, which of course prevented much interchange of ideas or feelings ; for decanted *champagne frappé* is not flatter or colder, than conversation thus carried on. If in his relations with foreigners he was unsympathetic, in his conduct towards his own people he was arbitrary, rapacious, and cruel to the last degree. The possession of wealth was often only a passport to Fazougli (the Egyptian Cayenne) for its proprietor, and the confiscation of the property, "for treason," to the State (that is, the viceroy's) coffers.

With foreigners he could not meddle—they were safe under their consular protection—nor could he expel them for the same reason; but trade was crippled under his reign, since even his avarice, which was great, could not conquer his prejudices, and induce him to encourage and foster the commerce of the country. With his own people his will was law: for he paid heavy backsheesh to Constantinople, partly to be let alone, and partly in the hope of changing the succession in favour of his son, El-Hami—a dream which every viceroy has indulged in, and which the Khedive has finally made a reality.

El-Hami was afterwards married to one of the Sultan's daughters, and kept in splendid slavery at Constantinople—as the sons-in-law ever are—and was finally drowned while on a pleasure party; being of a gay and festive turn of mind, and much addicted to the wines as well as the customs of France.

During the reign of Abbas the Crimean war broke out, and the Sultan called on his vassals for men and money, to which Abbas promptly responded; and Egyptian blood and treasure were as freely poured out as water on the sands, then as now, to protract the death agony of the effete and imbecile dynasty of the Sublime Porte.

At the same time came an order from the Porte to expel from Egypt the entire Greek colony there, not enrolled as rayahs, or Christian subjects of the Porte; a measure the cruelty of which may be appreciated, when it is stated that the execution of this harsh measure would have entailed swift and sure ruin on that whole

community, numbering many thousands; among
whom were many of the oldest and most respectable of the foreign residents and merchants.
Their protests were not listened to, and they
were given but forty-eight hours to leave the
country. The consular corps, as a body, having
declined to interfere in their behalf, on account
of the political complications of their respective
countries, it was my good fortune to have been
enabled to take the responsibility of retaining
and protecting these luckless people during the
continuance of the war, by placing them under
the protection of my flag—a privilege accorded
all Christian Powers under the old capitulations—
after much trouble, and diplomatic and personal
pressure on the viceroy.

I must do Abbas Pacha the justice to say that
in this matter he showed either good feeling or
indifference, and did not press the execution of
the stern edict with zeal. On the contrary, when
representations came from the agents of other
foreign Powers, as to his non-execution of this
order, he simply shrugged his shoulders and said:
"What can I do? These people have obtained
another protection, and I cannot interfere with
them, without insulting a great nation." So, after
much diplomatic correspondence, the Greeks
remained in Egypt, and the order was practically
never enforced, except in a few instances where

the parties were noisily partisan in their demon-
strations or conversation. After the war was
over, the King of Greece proffered me the Grand
Cross of Sauveur, as a testimonial of his, and his
people's gratitude.

The character of Saïd was precisely the reverse
of that of his nephew. A bold, frank, fearless,
and reckless man, fond of foreign society, speaking French like a Parisian, and enjoying, of all
things, the witty turns of which that language
is capable; himself a wit of no mean calibre,
and equally irreproachable in his cook and his
cellar. It was like emerging from darkness into
sunshine when he succeeded Abbas, who, though
his nephew, preceded him under the provision
of the firman decreeing that the succession
should pass to the "eldest male of the blood of
Mehemet Ali." Abbas was a little older than
Saïd, and so inherited, owing his own succession
to the terrible tragedy which removed his father
from the line. That father having been sent by
Mehemet Ali to demand tribute of a semi-savage
chief in the Soudan, surnamed the "Tiger of
Shendy," having insulted and struck him, was
deliberately roasted alive in his tent the same
night, together with his whole troop, by his
treacherous and vindictive host, who surrounded
the tents in which they were sleeping with
dried corn-stalks and drove them back with

their lances into the flames when they sought
to escape.   The fate of Abbas was as tragic
as that of his father, he too perishing by perfidy
and violence; and the shadow of his coming
doom seems to have been stamped both on
his countenance and his soul.   He forboded
that fate, and took extraordinary precautions to
avoid it; and those very precautions rendered
its execution all the more easy, although he surrounded himself with guards, banished men on
mere suspicion, and ate no food that was not
prepared by his old mother's hands, or under her
immediate supervision.

Nothing is more indicative of character and
disposition than the choice and surroundings of
a man's residence.   Mehemet Ali, Ibrahim, and
Saïd, all dwelt much in the public eye, chiefly
at the palace of Ras el Tin looking on the sea,
accessible to all comers.   Their leisure hours
they solaced either in the lovely gardens of
Shohbra, where the plash of fountains, the scent
of roses, and the songs of birds created an
earthly paradise, which earthly houris were not
lacking to complete; or they rehearsed the game
of war under tents, with from 10,000 to 20,000
troops around them.

But Abbas lived as he died, alone.   Seldom
seen by his people, never by foreigners, except
from necessity, his favourite haunts were secluded

palaces, remote from cities and men, which he built in the desert. There, surrounded only by a few cringing slaves, and by the savage beasts he collected into menageries, he shrouded himself like Tiberius at Capri, and was as solitary in his death as in his life. He was strangled while he slept by two of his own slaves—boys sent him from Constantinople by a kinswoman—but the exact manner, as well as the inciting cause to his murder was, and is still, a mystery. The fact only is certain, as well as that of the ghastly farce which was played by the Governor of Cairo with the corpse of the dead man.

Summoned secretly and suddenly from Cairo, at the dead of night, to the Benha palace, twenty miles from Cairo, where the deed was done, Elfy Bey, the Governor of Cairo, gave strict orders that no one should divulge the death of Abbas. Ordering the state carriage to be brought to the private entrance, assisted by the head eunuch, he placed the body in a sitting posture within it, and taking his own seat opposite as usual, drove the twenty miles to Cairo, surrounded by guards and the usual state, in this ghastly companionship. He reached the citadel at Cairo with his mute companion, without exciting suspicion, aided by the habitual shrinking from observation which characterized his master; and once there, caused the guns of the citadel to be pointed on the city, strongly reinforced the garrison, and declared the truth, together with his intention of proclaiming El-Hami viceroy in defiance of the rights of Saïd. This purpose he was induced to abandon on representations of Sir Frederick Bruce, the English consul-general, and myself —both of us then at Cairo—and our friendly, as well as formal warning that such action on his part would be treasonable, induced him to abandon the design, and to invite and welcome the new viceroy to Cairo; whither he came and was installed, without delay. The days of that governor were not long in the land, as he died very soon and very suddenly thereafter: removed doubtless by some super-serviceable courtier— for the character of Saïd forbade even the suspicion of his complicity in any act of treachery or cruelty.

But throughout the East, from the rivalry produced among brethren, through the system of polygamy producing separate families under the same roof, with separate interests, and in princely families more especially, a man's worst enemies are often literally "those of his own household;" and hence there has been little love lost among the descendants of Mehemet Ali. Saïd collected the scattered sticks of the faggot which Abbas had divided; but on his death they were scattered again—the two nearest in succession, Mustapha and Halim, settling down at Constantinople, where the Porte promoted them to high offices, and kept them *in terrorem* over the head of Ismaïl. Of these, Mustafa, who was a great intriguer and able man, much distrusted by the Khedive, died but a year ago, and his family have been sent for and taken charge of by Ismaïl, who has also gained possession of his great landed estates, which Mustafa sold before his death. Halim is still alive; but his lands, too, including the Shoubra gardens, have also passed into the Khedive's hands. It is he whose succession was set aside by the Sublime Porte, in favour of Tewfik, the son of Ismaïl, but four years since. He holds, or did hold, one of the portfolios at Constantinople, and of him more anon; as, on the impending break-up of the Ottoman Empire, he and his claims may come to the surface again some day.

The young prince El-Hami was generously treated by Saïd, who allowed him to retain the bulk of his father's fortune, and showed friendly dispositions to him ; but he died early, and with him ended the line of Abbas, whose wealth, too, passed away like an exhalation, in the hands of his improvident and reckless son.

But Abbas, as a ruler, was to a certain extent

a success. He so managed the finances of
Egypt as to keep clear of debt. Under his reign
the railroad system was inaugurated—chiefly, it
is true, under English pressure—to meet the
wants of the Indian transit; agriculture was
encouraged and developed, and many of the
wild projects of his predecessor discontinued.
Little as he loved the foreigner, he was cunning
enough to see the uses to which he might be
put; and though he did not encourage immigration, he did not interfere directly or openly
with the trade and commerce carried on by the
foreigners. The foreign agents, with whom he
could only converse by proxy, were his bad
dreams, and he avoided them as much as possible—far less dreamed of entertaining them, as
did his successor, on a scale of truly princely
hospitality. Under him, Egypt increased and
prospered materially, but not socially or morally;
and the condition of the fellah during his term
was that of a dumb drudge, a patient ox, for
whose mental or bodily improvement his task-
master had no care. Such was the condition of
"the house of bondage" when Saïd succeeded
Abbas in August, 1854.

CHAPTER VI.

THE REIGN OF SAÏD PACHA.

Saïd Pacha's accession—The new era introduced by him—Reversal
of his predecessor's policy, and private conduct—Attempt to bind
together the family faggot—His social habits—His great *fêtes*—
His princess, Ingee Khanum—His personal appearance and character
—Resemblance physically and morally to " Bluff King Hal "—His
military mania—Life under tents, and black knights in chain armour
—His work in Egypt—A bright dawn and stormy sunset.

WITH the accession of Saïd Pacha a new era
may be said to have commenced in Egyptian
administration. He was one of the younger sons
of Mehemet Ali, by a different mother from
Ibrahim's, or the father of Abbas, and bore the
traits of his fair Georgian mother in complexion
and figure. Carefully educated by an accom-
lished French tutor (Kœnig Bey), who took
good charge of the morals as well as of the mind
and manners of his pupil, Saïd Pacha was
a gentleman in our acceptation of that term, a
good French scholar, with some knowledge of
English, a man of large and liberal views, and
extremely fond of association with Europeans,

whose manners and habits he had adopted in his private life: with the exception of course of his hareem arrangements.

In policy, as well as in his habits and modes of thought, Saïd was the direct opposite of his predecessor; and it was he who gave the first strong impulse to the improvements and progress which have, within the last twenty-two years, placed Egypt in the van of the great march of Western civilization eastwards, and given the performance as well as the promise of reform in administration and national life. For, in reversal of his predecessor's policy of isolation, he at once inaugurated a large and liberal policy of expansion. He invited and encouraged European immigration, and under his reign the foreign colony more than doubled its numbers. As late as 1854 the European residents at Alexandria did not exceed, if they amounted to, 20,000, and there were not more than 2000 at Cairo, with a few scattered over the villages in the Delta, representing Alexandrian houses. By encouraging foreign immigration, surrounding himself with European *employés* in the different administrations, inviting eminent engineers, and removing many of the restrictions on trade and commerce imposed by Abbas, the new viceroy gave a powerful impulse both to the agricultural and commercial development of the country.

As his great father made the first step in the creation of the country, so Saïd may be credited with the second in its expansion, as the Khedive is entitled to the credit of having done much more to perfect what his predecessors planned.   He recalled all the members of his own family from Constantinople and elsewhere, as well as many state prisoners languishing at Fazougli, and sought to make himself the father of his family connection, as well as of his people.   In regard to the latter, he was fond of repeating the wish of Henri Quatre, when he said the height of his ambition was "that every peasant in his dominions should have a fowl in his pot every Sunday for his dinner."   As far as he could, Saïd carried out this sentiment ; as I shall show when treating the subject of the Egyptian labourer later on.

The stranger who attended one of his receptions, or the entertainments which he gave on a scale of great magnificence, blending the European and the Eastern styles, and who fancied an Egyptian prince must be an Othello, with "a sooty visage," was ever surprised to find a counterpart of the portraits of Henry VIII. of England, in complexion, beard, face, and figure, in Saïd Pacha.   The similarity in temper, manner, and character was equally striking, though the bluff manner was redeemed and softened, on

public occasions, in the viceroy by that exqui-
site polish of manner, in which the Turkish
gentleman excels. Even as regards the multiplicity of wives, the Englishman was more Eastern
than Saïd : whose princess, Ingee Khanum, still
surviving and living in state as his widow,
one of the most charming and accomplished of
Eastern women, by the concurring testimony
of all who know her, shared his throne and his
affections exclusively to the end of his life.

Saïd Pacha was fair, with a ruddy complexion,
and reddish beard and hair ; his features were
regular, the expression of his face frank and
open. His figure was large and muscular, indi-
cating the immense personal strength which
increasing corpulence and illness marred in his
later years. His eyes though small were bright,
and he did not, like most Turks, keep them
habitually half closed ; but they had none of the
sleepy langour of his race, but flashed with fun
or blazed with anger, as his excitable temper and
changing mood moved him. Neither did he
avoid a direct glance at his interlocutor, in
Eastern fashion, but looked straight in the face
of the person with whom he was conversing.
His readiness of wit, and the charm of his conversation (conducted in French, which he spoke
as his mother tongue), rendered him a delightful
companion ; and he was convivial at the table,

without going into excess — drinking wine in moderation, ever of the most superior quality. His "French cook," who was an Arab, used to prepare for the breakfast dishes worthy of the most famous Parisian restaurants ; Saïd appearing in the loose Turkish summer dress he wore in private, which made him look like a huge bale of cotton, being all of fine white linen. Generous to a fault, and liberal to prodigality, he pushed those virtues to excess, and was deceived and preyed upon by many whom he rewarded and trusted, until, like most princes, he became soured and distrustful in his later days. After a long and most intimate acquaintance with Saïd Pacha, without being blind to his faults and shortcomings, I can truly say that, in my widely varied experience of men and countries, I have met no nobler and manlier nature than his, either Christian, Turk, or infidel; and in his early prime, before disgust and disease had warped, though they never obliterated, his higher traits of character, he was every inch a king and a gentleman by God's own patent. In imitation of Mehemet Ali, and in direct contradiction to Eastern etiquette, Saïd Pacha courted publicity, and was more easy of access than European monarchs, hedging himself in with as few formalities as he possibly could, in consonance with the prejudices of his people, who are strong believers in "the divinity that doth hedge a king." He gave grand *fêtes* continually, to which all European men were free to come, whether invited or not, at which he entertained the foreign consuls-general and distinguished visitors to Egypt right royally. His open-air *fêtes*, in which thousands participated, renewed the recollections of the "Thousand and One Nights," with the variegated lamps suspended from the trees of his palace parks, and the Oriental costumes of his courtiers and people. To these the European ladies passing through Cairo frequently came, but uninvited; the march of Frank customs not having yet been accelerated to the pace now followed by the Khedive, whose balls at Ab-din every winter are exact copies of European royal entertainments.

Saïd Pacha's natural instincts were those of a soldier, and as happily he had no opportunity of indulging them in actual warfare, he amused himself with its mimicry—paid great attention to the recruiting, equipment, drill, and manœuvring of his army, which he raised to the number of 50,000 men, and spent much time under tents, taking a large force with him into the desert to drill and manœuvre. He changed the Stambouli or "Frank" uniform, adopted by Abbas, back into the more appropriate Eastern costume; and in addition to his 30,000 or 40,000 infantry in

baggy breeches, and jackets of white with metal
buttons, equipped several squadrons of horse in
fancy style.

One of the most striking of these was a troop
of gigantic Nubians, clad from head to heel in
the chain armour of the early Crusaders, with
their black barbs in like panoply; and a grim
troop they looked, with their jet black faces,
black barbs, rolling white eyes, and rattling
chain armour. Another troop seemed sheathed
in gold, with bright brass breastplates on horse
and man, and glittering brass helmets on the
riders—preserved from sunstroke, under that
burning sun, by special grace of Allah alone.

His dinners were frequent, and the effect
produced by alternate layers of European and
native down the whole length of the long
festive board, presenting such striking contrasts
in costume and nationality, was curious in the
extreme. The viceroy and the foreign agents
dined at the head of the table on a raised platform, and the entire service at each remove was
of gold, the epergnes, candelabra, etc., being all
of the same precious metal. The ladies of the
hareem, of course, were never visible; but, invisible to us, bright eyes looked down and
watched the repast from peeping-places above,
the hareem wing giving a view of the banquet-
ing hall, so that the princess and her visitors

H

could amuse themselves with the spectacle, without the trouble of entertaining the guests.

His restless nature kept him as busy in work as play. He was ambitious of leaving a high record behind him, and lent an ear to all schemes of public improvement and utility. He summoned Robert Stephenson, and a small army of engineers, to make several lines of railway, in addition to the one commenced under Abbas, which at his death was completed only to Cairo; and during his whole reign that work went bravely on. He employed the famous French engineer, Mougel Bey, to carry out the great breakwater, the Barrage of the Nile (to this day unfinished). He caused new canals to be cut and opened for irrigation; improved the condition of the fellahs, and tried to make large landed proprietors out of the more intelligent among them; removed onerous taxes and restrictions; built model villages for the fellahs; and finally, when M. de Lesseps returned to Egypt—after leaving the French diplomatic service, in which he had served before in Egypt, while Saïd was a youth—took him under his patronage and protection, gave him the concession for the Suez Canal, which has made the fame and fortune of that energetic and adroit projector, and gave such practical aid, pecuniary and moral, subsequently to De Lesseps and his work, as insured the

success of both; in commemoration of which
the Mediterranean mouth of the canal bears his
name. He also adopted the telegraph, extending
the wires, not only from city to city, but high up
the Nile—a startling innovation in Egypt, where
the old semaphore signals had hitherto been
regarded as the perfection of telegraphic communication. He introduced steam pumps and
steam machinery of all kinds, for agricultural
purposes, into Egypt, and kept Father Nile within
his bed, out of which, as now, he annually at
a given time roused him, to take a run over
the country, instead of allowing him to tumble
out himself in primitive fashion. The annual
revenues of Egypt rose, under his judicious
management, from its imports and exports, to
£6,000,000 per annum—an increase to which the
American civil war conduced, by creating a great
demand and higher prices for Egyptian cotton.
Remarking to me, on the breaking out of that
war, "Well, if your people stop growing cotton,
I shall be glad to supply their place," he did
strain every nerve to do so, greatly enriching
Egypt by the increased production of that
staple.

Before that war he had sent large orders to
America, and obtained large supplies of American
locomotives and open railway carriages, which he
considered best adapted for the hot climate of

Egypt : ordering a very grand one for his private use, including house and kitchen as well.

He had connecting lines of rail run up to the back doors of his palaces, and when bored by visitors or consuls-general, would slip away in this house-carriage and stay somewhere on the road for several days, as a practical joke. I saw him last shortly before his death, in the summer of 1862, at Paris, whither he had gone to consult a famous surgeon as to the internal disease which was then destroying him. His increasing feebleness was rendered more perceptible from the huge bulk of his body, swollen and flaccid by disease. But his mind seemed still vigorous, though his eye was dull; and his manner had lost little of its old charm, and his powers of retort were as keen and caustic as ever. He saw and submitted to his rapidly approaching doom, with the blended stoicism of the fatalistic Turk, and the resignation of the French *philosophe*, both of which characters were blended in his.

He died not long after, and was interred, not among the others of his line, who have stately mausoleums near Cairo, but in the burying ground of a small mosque in the centre of Alexandria, where his mother's remains also rest.

If the early morn of Saïd Pacha's reign was bright and smiling with promise, its close was dark and dreary enough to add another to the many examples, from "Macedonia's madman" to the Swede, to prove the vanity of human hopes, and the nothingness of human grandeur. He mounted the throne of Egypt in 1854, a gay, hopeful, ardent man, with vigorous health, boundless power, and almost inexhaustible wealth. He left it but nine years later for a premature grave; his strength wasted to childish weakness by disease and trouble ; hope, fortune, friends, all lost; and, with a soul as sick as his body, welcomed death as a release from suffering.

At my last interview with him, he expressed deep regret that he had saddled his country with a public loan and a public debt ; and that he repented of it. When he died, I believe the public debt of Egypt did not exceed £5,000,000. What it now is, under the fatal facility of credit, and the new system of "financing" introduced into Egypt, and flourishing like a poisonous fungus for twelve years past, the world has been informed through the reports of the financial surgeons sent from Europe to probe and cure, if possible, the gaping wound.

In justice to the Khedive of whom, once the spoiled and petted favourite of Europe, few now have a good word to say, it must be stated that he treated Saïd's royal lady, and his only son, Toussoun Pacha (who died the other day), like

a king and a kinsman; and still continues so to
do to the surviving widow, who keeps up a state
and commands a respect second to none in the
reigning house, and is treated with equal consideration and courtesy by the Khedive himself.
Toussoun he married to one of his daughters,
and made Minister of Education. He was much
respected and beloved, possessing his father's
traits of temper without his force of character.

Of Saïd Pacha, in conclusion, it may be said
that, as he was human, he sinned and suffered,
both as a public and a private man. His faith
was that of Islam; many of his ways were not
as our ways; his civilization was blended with
barbarism; but he was a brave, true-hearted
man, a staunch friend, a forgiving enemy, a
just, humane, and judicious ruler over the
country which Providence had confided to his
care. *Requiescat in pace!*

THE GRAIN MARKET AT SUEZ.

To face page 103.

CHAPTER VII.

THE FOREIGN COLONY IN EGYPT IN OLDEN TIME.

The foreign colony in Egypt, under the earlier viceroys—Classification of them—The merchant princes—The European army officers— Suleyman Pacha, or Colonel Séves, commander-in-chief—Some anecdotes of him—Other conforming and non-conforming officials—Some curious specimens—Talking only Arabic!—Peculiar privileges of foreign consuls-general and their *protégés*—The new mixed tribunals superseding consular authority—A few words about them, and the old doctrine of " Exterritoriality."

I HAVE already stated that the foreign element in Egypt, composed of Europeans and of Greeks educated in Europe, played a conspicuous part in the early history of Egypt, and that their numbers were largely recruited during the reign of Saïd Pacha, in consequence of his encouragement to and patronage of them. I have also slightly sketched the first pioneers of this tide of Western civilization, the merchant princes, in the preceding chapter. Of these, who came in with Mehemet Ali, and gradually lost both their monopoly of the trade, as well as of the heavy commissions attendant on royal orders for machinery, cotton goods, and other Western productions, in consequence of the competition of the later arrivals, it is unnecessary to say more.

Let us cast a hasty glance over the other classes composing this advanced guard of civilization, presenting as they do many curious subjects of contemplation and observation. Among these there were not many who found it necessary to become renegades, or profess or practise the creed and habits of Islamism.

In the army was the Count Galeazzo Visconti, of Milan, a scion of the old Italian Viscontis, who held a captain's commission for years, but who never owned a uniform, put on a sword, or saw a review of troops, during his long stay in Egypt. Lord Palmerston's recommendation had obtained him his nominal rank and duty ; and there were a legion of such. Polish, Hungarian, Italian, Austrian, and Venetian refugees came and settled down in swarms ; some to useful pursuits, others to nominal ones, or sinecures under the Government. Among this latter class was one man of rare ability and acquirements, the Chevalier Geronimo Lattis, who, with Manin, had been one of the triumvirate of the short-lived Venetian republic. His scientific abilities found a useful field in Egypt, and he was much consulted in agricultural matters by Saïd Pacha. I believe he still lives, and resides in Egypt.

Another set of Christian *employés* was taken from the class of rayahs, or native Christians, composed chiefly of Armenians, Syrians, Greeks, and Coptic subjects of the Porte. These, though little favoured by Abbas, were brought prominently forward by Saïd Pacha, who made Arakel Bey—the brother of the now famous Nubar Pacha, and like him an Armenian Christian— Governor of the Soudan; and Nubar himself his Minister of Foreign Affairs, though then quite a young man. The Copts, who seem to have a natural aptitude for figures and accounts, filled, as they still fill, the public offices; and the introduction of the railway and steam engine involved the employment of English engineers.

So that the foreign colony waxed fat, and became a most important element in the development of the new Egypt of the successors of Mehemet Ali: as it continues to-day, when the control of the finances, of the railway, of the docks and harbours, in fact of everything but the army, as well as the great products of the soil, has passed into foreign hands. The Khedive has allowed himself to be treated as Gulliver was in the land of Lilliput—tied down by thousands of small threads, until he can neither move hand nor foot of his own volition.

Will he long continue to submit to this abdication of the highest functions of government, and entrust them to foreign hands? Time alone can tell.

An idea of the Babel of tongues prevailing in Egypt, where all nationalities, Western and Eastern, are represented, and where a man should be a polyglot to prosper in trade or profession, may be formed from the statement that the transactions of legal proceedings there involves a knowledge of French, Italian, Greek, and Arabic, all four of which, together with other languages incidentally, must enter into the pleadings.

Mehemet Ali, as an Albanian, was really more Greek than Turk, though professing and reared in the latter faith, in which he brought up his family also. But he was no fanatic—even more liberal in matters of faith than most Turks, who are models in the matter of toleration, unless their fanatical fervour is violently roused—and so men served him faithfully, he cared little for the creeds they professed. The same liberality of feeling has ever been evinced by his descendants, with the exception of Abbas, who was supposed to be fanatical; although he never gave much practical demonstration of it, except by sanctioning by his presence the annual ceremony of the Doseh, when the returning head of the pilgrimage from Mecca rides over the bodies of a pavement of living men—a kind of Egyptian " Car of Juggernaut " ceremonial, which Saïd discontinued, and the present Khedive discourages; though I believe neither have been able entirely to suppress this cruel relic of barbarism.

In consequence of this toleration, but few of the foreigners who sought the Egyptian service conformed, and became Mussulmen in faith and in mode of life.

One notable exception to this was Suleyman Pacha, formerly Colonel Séves—a Frenchman who served on the staff of Napoleon in his Egyptian campaign, but remained after the French had left the country; and being a skilled soldier, and a man of talent and energy, rose to the rank of pacha and commander-in-chief of the Egyptian forces; dying at an advanced age, only a few years since, in that position. Suleyman Pacha did not do things by halves, but in all respects conformed rigidly to the tenets and practices of his new faith to the day of his death, diminishing his license in the way of wine, and increasing it in the way of wives; living in every way in true Mussulman fashion, and keeping up the old hareem usages. I knew the old man, and met him on several occasions; and a more thorough Turk outwardly, in appearance, manners, and habits, I never saw. Yet, when excited or irritated, the nature of the Frenchman would break through the conventional mannerism of the Oriental, and the old soldier of the Empire appear in full force. I never heard him speak of his old souvenirs, or make any reference to his past career. He avoided European society; and when forced into it by his official ·position, his reserve and reticence were truly Oriental. A stranger, watching the dignified old man in his Oriental costume, with his snowy beard falling on his breast, on which glittered. the Order of the Medjidie: his grave and composed manner, and thoroughly Eastern aspect, would have regarded him as the true type of the high Turk. But one who knew his history, and marked the occasional twitching of the mouth under the heavy moustache, and the flash of the steel grey eye, sharp as a scimitar, could detect the French irritability and frivolity which were masked under the Turkish phlegm.

He did his duty, however, thoroughly and well, and enjoyed the confidence of several successive viceroys, different in all respects; dying in harness at last, a very old man, in the full odour of Egyptian Pacha-dom.

He was a good soldier and a stern martinet, and greatly improved the efficiency and discipline of the Egyptian army. The present head of the army is the Khedive's son Hassan, who is also Minister of War, promoted recently in place of Ratib Pacha, a Circassian, who made so bad a mess of the late Abyssinian campaign, through incompetence or "want of stomach for the fight," or probably from a combination of the two qualities. Suleyman Pacha evidently took a leaf out of his old commander's book; for the first Napoleon was *philosophe* under the Directory, His most Catholic Majesty as emperor, and a most excellent Mussulman at Cairo.

There were other foreigners in the service who, without going so far as Suleyman Pacha, in dress appearance, and even in speech, commonly passed for Turks with strangers. One most ludicrous exemplification of this I have frequently witnessed with great amusement, in the time of Saïd Pacha, when an Englishman, got up in thoroughly Oriental style, and speaking Arabic like a native, used to sit solemnly on his divan at the railway-station, over which he presided, and gravely listen, *through his interpreter*, to the complaints made by British officers and travellers from India, *en route* for Alexandria to embark for Europe. "Ask that lazy old Turk to stop making a chimney of himself, and mind his business, or we will ask our consul-general to ask his master to kick him out of his place!" and other such flattering remarks would fall apparently unheeded on the ear of the functionary, who sat cross-legged smoking, while angry British officers used such and stronger language, through their dragomen, who in turn would translate into Arabic the supposed substance of the observation. But not even the movement of a muscle or the twinkle of an eye would betray the farce he was playing; for, had his interlocutors known he could understand their complaints, he would have been overwhelmed with them. Hence, he prudently kept his own counsel, and warned the dragomen not to betray him; and thus was enabled to smoke his pipe in comparative comfort, while the traveller fumed and fretted away his wrath, without venting it on the wearied ears of the unmoved official.

There were numerous other foreign *employés*, recruited from every land and language on which the Western sun has shone, and political refugees from all the countries of Europe, whom the year of revolutions (1848) had driven abroad, and who, under some foreign consular protection, sought refuge and bread in the remote land of Egypt.

The confusion of tongues, from the mixture of so many nationalities, still is made rubric on the walls of Alexandria and Cairo, where flaming posters are pasted up, either for advertising business or amusement, in at least three or four languages, French, Italian, English, and Arabic —these being the most universally current, and most generally understood.

Thirty years ago there were not more than 6000 foreigners in Egypt. At present, by the consular registers, there are near 80,000 recorded as residents in the country; and adding to these a number in the cities and villages who are not down on those registers, or resident only during the winter months, the business season in Egypt, the Khedive's own computation of 100,000 foreign residents, made to me, must rather be below than above the mark.* The population of Cairo is about half a million, of which probably 20,000 may be Europeans; that of Alexandria, about 250,000, of whom probably 50,000 are resident Europeans; though there are many Europeanized Greeks and natives, who cannot be strictly enrolled as foreigners, doing business there also; with a very large floating population annually visiting Egypt for business, health, or pleasure. The latter class spend much money in the country in various ways.

The new mixed tribunals present the most curious illustration of the confusion of tongues

* In Appendix marked D will be found the tabular statement, taken from the consular registers.

above referred to. They are as mixed in language as in law, and in the nationalities of the judges and clients, and require a small army of interpreters to act as intermediaries between their component parts. The native judges, who understand no language but their own, and no law save that laid down in the Koran, of course must find the sessions rather tiresome : but preserve a most decorous judicial gravity under the mask of their habitual Oriental seriousness. The foreign judges, several of whom, on arrival, were innocent of knowledge of any but their native tongues, when plunged into this seething cauldron of the French civil law code, expounded by Italian, Greek, and English advocates in such French and Italian as they could master, and set to try cases in which Greek and Arabic witnesses and papers contained the evidence, must have felt, and must still feel, that " ignorance is *not* bliss " in their case. They must frequently imitate that energetic American judge, who, not being able to find the law requisite for making a just decision in a particular case, when asked by his brethren on the bench where he got his law from covering the case, responded: " Well, I made that decision by main strength."

So must it often be in these mixed tribunals.

The existence of these tribunals, now the

overshadowing power in Egypt, superseding the consular authority which used to be omnipotent, as well as that of the Khedive, who was once the only High Court of Appeal in the country, but who now is (at least nominally) amenable to their jurisdiction, is due to Nubar Pacha. More than twenty years ago, in the reign of Saïd, he sought to persuade the consuls-general to divest themselves of their judicial powers, by consenting to the establishment of some such scheme. But neither the country nor the time was ripe for it ; and year after year, with dogged patience and inexhaustible resource, under different administrations, he persevered until his efforts were crowned with success. But by a strange fatality he was "hoist by his own petard." His unforgiven sin with his monarch is, that in tying the hands of the European diplomatic agents, and submitting all judicial decisions to what is practically an Egyptian tribunal, whose judges are paid out of the Egyptian treasury, he at the same time threw meshes around the Khedive, and imperilled if he did not destroy his sovereign prerogative. For the tribunal has affirmed its right to sit in judgment on the Egyptian Master of Legions, and decree against him, although declining to go through the form of insisting on enforcing judgments, for which it has not been put in possession of adequate means. Hence the anomalous and awkward position the two reciprocally occupy, *vis-à-vis* to each other. Under the old system—based on the doctrine of "Exterritoriality," which gave authority over the foreigner exclusively to the representative of his own Government, under the ancient capitulations—the consular courts exercised the power of pronouncing judgment, in contests between their own subjects and those of other nationalities, including the natives. Through the powerful pressure of their own personal influence on the Egyptian ministers and the head of the State, they enforced justice for their people. That power and right foreign governments have abdicated (at least for a term of five years, two of which have expired), and it remains to be proven by experience whether the substitute is a good and sufficient one.

It has certainly succeeded in clearing off much rubbish, in the shape of old reclamations against the Government, sitting as a court of claims, for which the Khedive should be grateful. It has also given the "happy despatch" to the multitudinous bankrupts, by a speedy and simple system of relief, in place of the complicated ones previously existing in consular courts, no two of which agreed; and for this the foreign colony, which has had very bad affairs ever

since the close of the American war, which
induced over-speculation and ruin, should be
duly thankful. These two kinds of work, I
believe, constitute thus far the bulk of business
done, except the settlement of small claims.

The intervention of the tribunal in matters
directly connected with the Khedive and his
creditors, has not been either as successful or
as satisfactory as in the two other matters, either
to the Khedive : the judge (Haakmann) who
pronounced judgment and tried to enforce it,
and was compelled to resign in consequence :
or finally to the creditors of the Khedive who,
believing they had been presented with the
oyster, have had to content themselves with
the empty shells, thus far.

But the test of time alone can show whether
the tribunals, like Marshal McMahon, can or
will be permitted to serve out their "quin-
quennate," and renew it for another term.
With the exception noted, thus far the machine,
though over-cumbrous, and enormously expensive, seems to have run pretty smoothly.*

The old system also of each foreign consulate
attaching to it, as *protégés*, a number of native
Christian rayahs, chiefly Copts, Greeks, and
Syrians, and affording them countenance and

---

* In Appendix C will be found some particulars relating to these
tribunals.

protection, which used to add so much to the power, influence, and prestige of the representatives of the Great Powers, and afford so much protection to the native Christians (though sometimes abused), has been almost if not entirely done away with under the new *régime*, to the great regret and loss of the class who used to be thus protected. The alleged evils of the old system I believe to have been greatly exaggerated, though there were some notorious cases of abuse of the privilege: as there must ever be when discretionary power is confided to incompetent or venal hands, and consuls-general must be supposed to vary as much in character and capacity, as all other public functionaries.

CHAPTER VIII.

THE KHEDIVE'S EGYPT.

ACCORDING to Cæsar's " Commentaries," all Gaul "was divided into three parts." So is Egypt, viz., into *Lower Egypt*, or the Delta, containing 2,650,563 feddans (acres) of land under cultivation, ninety-two towns and cities, and 2253 villages or communes; *Middle Egypt*, containing 827,616 feddans of land, six towns and cities, and 114 villages; *Upper Egypt* containing 1,146,041 feddans of land, fifteen towns and cities, and 658 villages; making a total of 4,624,221 feddans of land under cultivation, 113 towns and cities, and 658 villages or townships.

Besides Egypt proper are the provinces of Massawa, Souakim, and Taka, on the coast of the Red Sea, and that vast province termed the Soudan.

It is claimed that in the last fifteen years not less than 500,000 acres have been reclaimed for cultivation from the desert, being an average of over 70,000 acres per year added to the cultivated area of Egypt : and that 300,000 more are in process of preparation under the canal improvements instituted by the Khedive ; for, in Egypt, the desert may be made "to blossom as the rose " by the application of water only. The Central African annexations, under Gordon and his subordinates, bid fair to double Egypt's area and population.

The chief exports of Egypt are cotton, sugar, and grain. *Cotton*, the culture of which was only introduced in 1820 by a Frenchman named Jumel, is now produced to the annual amount of about 600,000 bales, and furnishes Europe with one-eighth of its entire supply—four-fifths going to England. Sugar comes next ; the largest portion of which is exported to France, the next to England. Then come the cereals, the greatest portion of which goes to England also, in the proportion of ten to one to any other country.

Egyptian statesmen remark, with just pride,

that their country, more populous in proportion than any country in Europe, is yet able to supply the inhabitants by her products, leaving an immense surplus for exportation; and they also refer to the fact that her exports are double her imports—£14,000,000 in value to £7,000,000. Certainly a most satisfactory state of things, and indicative of prosperity. Much of this is due to the indefatigable efforts of the Khedive, who was a most successful and enterprising planter before he became Khedive, and whose expenditure in improving machinery and agricultural appliances has been on a scale as gigantic as his planting interest.

Not to pile up here too many statistics, which are very dry reading, I shall add only a few figures which are curious and instructive, and then pass on to other topics. The number of domestic animals in Egypt (not including the mummied specimens in the bull, crocodile, and other pits, at Memphis and elsewhere), are estimated at about 300,000 horned cattle, 20,000 horses, 94,000 asses, 36,000 camels, and 2500 mules; of sheep there are 175,000, goats 24,000.

During the year 1872 (the year of the rinderpest)* 14,000 head of cattle and 200,000

* The horse disease broke out again at Cairo and the upper country in the autumn of 1876-77, supposed to have been imported from Abyssinia.

sheep were imported into Alexandria for food. The average price of cattle at the great annual fairs at Tantah and elsewhere is double that of horses, and the same as that of camels. The land-tax of Egypt anually rises to upwards of £4,500,000, that tax being about £1 per feddan (acre). The date palm is one of the great sources of the food of the country-folk, and about £200,000 per annum is derived from taxes upon its fruit. It is estimated that there are over 5,000,000 of date trees in Egypt of different varieties, producing about 20,000,000 cantars (cwt.) of fruit each season. The cactus is also cultivated on a large scale, and its pears eaten.

With regard to Egypt's new acquisitions in Central Africa, when the geographical position, fertile soil, and products of the Nile basin are considered, their value to Egypt and to European commerce may be understood; but the exact amount of that value depends on the uses to which its fertile soil and teeming population may be put. Its first effect has been to divert to Egypt the produce of the Nile basin through her great artery the Nile, reviving the trade of Cairo and Alexandria. When the railway com- munication is completed, penetrating far into the Soudan, that trade must be diverted from Zanzibar and the Red Sea ports to its natural outlets. With so vast an area of fertile soil, and such a teeming population, rich in flocks, herds, and grain, and the natural products of Africa, hitherto the spoil of native traders and slave-dealers (synonymous terms), the experiment can and will be tried on the largest scale; and Gordon Pacha is in earnest in his efforts to suppress the traffic of man in man, which makes Equatorial Africa a waste and a Pandemonium.

Egypt proper (not including its recent acquisitions in Central Africa, which have doubled its area and population) was, in 1872, about as large as Belgium, while its population was greater than that of that country, so prosperous and comparatively populous; as well as of that of Sweden, Holland, Portugal, Denmark, and Norway—the density of the Egyptian population exceeding any of these.

The population of Cairo is near 500,000, that of Alexandria about 215,000; and, in despite of the popular idea as to the health of Egypt (as the tables of mortality of its great cities, carefully collected and published by the present Government, show), the mortality, except during the prevalence of epidemics—now becoming more rare and almost disappearing—will compare favourably with that of European cities. The vast improvements made and making in Cairo, in Haussmannizing the old town, must

also increase its healthiness, though the climate
is too enervating to suit European children.
You see many people in the streets presenting
the appearance of great age : but whether they
are as old as they look I cannot say : for everything seems so precocious in this country, where
girls of ten and boys of fifteen are marriageable
and married.

As to the mortality among the rural population (or fellahs) it is exceptionally small, proving
that neither their condition nor their labour can
be quite so bad or so heavy as sentimental
travellers would persuade us : while their natural
increase is very great, another proof of at least
comparative physical well-being. Under the
two last rulers the condition of the peasantry
has been improved ; they have been not only
permitted, but encouraged to become land-
owners; and the subdivision of property has
commenced, which must increase with each
year. The stories of forced labour and forcible
recruiting, and cruelty to the fellahs by the
Government *employés* (who, by the way, are not
Turks, but men of their own race, often their
own fellow-villagers), I am told by old residents,
and myself believe, to be partly exaggerated :
although I do not doubt that the system is radi-
cally bad, and that there is immense room for
improvement, both in the condition and treat-

ment of the fellahs; nor that acts of hardship
and cruelty are frequently perpetrated by the
ignorant and often brutal agents of the Khedive
or his Government, on the persons and property
of his subjects. Travellers' stories, however,
must be taken with many grains of allowance,
owing not only to their lack of knowledge as to
the character and customs of this most peculiar
people, but also to their ignorance of the language, and the darkened medium of the dragomen through which both reach them; the crass
ignorance of most of these blind guides being
only surpassed by their mendacity and desire to
astonish or shock the "Howadji" under their
charge.

I have often listened to conversations at
Shepheard's *table d'hôte*, from the returned Nile
pilgrim, who had supped on the dragomanic
stories, and it has reminded me more of the
wonderful discoveries of French tourists in
London as to the manners and customs of the
English, which we find still circulated and swallowed across the Channel, than any other narra-
tives of travel within my knowledge. Then, too,
there is Smelfungus, who was met by Sterne
during his sentimental journey, "who travelled
from Dan to Beersheba, and found everything
barren." I am quite sure I have met him in
Egypt, not once but repeatedly. Only last

winter, at Cairo, he sat near me at *table d'hôte*,
and I am satisfied he must be the same man.
Loud of voice, arrogant in manner, big, burly,
consequential, and surly, he seemed to occupy
two places at table, and the growling thunder of
his voice drowned the more subdued sound of
conversation for some distance in his vicinity.
Sitting very near him at table were two of the
native *employés*, easily distinguishable by their
swarthy faces, straight-collared Stambouli coats,
and red fez tarbouches of the Government regulation colour. Their presence seemed only to
stimulate Smelfungus, who loudly abused the
country and the Government, and described in
harrowing terms the treatment of the fellah men
and women by the pampered officials, and by
order of the Khedive—relating instances of
cruelty and oppression, as the rule and not the
exception, which, if universal, would make Satan
himself the only possible counsellor to the Khedive. What impression as to Frank courtesy
and credulity Smelfungus produced on his unmoved Egyptian auditors, whose appetite his
diatribes did not disturb, and who apparently
took no notice of speeches they could not fail to
hear, the reader can judge as well as I.

It is indeed a great pity that Smelfungus and
his class could not be kept at home by parlia-
mentary enactment; for they are petty instru-

ments of mighty mischief, in exciting national dislikes and magnifying misrepresentations. But free countries cannot take the precautions which despotisms may; and which Russia did for many years, according to general belief.

Hence, when any " Egyptian horrors " are put in current circulation, it is well to see if Smelfungus, inspired by his dragoman, be not their author.

No government or population ever yet was improved by angry vituperation, or by " clothing them in curses as with a garment; " and righteous indignation subjects itself to suspicion when it deals in vague generalities of accusation, and does not discriminate between cases that are universal, and those which are exceptional.

I am no apologist either for the shortcomings or the sins of Egyptian administration in the interior: nor for the treatment to which the fellah population has been—and is, I fear, still—subjected by an arbitrary, arrogant, and irresponsible set of taskmasters and tax-gatherers, armed with almost absolute authority. Even to the heads of State themselves I have not hesitated to point out, nor (I must do justice to them) have those rulers, in response, frequently failed to admit and deplore, while declaring their inability to remove, the grievous burdens born by the fellahs in many ways, and the necessity of improving their mental, physical, and social condition. Both Saïd and Ismaïl have grappled with this evil, and have been met with the irresistible opposition of the terrible *vis inertiæ* of Oriental apathy and fatalism—that dumb stupidity, against which Schiller says "even the Gods are powerless"—as well as by the corruption and cruelty of subordinate officials.

Attempting to ameliorate the lot of the peasant, Saïd Pacha caused model villages to be constructed, with clean and comfortable dwellings, and, pulling down the fellah mud huts, transported the families to their new homes. Eighteen months after, I inquired how his model village was thriving.

" You will oblige me, the next time you pass on your way to Cairo, to stop and see ! " was his reply.

I did so, and found that the model houses had been deserted, and were rapidly falling to ruin, while, like sugar-loaf ant-hills, on the outer circle were again grouped the mud huts, in all their primitive dirt and discomfort, with their fowls and filth and prowling dogs : into which the villagers, with their swarming families, had squatted down. Against ignorance and prejudices well-nigh invincible, the fight is a hard one ; and when you reflect that similar ignorance and barbarism prevails throughout the

whole country, and embraces all classes—except
a very small circle in the cities and surrounding
the Court—the difficulties of the administration
may be comprehended, and allowances made for ·
shortcomings.

The substitution of the foreign in place of
the native official, as the means of improvement and better government in the interior,
thus far has not proved a success : as the long
roll of that "noble army of martyrs," the
African explorers, from Livingstone to Muzinger
Pacha proves. The path of exploration and
of civilization into Central Africa, like that
across the desert, may be traced by the bones
of the pioneers who have perished along the
route.

In the great Government centres, however,
of Alexandria and Cairo it has worked well,
although the selection of these foreign officials
has not always been made with great judgment,
nor has the state of the Egyptian exchequer
been consulted as to their salaries and emoluments. While men of such eminent administrative and executive capacity as McKillop
Pacha, of the British navy (long in the Egyptian
service, and of incalculable value to the Khedive
in many ways), receive the most inadequate
salaries, many of the recent importations, who
possess neither a tithe of his abilities nor ex-

perience of the country, receive four times the pay for not one-fourth of the work which he does so thoroughly and indefatigably. I have never heard him utter a syllable of complaint—he is too proud a man for that—but the facts have fallen within my own knowledge, and I cite his case simply as an illustration of a general truth; applicable also to many of the ablest and oldest of foreign officials in Egypt : but without meaning to cast any reflection on the new-comers, several of whom are undoubtedly most efficient and useful public officers.

It is certainly but just that the salaries of officials, transplanted there from England or France, should be greatly increased, perhaps doubled, in view of the probable increase of expense in living (enormously high in Egypt), as well as of the interruption of their former business relations.   But it really does not seem just, either to the old officials and *employés*, or to the "gentleman in difficulties" to whose relief they are called, that many of the higher officials should receive the salary of British ministers of State ! and that clerks should be paid in pounds what they got in crowns in England—from whence almost all these new *employés* are drawn, with only enough of Frenchmen to serve as a seasoning.

If charity begins at home, so should economy;

and however great the savings effected by the new administrators may be—and in some instances, as in the post-office and the customs. administrations, they have been considerable—they will profit the Khedive or his creditors but little, if they are swallowed up in the expenses of the machinery employed in their production.

Sitting at Shepheard's *table d'hôte* one day, I saw six of these new *employés* side by side, whose collective salaries amounted to more than £20,000 per annum, and but four out of the six held high positions : the other two being merely clerks in departments. Many of these gentlemen, doubtless very capable at home, verify the truth of Lord Bacon's axiom, that " he that goeth abroad without understanding the language goeth to school, and not to travel." For how people, to whom the old records and papers relating to new transactions, are literally " sealed books," being in Arabic, can possibly either comprehend, audit, or check accounts, I confess puzzles me ; for the interpreter—again to cite Lord Bacon—" having his hand full, truth may choose but to open his little finger." This fact accounts for much of the confusion in Egyptian accounts.

These comments are made in no invidious or hostile spirit towards the new *employés*, most of whom I do not know, and several who are known personally to me inspiring me with most

K

friendly feelings. But the truth should be told ; and when outcries against the Khedive's expensive administration of public affairs are so loudly made, it is but just that some of the leaks should be shown to proceed from other causes than his own personal extravagancies. The ordinary Egyptian official, whether foreign or native, has hitherto been so insufficiently and irregularly paid, that this contrast seems all the more striking ; and hence I have placed my finger as gently as I could upon this very tender spot.*

Several of the gentlemen personally interested, with a candour that did them honour, frankly admitted to me the justice of the complaint in this regard made by the old *employés;* but naturally were not quixotic enough to propose a reduction in the emoluments, with which they had been so liberally endowed by the Egyptian Government, out of its almost empty chests.

One of the greatest difficulties in the transaction of bureau or official business of any kind is the immense number of holidays claimed, and granted to *employés* in all the Government bureaux, which exasperate and annoy all foreign officials, and retard the progress of business : but which, owing to the number of fasts and feasts

* See Appendix C.

in the Mohammedan calendar, it seems impossible to diminish.

The fasts and feasts and holidays of the Greek, Latin, and Coptic rayahs (or native Christians) are fully as numerous and as punctiliously observed as those of the Mussulmen; and the accountants and subordinate *employés* in the different divans are taken largely from this class—there being really no Turks in Egypt, and the native Egyptians not being over fond of clerical or office duties. The latter however act as the heads of divans, with the intention of doing everything by proxy, and as little as possible personally. Thus, with both head and hands equally willing to be idle, this irritating interposition of newly arrived and zealous strangers can effect but little.

During these holiday times the Government officers and officials do no manner of work that is not absolutely essential, and the recurrence of these vacations is vexatious to the European heads of bureaux, who see at least two months in every year lost through them; not including the thirty days' fast of Ramazan, when all Mussulman Egypt is awake all night, and asleep, or half asleep, all day—making three. This is one of the ingrained old customs, which even Khedive Ismaïl, absolute as he is supposed to be, has contended against in vain; striving to limit and reduce these very liberal vacations so constantly recurring. But custom, which in the East is stronger, not only than law, but even than kings, will not be changed; and Egyptian *employés*, who benefit by these leisure days, from high to low, stickle for their perpetuation, and evade—when they do not dare openly to disobey—higher orders to the contrary.

Against any active opposition the Khedive's fiat is omnipotent; but against old customs, prejudices, and habits, stronger than any written law and more religiously followed, even his energy and efforts strike as vainly as a cannon ball directed against a floating silk banner, whose non-resistance is the secret of its remaining unimpressed by the force directed against it.

Time, education, and improvement may finally counteract the causes enumerated; but it will require the united efforts of the three to make Egypt like unto Europe.

Let us then give both the Khedive, and his new assistants from abroad, the benefit of good intentions and well-directed efforts; even though the progress actually made, in the way of practical and perceptible reform in the different administrations, does not seem very perceptible as yet, and though the performance falls very far short of the swelling programme: put forth in the hope of regaining the lost confidence of

Europe, both as to the Khedive's promises of reform, and his promise to pay. The first steps in the right direction have been taken, and, with patience, the goal may be reached at last.

CHAPTER IX.

HELOUAN.

An *Aix les Bains* in the desert—What and where is Helouan?—On the road to it—The grand boulevard to the citadel—Glimpses of interiors *en route*—The Mokattam Hills—Their quarries— Through the desert, in view of the Pyramids—Appearance of Helouan —Its sights and smells—The sulphur baths—The hotel—The view from its roof—An enthusiastic collector of antiques.

SITTING on Shepheard's balcony at Cairo, one soft spring morning this year, the idea struck us to visit the sulphur springs and baths of Helouan : one of the modern improvements undertaken and carried out by the Khedive, at his own expense, for the benefit of all native and foreign sufferers from rheumatic or kindred maladies. The existence of hot sulphur springs at Helouan, about fourteen miles from Cairo, had been known a long time ; but the merit of utilizing them, and creating a species of *Aix les Bains* in the desert, is due to Ismaïl Pacha : who not only established baths there of a most substantial description, but caused a fine spacious hotel to be constructed as well, placed a German manager and doctor in charge of it, and encouraged the creation of a little village in the vicinity, presenting building lots to all persons who would erect upon them dwelling-houses of an inexpensive description. He also caused to be built a palace for his mother, by way of example, and the little bathing-place has become quite the fashion already. So much so that visitors from Cairo have often to wait a week or two, to secure accommodation at the hotel during the winter season. When the great heats come on, I believe the hotel is closed, though the owners of the houses at Helouan pass the entire summer there; the dry air of the desert suiting some constitutions, and the nights being always endurable, from the winds which ever sweep across the empty waste of desert sand which surrounds the springs, which form an oasis in the solitude.

Since the opening of a railway line to Helouan, access to it is easy, several times daily; but until very recently the only way of reaching it was by donkey or by carriage, both of which modes of conveyance were slow and tedious, in consequence of the heavy sand over which the route lay. Now it is only a matter of an hour from the station, which is immediately below the citadel—that sleepless watchman over the city which lies nestling at its feet; and wherein grim old Mehemet Ali enacted that stern tragedy, which removed at once and for ever from his path the only stumbling-block to his direct march to the throne of Egypt, by the massacre of the Mamelukes. The spot where the last survivor of that savage soldiery, dying like wolves caught in a trap, leaped his horse over the wall, and rose living from the dead body of his steed, to be pardoned subsequently by Mehemet Ali, is still shown the stranger; and very near that historic site you see the small railway station, which speaks eloquently of the change that has passed over Egypt during that interval—the reign of slaughter and treachery having been succeeded by the more peaceful progress of civilizing agencies, the cannon by the railway.

But let us start from the hotel, either on one of the knock-kneed little donkeys, which still swarm around Shepheard's steps as of old, and make both day and night vocal with the "long dry seesaw of their horrible bray;" or in one of the street carriages, since all the European capitals seem recently to have spawned their most rickety and disabled vehicles on the "city of victory," drawn by animals modelled on Don Quixotte's Rosinante, whose blood may be dubious, but whose bones are irrepressible and stare you in the face.

Often, looking on these, the real "lean kine" of modern Egypt, is the traveller reminded of that remarkable animal described by Mr. Weller, which when put in stiff shafts and driven down-hill went admirably, because too weak to stop. Mounting one of these dilapidated vehicles, our party of four (of whom two were ladies) drove along the Ezbekieh Gardens—which French taste has now enclosed, clipped, pruned, and trimmed into the likeness of a miniature Bois de Boulogne—down through the Mooskie (both of which have already been described), until we reached the road to the citadel.

Formerly the route to the citadel was one of the most winding and tortuous in all Cairo, corkscrewing through the bazaars and the narrow streets leading out of the Mooskie, or quarter of European shops, and compelling a *détour* as picturesque as it was provoking to people pressed for time. But the spirit of Haussmann has seemingly descended on the Khedive, who, possessing the power as well as the inclination, has on a smaller scale followed in the footsteps of the French leveller. For not only here, but in other quarters of the old city, broad open boulevards, as wide as the French, have been cut straight through the old houses, with a most ruthless disregard for the prejudices or the prayers of the old house-holders, who loathe light, air, and sunshine, as well as publicity, as much as they do "plague, pestilence, and famine;" even although in-demnity is given or promised them for all demolition or damage to their premises. Nor are they entirely without reasonable excuse for grumbling at this arbitrary and compulsory change in their "ancient ways," narrow, damp, dirty, and gloomy as they seemed to the stranger. For here, where the sun gives more than enough of heat and glare from his rise to his setting, shade and coolness, alone attainable in narrow streets with but a small slit of sky visible between the projecting housetops above, are the chief wants of the residents, and it is questionable whether what is a real improve-ment at Paris, may ultimately prove so at Grand Cairo.

Already, waiving the practical features of the matter, the sentimental traveller has broken into objurgations on the modern Pharaoh, who has hardened his heart against the picturesque, and ruthlessly torn down the crumbling old mud houses, with their latticed wooden windows, through which peered the bright eyes of Egyptian Fatimas and Zuleikas—"making a hideous modern boulevard out of these once

Oriental streets, where one might admire the few remaining specimens of Saracenic architecture!" as one of the latest pilgrims pathetically remarks.

But unluckily the "specimens" referred to never were "Saracenic," nor at all resembling it, but purely Arabic, and barbarous Arabic at best; and so much more of the same style still is left in Cairo, that a little more of it might still be spared to the ruthless hammer of improvement.

The broad open road, leading in a straight line to the massive pile of citadel buildings which crown the hill, back of which towers the frowning and rugged chain of the Mokattam Hills, on the desert edge, is finished and in tolerably good condition. But with the usual careless way of doing things in the East, the demolitions on each side of the roadway have been but partially completed, or never repaired, in most cases; by the erection of new outer walls. So you pass through what looks like a city that has recently been shelled—houses in all stages of dilapidation, though still inhabited, giving most odd views of domestic interiors, frowning down upon you; while not even a screen, much less a wall, has been placed between the dilapidation and the street.

As the plan of most of these old houses seems

to have been modelled on that of a rabbit warren, from the multiplicity and perplexity of burrowing-places in them, this unveiling of the interiors, originally designed to be so private, gives odd glimpses into the inner life of the Cairenes; whose ideas of comfort puzzle us as badly as those of the disinterred Pompeians, judging from their homes.

We left the railway station at mid-day, and almost immediately found ourselves on the desert, though not a desert of billowy sand (as fancy ever pictures a desert to be), but one of hard gritty soil, on which however neither grass, shrub, nor tree was growing. On our right hand as we proceeded was a distant view of the Nile, and of the Pyramids; on the left towered up, apparently not half a mile distant, the rugged masses of the Mokattam Hills—huge quarries of stone, from whose embowelled entrails had already been drawn much of the building material of Cairo, and from which new drains were now being made afresh, to gratify the Khedive's constructive propensities. For, as he frankly said to the writer of these sketches but two years ago, "All men have their manias; mine is in stone" —"*J'ai une manie en pierre*," to use his own words; for he converses in French, not in English, not understanding the latter language.

We could see the square openings in the hill-

sides made for the excavations, presenting the
appearance of caverns for the habitations of
hermits, such as you see scooped out of the hill-
sides in Palestine, near the rock convent of
Marssaba, not far from the Jordan and the Dead
Sea; and this impression is heightened by the
desolation of the surrounding landscape, where
you see neither bird, nor beast, nor form of man,
his habitations or his works, for mile after mile.
Sometimes the sharp silhouettes of a long line
of laden camels are defined against the hills or
the horizon; the gaunt weird outlines of these
ungainly animals, led by the Arab driver en-
veloped in his grey abba, or cloak, with striped
silken bornous on his head, giving a pictorial
look to the desolate and dreary scene. For even
the vulture seems unable to pick up a living on
these wastes, and does not hover over them.
The camels and the ungainly oxen enjoy the
monopoly; and they are employed in the labour
of hauling the stone from the quarries.

Over this waste of wilderness beats down the
fierce flaming sun of Egypt, flooding earth, air,
and sky with a golden glare, almost intolerable
to the eye, unrelieved by glimpse of verdure or
of water, except at very rare intervals, where
a little strip of green may be seen bordering a
well or fountain on the route; and sometimes
you catch glimpses of the silvery and flashing

current of the Nile, with the fringe of verdure
on its banks; while, pointing heavenwards with
their sharp cones, the eternal Pyramids loom up
ever in the distance, with nothing to obstruct
the view of their towering proportions.

But the glare, the heat, and the dust became
so overpowering, after half an hour of this mid-
day ride through the desert, that we were compelled perforce to shut out the view, which was
becoming monotonous, by closing the curtains
of our railway carriage; and creating smoke-
clouds by puffing cigarettes of genuine Stambouli
or Turkish tobacco, the soothing effect of which
we soon experienced.

The transit from the station at Cairo to the
station at Helouan occupies about an hour.
Shortly before reaching the latter, we opened
the windows and curtains of our carriage, to let
out the smoke, and take another view of the
surrounding scenery. On our left hand now it
was all desert, unrelieved by the hills which we
had left far behind. On the right still loomed
up the Pyramids, but Father Nile had become
invisible. In front we saw a long, low, irregular
pile of buildings of considerable extent, enclosed
in high walls which might conceal gardens.
This, we were told, was the palace of the
Khedive's mother, to which she occasionally
came; and at long intervals the great man

himself honoured Helouan with his presence; when his courtiers thronged there after him, and gave life and animation to that ordinarily quiet place, whose hotel and scattered houses we could now discern and were rapidly approaching. The station is not more than 100 yards from the hotel, yet so averse are people here, both native and foreign, to pedestrian feats that an omnibus was in readiness to convey us that short distance.

Resenting the imputation conveyed on our energy and activity by such a proffer, we declined the accommodation; and strolled leisurely along over the desert sand towards the town and hotel, the latter of which presented quite an imposing appearance, contrasted with the small houses scattered around it, most of which appeared to have been rapidly run up on the Aladdin plan, in a single night, to present a proper appearance of a town to the visitor. An over-powering atmosphere of newness pervaded everything, which in this country of ruins and recollections seemed strangely incongruous. Sarah's unexpected and unhoped-for child hardly appeared more exceptional, than a brand-new and growing village, on the modern plan, seems to the traveller in old Egypt. Yet here was one the youthful appearance of which might have done honour to an American backwoods settlement, six months after the

first tree had been cut down by the earliest
pioneers from "the coast," except that there
never having been any trees here, there could
be of necessity no "stumps," the characteristic
feature of the new settlement in America. For
whereas the American pioneer regards the
tree as his natural enemy, to be removed as
a nuisance; here the first care is to set out a
young plantation for shade and as a screen from
dust; and around each house at Helouan the
occupant had carefully set out such trees as
could be procured in this treeless country, whose
greatest want is the want of wood. Dickens, in
his "American Notes," records the astonishment
with which he beheld a baby in one of the
Western cities, which seemed too newly built
to have afforded time for a baby to be born;
and we were reminded of his astonishment here,
on seeing a woman with a baby in her arms,
which really looked older than the town—if by
courtesy we may designate by that title the
fifteen or twenty buildings which constitute
"Helouan les Bains," as the large placards
posted up all over Cairo somewhat pompously
denominate it.

So rapid, however, is the growth of vegetation
under the Egyptian sun—even on the desert
sands wherever water can be supplied—that
already several of the houses were gracefully

decorated with climbing creepers even to the roof, and the gardens were already blooming with tropical flowers and grass, giving the place the aspect of an oasis in the desert; for all around it, far as the eye can reach, is flat sandy plain, unrelieved even by a hillock—the horizon bounding it on all sides as in a sea view, and the setting sun dipping as suddenly as he does over the waste of waters when seen from shipboard. We proceeded to the hotel, which the Khedive caused to be erected about a year ago, when he decreed the creation of *Helouan les Bains*, then alone possessing the bubbling hot sulphur springs, which long had trickled unnoticed over the sands, whose curative virtues the Khedive appreciated as soon as they were explained to him, and thus sought to utilize, as an additional attraction to the foreign visitors, who annually contribute so much to the life of Cairo and the pockets of its landlords and shopkeepers, foreign and native.

The hotel is a large square building, with an open court in the centre filled with flowers and shrubs, two stories high, with verandahs running all around the inner square, where one can take air and exercise during the mid-day, when outdoor exercise would be impossible or dangerous. By a winding stairway you ascend to the roof, which, as usual in the East, is flat, with a parapet four feet high running all around it, so as to make it a most pleasant lounging-place when the sun has set, and until midnight under these clear, bright, and starry skies.

The rooms are all so large and airy that the hotel cannot accommodate comfortably nearly so many persons as its apparent size would indicate: I believe not more than fifty at a time.

Its present manager is really "a host in himself," being a Greek formerly engaged in mercantile pursuits, which he has renounced for an enthusiastic love of antiquities, to the collection of which he devotes all his spare time, and Egyptian coins of modern stamp. His collection is already a large and excellent one, and every day adds to its extent and value; for the central position of Helouan between the two families of Pyramids, those of Gizeh and Sakkhara, and the long summer vacation, when there are no travelling Howadji or foreign collectors to snap up the "unconsidered trifles" which the fellah or Bedouin picks up in the ruins or turns up with his ploughshare, give the collector on the spot immense advantages, both as to the choice and price of antiques.

The amiable enthusiast who manages the hotel and baths of Helouan makes the most of these advantages, and is never wearied with exhibiting his treasures to his guests, and explaining their former uses or meaning; thus rendering a residence under his roof as instructive as it is agreeable.

Add to this pleasant host, whose good temper is inexhaustible, the attractions of an excellent *cuisine*, and a select society of all nationalities and all tongues, as well as the facilities for making numerous excursions on donkeys to the two sets of Pyramids and different interesting localities in the desert, with the sulphur baths in addition, and it is easy to understand why many persons, who are not invalids, desert the comparative city life of Cairo, for the repose and fresh air of the desert.

After resting an hour in the cool shady reading-room, well supplied with newspapers and magazines in English, French, and German, and divans and easy-chairs of all descriptions, we sallied forth to see the baths, under the guidance of one of the many medical men found at Helouan. For really the place seems to have attracted the medical faculty as much as the invalids: several of the profession, German, French, and American, having at least temporary residences here; although the hotel and baths have their regular medical man, attached to the establishment and salaried by the Khedive, to whom the whole thing as yet is a charge, or has been until this, the second season.

The bathing establishment is replete with every comfort—large rooms with white marble baths for ordinary bathers, furnished with divans covered with chintz, on which to repose after being steamed and sulphurized; with the inevitable Eastern accompaniment of coffee and chibouques. A separate set of bathing rooms, with a private entrance, has been prepared and reserved for the sole and separate use of the Khedive and his family; and these are fitted up and furnished with satin damask hangings, and divans covered with the same rich material. The bathing-places also are more richly and expensively arranged than those for the use of the public, and exclusively devoted to royal use; strangers being only shown through them as one of the sights of the place. From the moment you enter the door until you leave the building, which is a very solid and substantial one, the penetrating odour of sulphur assails your nostrils with a pungency that is almost overpowering; and you carry that most uncelestial odour away with you, and about your person, for a considerable time after leaving the baths. We did not bathe, but the doctor turned one of the spouts, and the water which poured into the bath-tub was hot and sulphurous enough to have bubbled up direct from Plutonian fountains close at hand, for a special bath for Queen Proserpina.

Several of our friends who essayed the experiment of the virtues of these baths for rheumatic, and other similar ailments, experienced great benefit from the treatment ; while the purity of the air, blowing freshly over the desert, is most unquestionable.

The chief drawbacks to thorough enjoyment arise from the heat and glare, which confine most persons to the house from 10 a.m. to 6 p.m. ; but the early morning, the evening, and the night are truly delicious, and make amends for the temporary imprisonment during the heated term.

If one could be pardoned the use of a "bull," however, in all Eastern travel or residence, save in mid-winter, the night is always the best part of the day, whether in a dahabeah on the Nile, in the city, or on the desert ; for an Eastern night, with its large and lustrous stars dispensing almost the light of day, though softer and more subdued than the garish daylight, with its soft, soothing, and balmy breezes, surpasses far the most delightful spring day in less favoured climes : and is the best time for exercise, enjoyment, and musing. Lord Lytton's German mystic, who lived in an imaginary life of his own creation in dreamland, while his actual daily life was to him as a dream, should have come to Helouan to enjoy uninterruptedly that existence ;

since no spot in the world offers finer facilities
for it.

A short distance from the building there is
quite a large pond—used for bathing also—
of fresh water, supplied from the Nile, about a
mile distant but not perceptible from the spot
on which we stood below. This pond is much
resorted to by the small population in and
around Helouan, in the evenings and nights of
summer or spring ; so that sulphur or fresh-water
baths are equally accessible to the sojourners
here.

But it is worth coming to Helouan to get the
view from the housetop at sunset, as we did, for
it is unique of its kind, and unlike any other in
the wide wide world. Ascending to the flat
roof by a spiral stairway of iron, you stand upon
the housetop, surrounded by a stone parapet
about four feet in height, and look around you.

On every side there meets the eye the grim
grey desert, stretching away into the distance—
a shrubless sea of sand, bounded only by the
horizon. In the distance the slight undulations,
which alone break the dead level of its surface
over which flows a thin vapoury mist of exhala-
tions from the heat, resemble the billows of
the sea ; but the restless movement of the waves
is wanting here, and the illusion is soon dispelled as the spectator still gazes over this sad

scene, enlivened by the presence of no living thing. Earth and air seem as tenantless as though creation's dawn had not broken, and the Creator's fiat had not yet peopled the world.

You turn and look in the opposite direction—and piercing the clear atmosphere with sharp distinctness of outline, you behold at once the sister Pyramids of Gizeh and of Sakkhara, both visible from this point, and seemingly very near; but if you mount your donkey, or plough through the sand to reach either of them, you soon find they are further off than they seem to be through the medium of this clear atmosphere, which is most deceptive. This is, in my judgment, by far the finest view of the Pyramids from a distance, taking in as you do at one *coup d'œil* these rival monuments of man's folly; for whether they are to be considered as royal mausoleums or, as later theorizers have pronounced them, astrological erections, equally must they be regarded as huge monuments of human folly, in such a waste of labour, life, and wealth as their erection must have entailed.

Straining the eye, you see a silver thread with what seems a fringe of vegetation around it, and after a time you catch a glimpse of the Nile; which is visible from where you stand, distant, I was told, two miles. But there must be some undulation on that side, for it was not very plainly perceptible.

This was all that was to be seen, and such a view might appear, from this most inadequate description, not to repay the trouble of seeking it. But what gives it so bizarre and peculiar a character is in fact indescribable; for it consists chiefly in the absence of what meets the eye in all other landscapes; for here, with the fiery globe of the sun rushing redly down to his rest, a globe of fire dipping down as though into the sea, the old Scriptural malediction on Palestine comes back vividly to the mind: "Thy sky shall be as brass, and thy land shall be as iron"—for of brass and iron seem both to be composed at this place and hour.

When we reached Shepheard's Hotel on our return from Helouan, it seemed to us that we could fully appreciate the feelings of the wanderers in the wilderness on reaching Canaan.

CHAPTER X.

THE KHEDIVE ISMAÏL AS A PUBLIC AND A PRIVATE MAN.

His lucky star—The accident that made him Khedive—Achmet
Pacha's closing scene—His character—A fatal *fête* and lucky illness
—Halim Pacha's peril and escape—What might have been but for
an open drawbridge—My early impressions of Prince Ismaïl—His
love for " Naboth's vineyard "—The man and the monarch, briefly
epitomized—Things he has done and things he has left undone—
His building mania.

THE Egyptians, like all other Orientals, are very
superstitious, believing strongly in luck—that
there are people born lucky and unlucky: apart
from their kismet or destiny, which they think
binds every mortal man in its iron chain from
birth to death, beyond his power of will or of
resistance. Thus the last king of the Moors in
Spain, Boabdil, during whose reign they were
expelled from that fair and beloved land, was
commonly called *El Zogoybi*, " the Unlucky,"
and verified the appellation.

So, until his late troubles and failures, Ismaïl
Pacha was regarded by his subjects as the most

lucky of human beings : and the earlier stages
of his career seemed to justify the common
belief. Even his occupation of the throne
was due to an accident, fatal to another, but
fortunate for him. Between him and the succession, after the death of Saïd should have
made a vacancy, there was another life—that of
his brother Achmet, a man but little older than
himself, of powerful constitution and regular
habits. Achmet was the eldest son of Ibrahim
Pacha, and the succession was his of right, under
the rule that then existed, but has since been
changed to the direct line from father to son.

Early in the year 1858, Saïd Pacha, then
viceroy, gave a great *fête* at Alexandria, to
which he sent invitations for all the members of
his family, including the sons of Ibrahim and
others residing at Cairo. Such an invitation
was equal to a command ; so all accepted and
came, except Ismaïl, who making illness his
excuse, did not accompany them. They attended
the *fête ;* and the princely party, at the head of
which were Achmet and Halim, a younger and
favourite brother of Saïd, were assigned a special
train to convey them back to Cairo, when the
festivities were over. Their retinue was composed of twenty or thirty friends and attendants.
Midway between the two cities the line of rail
passes over the Nile, at Kaffir Azzayat, where

there is a famous bridge, built by Robert Stephenson, with a drawbridge that opens and shuts to permit the passage of steamers or other craft. As the train bearing its royal freight came thundering down the slope that leads on to this bridge, the English engineer who drove it saw to his horror that the draw-bridge was open, leaving a yawning space over the deep and raging flood, full fifty feet below —but saw the danger too late to avoid it.

The carriages, with the princes and their train, were precipitated into the river, Prince Halim alone escaping through his superior ac-tivity and presence of mind; for while the carriages hung suspended for an instant over the flood, he forced the door open, called to his nephew Achmet and the others to imitate him, and plunged headlong into the river, as the sole chance of escape from a dreadful death. Skilled in all athletic sports and manly exercises, Halim thus saved his life, swimming ashore as soon as he rose to the surface; but Achmet, an awkward heavy man, did not follow his lead, but was drowned with his companions, leaving the succession clear for his brother Ismaïl, who doubtless recognized " his star " in the whole affair, as well as in his preservation from a similar fate to that of his elder brother. There was not wanting slanderous tongues at the time

to hint at the viceroy's complicity in this
dreadful casualty; and he himself bitterly complained to me that he doubted not such would be
the case, at the same time exclaiming, in the
spirit and almost in the words of Scripture, "Is
thy servant a dog to have done this thing?" and
adding that his hope was that the presence of
his favourite brother there might screen him
from so unworthy a suspicion. From my knowledge of his character, as well as from inquiries
made on the spot subsequently, I am convinced
that he was innocent of all complicity in the
transaction; which was the result of carelessness
—some might say of fatality. It is curious to
contemplate the very different state of things
that might be existing in Egypt to-day, had the
succession not been changed by this casualty,
and Achmet succeeded instead of Ismaïl. For
Achmet was by nature and habit one of the
most prudent and conservative of human beings
—the exact reverse of a prodigal; in fact, accused
of avarice and inordinate love of money; addicted not to spending but to hoarding, and in
character and temper exactly the reverse of his
brother, known to us as the Khedive, who however rapidly he has contrived to fill his hands,
has managed ever to empty them quicker still.
So far did Prince Achmet carry his economies,
that he often received his foreign friends, who

called at his palace in the evening after dark, by the light of no chandelier or lustres attached to the walls, but in a chamber illuminated by the ordinary "*fanous*," or glass lantern with two candles, borne by respectable citizens in traversing the streets by night, before patrols were instituted at Cairo. He would have economized the public funds, as he did his private fortune, which was very large; but Egypt would have stood still, not advanced, under his reign.

Yet, in justice to him, it should be added that he also possessed some truly princely traits to neutralize this weakness. He was a man of honour and of courage, most truthful and reliable in all he said and did, devoted to agriculture, and incapable of cruelty or dishonesty. But he was better fitted for a private station than a throne: and had he lived and reigned, most probably the Suez Canal, and the other great public works which will hereafter record the enterprise of the Khedive Ismaïl, long after his loans and the Egyptian debt have been forgotten, would never have been Egypt's dowry in her bridal with Europe.

Heir presumptive through this casualty, Ismaïl now bided his time, devoting himself to agricultural pursuits, shunning publicity through fear of inspiring Saïd's jealousy, and acquiring

real estate—one of his passions—until he became
perhaps the largest landed proprietor in Egypt.
In addition to his own large hereditary properties, he has absorbed those of his brothers and
cousins; and several of the loans which now
figure in Mr. Cave's report, were contracted for
such purchases before or since his accession to
the throne.

During that period I used to visit the prince
at his palace at Cairo, and found him a most
polished and courteous gentleman, fond of conversing on his European experiences of travel, in
French, which he spoke with perfect ease and
fluency, and producing the impression that he
was an amiable but not very able man. He
certainly played Brutus well while his Cæsar
lived; for even his intimates had no conception
of the hidden energy and grasping ambition
which that smooth manner and guarded speech
concealed. Saïd himself certainly had not formed
a fair or a just estimate of his probable successor,
whom he could not conciliate, but who kept aloof
from the Court which that merry monarch
assembled around him after the accident which
opened the way for him, and which probably he
regarded as a premeditated trap set for himself
and kinsmen—a suspicion which his knowledge
of Saïd's character should have dispelled.

So anxious was Ismaïl to learn, and the courtiers to communicate, the tidings of the last breath drawn by the dying man whose waning shadow still filled the almost vacant throne, that a high official, the head of the telegraph line (an Englishman), sat all night by the side of the telegraph operator, to send the news by lightning to the coming ruler, the moment life had left the body of the old one.

But Saïd, with his powerful organization, died slowly, and taxed the patience of the watchers. So the high official, tired out at last after several sleepless nights, summoned a trusted native clerk in the office, whom he believed to be faithful and devoted to him personally, and charged him to come immediately to his house and awaken him, should the news come during his absence, promising him a handsome backsheesh for his services. He then went home to snatch a little sleep. But the astute clerk, knowing as well as his master the custom of the country, which conferred rank and gold to the first bearer of such tidings to a new viceroy, when the news did come, during his employer's slumbers, hastened to take it himself to Ismaïl, and received at once the anticipated promotion and reward. Then, with the malicious cunning and avarice of his class, further to outwit the confiding Frank, he hurried away to awaken him and impart the news, without saying a word

as to the use he had already made of it. Full of
hope and joy, the official hastened to the palace
of Ismaïl with the glad tidings; but, to his infinite
astonishment and disgust, was contemptuously
dismissed without reward as the bearer of stale
tidings, and left to reflect on the perfidy of native
clerks, and the necessity of keeping very wide-
awake in Egypt. The perfidious clerk is now a
pacha; his betrayed employer yet a bey.

The accession of Ismaïl Pacha took place
early in January, 1863, and the educational progress during that period has been truly remarkable, and would be so considered in any country
of the globe. At the time of Mehemet Ali there
were but 6000 children receiving public instruction. During the first six years of the reign of
the Khedive the number had increased to 60,000,
a portion of the credit for which is due to Saïd
Pacha, his predecessor. In 1873 the figure
attained was almost 90,000, and at this time it
doubtless exceeds 100,000.

One of the greatest difficulties in educating
this people has arisen from the peculiar social
and domestic system prevailing in the country,
which renders access to the female children
(except those of the very poor, or fellahs) almost
impossible. Thus, of the 90,000 pupils in the
primary schools, but 3000 are girls—chiefly, if
not entirely, the children of Christian parents,

foreign and native. But the indefatigable Khedive has grappled with the difficulty. He has
instituted at Cairo, on a liberal scale (in the
name of one of his wives), the first school for
women ever known in the Ottoman Empire : and
various others also have since been established
elsewhere in Egypt for female education. He
has gone deeper, and established schools for the
female children of the fellahs, or agricultural
labourers, in the hope of elevating the social,
moral, and intellectual condition of this large
class of the labouring population, whose past
and present lot has been far less pleasant and
comfortable than that of the former Southern
slave in the United States. Should these comprehensive educational plans of the Khedive be
carried out successfully, the next generation of
Egyptians, male and female, will be an immense
improvement on their predecessors, and be able
to contrast favourably with the labouring classes
of any country. But even under the most
favourable auspices it will require a generation
to effect this result, even in part ; for the Khedive has to build up the mass of his people from
a very low level indeed : as all who know aught
of the life and labours of the actual Egyptian
fellah must acknowledge. Whether also education alone will suffice to correct imperfect
moral and social home-training, and the absence,

M

not only of the comforts, but even of the neces-
saries and decencies of life, on the part of
children born and living in such environments
as those which surround the Egyptian fellah
from infancy and accompany him through life,
constitutes another problem, to be solved only
by actual experience. The idea and the effort,
however, are both noble; and, whatever the
result may be, posterity must do justice to the
initiative of the absolute ruler capable of con-
ceiving, and striving to execute so comprehensive
a plan.

In the year 1862, under Saïd Pacha's administration, the Government appropriation for public
instruction amounted to less than £6000. In
1872 the Khedive's Government appropriated
£80,000 for the same object; added to which,
several private subventions, derived from the
Khedive and his sons, were given to private,
foreign, and native schools.

It is estimated that the number of native boys
old enough to attend school is about 350,000,
and that the proportion actually receiving instruction is about twenty-three per cent.; while
in Turkey it is about ten per cent., and in
Russia but three; and even in Italy it is
but thirty-one. The comparative civilization in
Turkey and Egypt, tried by this test, may be
judged of from these figures, and the distance

between them must widen with each successive year. Besides the schools already mentioned, the Khedive has established special ones for his army, now about 30,000 men, and every soldier now is educated, and well educated, too—privates as well as officers. The American officers declare that the aptitude of the Arab in acquiring knowledge, especially in mathematical and military science, is exceptional. It must be an hereditary transmission, since we owe our algebra to Arabia in the first instance. Unlike the negro race, the Arab seems susceptible of the highest culture; and opportunity has developed remarkable ability in many Egyptians during the present reign.

The Khedive is entitled to the denomination of merchant prince more than any one who ever bore that title, combining the two characters profitably for a long time; but attempting to add to it also that of a financier, he wrecked himself, and has come very near wrecking the country too. At once the great producer and exporter from Egypt of its most valuable agricultural products, with a virtual monopoly in the transit, by forestalling the market and fixing prices he was able to regulate production, price, and transportation, and reduce a monopoly into a mathematical certainty, without the possibility of rivalry. He enjoyed also the privilege of

commanding labour at his own or no price, by
corvée—practised habitually in Egypt, and but
recently restrained with fixed limits, but existing
still for all public works, and the Khedive's private property, too, unless he is greatly slandered,
and common report prove a common liar. But
this is a subject which will be more fully entered
into in connection with the land tenure, and the
actual condition of the fellah. For the present,
let us consider the personal characteristics of
the man who, almost idolized in Europe but
three years ago, is now proving the fickleness of
public opinion in his own person, by seeing the
reverse of the medal.

Ismaïl Khedive is a man of about forty-eight
years of age, under the middle height, but
heavily and squarely built, with broad shoulders
which during the last year seem to have become
bowed down by the heavy burdens imposed upon
him, under which he has so manfully struggled.
His face is round, covered by a dark brown
beard, closely clipped, and short moustache of
the same colour, shading a firm but sensual
mouth. His complexion is dark; his features
regular, heavy rather than mobile in expression.
His eyes, which he keeps habitually half closed,
in Turkish fashion, sometimes closing one
entirely, are dark and usually dull, but very
penetrating and bright at times, when he shoots

a sudden sharp glance, like a flash, at his interlocutor. His face is usually as expressionless as
that of the Sphinx, or the late Napoleon III., of
whom, in my intercourse with the Khedive, I
have been frequently reminded; for they are men
much of the same stamp in character and intel-
lect, with the same strong and the same weak
characteristics doing constant battle with each
other. The Khedive's voice is very characteristic—low, somewhat thick yet emphatic, well-
modulated, giving meaning to the most common-
place utterances; his words accompanied by a
smile of much attractiveness when he seeks to
please, and his mind is at ease. But under the
mask of apparent apathy or serenity, the close
observer will remark, that the lines across the
broad brow and about the strong mouth indicate
strong passions as strongly suppressed, and the
cares of empire intruding ever on lighter
thoughts : and judge the Khedive to be far from
a happy man.

Of his personal amiability of temper his attendants and old *employés* speak highly—another
Napoleon trait; and this natural humanity is
indicated by the cessation of severe punishments,
such as banishment, confiscation, and capital
punishment, during his reign,—with one remarkable exception, which has produced abroad the
opposite impression, and made one blot on what

would otherwise have been a stainless record. During his visit abroad, in the year of the Great Exposition at Paris, Ismail was quite a lion, and excited the jealousy of his suzerain, the Sultan, by the warmth of his reception, *in partibus infidelium*, both by the members of the European cabinets and crowned heads.

One of the most curious episodes of this visit —in which he was accompanied by his adroit and able Minister of Foreign Affairs, Nubar Pacha, whose reputation has long since been fully as European as Egyptian—was his reception of, and reply to, the deputation of the Anti-Slavery Societies of England and France; in which the tables were adroitly turned on his philanthropic petitioners, by the skilful and perhaps truthful character of the response, which covers the question both of the slave-trade and of domestic slavery in Egypt.

This deputation presented an address to him, calling his attention to the White Nile slave-trade, of which Saïd Pacha had decreed the abolition. The address was signed by Joseph Cooper and A. Chamerovezow on behalf of the English committee, and by E. Laboulaye and Augustin Cochin for the French. The deputation was introduced and presented to the viceroy by Nubar Pacha, his Minister of Foreign Affairs, who acted as interpreter, and translated His Highness' reply, according to Oriental etiquette, though the prince spoke French as well and fluently as any man present. The reply of the viceroy was as follows—and it would be difficult to find, even among the happiest responses of Talleyrand or his school, a more cutting, cool, and contempt-uous rejoinder, couched in language of apparent courtesy. Nubar Pacha, acting as the mouth-piece of the viceroy, said—

"The Viceroy felt gratified to receive the deputation, and was much pleased this step had been taken, for he was most anxious to put down the slave-trade. He had adopted the strongest measures for that purpose. But *although he could act against his own people, he was powerless to do so against Europeans, who were the chief delinquents.* They carried on a trade in ivory; but this was a mere pre-text, their real article of merchandise being slaves, who were conveyed down the river in boats. If these boats had no flag, or sailed under Egyptian colours, they were liable to be overhauled, and if slaves were found on board, boat and cargo were confiscated and the traders punished. Within the last six months he had caused to be shot a commandant and a colonel, who had disobeyed his orders and favoured the slave-traders. But the slave-trading boats gene-rally hoist European colours of some sort, because their owners are Europeans, and if any question respecting the cargo arises, the answer is, that the men are part of the crew, the women their wives or concubines, and the young persons their children. The Egyptian authorities could not do anything under these circumstances, as they were debarred from the right of search. Within the last thirty years European influence had transformed Egypt, and if he were free to act against European slave-traders the slave-trade would soon disappear. *The European Powers should give him the necessary authority to exercise the right of search* as regards boats sailing under European colours.

" The extinction of slavery was another and distinct question. Slavery had existed in the country for 1283 years, and was mixed up with its religion. It was a horrible institution, and he desired to see it extinguished. But it was not to be done in a day. He considered that the civilization and progress of Egypt depended on its abolition : and were the slave-trade stopped, slavery would disappear in fifteen or twenty years, or very few traces of it would remain, because it would not be recruited from without. Of the actual slave population many would die in that time, many would be manumitted, and others adopted into families.

" He held the opinion—contrary to the views of his visitors—*that the slave-trade was the root of slavery in his country, and must be stopped before slavery could cease.* The abolition of the British consulate at Khartoum had certainly enabled him to act more efficiently against the slave-traders, *but the only effective mode of dealing with the traffic was to arm him with power to prevent Europeans from prosecuting it.*"

His introduction of Western civilization into Egypt; his Europeanising Cairo, the stronghold

of the vanishing Oriental type of city; his great
public works; his greater educational plans; his
filling his administrations with Europeans, and
placing them at the head of all the principal
bureaux; his remodelling his army under the
auspices of skilled and trained army officers,
invited from his *Ultima Thule*, America; the
broad religious toleration which has made Christian churches more numerous than Moslem ones,
in proportion to the relative populations of the
two sects, including the Eastern Christians
under his rule, to whom also he has given the
right and imposed the duty of bearing arms in
defence of the State (enrolling them in the army
in defiance of their universal exclusion elsewhere
throughout the Ottoman dominions)—all these
things are notorious, and constitute his claim
to the admiration of Christendom as a wise
reformer, a light newly arisen in the East.

But the financial embarrassments of Egypt
have come up like a cloud to eclipse these
glories, and he is now denounced in more un-
measured terms than he was lauded before,
and even his good deeds and good works
doubted and denied. My task is neither "to
bury Cæsar" nor "to praise him." I propose
simply to depict the man and the monarch as
I have seen and known him, and to do justice
at the same time to the ruler, and to his people,

not sparing the recital of his sins of omission
and commission, while giving a catalogue of the
benefits he has conferred on his country and his
people, heavy as may be the price which both
he and they may have to pay for them. This
Eastern prince is by no means " that faultless
monster the world ne'er saw," but a mere man
like the rest of us, and as such made up out of
a mingled yarn of virtues and vices. That he
possesses that sin by which fell the angels—
ambition—to which a moralist might add vain-
glory and rapacity, cannot be denied; that, in his
zeal for rapidly reforming his cities and his
people on the European model, he has gone
too far and too fast for his own comfort and
that of his subjects; that in annexing, and
seeking to annex, Equatorial Africa to Egypt
he has embarked on a dubious enterprise; that,
in looking solely at the ends in view, he has
often forgotten the means: and in the treatment
of the fellahs left much to be desired; and,
finally, that his expenditure has been greater
than his means;—all these charges cannot be
disputed.

As the father of a family, with four wive
and, I believe, twelve children, he has left
nothing to be desired which the most steady
bourgeois could demand; being a model head
of the family, on the Oriental plan of course!

Both his sons and daughters have been well educated by European instructors, and speak and write French, and perhaps other foreign languages, with ease and fluency. Both for sons and daughters he has insisted on the one-wife principle: his sons and sons-in-law being each but "the husband of one wife," according to the Scriptural recommendation. This is certainly a step in the right direction. But the young princes only appear in public, or at the Khedivial entertainments; the daughters still live on the hareem plan, for which their education has unfitted them.

The Khedive is an immense worker, and as it is one of the taxes on absolute power that its head must know and supervise everything, even to the minutest details, is compelled to get up early and sit up late at the labour he loves, of directing the whole State machinery; and these labours and cares are beginning to tell upon his health, as his personal appearance last winter attested, as well as his own admissions. Yet the rest and vacation which private men may freely take, are impossible to crowned heads, especially in such critical circumstances as those which environ the Khedive. The labours which used to constitute his pleasure have become an imperious necessity now. When he goes abroad, but little of the pomp and circumstance of royalty surround the handsome but simple equipage which conveys the absolute master of five and a half millions of Egyptians, and five millions more of Central Africans, through the streets of his capital. Clad in the Stambouli dress, only his fez cap indicates the Oriental; and half a dozen mounted guards, in his livery of chocolate, precede and follow the carriage, in which he rapidly. passes by, making salutations as he passes on, by a slight gesture of the hand to the Europeans, who raise their hats to him—the natives generally not courting his recognition, according to Eastern etiquette.

He lives in a fashion partly European, partly Eastern—European as to *cuisine* and mode of taking his meals, the latter of which he does in company with the chief members of his household, his chamberlains, private secretaries, physicians, and others immediately attached to his person, with invited guests very frequently. His *déjeuners à la fourchette* at mid-day, and dinners at 7 p.m., are in every respect worthy the admiration of the most experienced gastronome, both as to the dishes and the service, the wines included.

In a subsequent chapter some idea will be given of the character of these entertainments of the Khedive inside and outside of the hareem, of the latter of which, of course, I speak from hearsay, and from the report of a lady present at one of them, given on the occasion of a Khedivial wedding celebration.

The receptions of the present ruler of Egypt are far less formal than those of his immediate predecessors, who strictly adhered to all the old Eastern usages, and kept up many of the absurd and obsolete forms still in vogue at Constantinople. The unchangeable Abbas was only to be seen on compulsion by some foreign representative; Saïd, only when the whim seized him; and both carried the visitor through fatiguing formalities, pipes, coffee, commonplaces diluted through interpreters, and other annoyances.

Now the Khedive's receptions are less formal and more agreeable than those of any European Court; though the visitor must be properly introduced through his own representative at the Court, and be accompanied by him, if previously unknown to the Khedive. Access to the Khedive is wonderfully easy, through his head chamberlain, Zecchy Pacha, or one of the other chamberlains, all of whom are agreeable, polite, and accomplished men, speaking French fluently. Two of them, Zecchy Pacha and Tonnino Bey, have been employed in the same functions under the three last viceroys, which speaks volumes for their integrity and capacity, since no duties could be more delicate and difficult than theirs.

Any subject, however humble, may present his petition or grievance in writing to " Effendina," as they style the Khedive.

The winter receptions are usually given at the Khedive's favourite palace of Abdin, distant only two or three hundred yards from the large hotels on the Ezbekieh, on the outskirts of the city. There is a large open space before the palace, somewhat similar to the French *Champ de Mars*, where the troops are constantly drilling and exercising, their white tents pitched at the other extremity of the square; and as you drive up to the long low range of buildings which compose the palace, you are apt to witness military manœuvres going on ; and finer looking and better disciplined troops, of a light bronze colour, would be hard to find anywhere.

En route to the palace you pass through streets tenanted by small shopkeepers, Levantine and native—a most unattractive population of all nationalities, who, with their customers, neither attract the eye, nor woo the sense of smell with the " odours of Araby the Blest."

But violent contrasts of this kind, between the pomps and show of royalty and the ragged wretchedness of the lower class, are common everywhere throughout the East, where extremes meet more closely than in other countries. At Abdin, during the winter season when Cairo is full of strangers, the Khedive chiefly holds his Court, has his formal and informal receptions, gives his breakfasts and dinners to distinguished foreigners, and two or three *soirées musicales* or *dansantes*, to which ladies as well as gentlemen are invited.

His larger and grander palace of Ghezireh on the Nile, with its beautiful gardens, Eastern kiosque, and menagerie of wild beasts, is more a show place than a place of regular habitation for him; though occasionally grand entertainments are given there also. Here the Empress Eugenie had her apartments, as well as the Prince of Wales, when they visited Egypt.

The three chief passions of Ismaïl Khedive are his passion for real estate, his vaulting ambition which sometimes overleaps itself, and his mania for building, the latter of which he frankly admitted to me in conversation a year ago. "Every man," said the Khedive reflectively, speaking in French, as he always does, "is mad on some one subject. My mania is for building" —to use his own words, "*J'ai une manie en pierre.*" It will be well for him and for his people should he discover, ere it be too late, his two other manias, and set to work to curb and to correct them.

CHAPTER XI.

FOUR NATIVE MINISTERS AND HEKKEKYAN BEY.

Some of the Khedive's native ministers—Nubar Pacha—His life and work—Personal traits—A family of diplomatists—Cherif Pacha—Description of him—Riaz Pacha—The strange story of Ismaïl Sadyk Pacha, the Mouffetich—An Egyptian Wolsey—A visit to his three palaces, and what we saw there—The moral of his rise and fall—Hekkekyan Bey—His theory of the Pyramids.

In his reforms the Khedive has been greatly aided by his native ministers, most of whom are men imbued with European culture, or educated abroad, speaking fluently several languages—that of diplomacy, or intercourse with foreign agents, being the French.

The most active and distinguished of these ministers have been Nubar, Cherif, Riaz, and Ismaïl Sadyk Pachas, respectively Ministers of Commerce, Foreign Affairs, Justice, and Finance. The War Minister has also been taken from his own people, though that department has in fact been controlled by the American staff officers, about twenty of whom, on the Khedive's invitation, entered the Egyptian service about six or seven years ago.

As the jealousy of the Porte has forbidden the Khedive to have a navy, his fleet consists only of commercial vessels, with a couple of armed steamers to protect the commerce of the Red Sea, and suppress the slavers.

Nubar Pacha, though a man of only middle age, has been well and favourably known in Europe as an able statesman for twenty years past, entering the public service, in which he immediately took high rank, at a very early age.

Educated to diplomacy by his famous kinsman, Boghos Bey, himself one of the ablest counsellors of Mehemet Ali, his life has been spent in this pursuit. Speaking and writing almost all the languages of Europe with equal facility, and conversant with European affairs and their directors, he has steered Egypt free from the breakers that surrounded her, under two successive reigns: until falling about a year since under the cold shade of royal displeasure, he has since been virtually outside of public life, and travelling abroad as a private person.

Nubar Pacha's personal appearance is at once striking and prepossessing. Of medium height, with swarthy complexion, dark eyes and hair, regular features, and a most winning smile;

N

gifted with rare conversational powers, and courteous, almost caressing in manner and speech,
there is a persuasive charm in his manner with
which few men are endowed.

His firmness, however, is one of his chief
characteristics, and his frankness almost amounts
to rudeness at times; and it is most probably
this latter quality that has lost him favour at
Court, where words displeasing to the royal ear
are most unwonted and unwelcome sounds.

Nubar is an Armenian Christian, and that three
viceroys should have retained a man professing
and practising that creed for a series of years,
speaks volumes both for their liberality and his
own capacity; for he is the worst courtier I ever
saw, and always has been; his pride, which is
great, ever keeping him erect in mind and body
before his exacting and haughty princes, who
consider their wish as well as will should be
law: and that it is a kind of *lèse majesté* for a
subject to differ from either, even in thought.
His family have not only served but suffered for
the State, in the person of his brother Arakel
Bey—one of the most promising of the rising
statesmen of Egypt—who in the time of 'Saïd
Pacha was made Governor of the Soudan, and fell
a victim to the climate in his early prime; and
the son and namesake of that brother, the Arakel
Bey who, as Governor of Massowa, but the other

day accompanied Arendrup in the fatal expedition into Abyssinia, and perished gallantly fighting by the side of that ill-starred commander, to avenge whose death the second Egyptian expedition was despatched, which has but recently returned. Seldom has a single family, alien in race and creed to the ruling race, contrived to fill for three generations the highest places in the State, especially under the arbitrary monarchs of the East; yet to this rare distinction the family of Nubar has attained by sheer force of character and talent, without ever stooping to unworthy concessions, either religious or personal. The free institutions of England can boast of but one Disraeli at the helm of State, while absolute Egypt can point to Boghos Bey, to Nubar, and his brother and nephew, as illustrations of an enlightened liberality of sentiment, not usually credited to the Turk.

Perhaps, however, the great and crowning work of Nubar's career, which finally caused his exclusion from public affairs, was the establishment of the mixed tribunals: which at the same time placed a check on the absolute power of the Khedive, and crippled the influence and authority of the agents of foreign governments in Egypt, by depriving them of their former prerogatives under the old capitulations. At this work Nubar toiled with undiminished labour and patience more than twenty years, modifying his plan from time to time, but ever steadily pursuing the main purpose: and contending against the double current setting in against him, from the throne on one side, and the consuls on the other. Whatever success these tribunals may obtain, much of the honour will be due to their originator and fostering parent. Whatever defects or shortcomings may be visible in the practical working of this invention, Nubar cannot be justly made responsible for them, since his hand has been taken from the plough, at the very moment when most needed there, by the caprice of the Khedive; and he can neither supervise his invention, nor give his invaluable counsel to those who are trying their " 'prentice han's " upon it.

His relief from the cares of State has however reinstated health, that the unremitting labours of many years had begun to impair: for, meeting him recently at Paris, I was struck with the improvement in his face and bearing which his year's vacation had wrought. The name of Nubar Pacha was prominently brought forward at the time of the Conference, in connection with the appointment of a Christian governor for Bulgaria: but all of his affections and aspirations turn to Egypt, the land of his birth, in which his race—almost as much a standing marvel as the Jewish people in their dispersion and continued separate existence—has found a resting-place; and where he is a large landed proprietor and cultivator.

Cherif Pacha, the contemporary and rival of Nubar—the two having gone up and down, like two buckets in a well, in the Foreign Office for a series of years—has also spent his life in public service, in which he has grown prematurely grey.

While Nubar in character and manner resembles an Englishman, Cherif is thoroughly French in looks and address; probably understanding but not speaking English. He is a Mussulman by birth and faith, and conforms, though not rigorously, to Eastern forms of life and faith. His French affinities were strengthened by his marriage with a daughter of Suleyman Pacha (the French Colonel Séves), who for many years was commander-in-chief of the Egyptian army. In appearance, as in mind and character, Cherif is the direct opposite of Nubar—fair, florid, with light hair and eyes, the former of which is turning grey. His manner and address are frank and cordial, more those of a soldier than of a diplomat. He is a man to whom deception would be impossible; his easy careless manner and open face would betray him, if he ever attempted it, which he does not. He is clever and quick-witted, and a most agreeable companion socially: entertaining much and liberally. His strongest passion is for the chase; and like Nimrod he is "a mighty hunter before the Lord." His personal qualities make him universally popular. I do not believe he has any enemies, for I never heard any one speak ill of him, while the sterner character of Nubar repels as many as it attracts.

Cherif Pacha seem to have become an indispensable man in the Egyptian administration, sometimes filling one post, sometimes another: but chiefly the ministry of foreign affairs or of commerce, alternating with Nubar.

This fixity of tenure on the part of these two statesmen, under so arbitrary a government as that of Egypt, contrasts curiously with the perpetual change of men, as well as measures, under freer and more constitutional *régimes*. The Eastern Disraeli and Gladstone have only replaced each other in particular bureaux, from time to time, but both have continued consecutively in public service in some other department; and have not been allowed the leisure requisite for the weaving of romances, or cutting down of trees, in their interregnums: as Western statesmen have been permitted, both by people and monarch.

Riaz Pacha is a younger man, one of the new

generation. He is an *élève* of Nubar, who carefully trained him to the work, and enjoys a reputation for integrity and capacity. He has filled, and still fills, important posts, in all of which he has given satisfaction, and may be considered a rising man.

But the most curious and disastrous career, for the Khedive, the country, and finally for himself, was that of Ismaïl Sadyk Pacha (the Mouffetich), late Minister of Finance—a bright but baleful meteor shooting across the Egyptian sky, to be quenched in sudden darkness, and leaving gloom and terror behind.

Yet his story sheds so much light on Egyptian peculiarities, and on the strange blending of elements there, that I shall devote some space to a narration of the life and death, rise and fall of this Eastern Wolsey, who ruled not only the country, but seemingly his master also with a rod of iron for ten years, through some strange influence which no man in or out of Egypt can comprehend.

Ismail Sadyk was what Mr. Pitt was said to be, "a heaven-born financier;" for he was born and bred an Egyptian fellah, without training or culture, and to the day of his death spoke or understood no language but his own. He was a dark-coloured Arab, slight and stooping in frame, with sharp features, a face

devoid of expression, and a shifty cunning eye.
His manner was alternately fawning or brutal,
as he spoke to an equal or an inferior ; and at
first sight he inspired an instinctive repugnance,
which he was plausible enough to remove when
it suited his interest, although conferring
always with Europeans through his interpreter
(an old Frenchman), it was difficult to judge
of his conversational powers. It may have
been owing to this fact that he produced upon
me, in several interviews I had with him, the
impression of a crafty but ill-informed and short-
sighted man, unable to rise to the height of
a great argument, or even comprehend anything but an appeal to the most selfish motives
and interests, taking a narrow and contracted
view of everything not bounded by his own
immediate horizon. That he should, however,
have obtained and held so long a powerful and
controlling influence over the mind of the
Khedive (whose intellectual ability no one
doubts or denies), affords proof positive that
Ismaïl Sadyk was no common man, although
" his thoughts were low—to vice industrious,
but to nobler deeds timorous and slothful."
But he has proved the evil genius, the very
Mephistopheles of his master, who finally turned
upon and destroyed him, in mingled wrath,
agony, and fear, offering him up as a scapegoat

for the sins which he possibly may have devised, but in which he had many and very high accomplices, thus far escaping with impunity.

He commenced his career as a common fellah, but proving himself faithful over small things was rapidly promoted to the care of larger ones —the Khedive himself, as prince, employing him as the manager of one of his smaller estates. From thence, after the accession of his patron to the throne, he rose gradually to the post of Mouffetich, or Finance Minister : and under his evil auspices was commenced that system of loans and shifty expedients to raise money at any price from foreign or native money-lenders, which has plunged the Khedive and the country into that worse than Serbonian bog, from which both are now so desperately struggling for extrication. He was reputed, from his early training and experience, to understand better than any man in Egypt, how "to squeeze the fellah!" which meant to wring the last para out of the poor wretches by the threat or use of the terrible *kourbash*, or hippopotamus-hide whip, in the hands of agents as unscrupulous and merciless as himself—until a cry went up to earth and heaven against his oppressions, perpetrated in the name, if not by the authority, of his master, who has ever borne the character of a humane man, constitutionally averse to cruelty. It is but an act of simple justice to the Khedive here to say, that my own personal knowledge of his character from his earlier days had confirmed the popular estimate, and that it is difficult for me to believe that he sanctioned all the exactions and cruelties perpetrated in his name, through the agency of the bold bad man who had won his confidence, and acted for several years the Wolsey to his master — to meet a heavier retribution than his unknown exemplar in the end.

The atmosphere of an Eastern throne is favourable neither to the sight nor the hearing of its occupant ; and much that is common talk abroad never reaches royal ears ; so that although the Khedive could not have been entirely ignorant of the cruelties and exactions perpetrated in his name, and for a long time condoned them, we yet may give him the benefit of the doubt as to his privity in all the offences committed against the unhappy fellahs, nominally by his orders, under the direct supervision of the low-born oppressor of his own race and brethren.

The sole apology that can be set up for this wretched creature, whose fate has inspired an ill-deserved pity for him, is that his sudden and giddy elevation had driven him mad ; and that he was but partially responsible for his acts; and the reckless way in which he rushed upon his fate, which his own sane judgment should have foreseen knowing the country as he did, would seem to sustain this hypothesis. For the sake of human nature let us give him the benefit of this doubt as to his sanity; though his nature was ever what Carlyle terms the "vulpine"—one full of crafty suspicion, and tortuous ways to tortuous ends.

In the very height of his power, profligacy, and wealth, he was stricken down as though by a thunderbolt from heaven.

Seeing in the adoption of the financial schemes proposed by Messrs. Cave, Goschen, and Joubert, the end of his power and his illicit gains, he fought desperately against them, and rendered his own removal necessary to the Khedive, through the revelations he made, and threatened to make: whether true or false equally embarrassing and damaging to his master's credit.

But he mistook his man, and miscalculated his influence. Going a step too far on the path of resistance and intimidation, he toppled over into an abyss, from which living or dead he never emerged; for where his bones are no man knows to-day.

In the telegrams of the London journals there appeared one morning, what seemed to many a mere sensational statement—that the Khedive had personally taken the Mouffetich to drive, placed him securely in custody, and was to have him tried for high treason immediately. Those who did not know Egypt discredited the statement *in toto*; those who knew it immediately believed the statement (whose dramatic features made it more probable) and foresaw the end: although not the sudden and tragic *dénouement* of what, commencing in comedy, ended swiftly in sternest tragedy.

The next day, 15th November, 1876, the Egyptian public, which had been feasting on a thousand rumours of the most wild and improbable character concerning this event, read in the *Moniteur Egyptien*, the Government official journal, the following authorized communication in French :—

" The ex-Minister of Finance, Ismaïl Saddyk Pacha, has sought to organize a plot against his Highness the Khedive, by exciting the religious sentiments of the native population against the scheme proposed by Messrs. Goschen and Joubert. He has also accused the Khedive of selling Egypt to the Christians, and taken the attitude of defender of the religion of the country. These facts, revealed by the inspectors-general of the provinces, and by the reports of the police, have been confirmed by passages in a letter addressed to the Khedive himself by Sadyk Pacha, in giving his own dismissal. In presence of acts of such gravity his Highness the Khedive caused the matter to be judged by his Privy Council, which condemned Ismaïl Sadyk Pacha to exile, and close confinement at Dongola."

The *Phare*, a semi-official journal in French, in republishing this communication next day, adds :—

" The ex-minister, who had been kept on board a steamer on the river, to await the decision of the Privy Council, was immediately placed on board another steamer, which left forthwith for Upper Egypt."

From that hour to this the Mouffetich has been lost to the sight of man, and a thousand and one stories of the precise manner and time of his " taking off," many of the wildest and mostly improbable character, have been circulated and credited in foreign and native circles in Egypt.

Some time after his disappearance, a circular was sent to the foreign consuls-general, announcing the death of the ex-minister at Dongola, accompanied by a *procès verbal* from the governor of that province, testifying to the fact of his arrival and death, enclosing also an autopsy made by three physicians, who, after post-mortem examination, declared that he died a natural death from fatigue, grief, and excess.

But most of the Cairenes and Alexandrians shook their heads sagely over this statement, and persist in believing that the Mouffetich did not survive his arrest twenty-four hours: and that the steamer which passed up the Nile, with windows carefully nailed up looking like a floating coffin, encountered by Nile travellers, and said to be transporting the Monffetich to his place of exile in Upper Egypt, was only sent up for effect; and contained neither the living nor the dead ex-favourite and ex-minister.

So this must take its place among the other many mysteries of this most mysterious land: whose officials must shake in their shoes sometimes, in remote provinces, when thinking of their old superior and employer, the Monffetich, and the thick darkness that enshrouds his real offence and fate.

But however this may be, his removal from public station and private intercourse with the Khedive marks the vanishing point of the old system of extortion, fraud, and cruelty, of which he was the master, and the substitution of a more humane and wiser policy, which alone can save the Khedive and his country from the ruin that menaced both—whose ominous shadow has not yet disappeared.

Having reached Cairo shortly after the events above narrated, I availed myself of the opportunity of visiting the palace or palaces of the ex-minister, which were open on certain days for inspection.

The confiscation and sale of the effects and property of the Mouffetich, for the satisfaction of his creditors, had been advertized, and was going on in that leisurely way everything is done in this land of *bâde bukâra*, or day after to-morrow, wherein the poet Thompson should have placed his " Castle of Indolence." So we concluded to attend it, to see whether the rumours as to the boundless wealth and pro-digality of the Mouffetich were founded on truth. It took a short drive of fifteen minutes to reach there. Crowds of people were attending the sale, and walking over the acres of carpeting that covered the three vast palaces, which seemed insufficient to lodge this born-fellah, for another incompleted wing was in the course of construction at the time of his sudden and mysterious disappearance.

Wolsey, with his Hampton Court, that bluff King Hal considered " too great for a subject ! " dwindles into insignificance when compared with this more than regal robber, who sprang from a mud hut on the Nile, in less than ten years, into the possession of more palaces, jewels, women, and slaves, than Solomon in all his glory could boast of.

The three palaces are in the new quarter of Ismaïlieh—so named after the Khedive—are separate piles of buildings, though surrounded by a high wall, and probably cover with their gardens an area as large as that of the Pyramids. They are all built and profusely decorated in French style, without any regard to expense, and to walk entirely through them—for they are all vacant now—would take an entire morning. The carpeting, the curtains, the furniture, the decorations, must have cost untold money, as *carte blanche* must have been given the upholsterers, and all the thousand rooms these palaces are said to contain are furnished in the same splendid style — over-furnished in fact, .with enough gilt and glitter to dazzle one's eyes. All the window curtains were of the heaviest and richest satin, and the different tints of the same colour were perceptible, from chocolate even to pale .grey, each room being furnished *en suite* with chairs and sofas in French style. There were but few divans, and these in rooms evidently intended for reception of his native friends. The peculiarity was that each room shaded off in colour into the next, from dark to light, embracing every colour to be found in the rainbow. Great taste was displayed in these combinations, the *portières* on the doors and heavy curtains at the windows, of which I counted sixteen in one apartment, being of the same description. Here this peasant-born, uneducated creature, who understood only theft and oppression squatted down, surrounded by his wives and women. Of wives, regular and irregular, he is said to have had thirty-six: each one of whom had six white slaves and a retinue of black ones. In fact the population of a small village was crowded into these piles of building, for the gratification of the pride or brutal passions of this low-born fellah. Stories of his corruption and cruelty were freely circulated after his fall, and whispered long before; but the "conspiracy," which was made the pretext of his death and the confiscation of his property, finds few believers in Egypt. They say he had earned and richly merited the dreadful doom which fell upon him, by a long course of crimes; but that neither the real reason, nor the real fate which befel him, has been given to the public; and that he was finally the victim of a State necessity, as inexorable as the grave.

The sale was going on briskly, in the midst of a Babel of confusion, at the first palace we entered, in the grand reception-room, crowded with people of all nationalities and colour. In the midst of this parti-coloured crowd a number of black and white slaves were moving about, with trays full of jewelry, and large cases containing every description of female ornaments, from *ceintures* set in diamonds to the value of

£7000, to cheap jewelry of the most common description. These were freely offered for public inspection, and were passed from hand to hand most carelessly, while the bearers were shouting out, at the top of their lungs, the bids already made for the objects exhibited. If you wished to increase the bid, your name and offer were taken down by a scribe at hand, and at the close of the day's sale these bids were jotted down and the article assigned to the purchaser, if the amount bid was considered sufficient by the person in charge of the liquidation. I was told the articles were bringing high prices : partly on the Eastern principle of investing in such portable values, and partly because the creditors of the Mouffetich were allowed to discount half on account; and probably thought half a loaf better than no bread.

The old Eastern principle of the inviolability of the hareem must have been broken in this instance, as this jewelry evidently was part of the spoils of the multitudinous wives and slaves of this Egyptian Sardanapalus. What had become of the fair or dusky owners of these jewels no one could tell me. The supposition was, they had been absorbed into other establishments of a similar description; but whether by sale or free gift, "nobody knows and nobody cares." If the taste of the Monffetich was as comprehensive in houris as in jewelry, he must have had a most miscellaneous collection of ministering angels. Personally he was a mean and dirty-looking Arab of low type, and to all who had ever seen him, the contrast between the man and his surroundings was startling indeed.

Such mushroom growths are possible only in the soil, where Jonah's gourd attained its wonderful growth in the shortest possible space of time ; but his rise and fall, and the relics of his luxury, must recall more the romances of the " Thousand and One Nights," than the sober experiences of modern Egypt in the nineteenth century.

The soil, in which such poisonous fungi can suddenly spring up and flourish in rank luxuriance, certainly needs draining and cleansing. Passing from the sale-room for jewelry into an inner apartment, or series of apartments, we saw tables covered with gold and silver plate —Eastern and European work—no less than precious metals serving the turn of this luxurious fellah. Even the ewers and basins, in which he and his guests washed their hands, or rather had running water poured over them, were of silver. The value of many thousands of pounds was deposited on the tables of one of these rooms alone. Another proof of the change

of habits among the rich here, even with those
who are not Europanized in mind or customs,
was the substitution of bedsteads for divans, on
which to sleep. The first palace was full of
these, intended probably for the use of wives
or guests; for the Mouffetich always presented
the appearance of a man, who wore by day
the clothes, in which he had slept on a divan the
previous night. The gardens in front of the
three palaces were very spacious and handsome,
and the value of the real estate must be large;
but what can possibly be done with these huge
barracks of buildings, crammed full of costly
furniture and curtains, almost valueless outside
of them? There is some talk of converting one
of them into public offices. They would serve
the purpose of hospitals admirably; only there
is too much of them, and the decorations are
too fine.

But as Mehemet Ali's old citadel palace, and
even his hareem apartments, are now appropriated to the army staff, it is more than probable
that the costly piles of the Mouffetich may come
to some such use at last. For the moment they
constitute the sole monument of the man, who
ruled Egypt with a rod of iron for eight years,
and died a dog's death at last.

One of the most curious objects in the palace,
or palaces, was a very large picture in a heavy

gilt frame, containing life-sized portraits of the son of the Mouffetich and his wife, an adopted daughter of one of the Khedive's wives. It was just such a picture as you would expect to find in a royal palace; and as neither wore the Eastern dress, the resemblance was still stronger. The man was sitting, the woman standing—he in ordinary Frank dress, without even the tarbouch; she represented in the fashionable European dress of the day, of rich blue velvet and lace, with a tiara of diamonds on her head resembling a crown. She was a very pretty and graceful-looking woman, and one would have mistaken her for a European—a mistake no one would have made as to her husband, whom we saw sitting placidly in one of the rooms, apparently watching the sale, and entertaining his friends with coffee; as though he were still master of the house, and had not been one of the chief victims of the heavy retribution, which had fallen on his father, and all connected with him by blood or interest.

Not only his fortune and prospects had been blasted, but even his wife had been taken from him: as she was promptly divorced after his father's fall. Yet there he sat, seemingly as cheerful and as unconcerned as though the family tragedy had been only a Christmas panto-mime, and himself a spectator, not an actor in it.

Practical philosophy like this Europeans might preach, but could never practise.

In order, however, not to present a bad specimen of the native-born Egyptian (and indeed a Mouffetich is always an exceptional type in every land), I shall conclude these sketches of Egyptians, with a brief notice of a man of whom any nation might be justly proud.

Hekkekyan Bey was one of that strange race which, like the Hebrew, has preserved its nationality without a country, and is as distinctive to-day as it was thousands of years ago. He was an Armenian Christian, a kinsman of Artin Bey, a former minister. Educated by order of Mehemet Ali in England early in the present century, he spoke English with the correctness of a native, and without the slightest accent ; he was a member and correspondent of several philosophical societies, as thorough an Englishman to talk to, as you might meet any day in Pall Mall or Piccadilly. Employed in the Foreign Office at home under that now remote reign, he fell into disfavour, being no courtier, and for thirty-five years spent his time in learned leisure, keeping up constant intercourse with foreign *savants* and societies, and occupying himself with abstruse philosophical investigations. Among other things, he promulgated a theory that the Pyramids—of which he asserted there had been a long chain — were intended as barriers to the encroachment of the desert sands: and not, as usually supposed, monuments to human pride, or the tombs of kings. To see him abroad in his Oriental dress, mounted on his favourite dromedary, scouring along the Shoubra road or over the desert, you would have considered him a veritable type of the old Oriental. But visit him in his house at Cairo, also thoroughly Oriental, embowered in gardens, and on his table you would see the latest scientific publications from England, together with the last English journals, evidently his favourite reading. Converse with him, and you would marvel at the extent and accuracy of his general information, and at the originality and boldness of his philosophic speculations; and leaving him, you would regret that powers so rare had been of so little use to himself or to mankind. He died at the age of sixty-eight, prematurely old, and like Swift "at top first." The men who knew Egypt and the Egyptians twenty years since, and more recent visitors, will remember him as a very exceptional type of the Europeanized Oriental.

CHAPTER XII.

THE LAND OF EGYPT AND ITS PRODUCTIONS.

Egypt nothing, if not agricultural—Contrasted with India and China—
Feeds her own population—"The life of Egypt"—Five million
acres under cultivation—How cultivated—Flax culture—Cotton
culture—Sugar culture—Extracts from recent report on Khedive's
sugar estates—Curious facts and figures relating to it—The grain
crops—The date and fruit culture—Land taxation—A painful picture
of a year's work in the fields.

EGYPT is nothing, if not agricultural. There is
her strength, her substance, her existence; and
so has it been with her since the days when
Joseph was Pharaoh's chief counsellor, and she
was the unexhaustible granary of the world.

Reference has already been made to the wild
and fruitless efforts of Mehemet Ali to change
her natural bent and bias, and introduce manufacturing and mining industries by main strength;
resulting only in a great waste of time,
money, machinery, and labour. Similar lessons
have been given to those of his successors
who sought to imitate his example: and the
conclusion has been forced upon unwilling

minds that in the soil alone lies the strength and the wealth of Egypt. The whole extent of land under cultivation at present is nearly five millions of acres, of which about 719,000 are devoted to the culture of cotton; the rest is devoted to rice, sugar, beans, barley, maize, and clover (*bersim*). From two to three successive crops can be made off this land each year, owing to the peculiar features of climate, soil, and cultivation.

It has often and justly been said that "the Nile is the life of Egypt!" for it is owing to the aid of its fertilizing waters that Egypt is, and has ever been, such an exhaustless granary and storehouse of food for man; while farther east we hear, year after year, the despairing cry of famishing millions echoing across the wide waters, "Give us bread or we perish!" Yet hands are far more numerous in India and in China—labour far more plentiful and cheaper than in Egypt. But the great artery of Egypt's life is lacking to them; they have no Nile, bearing down from Abyssinia, and regions yet unexplored, the rich deposits with which it annually fertilizes the favoured land of Egypt, and renews the exhaustion consequent on the cultivation of untold centuries. In more primitive times the great river was allowed to follow its own sweet will, and annually overflow its banks, to place this deposit upon the surface inundated; but of late years engineering skill has been called in to restrain and direct that overflow by means of canals; so that the yearly cutting (the " Haleeg ") at Cairo, to let in the water from the Nile, has become one of the most imposing State ceremonials, over which the Khedive presides in person, in the midst of great and general public rejoicings.

There are certainly many advantages in the new over the old plan, one of which is that the natural inundation would keep a large body of the lands three months out of cultivation, if left to its own wanderings; but many old Egyptians contend that much of the fertilizing deposit is lost, by allowing it to settle in the bed of the river, when first brought down from Upper and Central Egypt.

Whether this be true or false, it sounds plausible; and the introduction of fertilizers of late years into Egypt, would seem to give colour to the theory. Man frequently mars Nature's plans by meddling with and trying to improve them; and the Nile is an exceptional stream, in more respects than in its reversal of the ordinary rule in running from south to north: in which caprice it has very few companions.

The whole extent of land under cultivation in Egypt Proper, may be roughly estimated as a little less than five millions of acres, out of which, according to Government statements, .719,000 are devoted to cotton; about 260,000 to sugar, a Khedivial monopoly; and the rest, as previously stated, to different species of grain.

The two last viceroys have done their utmost to introduce steam-ploughs, pumping-machines, and improved agricultural implements: and have introduced them on their own lands, as well as on those of their more enlightened subjects (unfortunately yet very few in number); but the native agriculturists, the fellahs, on their small holdings, prefer and adhere to the ways of their primitive forefathers, with a mild obstinacy that is impossible to overcome. They insist on holding fast to the groaning water-wheel (or *sakkia*), turned on its creaking wooden beams by the plodding water-ox; they prefer scratching the ground with the rude wooden contrivance that they term a plough; and the "ox that treadeth out the corn," in the Old Testament, has bequeathed his duties to his descendants, on the threshing-floor of the bare earth, where now as then the Egyptian rustic cleanses his grain. Yet such is the climate, and such the soil, that even with these primitive contrivances, and no fertilizer beyond the Nile water, the most bounteous harvests repay the toil of the fellah: and he has not one only, but two or three successive ones, in the course of one revolving year.

In the earlier days of the new Egypt, the cultivation of flax was carried on very largely and profitably; but has since been supplanted by that of cotton. Ibrahim Pacha was in the habit of selling his crop of flax, in three different parcels to three different purchasers, at different prices and at different times. He used then carefully to compare the three sales, so as to decide where and from whom he could get the best price.

When he paid his short visit to England, he suddenly announced to his suite his intention of visiting Belfast; and did so, that he might examine the machinery, and some new methods of preparing the flax adopted there.

Saïd Pacha did not in person either superintend the cultivation or the sale of the products of his properties, which were never very large. He was too much absorbed in other matters, for which he had more taste. During his time the fellah was left pretty much alone to cultivate his lands, but Saïd took from the peasant proprietors much of the land called Abadiehs; i.e., land which could not be sufficiently or efficiently worked, in consequence of the insufficiency of hands in the neighbourhood, owing either to the want of dense population, or removal of the men from the fields for enlistment in the army, or working by *corvée* on the canals; both of which were very heavy drains on the population. He also laid heavier taxes on the fellahs, but being at heart a generous and a just man, discouraged and punished all oppression or peculation on the part of the tax-collectors or governors of provinces, when proven to his satisfaction.

The cotton plant is indigenous to Egypt, and has been cultivated time out of mind on the narrow strip of fertile land which fringes the Upper Nile, beginning at Thebes. But this native cotton is of inferior quality, short in staple, coarse in fibre, and fit only for the manufacture of the coarse stuff worn by the fellah men and women. Its cultivation was very limited, and until the year 1819 it was the only kind grown in Egypt, and was exclusively used for home consumption. In this year, when the energetic rule of Mehemet Ali was reviving old Egypt from its ashes, a Frenchman named Jumel, walking in the gardens of Mako Bey, at Cairo, observed a curious plant, the leaf and flower of which were unfamiliar to him. He questioned the gardener, and learned it was the cotton plant, a few specimens of which had been brought from India, to give variety to the shrubbery of the garden. Seeing the great superiority of this plant to the common kind cultivated in the upper country, M. Jumel brought the matter to the attention of the viceroy; who by his aid and co-operation, succeeded in making its culture general in the fertile lands of the Delta of Lower Egypt: whence the great bulk of the crop is now obtained.

It was not until 1840 that the experiment of introducing the American sea island cotton seed was attempted. Since that time it has been largely introduced, and the yield has been fully equal to that of the best sea island. From some peculiar quality of the soil however, or possibly from the system of irrigation adopted, it has been found necessary to procure new sea island seed every two years; and the Jumel or Mako cotton has therefore been preferred by the Egyptian cultivators.

There are therefore three species of cotton grown in Egypt:—

1st. The native cotton, short staple, coarse.

2nd. Mako or Jumel, long staple, fine.

3rd. American sea island, ditto.

These varieties are all perennial, but are sown annually, except the Mako, which will last two years. The Mako is greatly preferred, although the cotton it produces is not quite equal to the best sea island, but rather better than the best American upland cotton.

The two latter species alone are exported;

the first, or native cotton, cultivated on the Upper Nile, being used chiefly for stuffing divans—the Egyptian substitute for our chairs and beds, and which serve the double purpose of seats by day and couches by night, even among the richer classes. It is also used to make the " Nizam " or soldiers' uniform, as well as the single blue shirt which constitutes the entire toilette of both male and female fellah. The culture of this species is not extensive, nor are these fabrics now manufactured as largely as formerly. Mehemet Ali, who entertained the idea of manufacturing on a large scale, established twenty-four large factories, employing 24,000 operatives, but it was soon found to be unprofitable; so that in 1852 all that remained of his great enterprise were one large mill worked by steam, and three small ones worked by ox power, manufacturing chiefly army uniforms, and consuming on an average not more than 10,000 bales of cotton per annum.

The rapidity with which the cotton culture developed itself, after M. Jumel's walk in the garden at Cairo, may be inferred from the following statement of exports :—

In 1821, Exports were 60 bags, of 100 lbs. each.
　　1822　　,,　　,, 500　,,　　　　,,　　　　,,
　　1823　　,,　　,, 1200　,,　　　　,,　　　　,,
　　1824　　,,　　,, 1500　,,　　　　,,　　　　,,

This too while Mehemet Ali's experiment of manufacturing was going on, consuming an amount of which we have no means of judging, as statistics are a modern innovation in Egypt. In 1852 the annual exportations of cotton had risen to about 44,000,000 pounds; in 1856, to 57,000,000; and in 1865, to the maximum of 560,000 bales.

Quite recently a new kind of cotton has been discovered and successfully cultivated in Egypt, which is said to yield much more than any previously known. Indeed, it is claimed that the yield is four times as great as that of the ordinary kinds. I was told that this cotton has this peculiarity, that the bolls instead of being ·attached to the branches of the plant, adhere closely to the stem. I was not fortunate enough to be able to obtain any specimens of the plant itself: but the seeds were in great demand, and some have already been sent abroad. The lucky discoverer is a native planter, and the new cotton is causing some excitement and very "great expectations" in the breasts of the excitable Alexandrians, to whom cotton still is king! in despite of the heavy losses their over-confidence in that plant and its products has caused them. From one of these gentlemen, who probably understands the business, and the cotton culture in Egypt, better than any man there, I

P

obtained the statement, which will be found in
the appendix: and which, coming from a private
and reliable source, may be more thoroughly
depended upon than the statements made by or
through the agents of the Government, who
often have their own private reasons for increasing or diminishing the annual yield, or exportation, from private or public considerations.*

While cotton brought high prices—it rose to
half a crown per pound during the American
war—it paid well; but at 7*d.*, as it now is, it
is hard to see how it can bring a profit on its
production.

SUGAR.—The culture of the cane, and the production of sugar, have been the great hobby of
the present ruler of Egypt: who has devoted to
them an immense sum of money, and a very
great quantity of the labour of the country,
diverted for that purpose from far more profitable
pursuits. This labour, if it cost him personally
little, has cost the country and the fellahs
prodigiously dear, and has excited great discontent among these patient people throughout
Upper Egypt, whence the *corvées* for it have
been drawn, (if I am correctly informed); for
of this I do not speak from my own personal
knowledge.

How much this experiment has cost, it is

* See Appendix H.

impossible even to form an idea of: but the
enormous amount of useless machinery purchased and never used, or used unprofitably;
the vast sums expended on the preparation of
the lands, and the creation of a canal, on which
it is estimated a fourth of the labour devoted to
that of Suez had to be employed, constitute the
direct expenses. The indirect outlay may be
computed at a very large sum, and is represented
by the labour of the fellahs for three months
every year upon these lands; which labour, if
bestowed on their own fields, in the production
and rotation of their grain crops, would produce
far more profitable results,—not to speak of the
improvement in their condition. Even were they
paid for their labour on the Khedive's lands—
which I am credibly informed they seldom if
ever are, and in food if at all—the public loss
must be equally great in the diminution of the
crops; theirs being the only available labour.

I am not aware that any of the reports on the
Khedivial debts and property touch on this
point, which is certainly a very delicate one.

A very full and apparently fair report on these
sugar properties has recently been made by two
foreign experts, who have lately visited them,
from which I shall make a few extracts, never
having personally visited the place.

They report an abundant supply of water, a

good railway system for conveyance of the canes, etc., and a quantity of machinery vastly exceeding the wants of the mills, of which also there are many more, both in and out of working order, than there is any necessity for. " The scarcity of labour alone prevents the extension of the plantations " in their judgment.

The Khedive's sugar estates, on the line of railway from Cairo to Assiout, extend over a tract 100 miles in length, and from twelve to sixteen miles in breadth, chiefly on the west side of the Nile.

Canes are grown on the same land two years in succession without replanting, after which the roots are ploughed up, and the land either left fallow for a year, or a grain crop put in. The visitors consider the canes to be planted too close together, viz. but three feet apart : whereas in the West Indies six feet are allowed. The mode of cutting down—hacking with a blunt hatchet—is also objected to. Steam ploughs are in use there. "Complete machinery for twenty-two factories seem to have been imported, some of which are partly erected, others becoming gradually buried in the sands on the river's banks. There is a skeleton factory near the Feshu station, of which the machinery has been three parts erected, but the walls were never commenced, and the machines left to ruin.

Original cost in Europe for machinery for larger factories is said to have been about £130,000 each."

A large amount of unused extra machinery is lying scattered about over the whole country, arising from French and English rivalry in the erection of factories. The total cost of the factories is roughly estimated at £5,000,000; add £2,000,000 more for cost of rolling stock of the estate railway, pumping engines, etc., and the total cost rises to £7,000,000. There is a system of railway all over the estate, connecting the different factories. This is the only way in which the cane can be brought in fast enough; 18,000 cantars, or over 800 tons, per day being required to keep the large factories going, working day and night for sixty or seventy days, commencing at the beginning of the year, as the canes must be crushed up immediately on ripen-ing. The factories are under the management of the engineer, the only European now employed on these works; the management of the estate being entirely in Arab hands, each separate manager looking exclusively to the private interests of his section, regardless of the general welfare. Their *feddan* is elastic, and their habit is to return a larger quantity of land than is really under cultivation, to make their profits out of imaginary disbursements for labour, etc.

Speaking of the improvements that might be made under European administration, the report says—" Certainly a higher rate of wages would have to be paid than that now paid by the Daira; and there would be probably an insufficiency of labour, owing to the thin population of this part of the country, and *the aversion of the people to the work. At present all the labour is compulsory.*

" At Assiout we saw some small *corvées* working on the above-mentioned canal banks. Small children, and boys and girls as young as seven or eight years, were walking all day up and down the banks, with their baskets of earth. Their pay was a daily supply of bread, which has certainly improved in quality on that supplied them last year. We visited the bakery, and saw that it was made simply of coarsely ground wheaten flour, but the Nile mud and chopped straw had not been too carefully extracted. It was lightened, more or less, by sour dough. Still it was comparatively good and wholesome. The man in charge confessed the quality to be superior to that of last year, but attributed the reason solely to the improvement in the wheat; a doubtful reason, seeing that they are still using last season's wheat, which they were then using in its new condition. The children looked very thin and miserable, and their extreme poverty was evinced by the unbounded delight exhibited by a small boy, on receiving a coin equal in value to one-sixteenth of a penny."

This is certainly not a flattered or a pleasing picture, nor can it be regarded as an exceptional one. "There are a dozen sets of large fixed pumping engines, with fine brick building and tall chimney each, on the Nile banks; but their use has been destroyed by the new canal, called the Ibrahimieh, which is cut from the river at Assiont by fellah labour: twenty-five to thirty yards in average breadth, with rows of fine bridges, locks, and sluices dividing the canal into three large branches and two small canals. The cost of these disused pumps was probably not less than £500,000. This new canal is one of the largest, finest, and most costly in the country. Its chief use is to supply water to the Khedive's estates." No statement or estimate as to its cost is given.

The labour question is thus touched on in this report, from which it appears that some pay is given or promised to the labourers, which is "paid in kind—grain or molasses—on which the Daïra makes a profit;" thus reducing the pay, wretched as it is. In fact, the skilled labourers are the only ones who really get, or are promised, anything beyond a little coarse food—"grain or molasses"—which can keep a man or boy in that climate in bad working order. The report says—

" The wages received by the ordinary hands in the factories are 7d. to 7½d. per day for men and 4d. for boys, and by the hands working in the fields 4d. per day for men and 2½d. for boys. They are always paid in *kind*—grain or molasses—on which the Daïra as a rule makes a profit. As mentioned above, *they are compelled to work.* Their condition is exceedingly miserable, and their appearance much more savage than the fellahs of the Delta. Skilled Arab labourers, such as men that attend to the engines and such like work, receive 20s. to 25s. per month. Men driving the locomotive engines receive from £3 to £5 per month, and stokers about 30s. per month. The pay of all is allowed to get much in arrear."

The grain culture in Egypt—which is so large as to suffice not only to feed its own population, but to export largely to other countries—together with the cotton culture, occupies the exclusive attention of the fellahs, when they are not drawn from it by requisitions to work on the canals or drafted into the army, the conscription being practised in a most irregular and sweeping manner. In peaceful times, however, a large proportion of the soldiers are sent back on leave to their villages to aid in tilling the ground; and

even while in actual service their labour is often
utilized by their being set to work in squads
in the fields, under command of non-commis-
sioned officers. It is said their labour is far
superior to and more reliable than that of the
ordinary fellah, who is a steady but not a fast
worker in the old style. This conversion of the
bayonet into the plough, is one of the most
sensible things which is done by the Egyptian
Government; and a permanent change in the
occupation of thousands of the stalwart young
fellows, who constitute the army of Egypt, by
their return to peaceful pursuits, would prove a
blessing to them and to their country; since war
is a game at which only powerful monarchs can
afford to play. The land now pays an annual
tax of almost, if not quite, £4,000,000, including
the Moukabaleh—of which explanation will be
given in the chapter on finance—a taxation
which, on 5,000,000 acres (one-fifth of which,
being royal property, only nominally pays the
tax), must be admitted to be very onerous
indeed.

But, unhappily, this is only one of the Government impositions on the landholders, as the
annexed statement from a most reliable source
will show. The value of the crops on average
lands on the two years' system of rotation is as
follows:—

	P.T.		Expenses. Water.		P.T.
"Cotton, 3½ cantars, at ...	260	equal to	910 less	260 equal to	650
Wheat, 6 ardebs, at ...	50	„	240 „	70 „	170
Maize, 3 ardebs at ...	60	„	180 „	100 „	80
Bersim (clover), per crop	—	„	600 „	140 „	460

P.T. 1360

£13 19s. 0d.

"In the three years' rotation these figures
would, of course, be altered, but as I am only
considering the fellaheen cultivation it is unnecessary to give the three years' figures in detail.
Thus the gross annual receipts of the two feddans,
at the present price of cotton, only come to about
£7. The expenses which must be deducted, in
addition to the watering, in order to arrive at
the net result, such as the price of seed, labour,
and carriage, are difficult to arrive at, and vary
according to circumstances. Thus the cattle
plague of this year has swept away two-thirds of
the horses in the country, and has enormously
increased the expense of carriage to railway,
canal, or warehouse. But the ordinary calculation is that the wheat, maize, and clover crops
pay all working and living expenses, and the
value of the cotton—£6 13s. 6d.—goes to pay
the two years' taxes. The living expenses are
marvellously small. Bread and vegetables are
the food, Nile water the drink, an annual cotton
gown the clothing, a mud hut the shelter.
There could not be a creature of fewer wants

than the Egyptian fellah. It will be a sign of progress when he is less of an animal and his wants are more complex.

" Now, as regards the amount of taxation, I am informed on very good authority that the taxes levied on land during the last two years in the Delta, including the Moukabaleh, the National Loan, and a small war tax, have exceeded P.T.400* per annum. The taxation has therefore been in actual excess of receipts, and although the fellah and his family have slaved in the fields from sunrise to sundown, he has failed to make the two ends meet. In many cases loans from Europeans at usurious rates have furnished the means of payment. Pay-day has now come. The capitalists are encashing what they can, and the tribunals are full of such cases. In fact, it is going hard with the fellaheen—beasts, produce, goods, hareem jewellery where it existed, and even the land itself are being sold to meet their debts. One does not like to believe that even this enormous fiscal charge has been increased by irregular exactions, but all informants concur in saying that this has been so."

This is not a pleasing picture, but my own observation and inquiries induce me to believe that it is unhappily, a true one.

* We may roughly reckon 100 piastres to the pound sterling, which would bring the taxation up to £4 per annum.

The Khedive ought not justly to be saddled with the whole responsibility of this, for he is the heir to a vicious system, and the clamour of his creditors, public and private, has driven him almost to desperation, and desperate diseases often demand desperate remedies.

The creditors of Egypt, however, who are the instigating cause of these exactions and oppressions, should have sense enough to see that no goose, however golden, can long survive such treatment—no people, however patient and long-suffering, live and work under it. The speedy end of persistence in a policy at once so cruel and so fatal should at once be insisted upon, even at the cost of a reduction of the interest now paid them out of the sweat and blood of the fellaheen, and by impositions, ordinary and extraordinary, which no country or people on earth could long endure.

Gladly indeed, if he could safely do so, would the Khedive diminish these burdens; and his offer to assign over his sugar estates to his creditors, and wash his hands of all responsibility, proves at once his humanity and his sagacity.

Shall Christian creditors be less humane and less sagacious than this Mohammedan ruler? Will they make themselves responsible before heaven and earth of complicity in cruelties and exactions, which sicken even the callous hearts of the Moslem, who are, under their constraint, inflicting them ?

These are questions that the outside world, who are not creditors to the Khedive, will ask, and which they must be prepared to answer. For, I repeat, the solution of this stern problem rests more with them than with Ismaïl Khedive, "who is as clay in the hands of the potter," in the hands of his foreign creditors.

CHAPTER XIII.

˙THE FELLAHEEN.

Who is the fellah, and what is he?—His earlier history as written on
the tombs and temples, in the Scriptures, on stone and papyrus—A
letter three thousand years old concerning him, in the British
Museum—How Joseph treated him under Pharaoh—Origin of land
tenure in Egypt—Under the Mamelukes and the house of Mehemet
Ali, the new masters of his "house of bondage"—His treatment
under successive viceroys—His present condition.

ONE fundamental mistake underlies almost everything that has been said or written of the
Egyptian fellah, either by his sentimental or
indignant advocates, by kind-hearted women,
or sympathetic tourists, who, regarding him as
the dumb drudge—the serf, *adscriptus glebæ*,
attached to the land and not owning it—have
been entirely in error as to his true position and
stake in the country, which owes its wealth to
him.

Strange as it may sound to those who know
and have seen the fellah only by the wayside, or
working in gangs upon the *corvées* (compulsory
labour for public works), or whining out for

"backsheesh" at the railway stations, every man among them is or has been a land-owner or a land-holder by lease; and the bitterest taunt that one fellah woman can launch at another is this, in the Arabic vulgate: "Go! Poor woman! Your man does not own even a 'karat' (twenty-fourth part of an acre) of land!" So identical are property and "respectability," even among these ragged landed aristocrats!

The researches of Egyptologists have proved that the common belief, that the fellah is not the direct descendant of the Egyptian labourer, is equally erroneous. They have proved him not to be a spawn of the Arab conquerors under Amrou, but the original denizen of the soil: who, submitting to this last invasion, as he had to all preceding ones, ended by adopting the language and religion of the latest of his masters.

Not only do the recently deciphered papyri attest this, but an observant traveller to-day, turning from the sculptured faces in the processions in the temples and tombs, to the faces of the fellaheen who bear the torches by whose light he sees them, cannot fail to be struck by the similarity in type and outline between the two; still distinctly recognizable after the lapse of four thousand years.

The Copt is manifestly of the same ancient race, perhaps of a higher caste or class; or perhaps the differences of religion, culture, and occupation in cities for centuries, and sedentary and studious lives, may have occasioned the difference in the complexion and contour between the two: which in the upper country are not so perceptible as in the Delta, or in the cities. It is also probable that the Copt is of purer blood: for in many of the fellahs the intermixture of negro blood is plainly perceptible, both in complexion and conformation.

Discarding then these fundamental errors in the outset, and recognizing the fellah as the aboriginal Egyptian by blood and descent, as well as the landed proprietor, let us examine his past and present lot in the home to which he has adhered for ages, apparently as immoveable from it as the Pyramids, reared by the toil, sweat, and blood of his forefathers.

The condition of the man who aspires to no higher lot than a living earned by daily manual labour—of the daily drudge, tilling the fields from sunrise to sunset, demanding only " a fair day's wage for a fair day's work"—has in all ages and countries been a hard and a pitiable one, and is so still. It is so even to-day, in countries boasting the brighter lights of Christianity and civilization, separated as " the labouring class " are even there by a wall higher than the Chinese, from their more fortunate and richer brethren,

Q

whose own good fortune and merit, or that of their progenitors, has placed them higher in the scale, and relieved them from the debasing drudgery of incessant toil. Without preaching either Chartism or Communism, or declaring with the French philosopher that "all property is robbery," every candid and thoughtful inquirer into the problem of our modern social system must admit, that the unequal distribution of this world's goods, and the disparities in the lot assigned to the different classes that constitute the population of different countries from birth to death, prove that we are still far from securing "the greatest good of the greatest number," even by our model institutions, in this nineteenth century.

While Christendom can show, in its ripest fruit, such cankers as large bodies of daily labourers not only living "without God in the world"—like dumb driven cattle—but even ignorant of His existence, and dwelling underground in a darkness that is moral as well as physical—while large masses of peasantry all over Europe are as stolid and ignorant, and far more brutal, in their tempers and propensities, than the oxen they drive ; it cannot too loudly condemn Eastern rulers when a maddened labouring class, in the great centre of our civilization, can perpetrate the horrors of the Commune, and hundreds feast and revel in high places, while millions drudge and pine and starve in the midst of plenty. We, in our more favoured countries, may not hold up our hands like the Pharisee, and " thank God we are not as other men ! " when the fellah's lot is compared with that of the labourer elsewhere, dreary and forlorn as the fellah's lot may be.

But it is exceptional in this—that as his forerunners were in the time of the building of the Pyramids, when Moses led his people out of the " house of bondage," when Joseph was the favourite at Pharaoh's Court, and when successive waves of races swept over Egypt, each leaving its mark; even so is he to-day, the humble tiller of the soil, content with the scantiest supply of food and raiment and shelter, and the smallest wages for his daily work, that ever kept together body and soul, in any clime or age.

Coming down as late as the Norman invasion of England, the Saxon churl's existence was little if any better than the fellah's; for he was not even a free man, he wore round his neck the visible badge and collar that announced his slavery, which the fellah never did, being always nominally free : and was lodged and fed scarcely better than the swine he tended. But Gurth the swineherd has passed into tradition now, and the Saxon blent with the Norman blood makes the backbone of the country, the vigorous English yeoman. The continental peasant too has improved with the progress of his country into something more than a mere dumb drudge; but the Egyptian labourer has not risen much above the level of that life we see sculptured on stone, on the walls of the old tombs and temples, thousands of years ago. He is still the sole tiller of the soil, a tool in the hands of merciless taskmasters, "a strong ass crouching under burdens:" yet, strange to say, as contented and merry a creature, as apparently blind, deaf, and careless to his own wrongs and hardships and ill usage, as the patient ox and ass, who are his daily and congenial associates. To him the old "house of bondage" seems to have been a peculiar heritage, and to have lost many of its terrors; for, from generation to generation, he abides peacefully and uncomplainingly under the shadow of its palms, and performs his allotted task, if not unmurmuringly, at least patiently.

Modern research and patience, which have disentombed and deciphered the old papyrus records of the elder Egypt, have recently given us a curious proof of the unchanged and apparently unchangeable condition of the Egyptian labourer. A papyrus now preserved in the

British Museum contains part of the correspondence between Ameneman, the chief librarian of Ramses the Great, and the poet of the period, Pentatour, whose poem recording the achievements of the Egyptian monarch is engraved on the walls of the temple of Karnak at Luxor. In a letter written to this Tennyson of three thousand years since, Ameneman thus describes the condition of the Egyptian peasant of his day. As the translator justly remarks, "one seems to hear Fenelon or La Bruyère speaking of the poverty, the ignorance, the sordid existence of the French peasant under Louis XIV.," only the Egyptian's lot was far the harder of the two!

"Have you ever represented to yourself in imagination," says Ameneman, "the estate of the rustic who tills the ground? Before he has put the sickle to his crop the locusts have blasted part thereof; then come the rats and birds. If he is slack in housing his crop, the thieves are on him. His horse dies of weariness as it drags the wain. The tax-collector arrives; his agents are armed with clubs, he has negroes with him who carry whips of palm branches. They all cry, 'Give us your grain!' and he has no way of avoiding their extortionate demands. Next, the wretch is caught, bound, and sent off to work, without wage, at the canals; his wife is taken and chained, his children are stripped and plundered."

Without asserting or believing that the Egyptian fellah's lot to-day is truly shadowed forth in this terrible picture of the ancient Egyptian labourer, sketched by a contemporary observer more than three thousand years ago, I may still suggest that, in some respects and in some cases, it is applicable still, away from the great cities and thoroughfares, which rest under the eye of the Khedive and of the European population; giving the Khedive the credit of not being responsible for a tithe of the wrongs and outrages perpetrated under cover of his name. But the system that allows such outrages and oppression, in despite of the efforts of a reforming prince to rectify them, certainly demands a complete and radical revision, in his own interests, as well as in those of our common humanity.

Without crediting all the stories that are current, as to the treatment and condition of the fellah population in the upper country and remoter provinces, it must be evident to the eye of the most careless observer, who passes any time in the country—even in making the ordinary Nile voyage—that the fellahs are miserably lodged in huts of mud, with no pretensions either to cleanliness or comfort; that they are insufficiently clothed in dirty blue cotton shirts (men and women), and underfed; while, at the same time, they are overworked and overtaxed: and the proportion of those who are either comfortable in circumstances or condition is so small as almost to count as nothing in the calculation! This state of things certainly should not be allowed to continue as a reproach, not only to Egypt, but to our century; and something should be done to raise these poor creatures to the level of the labouring class elsewhere; low as that level unfortunately is in too many countries, calling themselves civilized and Christian.

This should be the Khedive's first care, and should take the precedence in his mind of grand schemes for the extension of his empire, or for public improvements, or for the erection of costly palaces or piles of stone and marble in his great cities; lest the old cry again arise from the suffering people, to curb his pride—" *We ask for bread, and you give us stones!* "

The " true believer," both Turkish and Arab, lays great store by the teachings and acts of the early Hebrew patriarchs, whose lives and environment assimilated so much to his own, and has deduced from both the rules which govern his society to-day. His version, however, of the utterances and doings of the early

Israelites varies considerably, in many instances, from our accepted version of them; and one of these discrepancies relates to the proceedings of Joseph during the seven years of famine that succeeded the seven years of plenty in Egypt, after his reading of Pharaoh's bad dream about the seven fat and the seven lean kine.

The Moslem version of Joseph's proceeding on this memorable occasion is, that he availed himself of the distress and famine among the people, and of his own superior foresight in laying up large supplies of grain during the years of plenty, by buying up from the starving people one-fifth of the land of Egypt, in consideration of corn supplied them at famine prices—an act more creditable to his head than to his heart, however it may redound to his business capacity. Hence the Arab conquerors of Egypt established in Egypt a "*vakf*," or ownership on the part of the Church of one-fifth of the lands, together with a *dime*, or tax in the shape of a tithe, upon the rest, which tax, varying in sum and substance—always heavy, and recently most oppressive—paid in kind or produce instead of money, and thus made as elastic as the conscience of the tax-gatherer, has continued to be levied until this day. The Eastern tax-gatherer, from immemorial time, has been a leech of the worst description; for even

Matthew, who afterwards was numbered among
the saints subsequently to his change of heart
on encountering Christ, is noted in the New
Testament as having been " an unjust collector
of taxes ; " and his lineal descendants in nature,
if not in blood, still abound throughout the
Eastern world.

When, following in the footsteps of the
Greek, the Roman, and the Goth, Amrou led
his victorious army, under the flag of the
Crescent, to take possession of Egypt, and the
Holy Land became also the spoil of the infidel,
the old land titles were left undisturbed, though
tribute and taxation were imposed on the
proprietors. Through all the anarchy that
succeeded the Arab occupation (including the
brilliant but oppressive sway of the Mamelukes,
and brief episode of Napoleon's memorable occupation of Egypt), the possession of the soil still
remained in the hands of the fellahs, with the
exception of a small portion held by the ruling
race, more for their occupation and pleasure
than for their profit. But when, early in the
present century, Mehemet Ali was named by
the Sublime Porte as Pacha of Egypt, and
after he had secured his absolute control of
the country and people, though still professing
allegiance to the Porte, by the slaughter of
the Mamelukes, he turned his attention to the

land question in most Napoleonic fashion. There were two kinds of land—one held in fee and cultivated by the peasant proprietors; the other the Abadiehs, or waste lands. Mehemet Ali finding or pretending that many of the lands of both qualities were insufficiently cultivated, or not at all, in consequence of the insufficiency of the population, and that consequently the taxes due his Government therefor were or could not be paid in sufficient sums to meet his wants—which were ever increasing—for the great schemes of public improvement he meditated, disturbed the existing arrangements by making large grants of land to his favourites to cultivate, taken partly from one class, partly from another, sometimes dispossessing the original proprietors.

When, after his long and brilliant rule of more than forty years, his grandson Abbas succeeded to the throne (the mere episode of the seventy days' reign of Ibrahim counting for nothing in this regard), there was an immediate and radical change of policy in this respect. For Abbas, with all his other faults, was the staunch friend and supporter of the fellah in all his ancient rights and privileges, which he revived and secured to him both by edicts and by practical action. While depriving the rich of the lands given them by Mehemet Ali, that they might revert to their original owners : despoiling the wealthy, to whom he was both unjust and cruel : and making himself an object of suspicion and terror to the members of his own family: he was the constant friend and patron of the lower class; which history proves to have been no exceptional case with despots.

Be this as it may, however, the fact remains, whatever the prompting reason may have been; and the Egyptian fellah really has more cause to-day to bless the memory of the gloomy and cruel Abbas, than that of the generous-tempered, open-hearted Saïd, in so far as this land question is concerned.

For Saïd reversed, and to a considerable extent undid the restitution made by Abbas in respect to the land tenure; reverting more to the policy of his grandfather—imposing additional burdens of taxation upon it, and parcelling out again much of what he declared to be public lands, because their proprietors could not cultivate or properly utilize them.

The policy of Ismaïl Khedive has differed from that of all his predecessors; for, while he has imposed more and heavier taxes upon land, its products, and its occupants, so as to wring treble the revenues out of it ever obtained by Saïd, his immediate predecessor: he has secured for himself, in his own name and those of his

sons and daughters, fully one-fifth of the best
and most valuable of the lands of Egypt under
· actual cultivation; but one-half of which, the
title being in his own name, he offers to his
personal creditors, in extinction of his Daira
debt.

When he mounted the throne in 1863—just
fourteen years ago—his personal real estate was
comparatively small in quantity.   Since that
time he has bought out the property of his half-
brother Mustafa and his uncle Halim, for many
millions respectively, for which two of the
Egyptian loans were issued; thus creating the
confusion between the public and private indebtedness, which has rendered the task of successive financiers, sent from abroad to clear up
these accounts, so difficult and perplexing.*

The present condition of the fellah, and of
the real estate of Egypt is as follows :—There
are 5,000,000 of feddans under cultivation.   Of
these, 1,000,000 are Khedivial or family property;
the rest, outside of a few large landed proprietors,
such as Nubar and Cherif Pachas, and other
high dignitaries of the Court or distant members
of the blood royal, amounting to say 3,500,000
feddans, is still the property of the. fellaheen, or
native peasantry.   Their lands are subject, how-

* See Mr. Sandar's statement of the Khedive's Daira property
and the supposed income therefrom in Appendix.

ever, to a most grinding taxation, varying from £1 10s. to £3 10s. per feddan per annum—some say even more—by irregular impositions; in most instances giving the cultivator, or peasant proprietor, only enough out of his earnings to eke out a bare subsistence, and afford such scanty and insufficient shelter, food, and clothing as keeps life together in himself, his family, and the camel, ox, or ass he employs in his daily labour.

The taxes, too, are taken in kind, not in cash; so that the tax-collector can levy an additional amount by his valuation of the crop.

Then too comes the new tax borrowed from France—the octroi, which is estimated at eight per cent. *ad valorem;* and is also liable to increase the same way.

There is also a tax upon date-trees bearing fruit, a tax upon trades and professions, a tax even upon donkey-boys, who have to pay for their badges. In fact, taxation seems modelled upon the old Roman model, as mentioned in the Scripture, where the edict went out from Cæsar that "all the world should be taxed;" and that relic of the old Roman rule has certainly survived in full force and vigour in Egypt, supplemented by more modern inventions, such as the octroi.

But the heaviest imposition of all is that of

the *corvée*, which, nominally abolished, except in case of necessary labour on the canals for irrigation, is still enforced on a large scale in the upper country, for the benefit of the Khedive's sugar estates, and those of his family and particular favourites: where for three months in the year large bodies of men are taken in gangs to work, receiving neither wages nor food for themselves and their camels—their wives having to bake and bring bread for their husbands, and the men to supply and feed their own cattle.

Domestic slavery in Egypt, and the internal slave-trade which has long supplied its demands and those of Turkey in Europe—against which European philanthropy raises its voice so loudly, and against which all its shafts are levelled—great as their abuses may be, are far more difficult to reach and remedy, than this other cancer in the breast of Egyptian society, to extirpate which might be a slow, but would certainly be a comparatively easy task, as well as a profitable one, to the Khedive and his country. Now that he has offered to surrender up the management and proceeds of his vast sugar estates to his creditors, that they may be placed under European control and direction, the main cause for the continuance of the *corvée*, or of compulsory labour, either in the fields or on the private canals which irrigate them, will cease to exist; and the Khedive himself no longer be tempted to resort to it, under pretexts however specious.

Let us therefore hope that, under these new circumstances, the fellah's lot may be ameliorated, and his opportunity of getting "a fair day's wage for a fair day's work" out of his own fields be no longer prevented; as well as that, in providing for the payment of the foreign creditors, and presenting a good showing in the monthly receipts in the *Caisse* presided over by the European controllers, equal consideration may be shown for the native tax-payer, as for those he is made to pay out of the sweat of his brow, for money which never profited him.

I find some statements so *à propos* to this in the Alexandria correspondence of the *Times*, of a recent date, that I cannot forbear to quote it in confirmation of my own comments on this head. The correspondent says—

"The war-tax which was voted by the Egyptian notables is being rapidly encashed, and the usual mode of collection is being followed, as regards that portion which falls on the land. The sheikhs of the villages are summoned to the chief towns. The moudirs, or governors, tell them how much is needed and when. A rough assessment is nominally followed, and the authorities are supposed to be guided by certain fiscal regulations. But these paper restrictions are not too strictly observed; all the moudir really insists upon is that the money be forthcoming; and it goes hard with the sheik who fails to squeeze the right amount out of his people. The tax is levied as an increased charge of ten per cent. on all previous imposts, after the manner of the *centimes additionels* which provide for provincial administration in France. It will realize about half a million sterling. But that amount is increased by a voluntary subscription, a patriotic fund, raised from the native moneyed class, which will provide an additional £100,000."

The simplicity of this contrivance for squeezing the fellah, is only equalled by its completeness. Appeals to " patriotism," made in such a shape, cannot fail to meet a satisfactory response; but can the fellah bear these additional impositions, broad as his back may be?

The correspondent goes on to confirm yet more strongly my previous assertions as to the present condition of the labouring class, and his testimony coming from a witness on the spot carries conviction with it. He says—

" A contract was concluded yesterday by the Government with a Manchester house, which much improves the prospect of the July coupon;

£500,000 is to be advanced, one-half now, one-half in London, on the 10th of July. The Government on its side undertakes to deliver by that date, in successive deliveries of 50,000 *ardebs*, 600,000 *ardebs of wheat and beans, which are to be paid for at the market price of the day in Alexandria. This produce consists wholly of taxes paid by the peasants in kind;* and when one thinks of the poverty-stricken, over-driven, underfed fellaheen in their miserable hovels, working late and early to fill the pockets of the creditors, *the punctual payment of the coupon ceases to be wholly a subject of gratification.* The fellah would open his eyes if he were told that taxes are only payment for benefits received; a contribution to a fund which is wholly expended for the public good?"

With this confirmatory testimony as to the fellah's actual condition and prospects, under the existing state of things, I close this chapter, which could readily be made a volume, and even then the half would not have been told.

To see the Egyptian fellah as the traveller sees him, he is a most amusing, picturesque, and Oriental object, in perfect keeping with the scenery which surrounds him—whether jogging along on his small donkey, his feet almost touching the ground, in his peculiar costume, which scanty as it is suffices for his comfort in that

R.

climate ; or labouring in the fields, accompanied
by his strange-looking water-ox, half cow, half
hippopotamus in appearance ; or, when his day's
work is over, squatting upon his hams in that
position which only he can comfortably assume,
and which would certainly entail a cramp in the
leg or a back somersault on any less-experienced
practitioner. In spite of his dirt, his rags, his
half-starved appearance, he looks happy, or if
not happy content with his lot, hard as it seems
to the stranger. If "happiness be indeed our
being's end and aim," then must the poor fellah,
who so many have compassionated and so many
more despised, truly have more nearly attained
that end and aim, than the wise and great ones
of the earth, to whom increase of knowledge and
of worldly goods and honour have only brought
increase of care. But should curiosity, or some
higher motive, prompt the stranger to follow him
home and carefully picking his way through the
filthy narrow paths that cannot be called streets,
peer into the interior of the mud hut—into the
single apartment where his family and all his
visible worldly goods are crowded, half hidden by
the smoke which fills the windowless den, without
chimney or other aperture to admit light or air,
save the open doorway—all his senses of sight, of
smell, of hearing, of touch, of taste, will be equally
revolted. Yet in huts like these do the great

mass of the fellah population live, and propagate blear-eyed and unhealthy children, from generation to generation ; secreting and hoarding what money they may earn, without any attempt or desire to improve a condition and style of life which would prove utterly unbearable and immeasurably wretched to any other agricultural class in the world. Yet the almost untold millions squandered by Egyptian rulers on works of vanity, and on useless expeditions for centuries past, have been extracted out of this apparently impoverished and half-starving population, and each year renews the ever-recurring miracle, to the astonishment of the rest of mankind.

Is it not time this tragi-comedy, which has in it far less of laughter than of tears, should be brought to a conclusion ; and the curtain be allowed to fall on a redeemed and regenerated race — even though residing still in the old " house of bondage " ?

CHAPTER XIV.

SCIONS OF THE ROYAL HOUSE OF MEHEMET ALI.

The sons of Ismaïl, and other scions of the royal house, yet surviving
—The sons of Abbas and of Saïd Pachas blasted in the bud—The
sons of the Khedive—Mohamed Tewfik, heir presumptive—His
brothers Hussein and Hassan—Characteristics of each—The younger
sons—How the Khedive is educating his children—Their uncle
Halim Pacha, formerly heir apparent under the old rule—His
character—Description of how he hunted the gazelle with hawk
and hound—Revival in Egypt of a mediæval sport—Halim's
prospects.

THE sons of the Khedive have been most carefully trained and educated, and if they do not
prove clever and useful men the fault is theirs,
not his ; for neither expense nor care has been
spared on their intellectual and physical development. European tutors have been furnished
them from a very early age, who have indoc-
trinated them in the usual branches of a liberal
education, including the languages of Europe, or
at least a portion of them ; and the younger
ones have also been sent to schools and univer-
sities in France, England, and Germany, to

learn as much as it is possible to prevail on princes to acquire—moral suasion only being possible in such cases; the more stringent methods adopted with " common people," of course, never being dreamed of where " blood royal " is concerned.

I believe the heir apparent, Prince Mohamed Tewfik, has never enjoyed the advantages of foreign travel, nor a foreign curriculum, but has been brought up and educated at home. Yet he does credit to his teachers, both as to mind and manners, being one of the most modest and at the same time one of the best-informed young men to be met with anywhere; universally respected as well as liked by foreigners as well as natives: though he shrinks from rather than courts observation or society. Whether this proceeds from native modesty or from policy, the position he occupies being a more delicate and difficult one in the East than elsewhere, I am not sufficiently intimate with him to say; but my impression, formed from my own opportunities of observation, was that the former cause had as much to do with it as the latter. Yet his modesty and retiring manner by no means indicate a lack either of will or of firmness; on the contrary, I should judge he was naturally obstinate, and very hard to move from the path he had selected, either by persuasion or threats. Less politic and plausible than his father, Prince Tewfik impresses you with belief in his sincerity, and that he means what he says —qualities which very clever men often are deficient in. He does not affect so much of the Western air and habits as do his father and two brothers, although he wears the Stambouli costume; and is reputed to be a conscientious though liberal Mussulman in creed and practice. His private character is above reproach. In the great whispering gallery of that Court, and of the Frank community at Cairo, I have never heard a whisper breathed against his domestic virtues or private character. In short, if I were asked to point out the model gentleman among the younger native generation at Cairo (in the higher sense of that much-abused word), I should select Prince Tewfik as one of its most superior types; although in the graces, and in the social circle, one of his brothers may surpass him.

Prnice Tewfik is decidedly Oriental, both in face and figure; of the Circassian type, with square head, heavy frame, dark eyes and hair, and with something solid and substantial stamped bodily and mentally upon him. Devoid apparently of some of the more shining qualities, slow and even hesitating in speech, and not affecting brilliancy or even smartness, his face, eye, and smile inspire confidence. You feel that here is a man whom you can trust.

He is the husband of but one wife, and reported to be very domestic in his habits and tastes. He is Minister of the Interior, and said to be an energetic and indefatigable public officer. Should it be his fate to mount the throne of Egypt, I predict that he will prove a prudent, humane, and sensible ruler, and do credit to himself and good to his people; although I have seen such strange and sudden transformations take place in Egyptian princes after becoming viceroys, that my prediction is made with some hesitation.

The next eldest son is the Prince Hussein, at present Minister of Finance, *vice* the late Mouffetich, departed. He, in appearance, manners, and character, is the reverse of his elder brother. Slight and wiry of frame, with an active and springy step and quick movements, with sharp, shrewd features and restless eye, Prince Hussein is a man who impresses you as well fitted for intrigue; with boldness enough to carry out what he had planned without regard to the consequences. He seems to have inherited much of his father's restless spirit, without the caution which has ever accompanied it in his progenitor; and is certainly a quick, clever young man, though he does not impress you, with all his boldness, as being as open-hearted and sincere as his brother Tewfik. Although, I believe, he has never visited Europe, he is quite French in his dress and address, and figures in the quadrilles and even the waltz at the royal balls, with the grace of a practised man about town. In fact, he is quite French in appearance, and can rattle off *calembours* as fast as any *petit crève* of the boulevards. He is also said to be an extremely good business man, in so far as he is allowed to exert that ability—the Khedive being king and all the ministers echoes, since the death of the Mouffetich, the only one among them to whom he gave more than the shadow of power, after Nubar Pacha (who refused to be a shadow) got his *congé*. The young prince has no pleasant position, being compelled to act as a financial "buffer" between the irate creditors of the Government or the Khedive, and his father. The latter (who is by no means so visible nowadays as he used to be) is ingenious enough to put much of the burden of "to-morrow and tomorrow," sung to the creditors, on his son, whose nominal duties as Finance Minister are really performed by the foreign commissioners, Messrs. Romaine and De Malaret, one of whom receives, and the other of whom disburses, all of the hard cash to be collected in Egypt.

If Prince Hussein resembles a Frenchman,

his brother Hassan, late Minister of War, and now in command of the Egyptian contingent in Turkey, is more like a German in appearance and address; his manner of pronouncing English, which he understands, having been some time at Oxford University, being decidedly German. The same may be said of his manner, which is short and abrupt, though he has enjoyed greater advantages than his brothers. Of his capacity, either civil or military, he has as yet given no proofs. He may show the stuff he is made of, in his present position.

The mystery which still enshrouds the Abyssinian campaign, in which he participated, veils also the part he played therein, the accounts of which are very conflicting, and by no means confirmatory of the florid accounts given in the despatches of the Egyptian generalissimo, Ratib Pacha, who is generally believed to have imitated Falstaff more than Hotspur in his conduct of that most unfortunate and fruitless campaign. The prince has now an opportunity of winning his spurs if he pleases, for if he goes to the front he will have to show the mettle he is made of, against the hereditary enemy of his race.

His duties as War Minister were chiefly nominal; the real management of that department, for the last six or seven years, having been in the hands of the American staff officers, at the head of whom is General Stone (now Stone Pacha Ferik), and General Loring (Loring Pacha Ferik), who has had a separate command at Alexandria, covering the protection of that place, and the line of sea-coast from Alexandria to Port Saïd.

These old and experienced soldiers, military men by early training and participation in bloody wars on the other side of the Atlantic, aided by a picked corps of younger officers, chiefly Americans, have brought the Egyptian army into a fine state of organization and discipline, and made the coast fortifications very strong and effective against any fleet or force seeking to invade Egypt—a contingency happily not likely to occur during the present war, if the solemn assurances of Russian diplomacy are to be relied upon ; but against which, nevertheless, the Khedive is and has long been preparing his troops and defences.

Three or four other younger sons of the Khedive are being as carefully trained and educated as their elder brothers. I believe most of the brethren are by different mothers, but the Khedive is certainly a good father, however miscellaneous his taste in the matter of mothers.

His daughters he has married chiefly to their cousins, richly endowing them all, and insisting

that their husbands shall have no other legal
wives—the Mussulman law allowing four at a
time to all "true believers;" a privilege of
which the Khedive has fully availed himself,
and probably deprecates for his sons and sons-in-
law, from the fruits of his own experience.

One of his daughters married Toussoun Pacha,
the only son of his predecessor Saïd, to whom
Ismaïl behaved well and generously, making
him Minister of Public Instruction, and furnishing him liberally with lands and money. He
died about a year ago, much regretted for his
amiability and generosity of character, in which
he resembled his father, without possessing his
stronger qualities. The son of Abbas also
died young at Constantinople. Mustafa, the
Khedive's brother, who was set aside from the
succession by the new firman from the Porte, is
also dead, and his family were sent for to
Constantinople, and treated in a most princely
manner by the Khedive. But Halim Pacha,
the younger son of Mehemet Ali and uncle to
Ismaïl, still lives, and casts a shadow over the
succession of Tewfik, to secure which his claims
under the original firman granted Mehemet
Ali were set aside by the late Sultan Abdul-
Aziz. Halim, like Mustafa, has been kept at
Constantinople, where both were in high favour,
and given high positions in the Government, as

a rod *in terrorem* for the Khedive and his sons, should they prove refractory, or stint the supplies of backsheesh, which every " Commander of the Faithful " has an undying thirst for, unquenched and unquenchable by any millions however often repeated. How much of the gold extracted from the sweat and blood of Egypt, or from the pockets of the foreign creditor or bondholder, has passed into the capacious maw of the ogre at Constantinople, during the last twelve years, while these two princes of the blood were held as hostages and rods at Stamboul, no one knows save one man, and he doubtless will never divulge it. But certain it is that many millions of pounds annually have been sent there, as sops to the Cerberus, for favours granted in return, or preservation of the *statu quo*.

Mustafa Pacha was a great political intriguer, and probably played his part in these proceedings; but the bold frank character of Halim Pacha frees him from similar imputations. Personally he is one of the most remarkable men of his line, prolific as it ever has been of strong men and original ones.

Born of a Bedouin mother, the wife of Mehemet Ali's vigorous old age, Prince Halim partakes of the peculiarities of his mother's race, being originally spare and wiry in frame and

muscle, lithe as a leopard, a hunter like Nimrod,
a horseman unequalled even among his mother's
centaur-like race, with quick flashing eyes and
sharp features, dark eyes and hair, and Arab
complexion. He has grown stouter and heavier
since residing at Constantinople, but his original
type was such as I have described. He was an
excellent French scholar, and a man of considerable culture, as well as vivacity; extremely
hospitable, and fond of entertaining his Frank
friends at his palace at the Shoubra Gardens, left
him by his father as an inheritance, but which
has now become the property of the Khedive,
who has suffered the palace to fall into ruins,
and the gardens to go to decay. Here Halim
Pacha used to live and enjoy life, until quarrels
between himself and the Khedive drove him out
of Egypt, and caused him to sell out his
property there to the Khedive, for which one of
the outstanding loans was issued. I am not
aware that Halim has, in any manner, formally renounced his pretensions to the Egyptian throne
under the original firman; neither do I know
whether he still cherishes hopes in that regard,
for I have not seen him for many years past.
He was in London recently for a short time, and
it was then whispered that he might possibly
have been sent or have come on a political
mission, relative to the Egyptian succession.

I imagine however that the general acquiescence of the Great Powers to the change of the succession, informal as it may have been, will prove a bar to the claims of Prince Halim, even should he strive to press them : and that the accession of Prince Tewfik is as safe as any political possibility can be.

Of the narrow escape of Prince Halim from death, through his own quickness and presence of mind, when his nephew Achmet was drowned in the Nile, I have already spoken ; and shall conclude this sketch of him with a detail of the manner in which he used to practise his favourite sport, in chasing the gazelle with hawk and hound over the desert.

Although the fleetness of the Arab horse and Syrian greyhound are proverbial, and seem capable of outstripping anything but the wind, yet, fleet as are its pursuers, the gazelle is fleeter still ; and hence the revival on these Eastern plains of the mediæval pastime and "joyous science" of hawking ; bringing the children of the air in aid of hunter, horse, and hound, and assailing the helpless quarry from earth and sky at once.

It was a gay sight to see this Eastern knight on his fleet Arab courser, attended by a princely retinue of friends and followers (but "no lady fair," which Eastern etiquette forbade), sally forth at early dawn from his residence in the famed

gardens of Shoubra, with hawk on fist, and the
Syrian greyhounds in leash, led after him, only to
be unleashed when the quarry was raised on the
desert, a few miles distant.

The Prince himself, usually attired in French
costume—for he is an educated man, and very
French in his tastes—on these occasions wore
the native dress; and his suite, with their gay
and picturesque costumes, and costly trappings
bedecked with gems and cloth of gold, presented
a most gallant and striking appearance; for
among these semi-civilized nomads of Egypt
and Syria, the passion for the chase is only second
to that for war, the children of Nimrod and of
Ishmael retaining still the tastes of their remote
progenitors.

The Syrian greyhound is a very beautiful
specimen of the race. Smaller and with less
length of limb than the English greyhound,
and consequently with a shorter stride, the
rapidity of his movements, and the toughness
and tenacity of his muscles, render him no unworthy scion of the stock to which his British
cousin belongs. Moreover his long feathery-
tufted tail seems to act as a rudder to him, when
in full flight across those breezy plains—for a
strong wind is ever blowing over the desert—
an advantage which marks the difference between the Syrian and other greyhounds, to

whom, in other respects, he bears the closest
affinity. In the eyes and faces of the choicest
specimens of these dogs, there shines an expression of winning and almost human intelligence;
yet, once launched in pursuit of game, they are as
blood-thirsty as the sleuth-hound. The dog in
Egypt, as throughout the East, with this exception is a homeless and houseless vagabond and
semi-savage, prowling in packs, acting as scaven-
ger only, and never domesticated, because considered "unclean" by Mussulman law and
custom. The Prince Halim had the courage to
brave this prejudice, and kept his greyhounds
for the chase. But he also kept another and
more curious class of creatures for the hunting
of the gazelle, probably the fastest in its movements of any wingless animal, viz., his hunting
hawks, which seemed the genuine descendants
of the "falcon gentle," which was wont to afford
such rare sport to our ancestors in the Middle
Ages. As the cavalcade pranced forth from the
gates of the city, and especially from the old
Bab el Nasr, or "Gate of Victory," which
leads to the desert—past those beautiful but
crumbling castellated memorials, the tombs and
palaces of the Memlook sultans, now falling into
ruins—the hooded hawks, perched on the right
hands of the prince and his friends, constituted
a curious feature of the knightly retinue.

The hawk used for this purpose is not the ' ordinary large Egyptian one, which hovers over the city of Cairo, poised in air on its wide wings, or circling around in search of its quarry; but a smaller and fiercer bird, desert born and bred, with keen eyes and sharp talons, of which the larger brother stands in wholesome awe. These birds, trained much as were the mediæval falcons, seem to love the chase as much as their master, although their quarry be not the heron, but the gazelle. Their services were only brought into requisition after the chase had continued some time, and as an adjunct to the pursuit of men, dogs, and horses, all concentrating their energies against the life and liberty of the most lovely, graceful, and inoffensive of wild creatures, almost the sole tenants of these arid wastes.

After advancing a few miles into the desert, which presents one flat, dead, unbroken level of hard gritty soil (not sand), unrelieved by any shrub, grass, flower, or tree, bounded only by the horizon, and producing almost the illusion of a sea view, suddenly half a dozen slender shapely forms spring up, and stand in bold relief against the sky, with heads erect like statuary, some half mile distant.

The sight seems at once to infuse new fire and vigour into the horses, dogs, and men, all

of whom are immediately launched like thunder-
bolts in the direction of the quarry, which
pausing motionless for a moment, break into
full flight the next, bounding marvellous dis-
tances each spring, and soon leaving even the
fleet greyhounds toiling hopelessly in the rear :
the distance between them visibly increasing,
as the tireless gazelles almost fly forwards, inspired by fear. The scene now becomes a most
animated, exciting, and picturesque one, with
the floating burnouses of the Bedouin or Egyptian riders, and the gay attire of horse and man,
and the gallant Arab coursers stretching out
to full speed, with expanded nostrils and pro-
truding eyes, and the feathery tails of the
Syrian greyhounds waving like banners, as they
bound after the flying gazelles.

But vain are the efforts of all their enemies
to gain upon, or even to keep pace with, the
graceful children of the desert. Horses, men,
and dogs are falling rapidly behind : and even the
forms of the gazelles are becoming indistinct
and with difficulty discernible, except to the
eagle eyes of the prince and his Bedouins, when
a new ally is summoned to the assistance of the
hunters, and a new foe launched at the heads
of the triumphant fugitives.

Rising in his shovel-stirrups, in full career,
with the grace and dexterity of an Eastern rider,

Prince Halim, slipping off the hood from the head of the hawk he carries on his right hand, with a peculiar shrill cry launches the bird into the air in the direction of the fast-disappearing quarry. Thus released, the hawk circles rapidly upward until almost lost to sight, a mere speck suspended in blue ether, and seemingly motionless in the cloudless sky, blazing under the fierce Eastern sun in a flood of light. A moment later, the hawk can be seen shooting downwards like a lightning flash on the gazelle, buffeting its head and blinding its eyes, with the rapid blows of its strong wings. Almost frantic with fear and fury, the gazelle soon frees itself from its feathered assailant by striking its head upon the ground, and then resumes its flight; but the relief is only momentary, for the pertinacious assailant as soon as shaken off renews the assault; coming down on the antelope's head again and again, releasing it only long enough to avoid being crushed or impaled upon its sharp brow horns. Blinded at last and wearied by these attacks, confused by the cries of the approaching huntsmen, the terrified and exhausted gazelle falls an easy prey to the greyhounds and pursuing horsemen.

Sometimes a young or badly trained bird would fall a victim to his interference: for the efforts of the gazelle to destroy as well as shake off his tormentors, inspired by the instinct of self-preservation, are often as energetic as piteous to witness.

The hunt of Prince Halim over, the grey-hounds re-leashed, the hawks hooded once more, the heads of the panting Arab steeds are again turned homewards; though the desert-born horses, snuffing eagerly their fresh native air, seem reluctant to return citywards, fretting and chafing under the powerful bit and shovel-spur which compel obedience. This bit is strong enough to break a horse's jaw, with a cruel, sharp iron spike pressing on the tongue, so that a rider who sharply reins in his steed in full career draws blood, and lacerates the horse's tongue. The shovel-shaped stirrup, too, with its sharp edges gores the side of the animal, when spurred, like a knife; so that obedience to the rider's will is easily enforced by a reckless or cruel rider.

Returning at mid-day through the desert under the blazing sun, whose insufferable glare blinds and dazzles European vision, and against which even Bedouin or Egyptian protects himself by the projecting *cofia* or silk shawl drawn over the head and face like a projecting hood, the stranger, if fortunate, may witness the strange and startling optical delusion of the *mirage*, so often described, yet of which the reality is so immeasurably superior to the description. For suddenly, out of what was a moment before but void space bounded by a distant horizon, seems to rise as if by enchantment the semblance of stately cities, with domes, mosques, and minarets, and long moving processions of men and camels; or, more mocking still to dizzy brain and parched palate, the counterfeit presentment of clear pools of water, embowered in shady palm groves. The Turkish bath, the midday siesta preceded by chibouque or nargileh of Latikia or Persian tumbac, constitute the fit pendant to the day's chase.

Such used to be the favourite sport of Prince Halim's youth. He is now a middle-aged man, but a year younger than the Khedive, and they tell me has grown stout and indolent in the enervating air of Constantinople.

But as the last surviving son of the great founder of the house that has ruled Egypt for the last half century, a certain interest attaches to him; to which the future of Egypt, dark with clouds, must add a keener edge. For the present it is the policy of the Great Powers to preserve the *statu quo* in Egypt, and to sanction the change of succession.

CHAPTER XV.

IRRIGATION AND THE BARRAGE.

"The life of Egypt"—The barrage—Proposition to pull down the Pyramids to construct it—A French engineer's perilous predicament —How he extricated himself—Saïd Pacha's new city on a medal !— Egyptian irrigation—How it is managed—Proposed substitute for the irrigation of the Delta—Something about the barrage.

IN former days, before there was railway communication with Cairo, little more than twenty years ago, the traveller who ascended the Nile in a dababieh or small steamer used to be struck by the sight of what seemed at once a turreted castle, a bridge, and a breakwater across the stream. This was the barrage, commenced by Mehemet Ali, continued by Abbas fitfully, and abandoned by Saïd; although at one time he conceived the idea of completing this great work, on which both Mougel and Linant Beys, the Franco-Egyptian engineers, spent much time and labour, and to. which, I was told, about three millions of pounds sterling had been contributed. Saïd was so full of the idea that he actually founded a city there, gave a three days' *fête* on the spot, and struck off a silver medal to commemorate it ; but the city stopped there, and so did the works.

A curious story was told me by one of the French engineers, in connection with the barrage and Abbas Pacha. Summoned by the viceroy to one of his desert palaces hurriedly, the engineer repaired with all speed to see him. He was at once greeted with this suggestion :—

" You are always troubling me about your barrage," said Abbas, " and an idea has struck me.   Those great masses of stone, the Pyramids, are standing there useless.   Why not take the stone from them to do the work ?   Is it not a good idea ? "

" Pull down the Pyramids ! " stammered the amazed engineer, aghast at the idea that his name would go down to posterity in such a connection.

" Yes," impatiently repeated Abbas.   " Why not ?   Are you silly enough to attach any reverence to those ugly, useless piles of stone !   See if you cannot make use of them for the barrage. They have helped to build Cairo already."

The Frenchman made his salaâm and retired in despair.   What was he to do ?   The obstinacy of Abbas was ever proof against argument, and he brooked no contradiction to his will, however

extravagant the whim that prompted it. To
refuse to carry out his orders would be equivalent to losing his place; to obey would, to his
excited imagination, stamp his name with an
immortality of infamy, as the destroyer of the
Pyramids.

Tossing restlessly on his sleepless bed all
night, a bright idea flashed upon him. He
would appeal to Abbas's avarice, to escape the
desecration of the great historic monuments of
Egypt. Taking a large sheet of paper, he
covered it over with long rows of figures and
calculations, and armed with this, returned to
the viceroy the next day.

" What is all this ? " growled Abbas, glancing
suspiciously at the sheet covered with what to
him were cabalistic figures, and frowning darkly
on the engineer. " What rubbish is this you
bring me ? "

" Highness ! " was the reply, " after receiving your orders to remove the stones from
the Pyramids for the barrage, I deemed it my
duty to make a rough calculation of the cost;
and here it is."

" Well, well," said Abbas impatiently, " what
do I know about your hieroglyphics ? Tell me,
what will it cost ? "

The engineer immediately named an enormous
sum for the cost of taking down and transporting

the stones; and after some severe cross-question-
ing from the viceroy, who seemed suspicious of
his good faith, finally persuaded him to abandon
the design of pulling down the Pyramids—
sooner than aid in doing which, he swore to me,
he would have resigned and left the service.

"*Figurez vous, monsieur!*" he said, with
flushed face, and eyes almost starting from their
sockets, as he recalled the recollection. "Fancy
your own feelings, at the thought that your
own children would be pointed out everywhere
as those of *the man who destroyed the Pyramids!*"
and his hair bristled on his head with horror, at
the thought of the peril he, and his children (he
had none, by-the-by), had so narrowly escaped.

The Nile has often and truly been called
"the life of Egypt," for the fertility of the soil
is derived from its deposits and irrigation. The
barrage was intended to irrigate the whole
Delta, and the design certainly was a grand one.
I am too ignorant of engineering, to express any
opinion as to the possibility of achieving the
purpose aimed at by such a breakwater: or
the reasons of the failure and abandonment of
the uncompleted work, in relation to which I
know the Khedive has lately consulted several
eminent English engineers.

The following particulars as to the great and
vital topic of irrigation in Egypt, and incident-

ally as to the barrage, I have procured from persons competent to give it, from long and careful study of both subjects. The whole matter is more simple than it seems; the chief question to be considered is the question of cost.

I believe it is estimated that £1,500,000 would put the barrage in successful operation.

As already stated, the whole cultivated area of Egypt owes its fertility to the Nile inundation. At high Nile the water is heavily charged with sedimentary matters, and these matters are deposited as the velocity of the flood-stream slackens; and so the bed of the river and the submerged lands on either side of it have been gradually raised. If the river were not carefully embanked, the lands immediately contiguous to the stream would be flooded to a depth of about three feet at ordinary high Nile, whilst those more remote from the river would be submerged to as much as three times that depth. These conditions are obviously all that could be desired for the effective irrigation of this country during high Nile, since it would only be necessary to lead canals from the river to the land to be irrigated, controlling the flow of water in the canals by sluices or barrages, formed at their intakes. But at low Nile the level of water in the river is some twenty feet below the surface of the land, so other means have to be adopted

to irrigate during summer. Three courses are
open for adoption :—

1st. To raise the water to the required level
by pumping or other mechanical means.

2nd. To tap the river at some point upstream,
and lead off a canal at a flatter fall than that of
the river, so that at the required place the water
will have attained the surface.

3rd. To dam up the waters of the Nile itself
by a great weir, or barrage.

The first course is that chiefly adopted in
Egypt: and the well-known shadoofs, sakiehs, and
natalahs are the mechanical means most in vogue,
though Cornish pumping-engines and centrifugal
pumps are also common enough. The second plan
of high-level canals is ill-adapted to the conditions in Egypt, because of the small fall of the
land.   Thus, the Nile valley falls at the rate of
five inches per mile; hence, since the inclination
of the canal could hardly be less than one inch
and a half per mile, it would require a length of
nearly seventy miles of canal before the water
would have attained a sufficient height, relative
to the adjoining land, to irrigate without pumping. Canals of this length and of the required
capacity would cost many millions, and even
then would do the work far less effectually than
a barrage.   It is no matter of surprise, therefore,
that the advisability of constructing a barrage

across the Nile at the head of the Delta was seen at a very early period; and that the work itself was undertaken by Mehemet Ali in the year 1847.

The barrage of the Nile is, perhaps, the most imposing engineering work to be found in Egypt; but unfortunately, from a variety of causes, it has not satisfied the anticipations of its projectors. From instability of foundations it has not succeeded in damming up the waters more than some five feet, whereas at least fifteen feet is required to do the work of irrigation effectually. The barrage across the Rosetta branch is 1525 feet in length, and includes sixty-one arches of 16′ 4″ span, and two locks of the respective widths of forty and fifty feet; the whole work presenting much the appearance of a railway viaduct of brickwork, with stone dressings. The Damietta barrage is 1787 feet long, with arches and locks of the same dimensions as in the other barrage. A large iron sluice-gate was to have been fitted in each archway, which when lowered would dam the waters back to a height of fifteen feet above low Nile level, and when raised would have allowed the floods to pass down unimpeded. Owing to the defect in the foundations, these sluices have not yet been furnished to the whole of the barrage; but temporary means are adopted for closing some of the arches during low Nile, and so slightly raising the level of the river above the barrage. The loss from the non-completion of the barrage works, and the consequent defective and costly irrigation of the Delta, is measured by many hundreds of thousands of pounds. Irrigation, which in India costs only a few shillings, in Egypt costs as many pounds; and the difference is almost wholly owing to the incompleteness of the irrigation works, amongst which the barrage is of pre-eminent importance. It is satisfactory to learn, therefore, that the completion of the barrage is seriously entertained by the Khedive, and that the whole question has been elaborately studied by Mr. John Fowler, his consulting engineer. Mr. Fowler, availing himself of the progress in engineering science since the period when the present barrage was commenced, proposes to put the foundations of his new works at a depth below the surface of the water which would have been impracticable thirty years ago; and so he will attain sufficient stability to dam the waters back to a height of fifteen feet, as originally intended, and as is necessary for the satisfactory irrigation of the Delta, without pumping.

So stands this matter of irrigation at present. Doubtless engineering skill, which has worked so many marvels, can dam up even the flood of Father Nile, and control its distribution; and former failure is no argument against final success, under the circumstances attending the experiment thus far. So that if the thing be really feasible and necessary, and will repay the cost—all of which are questions for engineers to solve—the completion of the barrage is now as certain as the perpetuity of the Pyramids.

CHAPTER XVI.

EDUCATION IN EGYPT.

What the Khedive has done in educating his people—The public schools—Their chief inspector, Dor Bey—Information derived from him—Slight sketch of the character and purposes of the new schools, civil and military—The Polytechnic School at Abbassieh—The Missionary schools—Miss Whately's school, and the German—Education for women—A queen worthy of her place—The coming race of Egyptian women.

FULLY to relate all that the Khedive has done for education would require a volume instead of a chapter; for his efforts in this direction are worthy of all praise: so much has he already accomplished within the last six or eight years. A volume has been written on the subject, and published by the Government, prepared by Dor Bey, the able controller and chief inspector of the public schools, giving full and accurate information and details on this most interesting topic. This gentleman was summoned by the Khedive from Switzerland, where he was performing similar functions, and is assisted in his duties by Mr. Rogers, formerly British consul at Cairo, but now in the Egyptian service.

From Mr. Dor's statements I shall merely extract a few of the most salient features of the new plan of regenerating Egypt, by educating and enlightening the rising generation—an Herculean task indeed, when the peculiarities of place and people are taken into consideration. The system is not to make education compulsory (which seems to me a mistake), and the advantages it offers have been confined thus far to the cities, and have not yet been generally extended into the country, where the rural population, who need it most, might avail themselves of the benefits of instruction, in something more than the Koran, free of cost. For the Arab child is remarkably bright and intelligent, and loves learning, when there is any possible chance of his acquiring it. Mehemet Ali made some attempt at such schools, as did also Abbas Pacha and Saïd; but the merit of greatly enlarging and perfecting them undoubtedly belongs to Khedive Ismaïl, who has summoned able men from abroad to assist him in the good work.

At some of the schools I visited I was struck by the quickness of the boys, and their memories seemed surprising, as well as their genius for mathematics and arithmetic. Standing before a black board, with a piece of chalk, the pupils would write down rapidly and correctly, sentences dictated to them in different languages. Men of all ages are admitted to prepare for teachers : some very mature ones I saw hard at work, grappling with school-boy tasks, with an iron gravity nothing could disturb. The colour of the pupils is as widely various as their types of face ; but I saw very few negroes among them.

Ophthalmia, the terrible scourge of Egypt, had left its mark on many of the boys ; but I was happy to hear that the virulence of this disease was abating under the new *régime*.

At the military training school at Abbassieh, where the number of pupils between the ages of sixteen and twenty was considerable, every possible appliance for instruction, both mental and bodily, was to be seen ; and some of the fencing I saw, both with foil and broad-sword, would have done credit to the professors of the art anywhere in Europe. Major Soliman Bey, an Egyptian educated at Paris and Metz, was at the head of the Polytechnic School of the Abbassieh, formerly the site of one of Abbas' desert palaces, near Cairo. Mr. Bourke, a gentleman of high culture and intelligence, was the English professor ; with two able professors of French and German as his colleagues.

One of the largest and most famous schools in the East, under Mahommedan auspices, has long

T

been in operation at Cairo, at the mosque of El Akhsar; but the course is chiefly if not entirely theological, comprising lessons from and instruction in the Koran. All the mosques also have schools attached ⸳ to them, where squat the youthful Arabs, shrieking out in Arabic at the top of their voices, all at the same time: and swinging to and fro as they shout, in chorus with their Arab instructor. These schools are not supported by Government endowment, but by the payment of a trifling sum from parents who can afford it. The Government, however, is helping these to better teachers, trained at its own normal schools and the course of instruction is being enlarged.

The public schools are composed of primary and Government schools. The primary schools have a course which extends over four years, and all who like to come, of whatever race or religion, are freely admitted, either as boarders or day scholars. The boarders who are able pay £26 per year; those who can pay a part only do so; the poor pay nothing. The same is the case with the day scholars.

The non-paying pupils however are subject to the call of the Government, which passes them on through the other schools, and prepares them for public service; and many are made teachers in the primary schools, besides being trained as doctors, engineers, surveyors, etc. There are also preparatory schools midway between the two classes above referred to.

The Government schools (so called) are of a special character, such as for medicine, the higher mechanics, and a polytechnic school for training officers of the army. Although so recently established, they have already laid the foundations for an admirable local education, and for the improved standard of the next generation of Egyptian youth.

As an indication of educational progress, the recent rapid advance of the American missionary schools may be cited. For nine years under previous reigns, a small but untiring body of these men, domiciled in Egypt, strove to get pupils, and only succeeded on a most limited scale; but their recent advance in this regard, within the last five years, has been wonderful. They are now erecting, opposite the old Shepheard's Hotel, an extensive edifice in stone, which will comprise a church in the centre and two wings, one for a male, and the other for a female college, capable each of containing several hundreds of students. The building, it is estimated, will cost £15,000 when completed, and will contain residences for the missionaries also.

From a statement made by these missionaries, they claim within the last twenty years to have

" gathered a community of 3000 souls ; to have established fifteen churches, with an aggregate membership of 600; and to have sold and distributed over 10,000 volumes of religious books and tracts in 1874." Their centres of operation are at Alexandria, Cairo, Mansoura, taking three angles of the Delta; the Fayoum in Middle Egypt, and Assiout in Upper Egypt. They number seventeen missionaries (ten male and seven female), twelve native evangelists, sixty-three native trained teachers, male and female, and a corps of native colporteurs. They have in active operation eighteen boys' schools and nine for girls, some of them boarding-schools; attended by Moslem as well as native Christian children, whose parents now permit them to attend to receive the benefits of education, if not of religious training. The Khedive has liberally assisted this work. He has not only exchanged for their old mission site on the Mooskie a most valuable lot near Shepheard's Hotel, but added £7000 in cash, with which the building has been commenced, and donations from other sources have raised that sum to nearly £9000; so that he may, in fact, be considered one of the founders of these schools, which are intended to instruct the children of Moslems as well as Christians.

The English chapel is also approaching com-

pletion, but on a much smaller scale : and not
combined with educational purposes. The
Khedive also gave the lot for the erection of
that building, and a large and valuable one it
is. In religious toleration this Moslem prince
sets an example to some well-known Christian
rulers and statesmen, who make religious opinions
a test of good citizenship, and who

> " Fight like devils for conciliation,
> And hate each other for the love of God."

The indefatigable Miss Whately, daughter of
the late Archbishop of Dublin, is devoting her life
and energies to the work of educating the female
fellahs, with a disinterestedness as rare as it is
noble. Her school will be her monument, when
her life and labours are over ; for England can
boast of few such women. She has given more
than money to this work of charity—the treasures
of her youth, the comforts of a home, the society
of friends and kindred. She may be termed the
Florence Nightingale of peace. Others have
sentimentalized over the fellahs, she has come
down to their level, in order to bring their
children up to hers. Luckier than most of the
self-sacrificing sisterhood, she and her work are
rightly appreciated both by Christian and Moslem : and by none more so than by the Khedive
himself.

The German church—the ground for which was also a gift from the Khedive—has been completed, and has a large school attached to it; but, I think, confines its instruction to the children of European parents.

I believe that very little is attempted or accomplished as to the conversion or religious instruction of Mussulman children; the so-called "converts" being chiefly seceders from the Coptic Church, which bitterly resents the interference of what it considers "latter-day" Christians, as compared to themselves.

During my experience in Egypt, most if not all the troubles and difficulties experienced by the missionaries in the upper country came from this quarter, and not from the Mussulman Government or people.

My friend Mr. Lansing, the able and zealous head of the American missionaries in Egypt for the last twenty years, I am sure will confirm this statement, having often frankly admitted the fact to me.

But the greatest innovation is the attempt to educate the native women which, under the auspices of one of the Khedive's wives, has been attempted on a considerable scale: and with very remarkable success thus far. Miss Whately and the American missionaries had been making a similar attempt previously, but the natural dread of the ignorant and fanatical natives, that the religious faith of their children would be tampered with by Christian teachers, restricted the benefit of their efforts chiefly to the children, male and female, of the native Christians; and many of these, through jealousy of the foreign teachers, would not patronize these schools. But when the wife of the Khedive took the matter in hand, it was a very different thing; for royal patronage goes as far in Egypt, as in more enlightened countries. But two years have elapsed since the Khedive allowed his third wife (I think) to make use of one of his numerous palaces for the purpose, of which he approved; and after preparations for the reception and comfort of pupils, and engagement of a staff of teachers, the mothers in Egypt of every class were invited to send their daughters to be lodged, fed, clothed, and educated, free of charge. There was a little hesitation at first, so startling was the suggestion, so utterly opposed to all precedents and Oriental ideas concerning womankind and her duties here below. But though for three weeks after the opening day the benches were empty, within three or four months the 300 for whom there was accommodation had filled all the vacant space; and more than double that number were pressing their claims for admission. This work is indeed

twice blessed—to her who gives and to those
who receive—and I regret that I do not know
and cannot commemorate the name of the princess, who is godmother to the first native female
school in Egypt, instituted under native auspices,
and endowed by native bounty.

Two years ago the Khedive, in talking to me
of his plans for the improvement of his people,
spoke of his educational ideas in reference to
the female children of his fellahs, who he proposed to substitute, in domestic duties of the
household, as servants in place of the slaves;
who, he declared, were more a necessity on
account of the want of a class fitted, by training
and intelligence, to take their places. "For,"
he said, "you know very well we have no such
class here; but let the fellah girls be educated,
and taught the duties of cleanliness and household virtues, and we can do away with the
slaves, who are a great expense and a great
nuisance."

The instruction in this school is based partly
on this idea, and partly on preparations for playing the higher part of mistress of the household;
for five days in the week are devoted to instruction in household duties and needlework, and
but two to intellectual culture. The entire
course covers a term of five years. The girls
are of all castes, colours, religions, and races,

even including negro slaves. French is the foreign language taught, and of course their own. The intelligence and quickness of the girls is even greater than that of the male portion of the population. With education they will make good wives and mothers, as well as good household servants; and the name of the Egyptian queen who has instituted this great reform (which must and will prove as the. first grain of mustard-seed with so imitative a people as the Arab), bids fair to go down to posterity burdened with the blessings of the male as well as the female portion of her people, who will enjoy the benefits and blessings of the reform she has so well and wisely· begun.

CHAPTER XVII.

SKETCHES OF TWO FAMOUS ANGLO-AFRICAN EXPLORERS.

Captain Richard Burton and Gordon Pacha at Cairo—Description of the men—Their latest work in Africa—The land of Midian—The Soudan—Burton's first appearance in Egypt—Some curious recollections—His last visit—What he was then and now,—Burton's discovery — Gordon Pacha's personal characteristics — His proposed work in Central Africa.

It was my good fortune last winter, at Cairo, to encounter and enjoy much intimate communion with two of the most celebrated of the Anglo-African explorers, still in the full vigour of mature manhood, and with ardour unquenched by the sufferings and perils, through which one of them at least has not passed unscathed. Captain Richard Burton and Gordon Pacha were both at Shepheard's Hotel during the winter; although unfortunately they did not meet there, Burton arriving only a few days too late to meet his younger colleague in adventure and fame. It would have been both instructive and amusing to have listened to a colloquy between these two men, who with the sole tie of love of adventure, are in all other respects as different as any two men possibly can be. Burton is a very old friend of mine; with Gordon Pacha my acquaintance is of recent date.

Many years ago, in the days of Abbas Pacha, a young officer in the Indian service came mysteriously to Alexandria, secluded himself in the gardens of some English friends, and diligently studied the language and customs of the lower classes of the Arab population. Then he as suddenly and mysteriously disappeared. Months afterwards there spread a rumour throughout Egypt, that an adventurous Frank, at the hourly peril of life and limb, had actually accompanied the pilgrimage into Mecca, disguised as a Mussulman, and penetrated even to the "holy of holies" in the city of the faithful, which no European ever had done before. But the story was discredited, and was ranked among the "thousand and one" fabulous stories which are the modern "Arabian Nights' Entertainments" in modern Egypt.

Passing my summer at Cairo in 1854, in common with several of the Frank residents (very few at that time, and composed chiefly of foreign officials, civil engineers, and foreign

officers in the viceroy's service), it was my
custom to dine frequently at Shepheard's Hotel,
for the sake of society. One evening at dinner
we remarked a rather dirty-looking native, in
Arab dress, sitting alone at the opposite end of
the table, yet eating in Frank fashion; apparently paying no attention to what was going on
around him, though we were struck by the
exceeding brilliancy and intelligence of his eye,
whenever he looked up. As it was not Shepheard's habit to allow natives, especially those
of a lower class, to sit at his *table d'hôte*, I
carelessly questioned him concerning this person;
but received only a vague answer, and dropped
the subject. But when we saw the man several
days in succession, in the same place, our
curiosity begun to be excited; fanned as it was
by Shepheard's hints, that we would "know
very soon who that Arab was, and might be
rather surprised!" At last, after playing this
farce for several days, doubtless tired of want
of companionship and enforced silence, Burton
(for he it was) dropped the veil, announced his
real name and character, and astonished us all
not a little by the announcement, that the
rumour we had heard and disbelieved was
founded on truth; as he had just returned with
the pilgrims from the (Haj) pilgrimage from
Mecca. He proved himself a most delightful

and welcome accession to our little circle in
the social wilderness of the Cairo of that day,
and was my guest at my Cairene house for
some time after: recounting in his own inimitable style, of which his written works convey
but a faint impression, his strange and startling
adventures.

Night after night would we sit together on
the flat roof of my house, or under the palm
trees in the garden, smoking our nargilehs
under the starlit heavens : while he revived his
daily experiences during that terrible trial, at
any moment of which detection would have
been death; and when he left us to prepare
his story for the public through the press, we
sorely missed his ready wit and exciting conversation. For he is a most admirable *raconteur ;*
and although not averse to the sound of his own
voice by any means, is an attentive listener,
and ready to take as well as give in conversation
—a very rare merit among clever men, whose
talk is seldom " relieved by occasional flashes of
silence," as Sidney Smith remarked on one
occasion of Lord Macaulay's.

Hence, when the familiar face of Richard
Burton, sadder and sterner, and bearing its
souvenir of past perils in the shape of a deep
cicatrice on the cheek, again greeted me at the
old place, and his strong hand grasped mine

again, it was like a resurrection of the olden
time; and we took up the thread of our long-
interrupted intercourse, where we had dropped
it more than twenty years before. In that
interval what countries had this, our greatest
modern traveller, not seen and described, from
Iceland to Sind, from Central Africa to Salt
Lake? and with what strange and diversified
memories must not that busy brain be filled,
never given to the world even in the library of
volumes, in which he has recorded his experiences in longer and more varied wanderings
than those of Ulysses, over lands undreamed of
by that ancient mariner?

I found Burton more changed in his outward
than in his inner man. Perhaps he was more
addicted to the utterance of very startling para-
doxes in his random talk, than formerly: and
even more fond of shocking people's stereotyped
prejudices than he used to be; but his manner
was less abrupt, and his tolerance of opinions
opposite his own much greater than in his
earlier days, when he was apt to be somewhat
dictatorial. The old charm of his conversation
was still there, increased by the stores of varied
information carefully gathered up and retained
by a most retentive memory. I have encountered
many clever talkers, in different languages, but
I really have never met Burton's superior any-

SQUARE OF MUDIRIEH AT KHARTOUM.

SARGENT

To face page 246.

where, in this respect. ˅ Physically he still •
retains the vigour and strength which he
formerly enjoyed. His arm is like a bar of iron;
and he keeps his biceps and other muscles in
constant training, by habitually carrying in his
hand an iron cane, which most men would find
fatiguing in an hour. He does this to keep in
training for carrying a heavy gun on his explorations.

For a long time he was mysterious with his
intimates, as to the real object of his visit to
Egypt: not knowing how the Khedive might
receive or assist in his search for the long-for-
gotten gold mines of the land of Midian. Three
days after I left Cairo for Europe, he started for
the land of Midian, furnished by the Khedive
with the means of conveyance and necessary
escort; and has again startled the world by new
revelations of new discoveries, more fully to be
explored and utilized, it is to be hoped, during
the ensuing winter.

Where Burton went, and what he saw, has
been briefly described in a letter from Alexandria
to a London daily journal, the substance of
which briefly is, that he went on a friendly
errand for the Khedive to survey the " land of
Midian," having informed the monarch of his
belief that valuable gold mines were to be found
there. On the eastern coast of the Gulf of

. Akaba, on the Red Sea, lies the ancient and almost forgotten land of Midian, famed of old for its mineral wealth. Thither went Captain Burton, a Government frigate and sufficient military escort having been furnished him; an able French mining engineer in the Egyptian service, M. Marie, accompanying the expedition.

The party left Suez on the 21st March last, and on the 2nd April arrived at Moilah, a port of the Gulf of Akaba, where an Egyptian garrison is stationed. The account goes on to state :—

" Thence they took boat to Eynounah Bay, at the entrance of the Wady, or Valley of Eynounah, a little to the north of Moilah, on the eastern side of the gulf. These wadys are curious. They are barren rocky places, with no possibility of much culture, and yet they all bear signs of abundant population in times gone by. Large towns, built not of mud, as Arab towns so often are, but of solid masonry such as the Romans always used, roads cut in the rock, aqueducts five miles long, remains of massive fortresses, artificial lakes—all these signs of wealth and numbers are reported by Captain Burton. According to him the reason of it all is not far to seek. The rock is full of mineral wealth. Gold and silver they found, and the former seems to exist in quantity sufficient to repay the labour of acquisition. Quartz and chlorites occur with gold in them just as they are found in the gold districts of South America. The party tested both the rock by crushing and the sands of the streams by sifting, and in each case with good result. Tin and antimony they also discovered, and they had evidence of the existence of turquoise mines. Each ruined town had its mining works; dams for the washing of sand and crushed rock were frequently seen; scoriæ lies about near ancient furnaces; in short, the traces are numerous of a busy mining population in a country which seems to be full of mineral wealth. From Makná (Mugna of the maps), the capital of the land of Midian, up to Akaba at the head of the gulf, Captain Burton reports the country as auriferous, and he believes the district southwards as far as Gebel Hassäni—a mountain well known to geographers —to possess the same character. He even goes so far as to say he has brought back to life an ancient California.

" M. Marie, a skilful mining engineer, also speaks with confidence. Of course Captain Burton has kept elaborate notes, and he maintains that they will bear out his golden views of the land of Midian. In any case they will be interesting, as the country is utterly unknown. No modern traveller has set foot there; even the map has yet to be made. It will be remembered that Moses fled from the face of Pharaoh and dwelt in the land of Midian, and Jethro, the priest of Midian, gave him for wife his daughter Zipporah. The Khedive, of course, is much interested in the complete success of this expedition, and is now very desirous to give practical effect to it. He has asked the Foreign Office to allow Captain Burton to return next winter to assist him in the development of his new gold fields, and no man could be better

U

chosen for the task. At the same time the Egyptian ruler is fully convinced that all schemes of development in his dominions must now be subjected to commercial tests. The success of the new mines will therefore depend on the opinion of European capitalists, and whether they find that the reports—which will be made in detail—of the results of the expedition offer a new field for the investment of capital. The Khedive himself will be satisfied with the payment of a royalty."

Physically and mentally, in appearance and manner, as well as in character and speech, Gordon Pacha is the direct opposite to Captain Burton. As habitually sparing of speech as Burton is the reverse, and of a shy reserved manner, and seeming absence of mind in common intercourse out of doors, when interested or excited, or in the vein with congenial companions, he can talk fast and fluently, and with great felicity of expression. He appears to most advantage when, breaking through his usual reticence, he frankly pours out his thoughts and feelings to the few whom he honours with his confidence. The real mettle of the man is then discernible, and the strong undercurrent of a singularly suppressed nature sweeps both speaker and listener along, on a tide of most animated and earnest talk : in which he seems to unburden his whole mind.

When this breaking down of the barriers of

reserve takes place, he seems to be swept away by the rushing flood of feelings and thoughts long pent up in his own breast: and you are impressed with the thorough earnestness of the man, in all he says or undertakes. For this, I take it, is the key-note to his character. He is a man terribly in earnest, and accepts life and its duties more in the spirit of an old Covenanter, than in the less serious one of our own days. The religious sentiment with him is very strong, the Bible being his constant companion in his tent, in the desert, or the wilderness, as I have been told by the companions of his explorations ; though he can be short and severe enough at times, as his Chinese record proves. In many of his peculiar ways and traits of character, he resembles much the famous Confederate chieftain, Stonewall Jackson.

Gordon Pacha is a man of middle height, sparely but strongly built, and giving little indication of the strength, both of sinews and constitution, which has borne him so far unscathed through so many hardships, and the African swamps, where the " pestilence walketh at noonday," and wherein so many of his pioneers have laid their bones. Neither in face nor in figure does he carry any traces of his conflicts with the treacherous climate, and more treacherous human wild beasts, among whom he had passed the two preceding years. Even his complexion, still comparatively fresh and fair, gave no hint of the kisses of the sun of Central Africa; and his eye was as clear and bright, as though he had just come from promenading on the shady side of Pall Mall. He is quite youthful in appearance, with regular features and dark brown hair. His bearing is not that of a military man, he affects no martial stride or measured step, but walks very rapidly, looking neither to right or left, in seeming abstraction, with head a little advanced, and with a slight stoop of the shoulders, his eyes cast on the ground. One who had never seen him before, would mistake him rather for an author, intent on embodying an idea or fugitive thought, than the cool and intrepid explorer of African wilds, the self-possessed ruler of African savages.

Yet this modest unassuming man has in him the stuff out of which great explorers and successful rulers of men are made—has proved it already; and if he lives, and is not thwarted in his settled purpose by treachery or death, will be very apt to achieve it. He has gone to the Soudan, clothed with absolute power as relates to the governing of that province, which extends from the first cataract to the Equator.

All the world knows the incidents of his earlier career, and how and why he received the *sobriquet* of "Chinese Gordon," when in conjunction with two American officers he rescued the "flowery empire" from its rebels, and gave the army they commanded the title of the "Invincible Army." Surviving his comrades, Burgwin and Ward, Gordon reaped a rich harvest of renown, and was invited by the Khedive to aid him in his Central African designs; with what results is also well known.

I had the pleasure of meeting him at Cairo, as he passed home on his brief *congé* at the close of 1876, and on his return early in 1877, when he presented his *ultimatum* to the Khedive, and was given all and even more authority than he demanded, within a few days after his arrival; leaving shortly after to assume his new functions, as governor-general for life of all the Khedive's actual or potential equatorial possessions. His work in Central Africa, thus far, has been simply preparatory to that which he now has set out to terminate, viz., to weld together under one government the scattered outlying provinces, and more recent acquisitions loosely termed The Soudan : a territory larger and more populous than Egypt proper, to which it acknowledges the most indefinite kind of obedience— offering, both in its climate and its savage inhabitants, immense difficulties in the way of regular government or improvement. But the main object of Gordan Pacha's ambition, and the chief incentive to his taking his life into his hand, and returning to his province, is the suppression of the internal slave-trade; which feat he has pledged himself to accomplish, should life and health be spared him, and the inscrutable fiat of Omnipotence not forbid it. But neither he, nor those who know him best, believe that he will fail; although he has indeed a thorny path to tread, and a most difficult task to accomplish. All doubts as to the Khedive's sincerity in this matter, would seem to be put at rest, by the absolute authority he has given Colonel Gordon, and given for life, with no reserved right of recalling it; for it was on that condition only that he consented to go.

I do not know which, of the two tasks he has set himself, is the more difficult to accomplish. The Central or Equatorial Africans are terribly barbarous and savage, and as faithless as ferocious, with a wild sense of independence, and hatred of all the restraints of civilization. As to slavery and the slave-trade, they have long been the cherished institutions of the country, the very foundation of their social system; and to eradicate either, or both, will be a task of greater difficulty and danger, than those unacquainted with the country and people can possibly imagine. Even without entirely accomplishing his self-appointed task, Gordon Pacha may do a great and good work, by reducing the existing chaos into some semblance of settled government: and paving the way, for at least the partial civilization of a people, at present given over to barbarism.

The first effect of the late stoppage of the slave-trade, has been to diminish the receipts of ivory, and other products of Central Africa; but once diverted by the river and railway communication to Cairo, that trade may become one of the most important resources of Egypt.

His seat of government will be Khartoum, on the White Nile, already a large and growing place of about 30,000 inhabitants, which the rapidly increasing trade of Central Africa, if diverted thither, should expand into a large city. He has no European or white man with him, save a Maltese dragoman, Tomaso Ferrante. His only lieutenants at present are Major Prout, a very clever American civil engineer, who has already been two years in Central Africa, and who will act as his deputy governor-general; and Colonel Mason, an equally experienced and clever officer, one of the ex-Confederates in the Khedive's service. Both of these last-named officers are good linguists, which is of great importance in their position. Colonel Chaillé Long, who was with Gordon in his first expedition (whose clever narrative of his adventures and discoveries excited much attention last year), is now at Cairo under medical treatment; his health having suffered severely from his trying visit to King M'Tesa. That potentate is said to be badly disposed towards the new governor-general, and may give much trouble; and disturbances are said to have broken out at Darfour, whither Colonel Mason was sent. The latest tidings of Gordon Pacha were, that he also was hastening to Darfour, to quell those disturbances. The extent of the new province, which is larger than Egypt proper, will render it a task of no small difficulty to keep it in subjection to the authority of one man; especially if the savage chiefs, like M'Tesa and the so-called King of Darfour, should rebel against or resist Egyptian rule. Whether or not success crowns Gordon Pacha's intrepid efforts to unite the scattered tribes under a stable government, and stop the slave-trade, his merit will be none the less; for, like the knight who set out in quest of the "Holy Grail," the purpose in itself would glorify even failure.

CHAPTER XVIII.

MIXED JUDICIAL TRIBUNALS IN EGYPT.

Efforts of Sublime Porte, for twenty-five years, to break down the doctrine of exterritoriality in the Turkish dominions—What exterritoriality means—Mixed tribunals attempted to be introduced, under "Hatti Houmaïon" of Sultan in 1856, and again tried by Egyptian Government in 1860—Why prevented by consuls-general on those occasions—Nubar Pasha's persistent efforts and final partial success—His plan as opposed to the plan recently adopted—My own action in the matter—The present tribunals entitled to a fair trial.

THE idea of mixed judicial tribunals is a very old one, originating a quarter of a century ago in Turkey; the Ottoman Porte thus seeking to shake off the anomalous, and, as it regarded it, degrading claim of the Christian Powers to deny the jurisdiction of its courts, and what it termed justice, on behalf of their subjects; resting their right on the old capitulations, which ceded that privilege, on the ground of the incompatibility of their law, based on the Koran, to people of other nations and different faiths. Hence arose the doctrine of exterritoriality, which simply signified the absence of local jurisdiction over the foreigner throughout the Ottoman dominions, and legal authority of their own diplomatic or consular agents over them, in all civil or criminal cases in which they might be defendants. For all cases in which they were plaintiffs, their representatives in the country, or on the spot, were bound to press upon the local Government their claims or rights : and the practice grew up of submitting such mixed cases to the local tribunals, in the presence of the *chancelier* of the consulate, or submitting them to arbitration.

The Sublime Porte, in its windy proclamations issued from time to time, attempted to shake off this *imperium in imperio* of the foreign agents, which doubtless was sometimes pushed too far, sometimes abused ; as will ever be the case when such great power is intrusted to men not always capable, or endowed with discretion or principle.

But, upon the whole, as far as my experience went, the system worked well, and insured speedy and substantial justice to foreign residents, in the absence of a better tribunal. As early as 1856, in the " Hatti Houmaïon " of the then Sultan, the substitution of mixed tribunals for the settlement of all difficulties between strangers and natives throughout the empire was decreed; and a copy of the firman sent to Egypt to be publicly read, that its provisions might be applied there, as elsewhere throughout the empire. On receiving it, Saïd Pasha shrugged his shoulders, and submitted it to the consuls-general, whose duties were diplomatic, the mere consular duties being attended to by the consuls and vice-consuls.

In a despatch to my Government, dated May 1st, 1856, the reasons that induced my colleagues and myself to refuse accepting this innovation were fully set forth. A few extracts from that document will suffice to show the justice of our refusal to countenance the change.

" With reference to the practical operation of the mixed tribunals proposed, an almost insuperable difficulty arises from the absence of a common language and a common sympathy between its constituent parts. Nine-tenths of the rayahs speak or understand no language but their own, the Arabic. Each foreign nationality is ignorant of the language spoken or understood by the other, as a general rule; while for communication with the natives a jargon composed partly of lingua Franca, partly of Arabic, is most current. The Maltese subjects of Great Britain, of whom there are a great many here, and constantly in litigation, have actually invented a new language, understood only by themselves, composed of French, Italian, Spanish, and Arabic.

"Men who not only live apart, but are careful even to be buried apart, regarding close contact in life or death as contamination, could scarcely be coupled together or confer very harmoniously. Imagine a tribunal composed of several Moslems, two Christian Armenians, two Latin and two Greek Christians (every native Christian sect here bitterly hating the other), and add two Jewish Rabbis, and you would have a most striking illustration of "the happy family" in the museums, composed of the most uncongenial animals possibly to be found. It would certainly require a liberal use of the most common instrument in the administration of Eastern justice, the *kourbash* (whip), to prevent them from throttling each other."

The indifference of Saïd Pacha, and the active opposition of the consuls-general to any change, quashed the project for a time. But, four years later, the idea was revived, and a determined effort made, with the support of a portion of the consular corps, to compel the introduction of mixed tribunals, on the Constantinople plan, into Egypt. This attempt was also frustrated, by the refusal of several of my colleagues and myself to consent to such a change on, as we believed, good and sufficient grounds.

In order that our action then may not be regarded as merely personal or factious, I shall make a few brief extracts from my communications on the subject to my own and to the Egyptian Governments, giving the reasons for our action. On July 7th, 1860, Cherif Pacha, then Minister of Foreign Affairs, transmitted to all the consuls-general a despatch, covering a printed programme of "A Mixed International Tribunal," which he declared had been "adopted by the representatives of the five European Powers signing the treaty of 1841 in accord with the Egyptian Government;" to which, in the name of the viceroy, he demanded our adhesion. The salient points of my reply to Cherif Pacha, in which all of my other colleagues, save the five above mentioned, concurred, were as follows :—

" Whatever may be the real or supposed obligations conferred on the Egyptian Government by any of the Powers in 1841, or at any other period, at this date every representative of a foreign Government here, great or small, enjoys the right of exclusive protection of his own subjects or citizens, under treaty stipulations, in which the rights and privileges conceded 'to the most favoured nations' place all foreign agents here on the same footing. Under such circumstances, as the representative of my Government

here, I never will surrender those rights, nor
resign into irresponsible hands, my high prerogative of demanding and enforcing justice for
my people, from prince or peasant, in Egypt and
its dependencies.

"A general convocation of all the consuls-
general has hitherto been the universal, as well
as the only just and proper mode of considering
proposed reforms, or changes affecting all nationalities; but on two separate occasions, within
my own official term, projects very similar to
this, but of wider scope, have been discussed,
and finally rejected by the whole body thus
assembled.

"Why, upon this occasion, a studied exclusion
of more than two-thirds of the consular corps
has been made, the Egyptian Government may
possibly be able to explain, if not to justify; but
it certainly relieves those thus excluded, from
the thankless task of volunteering opinions, after
the 'adoption' of a system, or of giving in their
adhesion to a tribunal, wherein they are to have
an occasional solitary representative, as an act
of grace only, when their own business is to be
settled by the numerous deputies of the Egyptian
Government and of the five Powers, with power
of appeal to another, a remote, and an alien
jurisdiction. The law too of such tribunals is
to follow the Code Napoleon, diluted by the

customs and usages of the country—a code in direct opposition to the common law, which regulates the affairs of sixty millions of American and English men. Apart from the radical objection as to the mode of its inception, the project itself does not obtain the sanction of my judgment, for many and grave objections as to its plan and provisions; which, at a proper time and place, and to a competent authority, I shall stand prepared to justify."

To the Secretary of State I gave those objections in detail, of which only the salient ones shall now be reproduced.

" 1stly. The High Court of Appeal from the judgments of proposed tribunal is to be Constantinople, where the laws, usages, customs, currency, and language are as widely dissimilar from those of Egypt, as those of England would be from those of Austria, and where neither judge, jury, nor witnesses would be accessible.

" 2ndly. Such tribunal is to adopt the Code Napoleon in its proceedings, where the usages and customs of the country prove insufficient, and is framed exclusively on French models and based on French law. When the Mediterranean shall really have become a 'French lake,' either by conquest or treaty, it will be time to adopt the French code as the supreme law of the Levant; but until then we prefer the common law, and an equitable settlement on the basis of justice, irrespective of forms, for our people.

" 3rdly. The representatives or judges appointed by the ' five treaty Powers ' only would sit in judgment on the rights and interests of all other nationalities in Egypt ; giving those ' five ' effectively a protectorate over Egypt, and all foreigners therein. In such case the continued residence of agents of other Powers would be a mere farce.

" 5thly. Under the printed programme a *bribe* is offered to the judges to protract, instead of hasten judgment : each receiving £5 for every sitting, and no limit being put upon their number ! Such litigation would be an expensive luxury.

"6thly. The large sum required to be deposited in advance by the claimant, for payment of expenses, costs, etc., would make this court the resort of rich speculators, not poor and honest creditors. To the same practical effect would be the extraordinary clause, that ' no claimant after commencing his process shall be allowed to settle his cause ! '

" 7thly and lastly. The creation of such tribunal is utterly uncalled for. The Egyptian Government exercises authority over the princes, who are Egyptian subjects, as well as over the rest of the natives ; and arbitration, the simplest and most honest mode of settling controversies, is always open to them, should this Government feel any delicacy in their behalf; while as relates to the Egyptian Government itself, I must bear testimony, after seven years' experience, to its good faith in the fulfilment of all *bonâ fide* contracts or obligations." ·

One of my colleagues concurring with me was the Sardinian, the list of whose consulate numbered 10,000 persons. The scheme was dropped.

The initiation of the existing judicial tribunals is due to Nubar Pacha, who for seven years laboured indefatigably with the foreign Powers and the Khedive to remove difficulties. In 1868 he laid down the basis of his project, in many respects widely differing from that which has been finally adopted, in a formal "Note to his Highness the Viceroy of Egypt on the Future Regulation of the Legal and Judicial Relations between the Foreign and Native Population of Egypt"—covering a report from · M. Manoury, of the bar of Paris, on the same subject—from which I take the following extracts :—

" SIRE,—The legal system to which Europeans in Egypt are subject, and which determines their relations both with the Egyptian Government and the inhabitants of the country, are no longer based upon the capitulations. Of those capitulations nothing exists but the name.

x

They have been replaced by a system customary and arbitrary, resulting from the character of each chief of the consular agencies; a system founded on precedents more or less improper, and one which the force of circumstances, pressure on the one side and anxiety to facilitate the establishment of foreigners on the other, have introduced into Egypt; a system which really leaves the administration without power, and the people without any regular justice in their intercourse with Europeans.

" The necessity of a reform is keenly felt as the European colony increases; the consular agencies themselves recognize the necessity of it, and even demand it. The Egyptian Government and the consulates are at one as regards the principle of this necessity; disagreement commences at the means of putting the principle in practice.

" The Government sees itself attacked by law-suits which frequently the consuls themselves are compelled to stigmatize as scandalous. The native population distrusts the European; the Government, which nevertheless sees progress in this same European, is obliged, for fear of being victimized, to keep aloof from him.

" For more than forty years the European has enjoyed the right to hold property in Egypt. His possession is said to be subject to the tribunals and laws of the country. The consuls in theory are agreed on this principle, but in practice, under pretext of the capitulations, which they say cover the European, the latter, being either owner of a house or carrying on a trade, pays no duties; and if being owner of an estate he does not pay land-tax, then the consul interferes, and his interference almost always ends in non-payment.

"This state of things, contrary to the spirit and even the letter of the capitulations, not only hinders the country from developing its resources, from furnishing to European industry and capital all that it is ready to furnish, but puts an obstacle in the way of its organization, and ruins it alike morally and materially.

"Your highness has thought that the only remedy to apply to this state of things is the organization of a good system of justice, which would present to Europe all the guarantees which it has a right to demand.

"Your highness has thought that *the foreign element ought to enter into the organization of our tribunals.* In fact, this element, which is not numerous at Cairo, is equal at Alexandria to the native element. A number of Europeans are permanent residents in the provinces. All are engaged in commerce or manufactures. They are therefore in daily, and so to s peak hourly communication with the population. Account must therefore be taken of this element in the organization of the tribunals, and upon principle even superabundant guarantees must be given, in order to inspire in that element confidence alike in the judges and in the administration.

"The main principle is the complete divorce of justice from the administration. *Justice ought to emanate from the Government, but ought to be independent of the Government. It ought to be alike independent of Government and of consulates.* In order to attain the end which your highness has in view, the Powers of Europe must be satisfied of the fact : ' Justice emanates

from the Government, but is independent of it.'
The means of inspiring this conviction are to be
found in the possession of a body of trained
judges. Knowledge of the law is indispensable
to the judge. It is matter of habitual study,
it is altogether an education. Our present
magistrates have a perfect knowledge of the law,
civil and religious, which sufficed when they had
but to render a uniform justice to a population
uniform in manners and requirements.

*" But to meet new contingencies we must have
new laws*, and the Europeans, in establishing
themselves in the country, have introduced new
usages and novel relations. A mixed system
has begun to find its way into our laws and our
codes, consequently we must have new men to
apply this new system. Egypt, to secure the
administration of justice, must do what she has
already done in so efficient a manner for the sake
of her army, her railroads, her bridges and high-
ways, and her sanitary improvements. The
element which is competent to the task, I mean
the foreign element, has been introduced. That
element has served to educate the native element.
That which has been done in the material must
be done in the moral world, that is to say, in the
organization of justice.

" I have the honour to propose to your highness the preservation of the two mixed tribunals
of commerce established at Cairo and at Alexandria; but in place of their being composed of
three members chosen by the consuls from
among the merchants of the European colony,
and of the three native members whom the
Government summons to it in turn, I would propose to your highness to compose the court of

only four members, of whom two should be chosen by the consuls from the most considerable of merchants, presenting the highest guarantees, and two others by the Government from the natives, whose course of business brings them into the closest relations with Europeans. These members, in accordance with the existing plan, would sit in turn. I would propose to your highness *to leave the presidency of the court to an Egyptian,* but to concede the vice-presidency to a judge chosen in Europe; and in order to have guarantees of his character, it would be well to apply to the minister of justice of the country from which he is taken. The latter judge would be appointed for life.

"Besides these two tribunals, it would be necessary to have a court of appeal sitting at Alexandria. That court would be composed *of three Egyptian members,* whom your highness could select among our young men who have studied law in Europe; and *three other members,* competent judges *obtained from Europe* by application to their respective Governments. This court would discharge its functions *under the presidency of an Egyptian.* By the side of the two tribunals of commerce, there would be two tribunals to decide in civil suits. Those might be composed of *two* competent members selected from abroad, and *two Egyptian members, also under the presidency of an Egyptian subject.*

" The court of appeal sitting at Alexandria would also enjoy as one of its prerogatives, the revision of judgments given by the civil courts. In causes arising out of questions of real property, Europeans have always been subject to our courts. These courts work well. Their

component members thoroughly understand the
subject-matter. Here the foreign element would
not be of superior competence. I therefore propose to your highness to leave these courts as
they are.

" About 1848 the consuls, under the pressure
of their countrymen, having usurped the office of
the law, found themselves powerless, erected
their own impotence into a principle, and by
degrees, by the force of circumstances, were
driven to the presumption of ousting the Government and holding trials themselves—at most
calling in a functionary of the native police ;
their pretext being that, as the penalty had to
be inflicted in their own country, the trial could
not be valid, except it were held in conformity
with their own laws.

" Such is really the state of things not only as
regards crimes, but even as regards offences and
simple infractions of the law. Justice is seen to
be altogether given up not to institutions, but to
the arbitrary will of individuals. The position
of the Government is no longer tenable, when
one considers that the police is powerless to
repress the smallest infraction of the law, to such
an extent as to be unable to enforce the highway regulations, or those which concern the
stations of the public vehicles. For, if some one
consul is disposed, upon the application of the
police, to call to order a refractory driver,
another consul regards the matter as a trifling
affair, sometimes for the very reason that the
other deems it worth attention.

" In short, what your highness demands,
whether in respect of the civil or the criminal
law, is a return to the capitulations ; and not

merely a return *pur et simple*, but, on the contrary, a return which would grant to foreigners guarantees superior to those which these capitulations presented to them.

"In effect, according to these capitulations the foreigner has a native tribunal, which hears and decides in the presence of the dragoman, a mere witness without a consultative voice.

"According to the projected reform your highness, in place of this silent witness, concedes to foreigners the guarantee of a tribunal, in the composition of which a European element enters; and of a code reduced into conformity with the penal and civil laws of Europe."

From this statement of the ideas and purposes of Nubar Pacha, it is evident, on comparing what he planned and what he achieved, that the Khedive and the Great Powers treated him as Homer's Jupiter treated the prayers of mortals— "one-half they granted, the rest dismissed into empty air." His plan was to curb at once the absolute power of the Khedive, and restrict the authority of the consuls-general, by establishing tribunals which should overrule the arbitrary decisions of both. At the same time his purpose was to give the controlling voice to the Egyptian element, and to extend their jurisdiction over the native as well as over the European population throughout the whole country.

As the tribunals are now constituted they are international tribunals only, with jurisdiction exclusively civil (extending only to criminal offences committed against their members), and not having jurisdiction over the five and a half millions of natives, who are still subject to the old Egyptian judges and the old system which has the Koran as its basis.

His avowed object was to make the system of general application; and while giving the European element a voice, to keep the control in Egyptian hands, but in educated and legal ones. The consular authority died hard; it reserved its criminal jurisdiction, and even its consular courts in certain cases, and claimed a controlling voice for its substitutes in the courts. The Khedive, ceding the mixed jurisdiction, has taken no steps to divest himself and his courts of absolute control over the native population, either in civil or criminal cases, in which no European interest is involved. Whether the consummation sought by Nubar will ever be reached, depends greatly on the success of the experiment, now being made on a limited scale, which might induce an expansion of its attributes and authority, in the creation of native courts founded upon a somewhat similar basis.

There are good lawyers and clever men on the existing courts, and they are honestly striving to remove the great impediments, which obstruct their usefulness, and their most strenuous efforts.

The pay of the judges I do not regard as exorbitant, under the circumstances; but I do think the costs and expenses of litigation are too great. Yet, even with the very heavy costs, the sum thus far gathered in, as I understand, has proved inadequate to relieve the Government from one-half of the expense of the very cumbrous machinery employed in working the new establishment. As the courts are organized on the French plan, there is a small army of subordinate officers attached to them; and if the whole affair could be simplified—reduced in numbers and in expense—I believe it would prove more manageable, and more in consonance with the wants and wishes of the parties chiefly concerned, namely, the tax-payers, the litigants, and the Khedive.

No machine so complicated and so entirely novel, both in construction and purpose, can be expected to approach perfection at the outset; and I venture, with hesitation, to make these suggestions, without impugning either the utility of the tribunals, within a certain scope, or the propriety and fitness of the selections made for their higher posts; the judges having been appointed upon the recommendation of their respective Governments, who, and not the

Khedive, must be held responsible for their selection. Doubtless, as the members of the tribunal warm to their work, and learn more of the exceptional country to which they have been called; as well as gain a mastery over the Babel of tongues prevailing there, the machine may act more smoothly and efficiently than it has hitherto done.

CHAPTER XIX.

EGYPTIAN FINANCE AND RESOURCES.

Absorbing interest felt therein—The doctors disagreeing—State of the patient in the eyes of a non-professional—A plain statement as to amounts actually received from foreign loans by the Khedive—What did he do with it?—Testimony of the *Times* partly exculpatory of the Khedive—Curious and instructive letter from a native Egyptian official, translated from the French—His statements ' of resources, and suggestions for their increase—A few facts and figures.

IT would seem strange that a book devoted to Egypt should make no mention of Egyptian finance, a matter which has probably attracted more attention, and created more painful interest in the minds of foreigners, towards the country and its rulers, than all M. Mariette's truly remarkable discoveries among the *débris* of its ancient and forgotten ruins; or the equally wonderful spectacle of an Eastern prince playing the *rôle* of reformer and regenerator of his public farm, for such Egypt had been to his family; the only previous efforts having been directed to the increase of its agricultural products, and the ways and means of increased taxation.

Where the most eminent financiers of all countries have been called into consultation, and have proffered their panaceas, it would be presumptuous indeed in one whose mind has been engrossed, and whose life has been spent, in other duties, dogmatically to pronounce either on the symptoms or the condition of the patient, over which these most learned doctors have only "agreed to disagree."

I shall, therefore, on this topic briefly cite the opinions of those who are best qualified to pass judgment, both as to the disease, the remedy, and the actual state and prospects of the patient; who I have never believed to be half "the sick man" his cousin at Constantinople long has been, and who, under proper treatment, and the exercise of forbearance on the part of his dry-nurses, can and ought to be restored to even more than his pristine vigour, if time only be given for the cure, and undue pressure be not put upon him in his present shaky condition.

And firstly, as to the amounts received and squandered, or invested in public works as yet unproductive—have they really amounted to the very large figure, rising to almost £100,000,000, for which the Khedive and his country are debited by the foreign accountants, and his own admissions. It is safe to say that not one-half of this amount has the Khedive ever netted out of his various loans, and that the outside dead loss to the foreign investor — chiefly English and French—supposing the Egyptian Government absolutely bankrupt, excluding the funding loans and floating debt, would not exceed from £15,000,000 to £20,000,000.

But recent experiments, under Mr. Goschen's scheme, have proved that the country is by no means bankrupt, and is astonishing everybody, even those who thought they best understood the limits of her resources, by meeting the enormous payments due in January and July, under the most stringent and onerous conditions ever imposed by creditor on debtor; and, crucial fact of all, that the Khedive has acted in perfect good faith towards his foreign commissioners of the Caisses for receipt and disbursement of the public funds; doing more instead of less than he was called upon to do.

For the statement I have made as to the actual receipts and expenditures, for public benefit, from the loans originally made by the Khedive, I quote from the money article of the London *Times* of 19th May, 1876, the following pregnant admissions; the more weighty because that journal is not disposed to take a rose-coloured view, either of the Khedive, or of

Egyptian finance for some time past; Turkish
default having thrown its shadow over the
tributary, as well as the chief sinner, in the
Times' appreciation.   The *Times* says :—

" According to the statement of Mr. Cave's
report, the Khedive has only netted some
£45,000,000 on all the existing loans, State
and private, which have been floated for him,
and out of that he has paid back, including
the last April coupon, over £31,000,000. Of
the remainder, some £10,000,000 went to defray
costs connected with the Suez Canal and the
unjust awards of Napoleon III. connected with
it; so that but a minute sum remains which
the Khedive could by any possibility have spent
on improving his country.   He can hardly have
thus spent even that minute sum, because it
would be needed for commissions, discounts,
and market operations and for the ' service ' of
the debt.   Therefore, we have the huge floating
debt as the sort of lumber-room into which the
costs of all his extravagances have been flung.
The floating debts cannot reasonably be viewed
as an investor's loss at all, and, excluding these,
as well as part of the Turkish fives, and of later
funding loans of both Turkey and Egypt, we
believe a sum of £20,000,000 to £25,000,000
may safely be taken as the outside dead loss
of the investing public, not more than half of

which would fall on this country, supposing the
Turkish and Egyptian Governments to fail
absolutely."

In a very remarkable letter, addressed to the
Times from Paris, and published in French in
that journal under date of 19th May, a clear
and rapid *résumé* of the actual financial condition of Egypt, is given by an "ex-Egyptian
official then in that capital," who it was supposed could be none other than Nubar Pacha,
the former Minister of Commerce and Foreign
Affairs, whose knowledge and honesty no one
could doubt. I translate the closing portion
of his letter, which gives, in a nutshell, the
resources from which Egypt proposes to meet
her obligations, as I never saw them so briefly,
clearly, and intelligibly stated elsewhere:—

". . . . Having shown the efficacy of
the control established by the appointment of
the foreign commissioners, it remains only
to examine the financial side of this decree.
Can Egypt pay the interest she promises,
and, at the same time, meet the actual wants
of her internal administration? My answer is
in the affirmative. I entertain no doubts on the
subject. I adopt even the figures of Mr. Cave.
According to Mr. Cave's report the annual
revenues of Egypt are £10,500,000. He is
right in these figures, but he comprises in this

estimate the proceeds of the Moukabaleh, which amount to £1,500,000 annually; but as this is only a temporary tax, without it the regular revenues of Egypt would amount to £9,000,000. Yet were the Moukabaleh suspended, it follows that those who have paid but half the tax must also then pay the other half, which equalizes it, and restores the permanent revenue to £10,500,000.

"But you know that in Egypt there are two kinds of taxable lands, viz., the '*Kharadgis*' (under lease), and the '*Euchuris*' (tithe lands). The latter of these enjoy special privileges, and are not taxed to one-half the extent of the other. This certainly is not just, and the Government may well raise the rate of taxation in the latter case, so as to equalize the two.

"Now, as these privileged lands represent 1,300,000 feddans (acres), an additional tax of half a guinea on each acre, which would only raise the tax to the standard of the other lands, would give an immediate augmentation of yearly revenue to the amount of £650,000. You also are aware that the Europeans resident in the country pay no taxes. This enormity naturally must disappear, since the new tribunals have given them all necessary guarantees for their security. A tax of £1 10s. on each European (of whom there are 150,000 in Egypt) would augment the revenues £225,000, which, with that previously mentioned, would add £875,000 to the £10,500,000 estimated by Mr. Cave, making a total of 11,300,000.

" Granting that Mr. Cave has over-calculated by more than a million of pounds, even a million and a half, and we should have at least £9,700,000 and the interest of the debt defrayed, there would remain for the service of the State £400,000. But our actual administration never fairly costs this sum.

These are our true expenses, viz. :

For all the public administrations, except the army	£1,300,000
The tribute for Constantinople	700,000
Civil list of the Khedive	600,000
Leaving for the army	1,400,000
	£4,000,000

" But, in fact, the army only figures in the Budget for £700,000 ; hence the surplus of £700,000 must pass somewhere outside of the Budget.

" Should, however, the taxation and the receipts not reach the sum necessary for the payment of the interest on the public debt, have not the bondholders the right to say to the Khedive that he must sooner diminish his army expenses than their payments ? Have they not the right to say this enormous army is the ruin of the country ? Have they not the right to say to him that his civil list is six times as large as

Y

that of the Emperor Napoleon (the relative size of the two countries considered), and that, as proprietor of a fifth of the soil of Egypt, it would be but just for him to diminish by £200,000 or £300,000 his civil list, that his creditors might be paid?"

Owing to the anomalous attitude occupied by the Khedive towards his own Government and to the foreign creditor, arising from his double character as ruler of the country and private planter and trader, it has been found most difficult to separate his public and private indebtedness from each other, or to define the limits which bound one from the other. Hence all the European financiers, in their successive reports, have drawn a line between the two, in as far as they were able; although the affairs and obligations of the private Daira and the public debt seemed to be twined as closely together as the ivy to the oak. The clearest statement as to the personal liabilities of the Khedive, and his resources for meeting them, has been given by Mr. Sandars, the able lawyer who was sent out last winter by Mr. Goschen, in conjunction with M. Joson, a French lawyer, representing the French creditors, to perfect a plan already discussed with, and consented to by, the Khedive in his capacity of private landholder and agriculturist.

A very full report of the various estates belonging to the Khedive and his family, prepared by Mr. Sandars, was read by that gentleman, on his return to London in May last, to a meeting of the creditors, from which it appears that the landed property of the Khedive and his family embraced 435,000 acres, or "feddans," of which 258,000 were devoted to the sugar culture.

The balance-sheet of this vast property is given by Mr. Sandars as follows :—

INCOME.			EXPENDITURE.		
Lands let	...	... £130,000	Taxes	... ...	£150,000
Cotton ...	...	... 85,000	Agriculture expenses...		400,000
Sundries ...	...	... 85,000	Factory expenses	...	250,000
Winter crops	...	... 200,000			
Sugar	...	... 700,000			£800,000
			Balance ...	... ...	400,000
		£1,200,000			£1,200,000

The value of the sugar crop here given is admittedly taken at a higher rate than recent years have seen, but Mr. Sandars says that improved administration might so increase the yield of sugar as to compensate for a fall in prices. For the present year he places the probable yield at £800,000.

According to Mr. Cave's carefully prepared report, the Egyptian Budget for 1876 showed the receipts to be £10,772,611, and the expenditure £8,981,852, leaving a surplus of £1,790,759. As to the liabilities on the Daira or Khedive's private estate, the loan of 1870 showed that the unpaid capital is £6,032,620, and the floating debt £3,000,000. The present revenue of Egypt is arrived at under three heads—land-tax, £4,305,131; Moukabaleh, £1,531,118; other sources of revenue, £4,852,821; making a total of £10,689,070. As to the growth of the trade of Egypt under the rule of the Khedive, it is, to say the least of it, in the highest degree encouraging. In the thirteen years which elapsed from 1849-50 to 1861-2 inclusive, the exports rose from £2,043,579 to £4,454,425. The year 1862-3, the first year of the Khedive, began with a sudden bound to £9,014,277, and increased in the following year to £14,416,661. In 1865 the exports fell, but only to £9,723,564; they have never since been less than £8,000,000. Mr. Cave's report demonstrates as plainly as possible the fact of Egypt's solvency, should her finances be properly collected and administered, although in the judgment of those who ought to know the country best, she cannot afford to pay her creditors or tax her people at the rate of the existing arrangement, devised by Messrs. Goschen and Joubert, and thus far carried out with unexpected good faith and more than ordinary zeal by the Khedive himself, who—in justice it must be said—has from the first protested against the ability of the country long to sustain such heavy impositions, or so terrible a drain on its resources and productions, as this scheme involves.

Without professing any superior knowledge of finance, or even equal skill in that science (if such it may be called), to the many distinguished gentlemen who have ciphered up the Egyptian sum, I cannot forbear expressing my crude · opinion that Mr. Cave was wise, when he urged that five per cent. was the maximum of interest Egypt could then afford to pay her creditors at that time : since which her liabilities have so greatly increased, and her resources been so greatly diminished, that even that might now be difficult to meet, without more and greater sacrifices than that impoverished people are now making, and which it is impossible they can continue to make much longer; for flesh and blood cannot stand them.

My judgment is based partly on the exhaustive reports of Mr. Cave, partly on my own intimate knowledge of the country and its resources for the last twenty years, which confirms in all important particulars the correctness of Mr. Cave's facts and figures, and the deductions drawn therefrom.

Since the world began, was there ever a

population of the number of the Egyptian, from which taxation to such an enormous amount was annually wrung (even for a single year, much less for a series of years), increasing instead of diminishing, as the resources of the country became less and less, through the diminishing prices of their produce; grain alone, owing to mere temporary causes, having kept up in price, while cotton has ceased almost to pay the cost of production (if it does even that), and the number of hands employed in cultivation has been greatly diminished by causes already stated?

. Roughly stated, *five millions and a half of Egyptian fellahs pay, in direct and indirect taxes*, (besides extraordinary calls, such as war-tax and private pickings) a total of near SEVEN MILLIONS OF POUNDS STERLING per annum. To which must be added near a million more for what are termed "local revenues, taxes, and dues," embracing municipal taxes, canal, bridge, port, and other dues; and for the Moukabaleh (or anticipated land-tax) one and a half millions more; swelling up the total of taxation £2 per head all over Egypt. These figures I have adopted from Mr. Goschen's statement, the items of which I append; but in two items, the actual tax levied on land and that on date trees, the amount is understated very considerably.

When Sydney Smith drew his famous picture

of British taxation at the commencement of the present century, and showed how his countrymen, from the cradle to the grave, were the prey of the tax-gatherers, causing the great mass of those impositions to be removed, in the wildest flights of his fertile fancy he never soared to the naked realities of Egyptian taxation, as it is imposed and forcibly collected to-day, under European sanction.

CHAPTER XX.

EGYPTIAN NIGHTS' ENTERTAINMENTS.

The social life of Egypt—Native society unchanged—The ladies of
the hareem, and their adoption of French millinery—The root of
the evil—A royal wedding party in a Khedivial hareem described—
The Khedive's entertainments—His breakfasts, dinners, and *soirées
dansantes* at Ab-din.

THE social life of Egypt has undergone no
apparent change, in so far as the great bulk of
the native population is concerned. High and
low, rich and poor, they still shrink from social
contact with the foreigner, outside of the narrow
circle of the court and its immediate members
or *employés*. It is evident that just so long as
the present system continues to be the law of
the lives of this people, this must continue to
be the case. The isolation of woman from
general society involves the isolation also of
man, whose hearth and home are in the hareem,
where none but he may come. The cold civility
of the *selamlik* (or man's apartment), where
alone he may receive his guests or friends,

prevents familiarity or friendship, either with the foreigner or native; since into the charmed circle of the real home-life he is not allowed to enter.

It is true that the women of the hareem, especially of the higher class (which is very small in Egypt), have adopted for themselves and slaves the fashions and fabrics of France, discarding their own more picturesque ones; that instead of shuffling over the floor in slippers without heels, they now totter insecurely on the stilts of those hideous French boots, which make our modern belles as helpless and as tortured as the Chinese; and that some favoured ladies of the hareem have imbibed a sufficient smattering of French language and tastes to listen, half asleep, to the indecencies of Offenbach's opera bouffe; or stare with wide-awake eyes at the posturings and pirouettes of the imported ballet troupe, which outstrips and outrivals their own native *almehs* in agility and indecency. Yet even this chosen few still listen to, or view these things from a carefully curtained stage-box, where they can see and hear without being visible to the rest of the audience. A sudden flash of light from jewels, or bright eyes, through a rent in the envious curtain concealing these fair ones, gives the only indication of their presence at the opera or

theatre, where alone they are allowed even this
partial privilege of semi-publicity.

Ninety-nine hundredths of the Egyptian
women, however, still adhere to their old habits
and customs, and no woman of good character
in Egypt has yet dared to appear abroad without
her concealing veil or *yashmak*, or recognize or
speak to any man in public or in private, except
her husband or father.

The wave of progress and of civilization,
which has swept away from the Khedive's court
almost all the old forms and. usages, until it
approximates to those of Europe, has dashed in
vain up to the hareem doors; whence it has been
driven back in shattered spray, but could gain
no admission. The Eastern lady or woman may
put on Worth's finery, and clothe her attendants
in "Frank" dress; but there all similarity to
her Western sister ends.

She is unchanged in her thoughts and habits,
morals, and daily life. Until the slavery of the
hareem is abolished, there can be no hope of
the abolition of the domestic slavery it nourishes
and perpetuates, as a necessary essential to its
own continued existence. The Khedive enun-
ciated a great truth in his reply to the deputation
at Paris, already cited, when he boldly probed
this tender point; and those who have known
the East longest and best, look almost with

despair on the prospect of any real change in the position of woman there, so long as Islam, and polygamy (which is its offspring), are the laws of life to the female population.

But the external changes in hareem life, since the time when Lady Mary Wortley Montague wrote her inimitable letters from behind the hareem veil in Turkey, have been considerable; as foreign women, who have visited them twelve years ago, and recently, loudly declare. The complaint now made is that much of the glory has departed from the higher hareems, in consequence of these fair inmates having discarded their Oriental dress and usages, in the efforts to substitute "Frank" apparel and furniture for them; with the result ever accompanying half-way imitation.

Hence it may not be amiss, before the vanishing point has been reached, to give here a description of an old-fashioned bridal reception in one of the royal hareems, but three or four years since, on the occasion of a series of royal nuptials, in which the Khedive's sons and one of his daughters figured as the principal performers. As a matter of course, I cannot pretend to describe this festival as an eye-witness; but I have to thank a fair friend, who, as the wife of a high foreign officer in the Khedive's service, attended it, for the particulars. I cannot but regret, however, that I cannot reproduce her vivid account of the fairy-like scene, which has been marred in this attempt at repetition.

The *fête* specially described was given in special honour of the Princess Fatmeh Ahnem, the Khedive's eldest daughter, on the occasion of her marriage to Prince Toussoun Pacha (since deceased), at the queen-mother's palace at Cairo.

On leaving their carriages, the ladies who had been invited to the festival passed, first through an extensive garden, which was lighted *à giorno* by countless lamps of many colours, and following a marble paved walk, boarded on either side with trees and rare plants, they reached the entrance of the palace, where eunuchs were waiting to lead them into a large and richly furnished saloon. There they found the white female slaves of the hareem, half of whom were clad as men, and all in the most magnificent Eastern costumes. These slaves acted as ushers. Some were plainly dressed, carrying drawn swords in their hands, and having red tarbouches on their heads; whilst others were attired in splendid military uniforms; and my fair informant adds, that they presented a very martial-looking appearance—not a bad imitation of the genuine article. Having taken charge of the guests, they conducted them to a second saloon, where, for the amusement (and possible edification) of the visitors, dances were executed by the native *almehs* (dancing girls), to the music of their own castanets, and an orchestra composed of female performers. In other apartments other slaves performed a sort of ballet, with long wands, swords, and bucklers; but in this room only native dances were executed.

The guests passed thence through a series of apartments or long halls, in which all manner of refreshments were served. There, according to nationality or taste, each was served either in Eastern or Western style, with things substantial or sweet; and with those wonderful coloured drinks or sherbets, which are made of fruit, that Oriental hands alone know how to compose.

The princesses of the royal family presided over one table, which was reserved for the Pacha's wives and those of the foreign consuls and other distinguished foreigners; and in these apartments, as in the others, the sound of music and song was unceasing.

Refreshments partaken of, the guests were next presented to the queen-mother, who received them in a vast saloon, magnificently furnished, capable of accommodating thousands of persons. The visitors were preceded by the armed female slaves, and each formally presented by name and title by the European lady-in-waiting. The presentations concluded, the guests were shown to their seats—divans ranged along the walls and covered with rich silks—whence they looked on at the dancing and singing of professionals engaged for that purpose. The performance concluded, the dancers received rich gifts of jewellery and cashmere shawls, as a reward for their exertions; the wife of each bey or other dignitary invited to the *fête* having brought her present. At a sign from the queen-mother, the distribution of these gifts commenced, and as each was bestowed the name of the donor was announced, and a chorus of thanks returned by the recipients.

This ceremony at an end, the bride made her appearance in the following manner. The eunuchs of the households of the Egyptian ladies formed; from the foot of the staircase up the steps and to the door of the saloon, where the queen-mother sat, a long line, each man holding a candelabra, in which were many long wax candles of different colours. Through this avenue of bronze the bride passed, treading all the while on cloth of gold—no less costly carpet being considered worthy to receive her royal footprint. Dancing-girls, dressed in the bride's livery, preceded her; their costumes composed of silver gauze ornaments, with orange-flowers and splendid diamonds. Then came the bride, surrounded by her own women, followed by her mother and princesses of the blood, and another troop of dancing-girls. Next came the princess herself, moving slowly, with eyes cast down, and stopping a little at each step, as though to afford time for examination and admiration.

The guests stood up as the princess advanced; and as she passed along, girls, who were stationed on raised chairs behind the visitors, showered on them from baskets a quantity of small gold coins, struck off expressly for the purpose; many of which, falling on the head or garments of the guests, lodged in their hair or dress. My informant, on disrobing at night, found £3 or £4 worth in value of those pretty keepsakes. The native ladies, who were aware of this Eastern custom, had doubtless had their hair and garments prepared, so as to catch as much of the golden shower as possible. The magnificent saloon, draped in white satin and gold, ornamented with orange blossoms and roses, and blazing with innumerable lights—the dazzling brilliancy of the dresses and ornaments of the bride and her attendants—formed a spectacle of splendour worthy of the "Arabian Nights' Entertainments," and such as cannot ever be witnessed in our Western and more prosaic climes.

Three large chairs, covered with white satin, were placed on a raised daïs, and on these sat the queen-mother, the bride, and the mother of the bride. Worth, the famous man-milliner, was probably the maker of the bridal dress, which for execution was a marvel, and, apart from certain exaggerations, thoroughly Parisian in taste. It consisted of skirt, bodice, and train of the very richest white satin, and a tunic of the finest point lace. The train, five mètres in length, was carried by white slaves, who were richly attired. The bodice was entirely covered, and the tunic looped, with splendid diamond ornaments; and on her head the bride wore a magnificent diadem, also of diamonds. So arrayed, she might indeed be a fortune in herself, the value of her costume being something fabulous. Having received the felicitations of the royal and distinguished guests, she after a short time withdrew; returning to her own apartments with the same state and ceremonies as when she entered. The pageant over, the visitors descended to the first saloon, where refreshments again awaited them; and the ceremony concluded, they left the palace.

But I fear I am treading on delicate ground, in thus peeping (even by proxy) behind the hareem curtains; and, mindful of the fate of "Peeping Tom of Coventry," return to the more orthodox treatment of Khedivial hospitalities, which are fast and frequent during "the season" at Cairo.

The Khedive's entertainments comprise breakfasts, *déjeuners à la fourchette* at 12 a.m. (dinners in all but name); a formal dinner at 7 p.m.; *soirées musicales et dansantes*, to which ladies are invited; and open-air entertainments, with pigeon-shooting, etc., to which ladies also are invited, given in the gardens of the Ghezireh Palace.

His breakfasts and dinners are altogether *à la Française*, with an enormous display of plate; the letter " I " in gold, surmounted by a crown, being the only *chiffre* on the glasses, which have only a slight gilt rim, otherwise plain. Both the porcelain and crystal, and in fact the whole service, are in excellent taste. The native officials present at these entertainments are dressed and eat in European fashion. The wines are abundant, and of superior quality. The Khedive's "particular vanity," as Mr. Stiggins would say, seems to be Château Y'quem, though he is not disdainful of champagne on festive occasions. His balls and *soirées* (of which he usually gives several during the season), to which formal invitations are ordered by the chamberlains, may merit a short description, the place and persons figuring at them being considered. A sketch of one will convey an idea of all.

At nine o'clock the company assembled in the new wing of the palace, where the Khedive

z

received the guests with his usual urbanity, conversing with ladies and gentlemen, previously known to him, with much affability. About 150 invitations outside of his immediate court circle had been issued, and all the nations of Europe were represented by richly dressed women, and men in the sombre suit which the nineteenth century renders *de règle* for full dress.

About an hour was occupied in this reception business, and then the Khedive, with a lady on his arm, followed by the young princes, each escorting a lady, led the way into a long saloon prepared as a concert-room; where a concert was given by the best singers from the opera troupe, male and female. When this was over, the company moved back into the other apartments, of which there was a long suite. The chairs were removed from the concert-room, which was converted into a ball-room. The band struck up, and dancing began, which was kept up until long after midnight, when the doors of the supper-room were thrown open, and the *cuisine* vied with Terpsichore for a time. It was a very curious and picturesque sight, to see the strange blending of nationalities and costumes, Western and Eastern. The Khedive's officials and court were in gorgeous uniforms, their breasts sparkling with decorations. Save the three young princes of the blood, the natives did not dance;

but these footed it right merrily with the fair foreign dames; doubtless to the discontent of the grim grey pachas of the old school, who were there in considerable force ; since dancing, under the old *régime*, was considered not only effeminate, but disreputable throughout Islam, for either men or women of good character to indulge in.

What the ladies of the hareem, invisible to all our eyes, though probably peeping through some chink at these performances, thought of them it is impossible to say; but I should think that a *mauvais quart d'heure* may have awaited the young princes, on their return home to their hareems and their houris. The Khedive himself does not possess or flourish the fantastic toe ; his weight, both of person and character, preventing. The ball was kept up with great animation until the "wee sma' hours," the Khedive manfully holding his ground until the latest revellers had departed; being apparently as untiring in the pursuit of pleasure as of business.

The Khedive can play the pleasing host admirably when his mind is at ease, and really seems to enjoy society generally, as a distraction from his graver cares, and the daily drudgery of his duties, which are unintermitting. But I remarked last winter that his gaiety was frequently forced, his changes of mood too sudden to be natural; and that, in fact, on several of these occasions he seemed intensely "bored;" especially when pertinacious foreign representatives would button-hole him, and, leading the royal victim to a window, recall the recollection of his manifold perplexities, within earshot of the music and dancing.

What his private opinion of, or reflections upon, foreign women or society may be, he keeps to himself; but I have little doubt that he breathes a sigh of relief when "the season" is over, and he can retire within himself at Ghezireh, and enjoy such share of Eastern *keff* (repose) as his suzerain, the Sublime Porte, and the less sublime but closer consuls-general, and the unconfiding creditors, will permit Egyptian royalty to indulge in.

The Khedive certainly believes in, and practises the philosophy inculcated by a famous statesman, viz.: that the art of diplomacy centres chiefly in giving good dinners: and that the royal road to the heart is ever through the stomach; and if lavish hospitalities to the foreigner could cover his shortcomings, political and financial, would stop their mouths in more ways than one. There is this to be said of his, as of other royal entertainments—they promote trade, and please the shopkeeping portion of the community, as well as the invited guests. All annual visitors to Cairo hope these hospitalities may continue, however much the Khedive's creditors may growl at them.

CHAPTER XXI.

THE SOUDAN.

What and where is the Soudan?—Its first annexation to Egypt—
Conquest and occupation by Mehemet Ali—His visit there—
Establishes Khartoum as its capital—Abbas Pacha's treatment of it
—Saïd Pacha's visit—His proclamations—Attempts to connect it
with Cairo, by rail and river—Reasons of failure—Mr. Fowler's plan,
adopted by the Khedive—Some interesting extracts from his reports
—Present position and prospects of Gordon Pacha.

THE Khedive has been loudly denounced in
Europe, for an insane ambition, in extending
his explorations and annexations into Central
Africa, and most loudly by those who know
least about the matter; who counting only the
cost in cash expended, and the net results thus
far obtained, consider his projects in that direction as no better than idle dreams. Yet the
Khedive did not create, but inherited these
outlying provinces, to which indeed he has annexed others, and sought to annex more; but
his main purpose has been to make these dependencies of Egypt pay.

Whether he has adopted the least expensive

or most judicious means of effecting this, is a question on which opinions must and will differ.

Everybody has heard of Sir Samuel Baker's mission, of which he has himself, in his most interesting book, given such a graphic and exciting account. But the subsequent explorations of Gordon Pacha, through his "great talent for silence," which is habitual with him, as well as those of the American staff officers in the Khedive's service, are as yet sealed books, outside of the select circle of the Geographical Societies; and are not even guessed at by the loudest denouncers of the Khedive's "waste of men and means" in Central Africa. I regret that it is not in my power to give definite details of these explorations, of which I have heard much orally, but have no other knowledge of. It is said that Gordon Pacha's journals are in course of preparation by a competent hand; and the report of Stone Pacha to the Khedive, which will be found in the Appendix (marked F), will prove that the staff officers have not been idle, nor returned with empty hands from their difficult and dangerous explorations.

Hence it may not be out of place, in this book, briefly to sketch the origin and the peculiarities of these Egyptian acquisitions, from the time of Mehemet Ali, their first acquirer; as well as what has been done, or sought to be done, by successive viceroys in the Soudan; which still, to most people, is nothing more than a mere "geographical expression."

The annexation of the provinces, constituting what is termed the Soudan, dates back more than half a century. After the destruction of the scattered relics of the Mamelukes in Dongola, and the defeat of the Arab sheiks, Mehemet Ali, thus master of Nubia, ordered an exploratory survey of the provinces of Sennaar and Kordofan, and the countries remote from the two Niles, the White and Blue. This task he confided to Ibrahim and Ismaïl Pachas, giving each a large force. One expeditionary corps subjugated the country to the east as far as Fazougli, on the Blue Nile; the other pushed on to the subjugation of the people bordering on the White Nile. They had hoped to acquire much gold, which was reported there in large quantities, but found but little; and the washing of the river sands produced even less. Nevertheless, they brought back many slaves, and reduced Sennaar, and the tribes residing near the river, to Egyptian sway.

In 1839 Mehemet Ali in person visited his new acquisition, going as far as Fazougli—afterwards made an African Cayenne; banishment to which, in the days of Abbas, was considered equivalent to a death-warrant.

Mehemet Ali established the capital of the Soudan at Khartoum, declared the navigation of the White Nile free, established military posts on both rivers, encouraged adventurous men of science to explore the country, and sought to introduce commercial ideas, and civilization, into the minds of the negroes of Central Africa.

But his good intentions were frustrated by the perfidy and cupidity of those intrusted with their execution. The unfortunate negroes were made the objects of chase and of commerce by the slave-traders, and Khartoum became a slave-market. The consequence was that the natives rebelled, and were only held in check by military force; and the taxes required a small army to collect them.

"Such," says Dr. Abbate, who visited the country in 1857, in the suite of Saïd Pacha, "was the condition of the Soudan, when Saïd Pacha mounted the throne of Egypt. Agriculture almost abandoned, taxes out of all proportion to production or means, extortioners everywhere; the receipts of the Government barely sufficient to meet the expenses of supporting its authority, by reason of the military establishment which was essential; general disorder in the administration; an open slave-trade, almost as openly protected by those in authority on the spot."

Shocked at this state of the provinces, of which some rumours had reached him, Saïd Pacha, seized with one of his generous impulses, determined to go in person to right matters in the Soudan; and as with him to resolve was to act, carried the design promptly into execution.

Abbas Pacha had held on firmly to his authority in the Soudan, where he kept up always an imposing force, and exacted taxes from that unfortunate population, through terror and the unscrupulous agents he employed. It is more than probable however, that the expenses of keeping up an army in those provinces, which at the same time abstracted so much from the labour of Egypt (then as now insufficient, and rendered even more so by the necessity of sending troops to the Crimean war), amounted to as much, or more than the sums extorted from them in taxation, or by the commerce in slaves.

So the Soudan, for many years after its acquisition, was more an ornamental than a useful appanage to Egypt; and although it has figured in recent Egyptian Budgets to the figure of £100,000 per annum, grave doubts may well be entertained as to whether, as an investment, it ever has yet paid; taking into account the sums annually expended on its administration, and the cost of the expeditions of annexation or exploration, within or beyond its limits.

Saïd Pacha had been two and a half years on the throne, when he conceived the idea of following in the footsteps of his father, by making a tour of inspection in these provinces, then only five in number; and carrying out the purposes which Mehemet Ali had mapped out, but failed to have executed.

It is honourable to the memory of Mehemet Ali to have conceived, still more worthy of praise to his son to have executed, the reforms which partially rescued these provinces from the reign of terror and of barbarism, which seems to have been their normal condition, and from which they have not yet entirely emerged.

Early in the year 1857, Saïd Pacha carried out his design, and made a rapid tour through the Soudan; leaving Cairo 27th November, and arriving at Khartoum 10th February of the next year, making the trip in about two months and a half. An army of 5000 men, fully armed and equipped, with baggage waggons, accompanied him half the way: so that it was supposed he meditated more annexations in that direction; but he changed his plan, and fearlessly went on without them. Arriving at Berber, he summoned the chief men, and ordered them to meet him at Khartoum; he then verbally *announced the abolition of slavery, withdrew his garrison from the town,* and left the province under the guardianship of the governor. He then proceeded over the desert by Korosko to Khartoum, where he also summoned the notables of that neighbourhood; and in four remarkable "orders," addressed to the new governors, appointed by him over the five provinces of the Soudan—Sennaar, Kordofan, Taka, Berber, and Dongola—dated Khartoum, 26th January, 1857, laid down a charter of rights, and definition of their duties towards the Egyptian Government, characterized equally by liberality, justice, and wisdom,—by which, to use his own words, he sought "to insure the prosperity of the people, to improve their condition, relieve them from unjust burdens and abuses of those in authority, and at the same time point out their duties to them."

"When," says this generous viceroy, "visiting my provinces of the Soudan, I have seen the wretchedness into which the population has been plunged, by excessive impositions on their lands and *sakkias* (water-wheels), and especially their sufferings under the *corvées* (compulsory labour) and unjust taxes, I at once decided that justice demanded the abandonment of such a system, and that henceforward taxation should be apportioned to the means of the tax-payers; so that all apprehensions might be calmed, the country prosper, and no reason longer exist either for complaint, or expatriation on the part of its inhabitants."

Opening with these truly generous and princely promises, he then laid down the details of administration and taxation which, in his judgment, would secure them; and named new officials to carry them into effect; adding, " It is also a matter of urgent necessity, as well as my earnest wish, that regular and speedy communication should exist between the Soudan and my capital. You must therefore at once organize a postal service by dromedaries across the desert " —going on to give specific directions as to how it should be done. These admirable " orders " conclude with a promise, that if succour be needed from Cairo, from invading enemies, they might rely upon it when they called; and that if the inhabitants had good reason to complain of the governors, or the sheiks subordinate to them, " no guilty man should escape punishment."

Having performed these acts of justice and good administration with his usual impetuosity, Saïd Pacha returned to Cairo; and this, probably the most disinterested and patriotic act of his short life, and shorter reign, has left not even an echo behind it, either in Egypt or in Europe.[*]

Saïd Pacha also conceived the project of uniting his provinces to the central seat of his power, by railway or canal; and detached the French engineer, Mougel Bey, famous for his connection with the barrage and Suez Canal, to examine the best means of doing so; and also sent surveying parties to examine the possibility of removing the obstructions in the Higher Nile, but was deterred by the expense of these undertakings.

The idea was then abandoned, but in 1865–66 the present Khedive revived it; and a general study of the country, with a view to a railway, was made between Assouan and Khartoum by Mr. Walker and Mr. Bray; but little came of it.

In 1865 Mr. Hawkshaw, the eminent engineer, was consulted by the Khedive as to the canalization of the first cataract, and recommended the prosecution of that work. Mr. Fowler, whose opinion must carry greater weight from his personal survey of the spot, suggests that had Mr. Hawkshaw visited Assouan, he would have

---

[*] For the particulars of Saïd Pacha's visit to the Soudan, I am indebted to the instructive and able account of it by Dr. Abbate, of Cairo, an eminent physician and man of science, who was attached to the viceroy's suite during the expedition. His "Notes" of the tour (published by Plon, of Paris, in 1858) will richly repay perusal.

" shrunk," as he does, from the unknown cost
and consequences of excavating the large
quantity of excessively hard rock, which must be
encountered in the excavation of a canal, " of
which no trustworthy estimates can possibly be
made." Mr. Fowler's substitute is " simply to
use the mechanical powers of the descending
waters of the cataract, to draw the boats along
a ship-incline overland, between the top and
bottom of the cataract." Between the recommendations of two such high authorities in such
matters, the Khedive has found Mr. Fowler's
recommendation the best.

Some years later, early in the year 1871, the
Khedive called on the well-known English engineer, Mr. John Fowler, who had become Consulting Engineer-in-Chief in the Egyptian service, to make detailed surveys and estimates,
and report on the question of communication
with the Soudan. In accordance with those
orders Mr. Fowler sent out, with full instruc-
tions, a staff of experienced surveyors, who spent
five months between the first cataract and
Khartoum, bringing back full surveys and sec-
tions, and much useful information bearing on
the point. Under these surveys the present
projected Soudan Railway has been commenced,
and is already partially completed on the plan
proposed by Mr. Fowler, which embraced—

1st. A railway from Wady * Halfa to Shendy.

2nd. A ship-incline at the first cataract.

This plan Mr. Fowler has since modified, in 1877, by diverting the route and terminus from Shendy to Khartoum, laying down a single line of rails from Wady Halfa, near the second cataract, to Khartoum—the total cost of which has been estimated at £3,430,000, rolling stock, stations, and accessories necessary for working the traffic included. This line is among the possibilities of the future, dependent chiefly on the financial condition of the country.

In an extremely elaborate and interesting report made to the Khedive by Mr. Fowler in 1873, the route to be taken by the railway as then projected, together with the local and general objects of the work, and the traffic to be expected, are set forth with great fulness of detail. In Mr. Fowler's opinion, "the exportation of ivory and other Central African products will be increased and facilitated by such a railway; but they will sink into insignificance when compared with the grain, sugar, and cotton, which will be produced and exported from the vast alluvial plains of the Soudan." Mr. Fowler then proceeds to show how such a

---

* The wadys are ravines cut out by water running down from the desert plateau to the river, when sudden floods pour down during tropical storms. They are of great depth and extent, and very numerous.

railway, with the addition of a ship-incline over the first cataract, with a service of light steamers connecting Wady Halfa with the present terminus of the Egyptian railways near Rhoda (the Soudan Railway being extended to Massowah in the Red Sea), might shorten by three days the route to India, China, and Australia, and avoid the dangers and inconveniences of a part of the Red Sea passage. The chief traffic to be expected, after establishment of the railway, will be grain, sugar, cotton, gums, senna, dates, ebony, skins, gold, ivory, ostrich feathers. The return traffic southward would be cotton goods, machinery, cutlery, tobacco, coffee, rice, earthenware, beads, etc.

The present mode of conducting the traffic from Khartoum, its great centre, involves five changes in transit from Khartoum to Cairo—the cargoes being taken in native boats down the Nile, at Aboo Hammed; whence it is taken across the Nubian desert on camels to Korosko; again transferred to boats and carried down to the first cataract; thence on camels to Shelal, to Assouan; thence again in boats down the Nile to Boulak, the port of Cairo. From the Kordofan and Darfour districts a similar system, involving as many changes, has to be adopted.

The improvement of the river having been found impracticable, the railway scheme, in con-

2 A

nection with some plan for the passage of the first cataract, has engaged the attention of the Khedive and his engineer-in-chief; resulting in Mr. Fowler's recommendation of a railway of 3ft. 6in. grade, avoiding tunnels altogether, with very small quantity of rock-cutting, and, with the exception of a bridge across the Nile, no considerable work of difficulty on the whole line. Mr. Fowler concludes by saying, " I see no reason why every part of the railway, except the permanent way, rolling stock, and Nile bridge, should not be performed by Egyptians, under proper organization ; the work to be completed within three years from its commencement." The cost of the ship-incline and its adjuncts Mr. Fowler estimates at £200,000, and the time for its completion one and a half years. The latter should, if possible, precede the construction of the Soudan Railway, so as to give increased facilities for general intercommunication, and transport of men and materials. Mr. Fowler also states as " one of the national benefits to be conferred by this great work, the facility of transporting, under proper regulations, the surplus labour from Equatorial Africa to the cultivated districts of Egypt."

I give these as the views of this experienced and eminent engineer, without endorsing or discussing them, for the purpose of showing the inducements and the purposes for which this Soudan Railway has been projected.

The wadys, the rains, the floods the drift sands, the desert, and the white ants, are the chief obstacles the engineer will have to encounter, not to mention the wandering Bedouins, the Rob Roys of Africa.

The plague of ants, those apparently insignificant but really terrible enemies to man and his work in Central Africa, is thus described by Mr. Fowler's engineer: " Along the whole route (from Om-Badhr to El Fascher) white ants are very numerous. All kinds of wood are eaten; even the largest trees totally destroyed. Ordinary wood sleepers for railways would not last more than a few weeks. Ant-hills abounded, some of which were four feet high and three feet in diameter; but eighteen inches in height would be the general average."

This country is the paradise of the hunter, all species of game, from the lion and leopard to the hare and antelope, being abundant. The locusts abound here, and are eaten by the natives; while birds, from the ostrich and guinea-fowl to wild duck and snipe, equally abound. Cotton is grown in small quantities, but it is small and coarse. The staple food of the whole people is *duku*, a somewhat similar plant to the *dhoura* of Egypt. It is smaller and not so sweet as the *dhoura*, but an excellent food. The country is well wooded, but the timber is small and only fit for fuel, four inches in diameter being the average size of the main stems. In the wadys near Khartoum, sheep, goats, and cattle abound; there is good land, but cultivation is small for want of settled labour.

Mr. Fowler thus concludes his report :—" I should have been better satisfied if, before concluding this report, I could have added a calculation as to the precise amount of traffic and revenue to be expected from the railway. The largest portion of the traffic, however, as previously explained, will only exist after the accommodation for it has been provided, and therefore any calculation must depend on the assumption of figures for which there are not, nor can be, any existing data. . . . .

" In the particular case of the Soudan Railway and its probable traffic, it is a fact which cannot be disputed that the extent of land near its southern terminus, or within reach of it by navigable waters, or land carriage, which is capable of producing the finest crops of cotton, grain, and sugar, is practically unlimited ; and that during the time requisite for the construction of the railway, such area may be brought into cultivation as will furnish immediate and considerable traffic.

" The vast quantities of timber of various kinds which will become cheaply accessible to the proposed railway will supply fuel to the locomotives for a long period of time, and one of the most important items in the working expenses of the railway will thereby be largely reduced.

"Assuming the working expenses of the Soudan Railway to be sixty per cent. of the gross receipts (which is seven per cent. higher than the average working expenses of all the Indian railways), it can scarcely be doubted that the traffic from the local and through sources enumerated will yield a satisfactory return upon the small cost of the proposed railway. Under any circumstances, a large increase to the national wealth of Egypt must necessarily follow such an opening up of its undeveloped resources."

From the statements of this experienced engineer, it will be seen that the trade which is to pay for the construction and maintenance of this road will have chiefly to be created by it.

During the reign of the Khedive immense strides in Central African exploration have been made, with his assistance, and by his *employés*, both European, American, and native. Within the last four years Darfour has become a part of Egypt; the White Nile has been thoroughly explored and made navigable; the great equatorial lakes and the surrounding country have been traversed by the feet, and reported on by the ready pens, of the Khedive's adventurous emissaries, and efforts made to fix and define the very disputed boundary between Egyptian and Abyssinian soil. Colonels Colston, Purdy, Mason, and Prout, American staff officers, with Mitchell, the geologist—recently a captive in Abyssinian hands, but now liberated—have made very thorough explorations on different lines in the interior; the latter having discovered two ancient gold mines, the shafts still open, between the Nile and the Red Sea, near Kennar. Several steamers are now plying on the Nile, between Khartoum and Ragaff, above which the rapids render the river unnavigable.

The Khedive has possession now not only of several ports on the Red Sea, including Massowah, but about two years since obtained a very important one in addition, by purchase, from the then impecunious Sultan—the port of Zeila, situated at the extremity of a peninsula on the Somala coast, which opens rich districts, producing coffee, gums, ivory, wool, etc., to Egyptian trade.

The Abyssinian king, Johannes, has recently been keeping Massowah in a state of siege, and covets much the possession of that port, which would give him an outlet to the sea, which Abyssinia much needs. The latest tidings from that point indicate that negotiations were going on, virtually giving joint possession of that port to Egypt and Abyssinia, for all practical purposes ; but as yet no treaty has been concluded.

The Soudan has proved a graveyard for many governors and explorers, both foreign and native. Here perished the two Arakel Beys—father and son—the one falling a victim to the climate in early manhood, while governor at Khartoum, many years since ; the latter, as Governor of Massowah, accompanying the ill-starred expedition of Arendrup, and slain with him. Here also was foully slaughtered Minzinger Pacha, whose name and reputation rank with those of Baker and Gordon Pachas, as pioneer and explorer. Here, too, were left the mortal remains of the two gallant and promising sons of Linant Pacha, like the famous grenadier of France, their countrymen, dead on "the field of honour," in these fatal precincts. To give the long list of victims the climate and the barbarous natives have claimed, would make a long and mournful bead-roll. Let us hope that the new governor-general may enjoy better fortune than the great majority of his pioneers.

Gordon Pacha, when last heard from, had reached Khartoum, his seat of government, but was reported as having been threatened with annoyance from King Johannes, on the one hand, and King M'Tesa, on the other; while Darfour was also said to be in revolt. To bind together the scattered sheaves of his province will require no small amount of patience, skill, and courage; his friends claim all those qualities for him, and he has full power now to pursue his own policy.

Could the railway communication be once completed and opened between Khartoum and civilization, his task would be rendered far easier, and the province be made profitable to Egypt, as well as more manageable; until then the difficulties and dangers of his position cannot be overrated.

The Budget report of 1873 puts down the receipts from the Soudan at £100,000.

"History teaches us," says Mariette Bey, "that Egypt is bounded on the north by the Mediterranean, on the south by the Cataract of Assouan. But history, in imposing these limits, has not taken into account the indications furnished by geographical or race peculiarities. Over the north-west portion of the African continent stretches an immense zone of earth formed by the Nile, and fertilized by it alone. Scattered over its banks you find two different races, the one uncultivated, savage, incapable of self-government; the other a nation worthy the world's admiration for its glory, its industry, and all the elements of civilization that it nourishes in its bosom. History should say that wherever flows the Nile, there her rights and her dominion should extend.''

The language of the eloquent Frenchman, who has done so much to bring Egypt's buried history and treasures to light, seems to convey the dominant idea of three generations of the line of Mehemet Ali, and to account for the trouble, labour, treasure, and life they have squandered on the exploration and annexation of the Soudan. If it be a dream, it surely is a great and noble one, to reclaim to law, culture, and civilization the rich tracts now rank and pestiferous with jungle, and the plains over which still roams, as in the days of Abraham, the wandering nomad, with his flocks and herds; or, descending lower still, where man becomes a man-hunter, and preys on his own kind. The task to which Livingstone and so many other Christian men devoted their lives, surely cannot be unworthy of praise in a Mussulman ruler to attempt; even though ambition and love of gain may mingle with his higher aspiration.

CHAPTER XXII.

IMPROVEMENTS AND PUBLIC WORKS IN EGYPT.

Public improvements—Where some of the money has gone—General statement of public works and improvements during the present reign—Thirty or forty millions of pounds' worth accounted for—What and where are these improvements?—Harbour and lighthouse improvements—Gas and water works—Merchant marine—Thirteen hundred miles of railway completed in last twelve years.

THE statement has been broadly made, and as recklessly repeated, in print and in speech, that the Khedive "has borrowed and raised ninety millions of money, and has nothing to show for it but a few lath and plaster palaces."

Now, without attempting to act as the advocate of a prince, who certainly has been very wasteful of his own and other people's means, and has allowed his building mania to cumber the ground with a great many useless palaces for himself and family, justice compels me to say that the charge is as unjust and rash as it is false. This I shall proceed to prove by facts and figures accessible to every one who will take the trouble to look them up. The truth is that the improvements and public works begun and completed in Egypt during the past twelve years have been marvellous, and unequalled by any other country of quadruple the area and population of Egypt; and they have been of such a character as hereafter to enhance immensely the resources and prosperity of the country. But twenty-five years ago Robert Stephenson commenced the single line from Alexandria to Suez, little more than 230 miles in length. Now there are more than 1300 miles completed, and the Khedive is pushing his lines of railways and telegraphs into the very heart of Central Africa. The Soudan line alone will be 1100 miles long, if the engineer's plans be carried out; but of course it will require several years to complete so great a work: even should this line be carried out on the grand proportions suggested by the engineer, which I doubt.

1st. The completion of the Suez Canal, also was the work of the Khedive, although the heavy cost to Egypt was due to Saïd Pacha's imprudent concessions, and the indemnity adjudged by the Emperor Napoleon while acting as arbitrator. For these Ismaïl Pacha cannot justly be made responsible, the pressure put upon him being greater than he could resist. Still, that great work may hereafter indemnify the country when it becomes the property of Egypt; as in justice it should, if Egypt should continue independent, and be sufficiently solvent, at the expiration of the term agreed on, to meet her obligations to the company and enter into possession. The alleged cost of this enterprise to Egypt is estimated in the *Statistique*—a Government publication—to have reached £10,000,000, and other estimates, including incidental expenses, interest, etc., run it up as high as £17,000,000.

In other public works of more immediate utility to Egypt—such as the lighting the cities with gas, supplying water by means of extensive water-works, as well as pure air through street improvements—the reign of the Khedive has been a busy one, as well as in the extension of railway and telegraph lines, internal canals, docks, and lighthouses.

All these expenditures, it will be seen, were made for a great public purpose, and constitute part of the capital of the country, and may be considered as good investments. While Turkey has squandered the millions borrowed from Europe, and wrung from her own subjects, in extravagance and folly, in building palaces and buying ironclads exclusively, attending neither to the moral nor material advancement of her population or territory, Egypt can point to her great public works and improving people with just pride. Why Europe insists that Sinbad (Egypt) should carry on his back this " Old Man of the Sea " (Turkey), to the tune of £635,000 tribute per annum, is a political mystery which may soon be solved, or dissolved. In the name of Justice and Progress we may rejoice that these Siamese twins can be cut asunder without danger to the living one : and without calling Russia in to act as surgeon. Besides the great public works enumerated, more than a hundred new canals have been dug for irrigation purposes, two-thirds of which are in Lower Egypt; more than 500 new bridges built to facilitate transportation of the crops, one of which—that connecting Cairo with the island of Ghezireh—is a magnificent engineering work. Both at Cairo and Alexandria are gas and water works, supplying those cities, and large gasometers.

2nd. The cost of the railway constructions and repairs during the last twelve years may be estimated at about £10,000,000, and the fact that that portion of the public debt guaranteed by these railways is regarded and termed " a preference stock," proves that the investment has been a good one.

3rd. The harbour works at Alexandria and Suez, which are of great utility, and promise to improve greatly the commerce of the country, have absorbed several millions more, possibly £3,000,000 or £4,000,000. It is calculated that the revenues of the port of Alexandria may be raised to £200,000 annually, which would pay a handsome interest on the outlay, when added to those of Suez.

4th. The irrigating canals, several hundreds of miles of which the Khedive has made or improved during his reign, for the cost of which no statistics exist, must have absorbed much money; though I fear a great deal of fellah flesh and blood went into them, too, for very inadequate wages (if any), under the *corvée* system.

5th. The lighthouses erected on the Red Sea and Mediterranean coasts have supplied a great want to foreign and native commerce. Their cost has certainly been £200,000. The introduction of gas and water, improvements in sewerage, paving, and embellishment of Cairo, Alexandria, and Suez, are said to have cost £3,000,000 more.

6th. A fleet of merchant steamers to ply between Egypt, Greece, and Turkey, which is said to have cost £1,500,000; and

7th. The expeditions to Central Africa, and the Abyssinian campaign—works of dubious necessity and of no immediate utility—doubtless swallowed up £2,000,000 more.

So that, even from this rapid and imperfect

summary of public improvements, accomplished
within the last decade, it will be seen that the
Khedive really has something to show, more
than his palaces, for the millions expended;
although even his best friend or most obsequious
flatterer cannot venture to say he has shown
much judgment, or a proper sense of his own
means and those of the country, in many of the
works he has undertaken, or completed.

He can show public works to the value of
£20,000,000 or £30,000,000 for his twelve years'
administration of the country, as a visible proof
that, although he may have squandered some
of the public money, he certainly has not
thrown half of it away in ostentatious personal
extravagances.   Immense improvements also
have been made in the public roads leading
out of Cairo and Alexandria, as well as in the
streets of those cities.   The roads around Cairo,
for example, and the bridges in that neighbourhood are worthy of all praise, and must have
cost much hard cash, as well as indirectly
through the labour employed upon them, even
granting the labourers were not paid in money.

That Egypt is able to-day to astonish the rest
of the world by the immense revenues she is
able to dig out of her small area of soil—for all
the money must come out of the land—is due in
great part to the improvements made in irriga-

tion and railway extension, which at once greatly increase the produce of the soil, and render transportation of produce much quicker, easier, and less costly than it used to be. This much, I think, is due to the Khedive to admit, whatever his sins or his shortcomings may have been as a ruler and a financier, and however much of public money he may have wasted in needless extravagances for his own or his children's luxury or state.

CHAPTER XXIII.

THE ARMY OF EGYPT.

An indeterminate quantity—Curious exemption of Cairenes and Alexandrians from conscription—How the conscription is made—What successive viceroys have done for the army—The army and the military chest—Excellent drill and organization of the forces—The American and other foreign officers—The Khedive's true, and Egypt's wisest policy.

THE Egyptian army has always been a kind of indeterminate quantity, concerning which but little was allowed to be known to the world at large, or outside the immediate circle of the chief military men who controlled it.

Until 1873 its number was jealously limited by the Sublime Porte; but the persuasive powers of the Khedive, backed by the potential argument of "backsheesh," which insured his own elevation in rank and title, the direct line of succession, and his independence of Constantinople in so far as the internal administration of Egypt was involved, obtained also the concession of raising his army to any number that pleased him.

2 B

Of this permission the Khedive has made no great use thus far; having rather diminished than increased his effective force, as far as the facts can be known; and having returned to the cultivation of the fields, " on leave," large bodies of his soldiers, substituting for them in part the black recruits from the Soudan.

One peculiar feature of the Egyptian army is the incorporation of the native Christian element in its ranks; the levies from Upper Egypt being drawn chiefly from the Copt Christians, who constitute a considerable portion of the population in some of the provinces of Upper Egypt—many of the villages, especially on or near the Nile, being peopled by them. These men do not regard this exceptional mark of their equality with their Mussulman countrymen as a great favour: being a peaceful race, and preferring tranquil to warlike pursuits. Nevertheless the fact is not without its significance, as it shows the desire of the Khedive not to keep up invidious discriminations, prevailing everywhere else throughout the Ottoman dominions.

Another noteworthy peculiarity — although one of exclusion—is the exemption from military duty extended to the inhabitants of the two great cities of Alexandria and Cairo, in virtue of an ancient privilege exempting them from bearing arms. The reason for which this exemption was granted, I have not been able to discover; but in a country, and among a people, where custom has the binding force of law, the antiquity of the usage suffices to insure its perpetuation, even under a rule as absolute as that of the Khedive. Thus at least one-tenth of the population are exempted by this curious privilege from the conscription which, outside of the foreign element, is theoretically universal in its application to all classes and creeds of the community.

The exemption is unjust to the native population on many accounts; and because it throws the burden of this injurious system of recruiting on the rural population exclusively. The cities contain the great bulk of the element alien in blood and birth to Egypt—the trading, shopkeeping, and servant class, who drift into the cities from neighbouring countries.

Thus in Cairo you find a large population composed of an almost infinite variety of races, who should bear the burdens, as they enjoy the benefits, of the Egyptian Government; Europeans, who are protected by the capitulations, alone excepted.

Thus, at Cairo and Alexandria you see numbers of Syrians, of Copts, of Armenians, of Israelites, of Berbers, of Nubians, of Abyssinians, rayah Greeks, and Turks, all of whom numbering probably 150,000, are exempted from conscription in these two cities alone. This is one among the many unaccountable anomalies of the Egyptian administration. If you inquire of a high functionary why this custom is allowed to continue, he shrugs his shoulders and answers, " Who knows ? It was always so."

Apart from these exceptional cases however, the conscription is sternly enforced elsewhere, and theoretically with impartiality; but King Backsheesh can always interpose successfully here, through the venality of the agents employed, who always "make a good thing of it;" and hence the draft ever falls on that portion of the able-bodied population most wanted for the cultivation of the fields, especially in the upper country, where the population is sparse. Yet it is on this section that the twin abuses of Egyptian administration—the conscription and the *corvée*—weigh most heavily on the industrious poor, who cannot buy exemption through influence or money. In addition to the blinding effects of backsheesh on the recruiting officer, the recruit is allowed to return from service after one year's duty, on payment of a fixed sum.

As there are no territorial commands, or peace organizations into brigades and divisions, as in European armies, the system, or want of system

in the military organization, can be easily comprehended by military men.

There may be some pretence at rotation, and
as to an annual contingent; but in reality the
conscription is enforced "by superior orders,"
whenever the whim or the necessity for more
soldiers is felt by the Khedive; and then the
conscription is carried out much on the old
system, so often described by indignant tourists,
who have seen gangs of apparent convicts,
chained together, and driven by soldiers to the
place of embarkation, escorted by howling and
shrieking women, who see with them their
daily bread and that of their children taken
away. Those unpleasant sights and scenes have
not yet vanished from the Egyptian soil, either
for conscription or *corvée;* but it is high time
that they should; if reform is to be more than
a hollow show nd a mockery.

The acquisition of the Soudan has brought
some alleviation to the lot of the fellah, inas-
much as the savage blacks of Central Africa
have been found to make good soldiers; and you
now see whole regiments of these, who have
replaced the agricultural labourer, wisely sent
home to till his fields and take care of his
family. This is the first actual benefit accruing
to Egypt from these acquisitions; and it may
be greatly extended, by drawing on that savage

swarm of humanity—warriors by instinct—and releasing the gentle fellah from a duty, for which neither his nature, nor any amount of training can fit him. The secret of the domination exercised over the Arab race by a mere handful of Turks, in garrison towns throughout Egypt and Syria, establishes this truth incontestably.

The successors of the warrior kings, Mehemet Ali and Ibrahim, have made efforts to keep up an army of respectable proportions, in so far as the jealousy of the Sultan would permit. Abbas kept up more than the regulation number, including a large force to overawe the Soudan, and the contingent sent to the Crimea; at one time said to have risen to 100,000 men.

Saïd Pacha, in the early part of his reign, "played soldier" a good deal; but failing health and other causes induced him to neglect and greatly diminish his soldiery, in the latter part of it, until it is said to have dwindled down, in peace times, to about 5000 men (the war strength to 15,000) actually under arms, or immediately available. The Khedive has been busy in this, as in all other matters of internal administration; though what the actual strength of his army has been, or may now be, is known only to the Chief of Staff, Stone Pacha, who can keep a secret as well as any man alive.

Theoretically the military force of Egypt consists of—

1. The regular army, with its reserve.
2. Irregular or local troops.
3. The gendarmerie, uniformed and mounted.

There are stated to be eighteen infantry regiments, of three battalions each ; four battalions of rifles ; four regiments of cavalry ; and 144 guns—among them some large Krupps and Armstrongs.

The number of men in the regiments and batteries varies so much, in consequence of constant practical disbandments (in the shape of leave, when the military chest is empty, as it often is), that it is impossible even to guess, at any time, as to the actual effective force of the Egyptian army.

Of their admirable training, drill, and discipline, under the supervision of the exceedingly able staff of American, and other foreign officers, in the Khedive's service, as well as of the instruction given officers in the polytechnic schools, foreign military observers speak most highly ; and the fact is obvious to the most careless observer, as these troops march past the hotels. A finer looking soldiery can be seen nowhere ; and that some of the native officers at least are clever, an inspection of their drill, and a visit to the monthly *séances* of the Geographical Society, where one of them occasionally reads a report of his explorations, will prove to the most prejudiced stickler for caste and colour.

I am told that at present their weak point is in their officers; but my own private opinion is that they are not the stuff good soldiers are made of, except the Soudanese, and had better be devoted to the arts and pursuits of peace, than to the right royal trade of murder by wholesale.

The infantry are chiefly armed with the Remington rifle; and of arms and ammunition the Khedive has laid in so abundant a store, as to have sent millions of fixed ammunition to Constantinople as a present, in addition to his contingent of troops and their supplies.

Each cavalry regiment is armed partly with the lance, partly with the carbine.

The irregular cavalry is supplied by the Bedouins, who furnish their own arms and horses, and are commanded by their own chiefs. They resemble the Cossacks in appearance, and in more particulars than one.

We learn from foreign sources that "Nothing more than a' rough estimate of the Egyptian army is possible, but it has been calculated that with regiments filled up from the reserves, the fighting strength of the regular army would be about 60,000, with 144 guns. There would remain a reserve of about 30,000, and an irregular force of possibly 60,000 more; but the probability is, that the strength of the army would entirely depend at any given moment on the amount of money in the possession of the Khedive at the time and the conscription three years previously."

As far as I have been able to pick up any information on this jealously guarded secret, the above estimate is in the main correct.

The chief use of the Egyptian army, outside of the "gendarmerie," or local police force (which is well armed, uniformed, and disciplined, and preserves peace and order admirably), is for the protection of the frontier against the desert Bedouins on the one side, and from the Abyssinians on the other; both of whose raiding propensities are very great, and require to be constantly kept in check.

I do not propose here to enter into a discussion on the Khedive's little wars with his neighbours, which I sincerely believe were forced upon him, as he is more a man of peace than a man of blood; but those who are curious concerning the last and most costly of them, will find a truthful account of it, taken from the notes of a staff-officer, in the July number of *Blackwood's Magazine*, in which the whole story is intelligibly and impartially told. It is probable, however, that this disastrous experiment will not soon be willingly repeated by the Khedive.

The duties of the foreign staff-officers are not confined to the drilling and instruction of officers and privates, and organization of the army. They have been busily and usefully employed in the work of exploration in the Soudan, and elsewhere; and have done immense service in ascertaining and reporting on those portions of the Khedive's Egypt, of which little or nothing was previously known. The report of the Chief of Staff, Stone Pacha (as yet, I believe, unpublished), to be found in the Appendix, will show where they have gone, and what they have done.*

In a letter from one of those officers to me, he says :—" Egypt is abused for spending money on the Soudan Railway; but the reconnoitring officers find hundreds of thousands of cattle, fat and sleek. Now, when the railway shall be finished to Dongola, in three or four years, that station will be within easy driving reach of those vast herds, and instead of importing many thousands of thousands of cattle every year from Greece to Turkey, Egypt can bring down her own cattle from her own provinces, and that so cheaply that she might even export cattle to Europe."

See Appendix F.

The Khedive is shrewd enough to see and know that the safety of his patrimony, and integrity of Egypt, do not depend on and could never be protected by arms alone; but rest on the determination of the Great Powers of Europe, who gave and can take away his heritage, should they ever deem it necessary to change the Egyptian *status* for selfish or for State motives. He further understands, better than most princes, the wisdom of the saying of Lysander, that "when the lion's skin is too short, it may be eked out by the fox's!" and both his precept and his practice have accorded with this ancient maxim: which possibly he never heard of, though he has acted upon it.

In European jealousies lies Egyptian safety— not in arms or armaments, nor in the wish or will of the dying dotard at Constantinople, whose ominous shadow has so long veiled the light and life of Egypt, the blood of whose peaceful people is even now being poured out on foreign battle fields, that the waning Crescent may not utterly disappear from the Western sky.

If Ismaïl Khedive is wise, he will turn his attention henceforth more to the arts of peace than to those of war; although he does well in keeping up a sufficient force for the internal protection of his territory and people, against his lawless border neighbours; and in securing the best military talent from abroad, to make a small but efficient army do the duty of a larger one.

CHAPTER XXIV.

THE SHADOW OF THE STRANGER.

Egypt's experience—Her three periods: Pagan, Christian, and Mussulman—International jealousies—Shall the Mediterranean be a French or English "lake"?—Curious history of this rivalry in regard to the overland transit—Cost to Egypt of conciliating the rival nationalities—Mariette Bey's characterization of the Egyptians—The irony of their destiny—The shadow of the stranger eclipsing native government—*Laissez nous faire!*

EGYPT, during her long life of many thousands of years, has passed through three periods: Pagan, Christian, and Mussulman. The first is supposed to have endured for upwards of 5000 years, terminating A.D. 381; the second lasted 259 years, ending A.D. 640; and the third commenced at the latter period, and endures to the present time—Egypt continuing subject ever to Constantinople, until her quasi-independence was obtained by Mehemet Ali, and under many different phases, resolutely maintained by his successors.

Her future lot, at this moment, he would indeed be a bold man who would venture to predict; for clouds and darkness now veil her horizon.

During the reigns of successive viceroys, England and France have alternately exerted the greatest influence at the viceroyal court; and until the fatal day of Sedan, the latter, assimilating more in character and language to the successors of Mehemet Ali, had certainly enjoyed the greatest favour, and shaped more visibly the political action of the viceroys. But since that disastrous time the star of France has waned, that of England risen on the Egyptian firmament; until the wish or will of the British Cabinet has become a làw unto Egypt, almost as binding as the ancient "laws of the Medes and Persians" were said to have been.

How France and Frenchmen chafe at this, may be seen in their jealous insistance on more than equal representation on the new tribunals, for their nationality; as well as in the late financial arrangements, where if English agents have the collection, French agents have the control over the disbursement, of the public funds; and whereas England sends to Egypt gentlemen skilled in public accounts, France sends her most practised diplomats, to be near the Khedive.

This international jealousy is not confined to the two nations named, for it exists in other

nationalities, who have, or suppose they have, a
political or commercial interest in Egypt ; yet
its greatest manifestation has hitherto come
from the two great Powers, whose struggle for
the last half century has been, whether the
Mediterranean was to become a French or an
English " lake."

A curious exhibition of this feeling has just
been made in France — rendered more keenly
sensitive by the sense of lost *prestige* and power,
since she dashed herself against the German
Colossus.

Reports having been generally circulated, of
the initiation of negotiations between England
and the Porte, for the purchase of the eminent
domain in the land occupied by the Suez Canal,
the *Moniteur* (always regarded as the mouth-
piece of the existing Government of France)
published conspicuously the following remarkable comment thereupon, towards the end of
June in the present year :—

"A rumour reaches us from London which,
no doubt, is without foundation, but to which it
appears to us important to call attention. It is
said that the Ottoman Government has offered
to make over to England for twenty-five millions
of francs the Sultan's 'territorial rights' over
the Suez Canal. In the first place, we wish to
remark that the Sultan has had no 'territorial

rights' in Egypt since 1840, when the Sublime
Porte, with the assent and sanction of the
Powers, made the viceroyalty of Egypt the
exclusive and hereditary *apanage* of the family
of Mehemet Ali. We will also add that the
Khedive, as master of Egypt, and consequently
of the territory which the canal goes through,
has undertaken to '*exploiter*,' in common with
the Suez Canal Company, the land on both
banks of the canal for a period of ninety-nine
years. It would be requisite, to realize this
news from London, to assume that, in the
first place, the present Sultan should revoke the
hereditary rights held by the Khedive since 1840
with the sanction of the Powers; and next, that
a new code should permit a sovereign to sell, for
his own benefit, the private estates existing in
his empire." *

The significance of this note consists in its
publication by the semi-official organ of the
French Foreign Office. Its *animus* is evident;
and it truly represents French feeling in and out
of Egypt.

So long as the two Powers were in equipoise,
successive viceroys were adroit enough to play

* The key to this semi-official note is, most probably, the publication, in the *Nineteenth Century* magazine, of Mr. Edward Dicey's
very powerful article, advocating England's immediate appropriation
of Lower Egypt and the Suez Canal, by purchase or otherwise, as a
measure of national safety.

AN EGYPTIAN STUMBLING-BLOCK.   385

the one against the other, for their own protection; appealing to the outside Powers as make-weights. But recently, as before remarked, the one has preponderating influence; and hence the ill-concealed jealousy of the other; which hereafter may find anew its battlefield in Egypt, when France recovers from her present political eclipse in the Orient.

One of the greatest stumbling-blocks in the path of Egyptian progress has been the necessity of conciliating, at very heavy cost, all the rival nationalities in Egypt, representing in all about 100,000, out of her population of 5,500,000! For this small quantity of leaven is made to leaven the whole loaf, and swell enormously the annual Egyptian Budget, by the heavy additional expenditure imposed on Egypt, by the presence of the stranger on her soil.

A shrewd observer, recently writing from the spot, has remarked that the great cost of the new reform measures has arisen from this cause, which "*compels the Khedive to employ half a dozen persons to do the work of one!*" citing the fact of twelve nationalities being represented on the judicial tribunals; to which he might have added, that some of the most favoured of these have three or four to their share; besides a crowd of minor officers of court. The same is the case as to the public debt commission, the

2 c

railway, and other administrations. Very curious manifestations of this rivalry are constantly being made, adding greatly to the perplexities of the Khedive, and to the cost of his administrations. It is difficult to see how this evil is to be done away with, so long as the causes for it exist, and Egyptians and Foreign Governments occupy the same relative positions. Yet, probably, the permanence of the dynasty of Mehemet Ali has been due as much to the eternal intermeddling and undying jealousies of the foreign Powers, in regard to Egypt, as to the ability of his successors, who certainly have played that card very skilfully, however much they may have erred as to other points of the game. To-day the necessity of continued interposition in Egyptian affairs, both political and financial, seems to be inevitable; in consequence of the existing complications, familiar to all the world.

Whether the present anomalous condition of things can continue; whether an *imperium in imperio*—through which a practically absolute ruler is divested of his authority and control over all his administrations, and his treasury, by a foreign commission, and a foreign judicial tribunal, appointed and paid by himself to sit in judgment on his acts—can be preserved in Egypt: and the grandson of Mehemet Ali be long content to rest in this attitude before his own people and the world, is a question that time alone can solve.

The shadow of the stranger, projected over Egypt, now hides both the throne and the native administration. Whether it will ever again be removed, and throne and country pass under the protectorate of one, instead of many foreign Powers, or its present ruler resume the powers he has temporarily abdicated, with renewed *prestige* and replenished treasury, is an Egyptian riddle, more puzzling than any ever propounded by its ancient Sphinx.

When the tardily appreciated, and unrewarded enterprise of Lieutenant Waghorn, had demonstrated the feasibility of the overland transit through Egypt, and England sought to utilize it by a line of railway from Alexandria to Cairo, French jealousy immediately strove to bar the way; and for some time did so successfully. From a curious pamphlet, published by an old resident of Egypt, in 1851, the following particulars of this struggle are taken—rendered doubly interesting at this moment, in consequence of the impending struggle over the Suez Canal property, foreshadowed by several recent indications. The writer says :—

" The first care of France, after the settlement of 1841, was to remove from the mind of Mehemet Ali the bad feeling he naturally entertained towards her, for the non-performance of those promises, on the reliance of which he had risked his very existence. It was a difficult task; but by working alternately on his *amour-propre*, and on his fears, she ultimately succeeded. The most marked and delicate attentions were resorted to by Louis Philippe, and the members of his family; while at the same time, the French *employés* in Egypt, and the French party in the native ranks, constantly held out that Great Britain had aggressive views upon Egypt, and that being the half-way house to India, she would never rest until she had made it her own. Her progress in India was constantly referred to, and her gradual steps from commercial relations to exclusive sovereignty and military possession, were daily urged upon the Pacha's notice. At the same time he was taught to believe, that France alone could save him from similar consequences, at the grasping hand of England. A host of Frenchmen were taken into his service, some of whom were to be met with in every administration; many of them holding important posts, with the rank of pacha and bey; and these, aided by such Turks and Egyptians as had received their education at Paris, established an all-powerful influence on the action of Government—an influence whose force was strained to the uttermost to thwart any measure which seemed, in the most remote manner, to forward British interests.

"To Great Britain the immense importance of railway communication between the two seas, was one of those occasions which seemed to call for the most energetic exertion of this influence; nor did French jealousy fail to appreciate it. Accordingly, the opposition of France to this railroad, has ever been of the most determined nature. Its existence, or its non-existence, seemed the point on which her policy turned; and eventually it became a question involving her support or her hostility.

"Twice the French party succeeded in inducing Mehemet Ali to abandon the project: although at one time more than thirty miles of rail were actually bought, and for fifteen years were lying unused in the Government stores.

"It was the same party, and the same influence, which planned, and caused to be executed, the fortifications of Alexandria, and the whole sea-coast of Egypt. . . .

"An English company had been formed for the transit of passengers and goods through Egypt, in connection with the steam communications to Alexandria and Suez. Great privileges had been granted it by the local Government; a large capital was embarked in building station-houses in the desert, in providing steamboats,

carriages, horses, and other means of conveyance. . . . Its growing importance attracted the
jealousy of the French party, and its removal
from English hands was decided upon.

"They persuaded the Pacha, that the existence
of so powerful a foreign company was detrimental
to his interests; and that some day it might
become a stepping-stone for the aggressive views
of Great Britain upon Egypt. The station-
houses, they said, would form the nucleus of
forts, and the steamers on the Nile might,
with little difficulty and upon some trivial pretence, be easily converted into vessels of war.
With such arguments they persuaded Mehemet
Ali to take the transit into his own hands, and
partly by force, and partly by promises of large
compensation, he became the proprietor.

"These facts suffice to show to what extent the
mind of Mehemet Ali was held in subjection by
his French allies. In return for this compliant
submission to their authority, he received, it is
true, more solid proofs of friendship than those
conveyed in the shape of presents, flattery, and
courteous attentions. They lent him their firm
support at Constantinople; and to the day of his
death aided him in resisting every semblance
of encroachment on that freedom of action,
guaranteed to him, and his successors, by the
firman of investiture. . . .

"During the lifetime of his grandfather, Abbas had invariably protested against the undue influence of France; and from the day he came into power, he resolved on relieving his country from so grievous an incubus. His first act was in that sense; and after hurrying through the form and ceremony of investiture at Constantinople, he no sooner returned to Cairo than he set to work in earnest. He commenced by dismissing from his service, and pensioning off, a number of Frenchmen, and other Europeans, who for years had enjoyed the rank and drawn the emoluments of beys; but the exact nature of whose duties it was difficult to define. Amongst his own officers there were many, holding high rank and important posts, who had been gained over, heart and soul to the views of France. These he recommended 'to retire to Constantinople' " (*i.e.*, banished).

English influence at length prevailed, and the road was constructed; and under the Empire, France patronized the Suez Canal, as a political equipoise.

History repeats itself oftener in Egypt than elsewhere, and the old rivalry is neither dead nor sleeping to-day, as living men may see. In addition to the former rivalry, new ones have been created. Until the Russo-Turkish war removed her representative from Cairo, Russia was busily agitating in Egypt, with the assistance of Panslavist envoys, whose correspondence has been intercepted and published. The new kingdom of united Italy, whose subjects almost equal those of France, and double those of England in Egypt, claims a consultative voice in the councils of the Khedive in all matters of foreign concern. Nor is there any foreign agent there who does not aspire to have his finger in the pie, and exert some influence at the Court to which he is accredited—the functions of consuls-general being purely political, except in cases of appeal from the action of their subordinates.

Egypt seems to have been set apart by destiny as the battle-ground of races, and so continues still; her native population having far less voice in her councils, and far less of the profits derived from their labour, than the " stranger within their gates," of any alien race whatsoever. And yet, there never was a race, as Mariette Bey has justly observed, more naturally conservative, and less disposed to strife, than the native Egyptian is and ever has been from his earliest recorded history; which however has been a history of change and of struggle always, the tide of events sweeping Egypt, in spite of herself, into the turbid torrent of perpetual revolutions.

" Egypt," says the close and experienced

observer of her monuments and history I have already cited, "through her admirable climate, which makes the mere act of living a luxury—through the fertility of her soil—through the gentle and docile character of her people, rendering the introduction of the arts of civilization so easy—is *par excellence* the most conservative of countries. Aggression, and the impulse of expansion and propagandism, so common to other races, are unknown to her ; and did not others come to disturb the tranquil repose which is the essence of her life, it is very certain she, of her own accord, would never stir to create agitations elsewhere. When she has been violently pushed into such movements, against her natural bent, they have proved but temporary·; and it is always sure, whenever the final catastrophe comes, poor Egypt must prove the loser."

" *Laissez nous faire !* " ("Let us alone") should be the motto, as it long has been the despairing cry of Egypt and her rulers; and until this perpetual meddling and muddling in her affairs ceases, and she is left to stand or fall alone, without so many super-serviceable friends pulling or pushing her in different directions, the shadow of the stranger will continue to shut out her sunshine from the natives of her soil.

CHAPTER XXV.

BY CAIRO TO EUROPE, *VIA* ALEXANDRIA.

By rail from Cairo to Alexandria—Disturbing a harem—The last of backsheesh—The country *en route*—Two rival capitals—How an Alexandrian feels at Cairo, and how a Cairene regards him—Something about the Egyptian Brighton—Old and New Alexandria—The place and people—The different routes back to Europe—The Brindisi route—Picturesque old places on the Italian coast—The Moorish pirates—Through Italy—Bologna and its museum—*La Belle France ;* and adieu to Egypt.

THE communication between Cairo and Alexandria is very intimate and constant, although the residents at, or near the latter city, affect to look down rather contemptuously on the former, as of mushroom growth, compared to their comparatively ancient colony, the nucleus and nest of the foreign settlement in Egypt. On the other hand, the Cairenes assume towards the Alexandrians, the patronizing and pitying demeanour, assumed by "fast" young gentlemen, on encountering the old friends of their parents, whom they regard as decidedly "slow," and ever treat with a mixture of deference and forbearance, which is very exasperating. This rivalry is curious to contemplate; and Shepheard's Hotel, where the English, and English-speaking element, most do congregate, affords daily exemplifications and illustrations of the bad blood engendered between the commercial and Court centres, during the present reign. Before that time this rivalry and jealous feeling did not exist. Mehemet Ali, his son, and grandson, preferred Alexandria to Cairo; and made it the capital. Abbas shunned both cities as much as he could, avoiding men and their haunts, that he might enjoy his own moody humour in the silence and solitude of his desert palaces.

The railway carriages struck me as very shabby and dirty last year, and the general administration of the railway, which had passed into new and foreign hands, was thoroughly slovenly and exasperating, involving a great waste of comfort, time, and temper on a transit of about five and a half hours' duration, which ought to be four—the whole distance being but little over 130 miles. It really seemed to me, that this line was far worse managed, than it had been fifteen years before; and although the heads may now be European, the hands (and very dirty ones) continually thrust into our railway carriage *en route*, were certainly those of Esau, not of Jacob—Egyptian, not European.

The journey may be described as a short one, elongated by perpetual stoppages, each of which is of considerable duration, time counting for nothing in railway calculations on this line.. The Suez Canal has hurt the railway lines, by diverting the great bulk of the passenger and goods traffic, which used to be transported from Alexandria to Cairo and Suez, under the old overland transit route; and the extension of the interior irrigating canals, also takes off another slice. The new Fresh-Water Canal to Ismailia will cut another large "cantle" off; and this may partially account for the general air of decay and dilapidation, which pervaded the entire service.

The route to Alexandria has been so often described in the books of the Nile tourists, who write as they run, that it would only fatigue the reader to recapitulate the oft-told tale; though there are views, constantly being framed in the carriage windows, that would make the fortune of the painter, cunning enough to catch and put them down on canvas. But Ismail Khedive has spent time, money, and influence in building up, and (as he thinks) beautifying Cairo, and has constituted it his capital and chief place of residence—rarely visiting Alexandria, where he also has palaces, or Ramleh, on the sea-shore near Alexandria, whose refreshing sea breezes

might woo him to pass the sultry Egyptian midsummer there.

The gossip of Alexandria whispers that a
superstitious dread keeps him away from the old
city, because it has been predicted he is to die
there; and a belief in such predictions is rooted
in the mind of every Oriental, whatever may
have been his instruction or training : and can
never be eradicated.

Be this as it may, it is certain that he has
ever smiled on Cairo, and given the cold shoulder
to Alexandria, which resents the slight, and
professes small affection for the Khedive ; and
where, in fact, the foreign element is openly and
bitterly hostile to the existing administration;
partly through the conviction that he has
already almost ruined the country, and themselves with it, and partly because of his treatment of them and their beloved city.

For, unlike the Cairene resident, who is only
a transient person, as attached to the Court or
some Government bureau, the Alexandrian has a
strong feeling of nationality apart from that of
his birth, owing to long residence and long
association, stretching back to the commencement of the present century. To him, therefore, the Cairene is but a *parvenu;* and
although he visits Cairo through policy, or by
business compulsion occasionally, he growls

at the city, and the Khedive, all the time he is
there.

At the grand new hotel, which is owned by the
Khedivial family, and therefore patronized by
"loyal" Levantines, you respire the odour of
loyalty towards the Khedive, "and all that is
his;" while at the Hotel d'Orient you may
fancy yourself in France, and at the Hotel du
Nil in the heart of the Rhineland—except that
the tropical plants of its pretty garden could not
bloom on the banks of that renowned river.

Leaving either of these hotels, by the express
train at 8 a.m., you are conveyed in an
omnibus to the station in a cloud of dust, and in
a few minutes are deposited on the platform of
the station, in the midst of a howling but good-
tempered mob of Arabs and Levantines, of all
conceivable nationalities.

The officious conductor of the omnibus registers your luggage, (on which you are always
heavily taxed for overweight, however small
your valise may be), procures your ticket, and
enters into a violent altercation with one of the
railway officials about your seat in a carriage :
insisting that as all others are crowded, one
with the curtains drawn must be unlocked for
your accommodation. High above the clamour of
contending voices, you hear the word "hareem,"
and apprehending that you may share the fate

of Orpheus, if you intrude on the hidden houris, implore your officious champion to get you some other place. Upon this he closes one eye, and whispers mysteriously, "Backsheesh!" You deposit a coin in his hand; he transfers it to the hand of the railway official; who, utterly oblivious of his previous statements, unlocks the door, ushers you into the empty carriage, and allows you the quiet enjoyment of all the seats, until another and similar performance is gone through on behalf of some other voyager, with similar results.

In despite of the dust, the heat, the glare, the flies, and the ceaseless shrieking for back-sheesh of the dirty little imps that haunt every station, with their *goolahs* of water, oranges, and dried dates, on which the flies are ever feasting, at every station, you feel you are really passing through the Lotos-land, with its wonderful varieties of verdure spread over the map-like stretch of tableland, over which the camel and water-ox are patiently plodding, and the half-naked Egyptians, on donkey-back in the foreground, make pictorial.

The first surprise awaiting the returning traveller is at Ramleh, which, from a small straggling sea-coast village of a hundred houses or cabins, has now grown into a large and densely inhabited town of many thousands of

permanent residents. There are no less than
two railway lines passing through and to it;
and a large proportion of the foreign colony
doing business at Alexandria now live there
winter and summer, going daily into the city,
about four miles distant. Every possible
variety of architectural caprice may be seen at
Ramleh, which squatting down on the sandy
sea-shore without trees, is all open to the
view—from Khedivial palaces, built in utter
scorn of all the orders of architecture, to Swiss
chalets, square boxes, and houses of as confused
plans, as the dreams engendered of undigested
suppers.

With the slight drawbacks of the absence
of all verdure, and a blinding glare from the
white sand all day, accompanied by a corre-
sponding degree of heat (only rendered endurable
by the stiff sea breeze), the absence of a casino
or other place of public amusement, and the
impossibility of doing much visiting until after
sunset—I should suppose Ramleh might be a
pleasant summer's resort for a person with a fine
faculty for sleep. Seriously speaking, however,
the place is a real godsend to the Alexandrians,
from the healthy character of its position, and its
refreshing sea breezes; and I am told that the
hotel of Beau Sejour there, is in every respect a
most admirable one; while the hospitality of its

residents would relieve any defects there, did they exist. The views from its high bluffs, of Alexandria and far out to sea, are very fine; and those who know the place and people best like them most, which certainly is a good sign.

On entering the railway station you see the first indications of Alexandria's improvement; for it would be considered a remarkably fine and spacious one in any capital in Europe; and everything is admirably systematized there for the safe and speedy transportation of passengers and their luggage to their hotels after arrival. As we drove through the principal streets to the Grand Plaza, on or near which are all the principal hotels, we remarked the great improvement and growth of the city in the last twelve years, in despite of the Khedive's small patronage of it; for high and solid blocks of stone buildings now occupy the spaces formerly void, or boasting only of small and shaky-looking houses, from the Rossetta gate down to the streets leading into the plaza. Around this plaza also improvement had manifested itself, in the shape of still larger and handsomer blocks of stone buildings, many of which are worthy of London or Paris. There was now a general air of freshness and bustle about the place, contrasting strongly with the drowsy aspect borne by place and people in the days when Saïd Pacha was

2 D

viceroy, and laid out and planted the open space
in the centre : now filled with trees and fountains, and whence old Mehemet Ali in bronze,
seated on horseback, looks down paternally, yet
grimly, on his favourite city.

For more than thirty years past Alexandria
has been substantially an European, not an
Eastern city ; the only Oriental features it possesses being its bazaars, which are by no means
fair average specimens of the article, and a population about half Arab, comprising chiefly the
labouring and small shopkeeping class.   So that
Alexandria, like Smyrna and many other cities
of the Levant, disappoints the traveller freshly
arriving in the East, from looking so European
—resembling rather an Italian than an Eastern
town.   Yet there is a great deal to be seen, and
more to be learned about the land and people of
Egypt from old residents there, than the mere
casual visitor would suppose.   The evidences
of capital in the buildings—chiefly owned by
Europeans—and of wealth displayed in the
houses and shops, are very striking ; and
although for a succession of years, since the
overtrading and high prices consequent on the
American war, business pressure and bad times
have prevailed there, and the merchants are
gloomy as to their future, the place looks
thriving and prosperous.

I do not doubt that, as Saïd Pacha predicted, the Suez Canal has injured Alexandria, by depriving it of the old transit profits, as much of Egyptian produce now passes out *viâ* Port Saïd. Yet the statistics show that Alexandria is still a busy port, and the costly improvements now making in her harbour may cause her to regain more than her lost ground, when completed.

Alexandria, representing as it does most of the foreign trade of Egypt, yet does not embrace more than three-fifths of the entire movement from the Egyptian ports.

This arises from the navigation from the other ports, chiefly from Port Saïd and Suez for direct transit, and from Damietta, Rosetta, and the Red Sea ports, which have the local traffic. According to the *Statistique de l'Egypte*, during the ten years intervening between 1863 and 1872 the number of vessels of all kinds entering the port of Alexandria amounted to 32,433, giving an annual mean of 3·243, each of 390 tons. This number was an increase of more than a thousand vessels over the preceding decade, and chiefly in respect to steamers ; a tendency which the Suez Canal, and the improvement of the port of Alexandria, will cause to manifest itself more strikingly still. The most remarkable feature with regard to the commercial movement to and from Alexandria, is found in the fact that the exports double the imports : which under sound principles of political economy, under a proper administration, ought to render Egypt the most prosperous country on the face of the earth.

There are two short routes, and several longer ones, *via* Malta and Gibraltar to Liverpool ; but the two favourite ones are *via* Brindisi, and by French *Messageries* to Marseilles. The screw steamers taking from twelve to fourteen days to Liverpool, are said to be very fair, and " werry fillin' at the price "—as Sam Weller says. From personal experience, I can speak of the other two lines, and can recommend both to those who wish to travel fast, and avoid long sea passages.

From Alexandria to Brindisi by P. and O. steamer takes but three days ; from Egypt to Marseilles by *Messageries* takes six days—giving two days' advantage on the trip to Paris by the former line, though a longer land travel by rail.

Leaving Brindisi, if lucky enough to travel by daylight, the traveller sees some curious scenery and very odd-looking old places, as he is whirled rapidly past the coast line, often in full view of the sea. Sitting in your railway carriage, there passes before you a series of panoramic pictures of crumbling mediæval old towns, each of which has its little history of the days when the Moorish cruisers used to descend on these coasts, harry the towns, and take away the men and women into captivity. Most of these places have a tower set upon a high hill, to which the people used to run for safety when the pirates came; and many have attempts at fortifications. They look more picturesque than pleasant as places of residence, and have a most decayed and mouldy look, even when viewed from a distance. They must appear terribly tumble-down old places on a near approach, for even distance could not lend enchantment to the view of them. The people looked half fisher-men, half pirate, with a strong dash of the beggar; and both places and people bore the stamp of poverty and neglect.

At Ancona and Bologna the traveller may sometimes stop for a few hours, and both will well repay a longer visit; the places being very quaint and curious, and the art treasures and antiquities of the museum at Bologna being exceptionally good and numerous. It was here the famous Cardinal Mezzofanti, so celebrated for his gift of tongues, presided, lived, and died; mastering more languages than any one man (or even woman) could possibly ever have use for. The old city is so very attractive to strangers that, like a mousetrap, once in it is very hard to get out of.

By the Brindisi route you also pass through

Turin, and that wonderful triumph of man over mountains, the Mont Cenis Tunnel; emerging from which again into bright sunshine and open air, after being half choked and stone blind in its gloomy passages, is like being born over again: adding a new and fresh charm to the beauties of nature unappreciated before.

At Modane, on the frontier line of France and Italy, the Custom-house nuisance again awaits the voyager—a troublesome and useless farce in most instances, and one which the civilization of the nineteenth century should mitigate, if it cannot (as it ought) entirely do away with it. Here you often see the mountain tops and sides, a rugged range, covered with snow; and then, after a tedious ride through wild but uninteresting country, with the worst food at the railway stations that ever tried the teeth, the digestion, and the temper of hungry travellers, you descend into the smiling plains and vine-covered fields of *La Belle France*—more lovely still by contrast with rugged, impoverished-looking Italy; whose most uninviting side you see during this twenty-four hours' railway travel.

Before descending, however, you feel that your Oriental dream-life is finished, and that you are returning to matter-of-fact places and people, and less sunny skies again. Before reaching the dividing line between Italy and

France, the broken character of the country, whose chief product seems to consist of rugged stones of various sizes, piled up in some places into high peaks whose crests never seem to doff their white nightcaps, and keen breezes that cut you like a knife, as you stand in a bare un- furnished room, where Custom-house officials search your luggage for tobacco or brandy, cause you to sigh at the memory of the sunny skies and soft breezes of old Egypt. As you rush more comfortably through France, the souvenir of Egypt is more pleasantly revived by the softer climate and serener skies; though the monotonous sameness of the scenery wearies both eye and mind. The same long flat stretches of field and wood, bordered with the prim rows of straight poplar; the same quaint old-fashioned towns and villages, looking precisely alike; the same ever-recurring types of population, plainly distinguishable each by its peculiar dress, as soldier or priest, *bourgeois* or countryman—offer little to excite or amuse the traveller, whirled by express through *La Belle France*, until he reaches Paris, the only city in the world where every human being feels himself at home.

As far behind us now in thought and feeling (though but a week has elapsed since we left her hospitable shores), as if centuries and the whole globe divided us, must Egypt now be to the

returned pilgrim of our widely different civilization ; but the memory of the land and of the
people, like the subtle perfume which still scents
the mummy-cloth after thousands of years, lingers
and must ever abide with those, who have visited
and dwelt in the " Old House of Bondage."

EGYPT'S FUTURE.

FROM the foregoing pages the reader will have been able to form an idea of what the new masters of the "Old House of Bondage" have done, as well as what they have left undone, for the country and people under their charge for three-quarters of a century.

As to the Khedive himself, who certainly has not come out "like refined gold" from the furnace into which his own short-sightedness and improvidence have cast him, his trials have brought to light the weakest, as well as the worst points of his character, viz., his egotism, his want of good faith, his vindictiveness, and his necessity of always leaning on some stronger will than his own for support.

He struck away his prop when he sent away Nubar Pacha, and since this removal has shown pitiable vacillation in his policy—if we may dignify by such a name the series of shifting expedients by which, before and since the removal and death of the Mouffetich, he has sought to regain some of his lost *prestige* in foreign eyes.

As he has virtually abdicated the absolute power, wielded so fatally for his people, in despite of the progress the country has made, we may now consider the Egyptian problem, irrespective of *the personality*, that so long overshadowed all else, and which has induced me to give the title to this book; for under the present reign it has been

"THE KHEDIVE'S EGYPT,"

and nothing else!

Proprietor, in his own name and that of his family, of *one-fifth of the best land in Egypt*, the sweat and blood of the fellahs has fertilized it; and even great public works have been made and used, solely to increase the wealth and pamper the luxury of the Khedive and his household; until even the much-enduring fellah now murmurs in revolt, and curses his task-master.

What Egypt needs, in my humble judgment, to redeem and regenerate her, may be briefly summed up in a few sentences, as follows:—

1st. Separation from Turkey, assigning the tribute to the creditors to whom it has been pledged, until that liability is liquidated; the privilege of regulating her own internal affairs, and pursuing the march of progress, under the direction of her own most enlightened sons, aided by foreign counsel. The Khedive might still act as titular head of the State, but as a constitutional ruler, shorn of absolute power.

2nd. The substitution of legality, and of the judgment of tribunals, for the arbitrary will of one man; following up the precedent which the Khedive has unwillingly established in his judicial and financial reforms; making those general and of universal application, which are now limited and restricted. So that the reign of Law may really be established in fact, as well as in name, throughout Egypt.

3rd. Publicity and responsibility in all matters appertaining to the different administrations : as well as in the discussions and recommendations of the body of Notables from the provinces (termed a Parliament), now sitting in secret session only, with an increase of their powers and responsibilities.

4th. Reduction and restriction of royal or public expenditures, and of the civil list, within reasonable limits : as well as of the building and improvement manias : and adjustment of the public machinery, in fit proportion to the work it has to do.*

5th. A more just and equitable system of

* No fitter and better heads for this duty could be found than the present commissioners, Mr. Romaine and Baron de Malaret.

taxation, administered or supervised by honest, educated, and responsible officials, and the abolition of all extraordinary impositions or forced loans, under any name or pretext whatsoever. Such new system of taxation to be devised and apportioned by the Assembly of Notables, who understand the country and the whole subject.

6th. The elevation of the fellaheen, by education and governmental aid, to a standard of equality, both in physical condition and political rights, with the labouring class of civilized countries; and the abolition of the *corvée*, and all forced labour, except in cases of absolute public necessity, in which latter case its objectionable features also should be amended.

7th. The gradual, if not immediate, abolition of slavery in Egypt; all the easier because only domestic slavery exists there, and is half abolished already. With its removal many of the social evils existing there would be ameliorated, the condition of woman changed, and her gilded slavery also approach its end.

Of course, in the present condition of the country, the initiatory steps in such reforms would have to be taken under foreign tutelage; but there is already a small educated class of natives, and so quick-witted a race as the Egyptian, can soon be taught sufficient to take at least a part in self-government.

These are not the dreams of a visionary, nor would the difficulties of putting such reforms into execution be half so great, as most people might imagine ; owing to the gentle and docile character of the race, whom centuries of cruelty and oppression have failed to lower or deprave.

Let us not, then, while giving the Khedive his due for such good as he may have accomplished, do injustice to the instruments through which he has achieved it. Let us not, to use the language of a famous writer on another occasion, "*while admiring the plumage, forget the dying bird.*"

The same external pressure which has already compelled the Khedive to relax his death-grip on the finances of the country, and partially to submit himself to the rule of law, as embodied in the mixed tribunals, might, in the great interests of humanity, compel the concessions shadowed forth above, and the liberation of an entire people from oppression. Then, but not until then, will the " Old House of Bondage " no longer deserve the name, which has clung to it from times older than tradition : and has unhappily continued to be a just appellation, whether its taskmasters called themselves Pharaohs, or Khedives.

APPENDIX A.

CONCESSION AND ALLEGED COST OF SUEZ
CANAL TO EGYPT.

No. 1.

The concession for the Suez Canal Company was obtained by M. de Lesseps in 1854, and in December and January, 1854-55, the preliminary surveys were made on the present line, about ninety-eight miles in length.

In November, 1855, an International Commission visited the isthmus, and their report was published in June, 1856. But the scheme dragged heavily for two years more; and it was not until 1858 that the Suez Ship Canal Company, under the name of *La Compagnie Universelle du Canal Maritime de Suez*, was organized, and not until March, 1859, that what were termed "preparatory explorations" were commenced, against which the viceroy issued his circular, prohibiting the commencement of the work before the consent of the Sublime Porte, which was a condition precedent, had been obtained.

From that period to 1869, when it was completed and inaugurated with great pomp and ceremony, the work went on, but with frequent interruptions arising from political and financial considerations, all of which, with the potent aid of Napoleon III., were finally overcome; the viceroy who granted, and his successor who confirmed the concession, having paid from first to last not less than £9,000,000 in cash, swollen by interest and other incidentals to £15,000,000 or £16,000,000.

The entire length of the canal is little short of 100 miles; 300 feet wide on top from one bank to the other, about 150 feet at the bottom, with an average depth of 24 feet. It connects four natural lakes—Mengaleh, Ballah, Timsah, and the Bitter Lakes—which had to be deepened to the requisite depth.

Two enormous jetties, one of 2700, the other of 2000 yards, with the distance of 1300 feet between their respective ends, constitute the protection of the canal against the choking up by the Mediterranean, and for protection of the shipping seeking transit through the canal, by the formation of a basin of 500 acres in extent, completely sheltered from storms.

The cuttings at El Guise, south of Kantara, are very heavy, extending five miles to Lake Ballah. Twenty-five vast steam dredges, and a large force of labourers, were employed on this work, and at some places the perpendicular depth excavated is upwards of 100 feet. The plateau on which El Guise stands is the most elevated point on the canal, and the labour of 20,000 fellahs for two years was required to cut a channel deep enough to float the steam dredges from the Mediterranean, and in filling the shallow basin of Timsah.

The Fresh-Water Canal from the Damietta branch of the Nile, originally extending to Zazazig, 50 miles west of Ismaïlia, has been extended eastwards to a point two or three miles west of Ismaïlia—then a part of the desert—and was of essential advantage in the construction of the canal, by furnishing the fresh water (which previously tasked several thousands of camels and donkeys to convey from Cairo) for the labourers engaged on the work. It is 26 feet wide, and about four feet deep. The Sweet-Water Canal now connects Ismaïlia and Cairo.

The northern end of the Bitter Lakes is ten miles from Port Saïd. The lakes themselves are about 24 miles long.

The cuttings at Toussoum and Serepeum, between Lake Timsah and the Bitter Lakes, next to those at El Guise, are the deepest and heaviest on the canal.

In October, 1867, the first steamer navigated as far as Ismaïlia from Port Saïd, as the pioneer of the fleet that within two years' time was to pass entirely through to Suez.

The Egyptian Government has gone to great expense in

constructing piers, docks, and basins at Suez, which must be added to the cost of its concession above stated.

Here is the Government estimate of the actual cost to Egypt of the Suez Canal, including interest and incidental expenses connected with the enterprise :—

COST TO EGYPT OF SUEZ CANAL.

Shares taken in the company by H. H. Saïd Pasha ...	£3,544,120
Award of Emperor Napoleon to compromise concession of forced labour	2,960,000
Paid to Canal Company for land and buildings near Cairo, called Cheflik-el-Wady	400,000
Paid to Canal Company to cancel concession of land on two sides of canal, as per contract, 23rd April, 1869 ...	1,200, 000
Paid to Canal Company for works executed on Sweet-Water Canal, and as compensation for relinquishing company's claim to that canal	400,000
Cost of works executed by Government in cutting Sweet-Water canal	428,927
Paid to French contractors for completion of Sweet-Water Canal by contract	815,833
Expenses of various missions to Europe and Constantinople in connection with canal, and expenses in opening the canal	1,011,193
	£10,760,073
Interest paid on above sums from respective dates to September, 1873	6,663,105
	£17,423,178

No 2.

THE receipts of the Canal of Suez for the first quarter, for four successive years, have been as follows :—

			Francs.
1874, receipts for first quarter			6,744,000
1875	,,	,,	8,212,000
1876	,,	,,	8,344,000
1877	,,	,,	9,071,000

The following figures, derived from authentic sources, will show the traffic :—

	Number of vessels passing through.	Tons measurement.
In 1875	1411	1,908,970
In 1876	1395	1,986,698

2 E

			Tons.
Of these, the English vessels amounted to			1,510,198
French	„	„	135,345
Holland	„	„	101,031
Italy	„	„	60,998
Austria	„	„	27,281
Russia	„	„	16,627

Thus, out of about 2,000,000 tonnage per annum, the proportions are—

English, a little more than . . 1,500,000 tons.
All other nations, a little less than 500,000 tons.

England thus contributing three-fourths of the entire tonnage.

APPENDIX B.

THE SUEZ CANAL AND THE ENGLISH GOVERNMENT.

The following correspondence with regard to the Suez Canal has been printed :—

No. 1.

" The Earl of Derby to Lord Lyons.

"*Foreign Office, May* 16.

" My Lord,—M. de Lesseps called upon me at the Foreign Office on the 10th inst., having, as he stated, come expressly from Paris to lay before Her Majesty's Government a project for regulating the passage of ships of war through the Suez Canal.

" I received him in company with the Chancellor of the Exchequer, and he handed to me the draft project of which I enclose a copy.

" After some conversation, I told him that the question of the position of the Suez Canal under present circumstances was a difficult and delicate one, and that I could not then say more than that the project which he had been good enough to submit to me should have full consideration.

"Her Majesty's Government have since carefully considered the project, and have come to the conclusion that the scheme proposed in it for the neutralization of the Canal by an International Convention is open to so many objections of a political and practical character that they could not undertake to recommend it for the acceptance of the Porte and the Powers.

"Her Majesty's Government are, at the same time, deeply sensible of the importance to Great Britain and other neutral Powers of preventing the Canal being injured or blocked up by either of the belligerents in the present war, and your Excellency is at liberty to inform M. de Lesseps that Her Majesty's Government has intimated to the Russian Ambassador that an attempt to blockade or otherwise to interfere with the Canal or its approaches would be regarded by Her Majesty's Government as a menace to India, and as a grave injury to the commerce of the world. I added that on both those grounds any such step—which Her Majesty's Government hope and fully believe there is no intention on the part of either belligerent to take—would be incompatible with the maintenance by Her Majesty's Government of an attitude of passive neutrality.

"Her Majesty's Government will cause the Porte and the Khedive to be made acquainted with the intimation thus conveyed to the Russian Government, and Her Majesty's Ambassador at Constantinople and Agent in Egypt will be instructed to state that Her Majesty's Government will expect that the Porte and the Khedive will on their side abstain from impeding the navigation of the Canal, or adopting any measures likely to injure the Canal or its approaches, and that Her Majesty's Government are firmly determined not to permit the Canal to be made the scene of any combat or other warlike operations.

"In stating this to M. de Lesseps, your Excellency will explain that Her Majesty's Government have thus taken the initiative in regard to the protection of the Canal on account of the pressing necessity, as regards British interests, of maintaining the security of the Canal, and they do not doubt that if the Canal were to be seriously menaced, the French and other Governments would adopt a similar course.

"I am, etc.,

(Signed)   "DERBY."

Inclosure 1 in No. 1.

"Memorandum by M. de Lesseps.

"The very clear declaration made by the English Government to the two Houses of Parliament of its resolution to maintain the freedom of the passage of the Suez Canal for its men-of-war has led me to believe that there might now be an opportunity of concluding an agreement with other Governments on this subject.

"As president of the financial company with which England is connected, I submit to Lord Derby a project simply expressing my personal views, which I have reason to believe the Duc Decazes would be disposed to adhere to after a private conversation which I had with him yesterday morning.

"Should the British Minister not think it well to initiate negotiations with the other Cabinets, I would make, at Paris, to the representatives of the several Powers interested, the overtures which I have made to Lord Derby and the Duc Decazes.

(Signed)   "FERD. DE LESSEPS.

"London, May 10, 1877."

Inclosure 2 in No. 1.

"International Agreement as to passage of Ships of War through the Suez Canal."

"Since the opening of the Suez Canal in 1869 the complete liberty of passage through the Maritime Canal and the ports connected with it has been respected for State vessels as well as for merchant ships, even on the part of belligerent Powers at the time of the Franco-German War.

"The Governments of —— now agree to maintain the same liberty to all national or commercial vessels, whatever may be their flag and without any exception, it being understood that national ships will be subject to the measures which the territorial authority may take to prevent ships in transit from disembarking on Egyptian territory any troops or munitions of war."

———

No. 2.

"The Earl of Derby to Mr. Layard.*

"*Foreign Office, May* 15.

"Sir,—I transmit to your Excellency herewith a copy of a despatch which I have addressed to Her Majesty's Ambassador at Paris, respecting a project, of which a copy is also inclosed, communicated to me by M. de Lesseps, for the neutralization of Suez Canal.

"Your Excellency will see that Her Majesty's Government have declined to adopt that project, but have informed M. de Lesseps of the intimation made by Her Majesty's Government to the Russian Ambassador that an attempt to blockade or otherwise to interfere with the Canal or its approaches would be regarded by Her Government as a menace to India, and as a grave injury to the commerce of the world, and that on both these grounds any such step—which Her Majesty's Government hope and fully believe there is no intention on the part of either belligerent to take—would be incompatible with the maintenance by Her Majesty's Government of an attitude of passive neutrality.

"I have to request your Excellency to acquaint the Porte with the intimation thus conveyed to the Russian Government, and to state that Her Majesty's Government will expect that the Porte and the Khedive will on their side abstain

* A similar despatch was addressed to Mr. Vivian.

from impeding the navigation of the Canal, or adopting any measures likely to injure the Canal or its approaches, and that Her Majesty's Government are firmly determined not to permit the Canal to be made the scene of any combat or other warlike operations.

"I have addressed a similar despatch to Her Majesty's Agent and Consul-General in Egypt.

"I am, etc.,

(Signed)   "DERBY."

APPENDIX C.

THE MIXED TRIBUNALS.

No. 1.

ROCKS AHEAD—SALARIES AND CONFLICTS OF JURISDICTION.

Lest I may be suspected or accused of captiousness or injustice in the remarks which I have felt bound to make in several places on two points of great public interest, viz., the extravagance of salaries paid some of the European *employés*, and the difficulties of the new tribunals in steering between Scylla (the foreign element) on the one side, and Charybdis (in the person of the Khedive) on the other, I cite the testimony of two witnesses upon the spot: one of whom is understood to be a gentleman holding a high official position on the new tribunals, and the other the English correspondent of a leading London journal. Such testimony must be regarded as unimpeachable, and it fully confirms my own on both points. From the letter of the *Times'* correspondent, under date of January 1st, 1877, I quote but a small portion of his comments on this topic. Speaking of the Khedive's economics, he says:—

"There is a further impediment, and a serious one, to the introduction of real economy in the matter of the salaries of the Egyptian Civil Service. Many of the higher posts are now filled by Europeans. In order to invite men of capacity and position in their own country, large sums have been offered as an inducement to come to Egypt, and contracts have been made, which insure the payment of such sums for a certain number of years. The new Controllers-General of Taxation, for instance, *are paid as highly as the President of the United States or a Baron of the Exchequer.* Even their deputies are to receive £2500 a year, while £3000 a year is not an uncommon salary to Europeans in other branches of the service. There is yet another obstacle to economy. International jealousy is strong in Egypt, and consequently *two or three men must be named to what is only the work of one,* in order that each nationality should have its proper influence in the country. Thus an Englishman and a Frenchman must attend to the taxation; two Englishmen and one Frenchman control the railways; an Englishman, a Frenchman, an Italian, and an Austrian attend to the public debt; and as many as twelve nationalities are represented on the judicial bench, which, however, is not paid on the scale of more recent appointments. Of course all this European talent is very highly paid, and the rate of these salaries to foreigners makes economy in the payment of the native functionaries a most invidious task."

The special correspondent of the *Daily News,* writing from Alexandria, February 19th, 1877, thus shows the "rocks ahead" of the judicial tribunals:—

"The position of the new tribunals has from the outset been one requiring great tact and delicacy, in order to avoid the extremes of manifesting too little independence, and so losing the confidence of the treaty Powers, on the one hand, and displaying too much, and thus bringing themselves into collision with the Khedive, on the other. How far these dangers have been avoided hitherto may be a matter of opinion, but anyhow the courts have passed through the first year of their existence, which is something to boast of. At the present moment, however, there are complications impending which can hardly fail to land them either on one horn or the other of a dilemma from which apparently there is no escape. The immediate source of trouble is a M. Brocard, formerly contractor for the Fresh-Water Canal at Ismaïlia, who, within the past week, succeeded in inducing the Cairo tribunal to award him £50,000 from the Government. Of course he failed to obtain payment, and in default ho proceeded to levy execution upon the Mallieh, or Treasury, where, as might from past experience have been anticipated, the officer of the court was resisted, and had to withdraw. . . . It is morally certain that the Government, having regard to the hundreds of similar cases pending, *can never allow the sentence to be enforced, and the only dignified course then open to the judges will be to perform the process known as the "happy despatch,"* and so close their own careers and that of the Réforme Judiciare at the same time. *Even supposing them to be willing to remain in office, and continue to act the part of mere lay figures in a judicial farce, the end would probably be none the less near or certain,* for it must be remembered that M. Brocard, the plaintiff in question, is a French subject, and that *France is one of the two Powers which refused to bind themselves to the Réforme Judiciare for any definite time.* She can, therefore, and doubtless will, at any period, withdraw from the convention upon finding that the interests of her citizens are not protected under it; and were France to abandon the new system, *Russia, which is similarly situated with regard to her obligations, would probably follow.* With the secession of these two important Powers, the integrity of the Réforme Judiciaire would be for ever destroyed—it would become practically unworkable, and its entire collapse must inevitably follow."

No. 2.

INTERNATIONAL RIVALRIES.

From a letter addressed to the *Times* from Alexandria, under date of May 27th of the present year, and supposed to emanate from a source worthy of credence, the following frank exposition of the internal dissensions and jealousies of the different constituent members of the new International Tribunal is taken. It gives a lively picture of the difficulties attendant on the creation and preservation of harmony or the merging of private piques and rivalries into the common interest, as well as the existing anomalies in the constitution of the tribunals.

"Mention has often been made of the international rivalry which goes on in Egypt. The French always strive to have more influence than the English with the Government, and the Italians and the Greeks enter into the same competition, though with less success; a struggle for predominance which has produced needless expense of administration, as the appointment of an Englishman or Frenchman has more than once led to the successful application from another nationality to have a similar nominee. In the new judicial body this international rivalry was appeased by a promise from Egypt that each of the seven Great Powers should have a nominee in the Court of Appeal, a second in the Court of First Instance, and a third in the *Parquet*, or Department of Justice. France, however, just recently has managed to obtain a small triumph by an ingenious evasion of this principle of equality of representation. The members of the *Parquet* were found of little use on account of the absence of criminal jurisdiction. Their only practical utility was as public prosecutors, and for that duty there is at present no demand. It was, therefore, proposed to the Powers to transfer these gentlemen to the Bench, where there is a want of power to meet the heavy and increasing demands for credit justice. All the Powers assented save France, who preferred, she said, to retain her nominee in the *Parquet*. Only six new judges were, therefore, secured. Then the French member of the *Parquet* complained of the inequality of his position *vis à vis* his recent colleagues. To satisfy him the post of Avocat-Général was created, and he now fills that office with an increase of pay. But this by no means contented the French party. They next protested against the infringement of the principle of equality of representation in the International Tribunal produced by the fact that all the Great Powers save France (and America, who never sent a member to the *Parquet*) had nominated two Judges of First Instance. The argument was found irresistible by Egypt, and a second French Judge of First Instance has been appointed. M. Bellet, Avocat-Général of the Court of Appeal of Toulouse, a man of high reputation and long experience, arrived here last week, and takes his seat at once on the Alexandria Bench, *where there is an appalling list of arrears.* The system and languages are at present purely continental, and this increase of the French element introduces the best working power. But there is a point which should not be lost sight of by

England. At the end of the first five years the whole system of the International Tribunals is to be subjected to revision, and the representatives of the large British interests in Egypt hope that certain changes may be made in favour of the English method of dealing with questions of fact. *The Anglo-Egyptians complain with reason that English law and English procedure should not have been wholly set aside in presence of the fact that two-thirds of the whole commerce of the country are English.* But if a reform of the codes were seriously contemplated, the English and American element in the courts would be of increased utility, and a predominant French party would only lead to difficulty."

APPENDIX D.
POPULATION OF THE FOREIGN COLONY.
No. 1.

It is difficult, if not impossible, to give an accurate statement as to the exact number and nationality of the foreign colony in Egypt. The consular registers are necessarily imperfect, in consequence not only of the neglect of persons to register their names and those of their families, but, in addition to the large floating class, agents of foreign houses scattered throughout the villages render the task more perplexing.

I subjoin a statement taken from the consular registers, showing only approximately the numbers and nationality of strangers resident in Egypt, which the Khedive himself estimates at about 100,000.

Greeks (not rayahs, or subjects of the Porte) ...	34,000
Italians	15,000
Frenchmen and French subjects	17,000
Englishmen and Maltese	6,000
Austrians and Hungarians	6,500
Germans	1,100
All other nationalities	1,390

Of Americans there are very few; a dozen missionaries, about 20 army officers, three judges of the mixed tribunals, and a small number of citizens. The number of American visitors annually is very great: larger than that of any other nationality except England.

No. 2.

Translated from the *Statistique de l'Egypte*, published by order of Government at Cairo, 1873 :—

No. 10.—FOREIGN SUBJECTS OF VARIOUS NATIONALITIES, RESIDING IN EGYPT.

Residences.	Greeks.	Italians.	French.	English.	Austro-Hungarians.	Germans.	Persians.	Spaniards.	Russians.	Dutch.	Belgians.	Swedes, Danes, Portuguese, Americans & Various.	Total.
ALEXANDRIA	21,000	7,539	10,000	4,500	3,000	600	100	150	127	220	40	40	47,316
CAIRO (suburbs inclusive)	7,000	3,367	5,000	1,000	1,800	450	400		103				19,120
OTHER LOCALITIES (Principally Isthmus of Suez and Delta)	6,000	3,000	2,000	500	1,500	50			210				13,260
Total ...	34,000	13,906	17,000	6,000	6,300	1,100			1,390				79,696

NOTE.—These figures have been taken by the respective consulates in 1870–72 from the registrations of each nationality, which at Alexandria represent about half the real number, or number supposed to be correct. For the Italian colony alone, the results of a recent and rather complete census, taken in 1871–72, has been used, but from this, no doubt, a certain number of residents have been omitted. The general total, 79,696, includes about 800 Swiss under the protection of various foreign Powers; it does not apply to the floating or travelling population, but only to residents.

APPENDIX E.

FIRMAN CHANGING SUCCESSION.

The firman of the Sultan changing the Egyptian succession was issued on 13 Rabi-ul Akhir 1290 of the Hegira—
equivalent to 9th June, 1873. In this firman it is declared
that "The Khedivate of Egypt passes to the eldest son of the
person who shall find himself clothed with the dignity of
the Khedive, or from him to his eldest son, and so on; that
is to say, that the succession is established exclusively by
order of primogeniture, as we are persuaded will be conform-
able to the interests and good administration of the Khedivate
and the welfare of its people. In case the Khedive shall die
without male issue, the Khedivate will pass to his younger
brother, or, if need be, to the elder son of his younger brother."
Provision is made in detail for a regency in case of the
minority of the heir presumptive, eighteen years being considered full age. This firman further recognizes the unlimited
authority of the Khedive to make internal laws and regulations for the government of Egypt, and his right to bestow
military grades as high as colonel, and civil grades as high
as bey. Higher grades must be issued from Constantinople
at his request. This firman, enlarging previous powers granted
to Egyptian viceroys, authorizes the Khedive contract to
loans without permission asked of the Sultan; to enter into
commercial or other treaties with foreign Powers, provided
such arrangements are not inconsistent with the political
treaties of the Sublime Porte; and also empowers him to
increase his army and navy, as he sees fit, with the exception
of ironclads, which are forbidden.

The annual tribute to Constantinople is fixed at 150,000
purses in gold, equivalent to about £680,000, concerning
which the Sublime Porte thus feelingly and forcibly speaks:
"Thou shalt also pay the greatest attention to remit each year
without delay, and in its entirety, to my Imperial Treasury
the 150,000 purses of tribute established, as fixed by the
firman of 1866"—the firman elevating the viceroy to the
dignity of Khedive.

APPENDIX F.

EGYPTIAN EXPLORATION OF CENTRAL AFRICA.

I am indebted to General Stone, Chief of Staff, for the following report, submitted by him to the Khedive last autumn, giving the results of staff and other Egyptian explorations in Central Africa:—

War Office, Bureau of the General Staff,
(*Cabinet of the Chief.*) *Cairo, 16th October, 1876.*

Summary of geographical and scientific results accomplished by expeditions made by the Government of the Khedive of Egypt during the three years 1874-5-6 :—

1. Accurate reconnaissance of the White Nile, from Gondokoro to Lake Albert.—Gordon, assisted by Watson, Chippendall, and Gessi.

2. Reconnaissance of the White Nile between Khartoum and Gondokoro, with greater exactitude than had ever before been accomplished, with the determination of five positions by means of astronomical observations.—Watson and Chippendall, under the orders of Colonel Gordon.

3. Observations of the transit of Venus, Dec., 1874. By Watson and Chippendall, under the orders of Colonel Gordon, at Rageef, near Gondokoro.

4. Reconnaissance of Lake Albert, 1876. By Gessi, under the orders of General Gordon.

5. Establishment of steam navigation upon Lake Albert. By General Gordon.

6. Verification of the course of the Nile between Lake Victoria and M'rooli, and the discovery of Lake Ibrahim. By Lieut.-Colonel Long, under the orders of Colonel Gordon.

7. Verification of the course of the Nile between the falls of Kamma and Lake Albert. By Linant, Gessi, and Piaggia, under the orders of General Gordon.

8. Discovery of the branch flowing from the Nile near Lake Albert towards the north-west. By Gessi, under the orders of General Gordon.

9. Discovery of the branch flowing from Lake Ibrahim in a northerly direction. By Piaggia, under the orders of General Gordon.

10. The accurate reconnaissance of the Nile between Foweira and M'rooli. By General Gordon.

11. Reconnaissance of the country between the White Nile, near Gondokoro, and the Makiaka-Niam-Niam country. By Colonel Long, assisted by Maino, under the orders of General Gordon.

12. Reconnaissance and completion of the map of the route between Debbé and Matoul, and between Debbé and Obeiyail. By Colonel Colston, assisted by five officers of the Egyptian staff.

Report upon the northern portion of the province of Kordofan.—Colonel Colston.

13. General reconnaissance of the province of Kordofan, and completion of the map to the 12th degree of north latitude. By Major Prout, assisted by five officers of the Egyptian staff. Lines of reconnaissance traversed, about 6000 kilomètres; seventeen positions determined astronomically.

General report upon the said province. By Major Prout.

14. Botanical reconnaissance (with large collections of plants) of the province of Kordofan. By Doctor Pfund, under the orders of Colonel Colston and Major Prout.

15. Botanical reconnaissance (with collections of plants) of the central portion of the province of Darfour. By Doctor Pfund, under the orders of Colonel Purdy.

16. Reconnaissance of the route between Dongola upon the Nile and El Facher, the capital of Darfour. By Colonel Purdy assisted by Lieut.-Colonel Mason and five other officers of the Egyptian staff.

17. General reconnaissance of the entire country of Darfour, and a portion of the Dar Fertit, as far as Hofrat el Nahass and Shekka to the south, as far as Gebel Medob to the north, and as far as the frontier of Wadai to the west, with the completion of the map and general report upon the country. By Colonel Purdy, assisted by Lieut.-Colonel Mason, Major Prout, and nine other officers of the Egyptian staff. Distance

traversed, over 6500 kilomètres; twenty-two positions determined astronomically.

18. Geological and mineralogical reconnaissance of the
country between Rudesiëh and Kinneh upon the Nile, and the
Red Sea near Cosire, with a geological map and profile, and
report. By Mr. Mitchell, assisted by an officer of the staff
and Emiliano, with large collections of specimens.

19. Topographical and geological reconnaissance of the
country to the south-west of Zeylah and near Tajurra. By Mr.
Mitchell, assisted by an officer of the staff and Emiliano.
Preparation of the map; collection of geological specimens.

20. Reconnaissance and completion of the map between
Zeylah and Hanar; map of the city of Hanar and of the
country neighbouring. By the Major of Staff Mocktar, assisted
by Adjutant-Major of the Staff Fouzy, attached to the expedition of Ranif Pacha.

21. Topographical reconnaissance of the country between
the coast of the Red Sea, near Massowah, and the plateau
of Abyssinia, with the completion of the map. By Colonels
Lockett and Field; Lieut.-Colonels Derrick and Balig; Majors
Duliu, Dennison, and Diuholy; Captain Irgens, and several
other officers of the Egyptian staff.

22. Geological reconnaissance of the country between Massowah and the Abyssinian plateau, with collections of specimens. By Mr. Mitchell, assisted by Emiliano.

23. Reconnaissance and survey of the country between
Berberah and Gebel Dobar, with completion of the map. By
Capitaine Abd-el-Rasach Nasmy, and other officers of the
Egyptian staff.

24. Reconnaissance and sounding, with completion of maps
of the ports of Kismaya and Dumford upon the coast of the
Indian Ocean. By Colonel Ward, assisted by Capitaine
Sidky, and other staff officers.

25. Reconnaissance of the route and completion of the map
between Siout (by the desert) and Aïn el Aghiëh. By Major
Diuholy, assisted by an officer of the Egyptian staff.

26. Reconnaissance between Tajurra and Aoussa. By the

Staff-Lieutenant Mohammed Igyat, under the orders of Munzinger Pacha.

27. Barometrical and thermometrical register taken by officers in the provinces of the Equator, of Kordofan, of Darfour, and in all the expeditions.

Respectfully submitted,

STONE,

General of Division, Chief of the General Staff.

APPENDIX G.

MR. GOSCHEN'S TABULAR STATEMENT.

DIRECT TAXES.

On lands	£4,302,400	
On date trees	189,300	
Licences on professions, etc. (contributions d'arts et metiers)	422,000	
		4,913,700

INDIRECT TAXES.

Customs	639,000	
Tobacco monopoly	263,900	
		902,900

REVENUES OF GOVERNMENT.

From salt-works (salines)	306,000	
Farming of fisheries (fermage du poisson frais, et Matarieh—poisson salé)	131,000	
		437,800
Sundry taxes and revenues in the provinces (Moudiriehs)	504,900	
Revenues of the province of Soudan	143,500	
Sundries	34,000	
		682,400
		£6,936,800

TOTAL GENERAL TAXATION.

Local revenues, taxes, and dues; municipalities, Cairo and Alexandria	£517,800	
Gonvernorats (governorships of small towns) and police receipts	202,400	
Canal, bridge, port, and other dues and tolls ...	165,600	
	885,800	
Railways	990,200	
		1,876,000
Amount received in anticipation of future land-tax (Moukabala)	1,613,000	
Repayments of advances made by Government and arrears	377,700	
		1,991,300
		£10,804,100

APPENDIX H.

EXPORTS AND PRICES OF EGYPTIAN CROPS.

Exports of cotton, grain, cotton-seed, and sugar for the years 1866, 1870, 1872, 1873, 1875 and 1876, from Custom-house returns:—

The exports of cotton were:—

Cantars.

In 1866	...	...	...	...	1,785,000
„ 1870	...	...	...	...	1,845,452
„ 1872	...	...	...	...	2,168,181
„ 1873	...	...	...	...	2,187,035

COTTON SHIPMENTS TO DIFFERENT PORTS.

Cantars.

Total shipments to all ports in 1874–75			.'.	345,794
„ „	Liverpool, same year		...	292,243
„ „	France and Spain, do.		...	38,014
„ „	Austria, Italy, and Russia, do.			35,447

2 F

The exports of grain were :—

		Ardebs.
In 1866	... ...	295,942
,, 1870	... ...	1,414,300
,, 1872	... ...	1,580,256
,, 1873	... ...	1,525,314

The exports of cotton-seed were :—

		Ardebs.
In 1866	... ...	750,877
,, 1870	... ...!	1,264,507
,, 1872	... ...	1,334,223
,, 1873	... ...	1,282,469

EGYPTIAN COTTON-SEED.

	Ardebs.
Total exportable crop (1875) estimated to be	1,450,000
Actual export	1,361,000

About half the crop went to Hull. About 90,000 ardebs estimated to have been retained for sowing.

The exports of sugar were :—

		Cantars.
In 1866	... ...	450
,, 1870	... ...	356,468
,, 1872	... ...	456,351
,, 1873	... ...	738,002

CROPS FOR 1876.

				Ardebs.
Wheat, Saïdi (100 ardebs equal to 63 imperial quarters)				817,219
Ditto, Behira	,,		,,	150,664
Barley	100	,,	62¼ ,,	125,697
Beans, Saïdi	...	...	...	934,737
Ditto, Behira	100	,,	65 ,,	83,183
Indian corn	100	,,	64 ,,	37,793
Cotton-seed	1000	,,	100 tons ,,	1,902,272

			Cantars.
Cake of cotton-seed (1 cantar equal to 93 lbs.)			108,374–49
Sugar	,,	,,	743,440-30

Cantars.

Cotton, from 1st of January to 31st of August ... 1,875,486–81
„ 1st of September to 31st of December ... 1,755,862–68

*3,631,349–49

AVERAGE PRICES DURING 1876.

Wheat .... 85 piastres Tarif, or 17s. the ardeb.
Beans .... 80 „ „ 16s. „
Barley .... 60 „ „ 12s. „
Maize .... 60 „ „ 12s. „
Cotton-seed ...... 75 „ „ 15s. „
Cotton-seed cake 20 „ „ £4 the ton.
Sugar .... 100 „ „ £25 „
Cotton .... 12 dollars the cantar, or 6d. per lb.

* This large export of cotton arises from the large quantity held over from 1875 for a cotton market, and from the hurried shipments in the autumn of 1876 to provide money. The crop of 1875–76 was 3,000,000 cantars, the largest ever known. The crop of 1876–7 was a smaller one —2,500,000 cantars.